ALICIA ALLEN INVESTIGATES 1

A MODEL MURDER

Celia Conrad

Barcham Books

First published in Great Britain in 2011 by Barcham Books, an imprint of
Creative Communications, Suite 327, 28 Old Brompton Road, London, SW7 3SS

ISBN 978 09546233 26 (0 9546233 2 0)

Designed by Andrew Dorman
www.andrewdorman.co.uk

Printed and bound by CPI Group (UK) Ltd, Croydon, CR0 4YY

For my loving family
and
in memory of Paul Marsh, my former literary agent,
who sadly died before this book went to press

Chapter 1

August 2005

'Strewth. You're soaked through!' she said as I stumbled through the outside door and into the entrance hall, fumbling with my keys, dripping umbrella in one hand and briefcase in the other.

'Sorry. Who are *you*?' I asked slightly awkwardly, looking up at the statuesque stranger standing in front of me. I pushed my wet hair out of my eyes as I shook the excess water off my coat. She was staring at me and all of a sudden I felt rather self-conscious. It was just typical to be caught in a summer thunderstorm, my umbrella to blow inside out and to return home drenched to the skin.

'Oh, excuse me. Let me introduce myself.' She extended her hand and smiled broadly. Although she spoke softly I could detect an Australian accent. She was striking looking with her shoulder-length, sun-kissed blonde hair, blue eyes and enviable tan. Dressed casually in a plain white T-shirt and hipster jeans, which showed off her long legs to perfection, she had an indescribable aura about her: confident but laid back. I suppose men would call it sex appeal. 'I'm Tamsin. But everybody calls me Tammy. We moved in yesterday.' She pointed to the door to the ground floor flat behind her. 'We're having a housewarming party tomorrow night. Feel free to drop by. You'd be very welcome.'

'We?' I smiled back at her, and shook the well-manicured hand.

'Kimberley. My flatmate. We're Australian.'

'So I gathered. I'm Alicia… Alicia Allen.'

'I know.' I looked at her quizzically. 'I bumped into that friendly Italian guy who lives on the top floor.'

'Oh, Cesare Castelli.' She nodded.

'He said he's a banker and works in the city. He told me you own the first floor flat and all about you.'

'He did?'

'Yes.'

'Then you have the advantage on me.'

'I understand you're a solicitor and that you're also Italian.'

'Half-Italian.'

'Which half?'

'My mother is Italian.'

'You speak the lingo then.'

'I do.'

'What area of law do you work in?'

'Private Client.' Her eyes glazed over.

'Tax planning, wills, inheritance and trusts.'

'Oh, right. Is that interesting?'

'Never a dull moment!' I paused for a moment. 'Did Cesare tell you about our neighbour Dorothy Hammond?' I asked, changing the subject. I felt that was enough conversation about me, for the time being anyway. 'She lives in the garden flat.' From the look on Tammy's face it was evident Cesare had not mentioned her. 'Only she's elderly, and I think she'd appreciate you letting her know about the party. Not that she'd mind or anything. But it would also be a good opportunity to introduce yourself.'

I was really fond of Dorothy who, at eighty-two, was as bright as a button and did not miss a trick. She had trained as a seamstress for Norman Hartnell and still enjoyed her dressmaking. I first met her a week after I moved in when I helped her with her shopping. Since then, on the odd occasion, I saw her for a cup of tea and a chat. I felt that she was very lonely since her husband had died from a stroke a few years before. She did not have any children and the only relative she ever mentioned was a niece who lived in Suffolk.

'Yeah, fair point. I'll call in on her later.'

'Are you settling in well?' Again I changed the subject. She nodded. 'Actually, I didn't even know this flat was being rented. Have you been in London long?'

'No. Only three weeks. We've been crashing at a friend's place but then this flat came up for rent and we grabbed it.'

'Why South Kensington?'

'Kim had a friend who worked here as a nanny and she said she loved the area.'

'It's a great location.' I stifled a yawn.

'You look bushed.'

'It's been a long day.'

'I don't want to hold you up, and I've kept you chatting far too long as it is.'

'That's all right. I've enjoyed talking to you.' She was very bubbly and chatty and I found her rather refreshing.

'I'd better run,' she said, looking at her watch, and gliding towards her front door. 'Don't forget the party tomorrow. Please come. Eight-thirty. Bring a friend if you want.' She turned, and hovered in the doorway.

'OK. Thanks for the invitation.' I started to walk up the stairs.

'Cool. See you later, Alicia.'

'Yes, see you tomorrow, Tammy.' I paused for a moment on the staircase and watched her waft back into her flat. There was no sign of her flatmate, but no doubt I would meet her at the party.

I bent down to pick the post up off my mat and glanced at my watch; it was already nine o'clock. As it was Friday evening I could lie in on Saturday morning and catch up on some much needed sleep. My week had been difficult because my secretary was ill and David Wagstaff, the Managing Partner, refused to call in a temp despite all protestations. I was about to unlock the front door to my flat, when I heard a familiar voice behind me.

'*Ciao, bella. Come stai stasera?*'

'Cesare,' I replied, spinning around and facing him. He was leaning nonchalantly against the banisters, hands in his jeans pockets and grinning at me as he always did. I gave him a wry smile. *'Così, così. Stai bene?'*

'Sì. Bene.' He bent down and kissed me on both cheeks. 'If you've no other plans this evening how about you come and have some dinner with me.'

I had known him since I moved in two years earlier, and we were good friends but, from the odd passing comment he made, I sensed he hoped for more. And although I was very fond of him my feelings for him were as a sister for a brother. In fact, he reminded me of my own brother, John, who had been killed with my father in a car crash ten years before and, like John, he was tall, had dark curly hair and bright blue eyes. I would never think of him as anything other than a close friend.

'That's really thoughtful of you. I'd like that. Give me half an hour to shower and change and I'll be with you.'

'Bene. I'll be waiting.' He winked at me and bounded off upstairs.

I pushed open the door to my flat and stepped inside. I dropped my briefcase and umbrella in the hall, placed my keys and post on the table, hung my coat up in the cupboard and walked though to the reception room and checked my answerphone. There was a single message from my friend Jo berating me for not returning her recent calls. Josephine Brook and I had met on our first day at senior school and we had been best friends ever since. I 'phoned her back and left a message.

I opened my post while undressing. It was mostly bills and junk mail, but there was a postcard from my sister Antonia. She was on holiday in the Bahamas with her latest boyfriend, Marco, whom she had met through her work as a public relations officer with Alitalia. The scene on the postcard looked idyllic and the thought of clear blue waters and running along a deserted stretch of sandy beach seemed very appealing as I enveloped myself in the warm running water of the shower.

After showering and throwing on jeans and a cotton top, I opened the French windows to the reception room and stepped out onto the balcony, which overlooked the garden square. It had stopped raining but the air felt hot and sticky. My 'phone rang, I ran to answer it, and in the process tripped over the mat inside the balcony door, knocking over a table and a green and white alabaster chess set my mother had brought me from Volterra. While I scrambled to pick the pieces up off the floor, my answering machine kicked in.

'*Ciao, Ally.*' It was Antonia and she sounded down.

'*Ciao, sorellina. Come stai?*' I said, picking up the 'phone.

'*Ally?* I thought you weren't there.'

'I was out on the balcony. *Che passa?* What's up?' I knew there must be a problem. Antonia would not call me from her holiday with her boyfriend if everything had been going well.

'Umm… Could you collect me from the airport on Sunday? I'm coming back early.' She used that 'do not ask me what is going on' type of voice. I knew better than to ask her any questions.

'Yes. OK. Give me the flight details.' I rummaged through my desk drawer for a pen and paper and took them down. 'OK, *carina*. See you on Sunday afternoon.'

I was on my way out when I heard my 'phone ring again. I paused for a second but decided to leave it because I was already late. Cesare was passionate about opera and, as I ambled up the stairs, I could hear the strains of *Rigoletto* coming from his flat. The front door was open and, on walking into the hallway, Cesare appeared at the reception room door.

'I thought I heard you. Ivano's here,' he said, beckoning me in. Ivano was one of Cesare's banking friends, though it had always seemed odd to me how they could be friends at all as Ivano was the complete antithesis of Cesare. I closed the door and wandered through to the reception room. Ivano was sitting on Cesare's cream leather sofa with his latest girlfriend. She was petite, like all the previous ones I had met, and had long curly brown hair and a curvaceous figure. With his height and dark good looks Ivano was used to charming women, and it was evident that he already had this one in his pocket; she was all over him and he was lapping up the attention. In the short time I had known him he seemed to have had a constant stream of women flowing in and out of his life *and* his bed. He had made it very clear to me on numerous occasions that he would like me to be one of them, but having singularly failed to seduce me with his charms, he still persisted at every opportunity. I felt sorry for his latest victim and wondered how long she would last. I suspected not more than a couple of nights and then Ivano would be seeking fresh conquests.

On seeing me he jumped up, grabbed me around my waist, and kissed me on both cheeks before I had the chance to move away. *'Ciao, bellissima,'* he said, standing back and ogling me. I looked at him with a bland expression. *'Stai bene?'* he continued, leaning forward and touching my hair. I turned my head and pulled away from him. 'Your hair is damp. Let me dry it for you.' His manner was suggestive.

'Buona sera, Ivano. Aren't you going to introduce me to your girlfriend?' I asked, ignoring the comment. I made a point of looking sideways at his companion who remained seated on the sofa, and had been staring at me hard since I had first walked into the room.

'Oh, Alicia, this is Maria.' He said it almost like an afterthought. I held out my hand to her, but it was not accepted. Her beady brown eyes continued to bore straight through me. She had no need to worry; I was not interested in her boyfriend. In fact, she was welcome to him so far as I was concerned.

'How do you do?' I was formal, but smiled at her hoping to break the ice.

'That's what I like about you, Alicia,' Ivano interjected. 'Your cool English reserve. But my view is that you are *too* English. You should loosen up and release the Italian in you. *I* could help you there!'

'That's a particularly bad chat up line Ivano, even for you.' I replied, rolling my eyes upwards.

'I've never had any complaints,' he snapped.

'You're wasting your time. I'm immune to your charms.'

'Red wine for everyone?' Cesare asked, popping his head around the kitchen door. He was holding a bottle of Chianti Classico in one hand and a corkscrew in the other. 'Everything OK?' He had obviously picked up on the tension between us.

'Ivano was leaving. He wants to spend some time *alone* with Maria,' I said, with the hint of a smile, but matter-of-factly. I sat down in one of the leather armchairs and placed my keys on a pile of magazines on the top of Cesare's low, oblong, glass coffee table.

'You should listen to this opera, Alicia,' he said, pointing to Cesare's CD player. *'La donna è mobile'* is fitting for you. *Ciao, bella!'* More like *'il uomo'* in his case, I thought, judging by his track record, but he and his girlfriend left.

Over dinner I asked Cesare about our new Australian neighbours.

'What did you think of Tamsin? I understand you spoke with her earlier. By the sounds of it you chatted for some time.'

'*Sì*. I met her on my way in. *Carina*. Very long legs.'

'You found *la bionda* attractive then Cesare?' I gave him a mischievous, questioning look.

'She told me she's a model,' he replied, shrugging his shoulders.

'That fits.' I laughed.

'Are you making fun of me, Alicia?' said Cesare, putting down his forkful of fettucine. He sounded indignant and clearly did not appreciate that I was only teasing him.

'*Ti prendo in giro*. I noticed that her nails were perfectly manicured. That's all.' I looked down at my own imperfect nails. 'Did you meet her friend Kimberley?'

'No. You?' I shook my head. I could not speak as my mouth was full. 'More wine?' he asked with the wine bottle poised ready to refill my glass. I placed my hand over it. He poured the remainder of the

Chianti into his glass. 'Are you going to their housewarming?' he continued.

'Umm... Yes,' I replied clearing my throat and placing my fork on the empty plate. 'I'm quite intrigued by Tammy.'

'*Perché?* What's so interesting about her?' he asked, scanning my face intently.

'I just have the feeling that things are going to change around here now that she and Kimberley have moved in.'

Although I had intended to sleep in late, I actually set my alarm for seven-thirty because I wanted to go to the gym before the Saturday morning rush. But as it happens I only managed to drag myself out of bed by eight. As I rounded the stairwell and looked out of the landing window I saw Dorothy watering her plants in the garden below. Knowing her as I did, she had probably been up since the crack of dawn.

I stopped off at the newsagent to buy a paper and when I arrived at the gym at twenty past eight, to my surprise it was not at all busy. Apart from myself, there were only two other people in there, each with a personal trainer. As I pedalled on the bicycle I was deep in thought, and totally unaware that Ivano had come into the gym and was watching me work out. It was only when I walked over to the leg press that I saw him in the mirror. He was standing behind me.

'*Ciao, bella.* For someone so petite you have very long legs,' he said, touching my left thigh.

'You don't give up do you?' I replied, removing his hand.

'Oh, come on Alicia. Stop playing hard to get. You *want* it as much as I do. We could be *so* good together.'

'Is that your idea of a joke, Ivano? Why can't you get the message? I'm not interested in you. Get over it.'

'There's *one* way you could help me get over you. Once won't hurt you. I bet you'd enjoy it too.'

'You have a very high opinion of yourself. You just won't accept anything that goes counter to your massive ego will you?' I raised my voice so that the other people in the gym would hear, and I might embarrass him into silence. I did not wait for his response but picked up my towel and stormed out of the gym, leaving him standing there.

I was about to put my key in the outside door when it opened. A jovial looking redhead wearing grey track-suit bottoms, trainers and a navy blue sweatshirt bounded out and almost knocked me flying in the process.

'I'm really sorry,' she said, stopping short and looking at me. 'G'day. You must be Alicia. I'm Kimberley.' She smiled broadly and I was struck immediately by her warmth. She had freckles across her nose, pale blue eyes and deep dimples which were prominent when she smiled. She wore her hair very short but it was the most fantastic shade of auburn.

'Yes. I'm Alicia. How are you settling in?' Kimberley was walking sideways down the steps as she responded.

'Fine. Please call me Kim. All my friends do.' I saw her looking at my sports bag. 'I was thinking of joining the gym to get into shape. I envy you being petite. Tammy's so thin too. I only have to look at a cream bun to put on weight.' She paused. 'Actually, I'm going out to pick up some bits for the party this evening.' She stopped at the bottom of the steps. 'You *are* coming, aren't you?'

'Yes.'

'Good. Catch you later then.'

'You will. Bye, Kim.' I watched her disappear down the street.

The 'phone call I had received on my way out the night before was from Jo. Again I rang her back but there was no answer on either her landline or her mobile. I left a message on both and set off for the supermarket.

The checkout queue was longer than usual. I felt my mobile vibrating in my handbag and scrambled to retrieve it from its depths. It was Jo.

'Hi, Ally. Where are you? I picked up your messages.'

'At the supermarket. How are you?' I asked, balancing my mobile between ear and chin, whilst struggling to pack my shopping and talk at the same time.

'I'm fine. I haven't heard from you for ages. You've had me worried. Do you want to meet up tonight? Will's working.'

Will Brook was Jo's husband and they had been married for eighteen months. Jo met him when she joined the police force ten years earlier. He was thirty-seven and she was nearly thirty, like me. Will was ex-CID and had recently left the force to set up his own private investigator's bureau and Jo was now working with him. I liked Will who reminded me of a burly rugby player with his rugged good looks and his shock of wavy blond hair that flopped down over his eyes.

I continued to pack my shopping, juggling my mobile between ear and chin. 'I'd love to, but I've been invited to my new neighbours' housewarming party.'

'New neighbours?'

'Yes. Two Australian girls. They're renting the flat downstairs.' I took my credit card out of my wallet and slotted it into the chip and pin PDQ terminal. 'Why don't you come, Jo,' I said as I punched the four digit pin onto the keypad.

'Umm… I'd love to.'

'Great.' I now struggled to put all my bags of shopping back into the trolley.

'Shall I come to your flat first?'

'Perfect.'

'What time?'

'About eight.'

'OK. Is Cesare going?' she asked casually.

'Probably. What makes you ask?'

'I just wondered how you two are getting along.'

'Still friends.'

'I always thought you'd make a great couple. It's obvious he's keen on you and he's such a lovely guy.' Jo was the inveterate match-maker.

'He is, and I intend to keep his friendship.'

'Hmm... I have to dash, but I'll see you at eight.'

'Look forward to it.'

'Me too.'

'*Ciao*. Bye.'

The party was in full swing when Jo and I arrived. Tammy was chatting to a couple of personable young Australians who seemed totally captivated by her. She looked simply stunning in a sparkly blue sequin halter neck top and black satin hipsters. I caught her eye and smiled and, as she beamed back, she glided effortlessly across the room to me.

'Hi. So glad you could make it.' She bent down and kissed me on the cheek. 'Help yourself to a drink.' The music was incredibly loud and I had to strain to hear what she was saying. She looked quizzically at Jo who was standing behind me, as if she was trying to place her. 'Do I know you?'

'Tammy, this is Jo.' I had to shout above the music to make myself audible.

'Pleased to meet you.' Jo held out her hand. 'Thanks for the invitation.'

'No worries. Are you sure we haven't met before? You're not a model are you?' she asked, shaking Jo's hand and scrutinizing her face. Jo shook her head. 'It's strange, but I'm sure I've seen your face in a magazine or something.'

'I must have one of those faces,' said Jo, laughing.

'With your looks and height you could be a model.'

Jo's paternal grandmother had come from the South of France and Jo had inherited her Mediterranean looks. Her *café au lait* skin gave her a natural, healthy glow. With her long and dark brown hair, deep brown eyes, regular features and five feet eleven inch frame she could well have been model material.

'Tammy has a point you know, Jo,' I said.

'No offence, but I don't think modelling is my scene and, anyway, I'm too old! When did you start modelling, Tammy?'

'When I was sixteen.'

'How old are you now?' Jo asked.

'Twenty. What do you do?'

'I work with my husband. He has his own private investigator's bureau. We both used to be in the police.'

'Oh. But you don't look like a policewoman.'

'No. You think I look like a model.' Jo laughed again. 'You know what they say about appearances being deceptive, "You can't always tell what people are like from their outsides." Is the modelling going well?'

'Back home it was. I'd really like to break into the London market though.'

'Do you have an agent yet?'

'I've been hiking my portfolio around the agencies. Something will turn up,' she said confidently as she tossed back her head and ran her fingers through her tousled hair.

I left Jo talking to Tammy and wandered through to the reception room in the hope of meeting someone interesting, but unfortunately I walked straight into Ivano. How on earth he had managed to wangle an invitation was beyond me.

'*Ciao, bella.* I knew you wouldn't be able to keep away from me,' he said, catching hold of my elbow.

'I suppose you've been eyeing up the talent in the room. Found any potential victims yet?' I asked curtly.

'I can't help it if I'm *irresistibile* to women.' He pulled me closer. 'But I can resist you so easily. You're incredible. Simply *incredibile.* You really are.'

'So *they* tell me, Alicia. It's your own fault you know.'

'Really? How do you make that one out?'

'You're a flirt in your flimsy little party dress,' he said as he pushed his fingers under the shoulder strap of my dress. 'If you weren't so tempting I could resist you more easily.' He placed his hand on my back. *'Fai gli occhi dolci a me. Sei una civetta!'*

'I'm not a flirt and, even if I was, I certainly wouldn't be flirting with *you*,' I snapped, pushing him back with both hands. 'Why don't you...'

'Please don't let the party degenerate,' he said, interrupting me in a sarcastic and mocking way as he grabbed hold of my right wrist.

'You do that all by yourself, Ivano. Let go of me. *Lasciami in pace.*' He released his grip of my wrist and I took a step backwards.

'I see the passion that burns within you, Alicia.'

'But I don't burn for *you*.' I turned away from him, and Jo was standing in front of me.

'You OK?' she asked.

'Yes,' I replied rolling my eyes up and laughing. 'Ivano can't help himself.'

'I thought that *was* the problem.' She winked at me. 'Where's Cesare?'

'He's not here. Maybe he couldn't make it after all.'

Will arrived so I left Jo with him, thereby avoiding any further discussion about Cesare, and wandered through to the kitchen where Kim was organizing the food. She was standing in front of the sink with her back to me.

'Do you need any help?' I asked.

'No. You're all right,' she said, spinning around and wiping her hands on a tea towel. 'I think I've got it under control. Thanks for offering.' She paused. 'Stay and talk to me though.'

She told me that she was working as a legal secretary. She was currently temping but was looking for a permanent position. She had been lucky, as the agency she had signed up with had found her work immediately in the litigation department of Crawford Taylor, one of the big city firms on Liverpool Street. She was enjoying it, even though the lawyer she worked for was a bit pompous.

'But what can you expect from a poncy lawyer?' I could not help but laugh. 'Oh, I'm sorry,' she said, holding her hand up to her mouth, 'Tammy said you're a lawyer. I hope I haven't offended you.' Kim's face flushed pink with embarrassment.

'No. Actually, I can't say I like lawyers much myself. Most of them *are* pompous. We don't have a very good reputation!' I gave Kim a big smile.

'Do you work in the City?'

'No. In the West End; for Simons, Snade & Brown. You probably haven't heard of them. It's quite a small firm. We deal with a lot of landed estates and inherited wealth. I enjoy the work but I'm not really happy there.'

'Time for a change?'

'Perhaps.'

'Is your boyfriend a lawyer too?'

'Boyfriend?'

'I saw that Italian guy talking to you earlier and I thought maybe you and he were an item?'

'Ivano?' I laughed. 'No way! As little said about him the better.'

Fortunately, Ivano left early with several of the other guests, but it was only after virtually everybody had gone that I espied Maria huddled up in the corner of the sofa at the far end of the room, very much the worse for wear. She smelt as if she had been sick, and from the look of her she had been crying as she had black mascara streaks on her cheeks.

'You OK?' I asked.

'He dumped me,' she said in between sobs. That was no surprise as Ivano was such a multi-timing bastard.

'Oh, I'm really sorry to hear that, but believe me he's not worth your tears. I'll get you some water.'

'I need to go home.' She tried to stand up but failed in the attempt and fell back onto the sofa.

'Where is home exactly?'

'Highbury.'

'We'll take her,' said Will, stepping in. 'It's not much of a detour for us and at least that way we can make sure she's home safely.' Jo and Will lived in Islington.

'What's going on?' asked Kim who had just come in to the room.

'Maria has had a bit too much to drink.'

'So has Tammy. She's crashed out on her bed.'

Will and Jo left with Maria and I offered to help Kim clear up.

'No worries. You're all right. I'll do it in the morning. You know something, Alicia, I have a feeling we're going to be good friends,' she said walking to the door with me.

'Me too. Goodnight, Kim.'

Chapter 2

'Where's Tammy tonight?' Kim was perched on my kitchen stool munching Pringles while I cooked the tagliatelle, and a cream and mushroom sauce. It was three months since Kim and Tammy had moved in and Kim and I had indeed become good friends. I liked her no-nonsense, down-to-earth attitude.

'Oh, she's gone for an interview at a club in Piccadilly. I'm not *exactly* sure what the job is. She was rather vague about it all, but that's Tammy all over.'

'Hmm... Yes,' I replied.

'I tried to talk to her about it this evening but she was running late and I didn't have the chance.'

At the age of twenty-six Kim treated Tammy as if she were her little sister, and she was inclined to cluck around her like a mother hen which Tammy found very frustrating at times. Kim was actually a close friend of Tammy's elder brother Tom, which was how the two of them had met.

'I'm sure she'll be fine,' I said reassuringly as I laid the table.

'I hope so, but she is *such* an innocent at times. The incident with the freelance photographer a few months back is a perfect example of how naïve she is.'

'What incident? You never mentioned anything,' I said, draining the tagliatelle and tossing it in olive oil.

'Tammy saw an advertisement in *The Stage* requiring models for photographic library work and sent off her résumé and photographs to the PO Box listed.' I served up the pasta and we sat down to eat.

'And?' I passed her the salad bowl and she helped herself to a serving of salad.

'A few weeks later she received a call from this guy called Nathan saying it was his ad and asking her to go for a test shoot. She did a few more shoots and then he told her he wanted to do a weekend shoot in Oxfordshire for a photographic library he was working on. This sauce is very tasty by the way. You must tell me how you made it. I love mushrooms.' She picked up a rather large piece of mushroom on her fork and perused it before swallowing it whole.

'Thanks. It's really easy. I'll write it down for you some time. You were saying that Nathan invited her to Oxfordshire,' I said, drawing her back.

'Yes. Well, that's where he told her they were going, but after he picked her up he said there had been a change of plan and that they were going to Studland Bay as he had a cottage there. To cut a long story short at the end of the day's shoot he said he needed more photographs and asked if she minded staying the night.'

'Oh, right. I think I'm getting the picture. No pun intended!' It did not take much imagination to work out what Nathan had in mind, even for those without very vivid imaginations. 'What did Tammy do?'

'She went to bed. The next thing she remembered was him on top of her, trying to have sex. He made some excuse about her being attracted to him and that's why she had gone down to Dorset with him.'

'You're right. She is naïve.'

'Tell me about it. The thing is, since then, she has refused to have anything further to do with him or to sign the modelling release for the photographs, so now he's hassling her. He has left a few aggressive messages on her mobile.'

'Hmm… Well he wants to sell them, but I guess if he's doing a photographic library he could sell them abroad and she wouldn't know anyway.'

'You know about all that legal stuff then?'

'It isn't my area of specialization. It's copyright law, so Intellectual Property, but I think what I've told you is correct. Coffee?' Kim nodded and followed me through to the kitchen. 'Skinny latte with sugar for you, isn't it?'

'Yeah. That's great. Actually, my boss does IP. I could ask him.'

'Why not do that.' I broke off some pieces of chocolate from a bar of Lindt Macadamia Nut and handed it to her.

'My favourite.'

'I know.' We wandered back into the sitting room and sat down on the sofa. 'Listen, Kim, I can understand why you're worried about Tammy, but she must be wiser now.' Even Tammy could not be *that* naïve. 'Why does she want the job in the Club? Isn't the modelling going well?'

'No,' she sighed.

'Really? But I guess it's so competitive.'

'How's Cesare? I haven't seen him around lately,' said Kim, changing the subject. She took a sip of her coffee.

'He's not. He was head-hunted by another bank and is on garden leave for six months. He went away a couple of weeks ago.'

'Where to?'

'Back to Italy to see his family, and then he's off travelling.'

'You must miss him.'

'I do. He's a good *friend*.' I knew what she meant. She was as bad as Jo. 'How's your new job going?' Kim had recently taken a permanent position at a firm called Wilson, Weil & Co. in Bloomsbury.

'It's different from the firms I temped at before. The Senior Partner Vincent Weil is a really unpleasant man. He shouts and swears at everyone and has a very short fuse.' I nodded in agreement.

'You know him?' She sounded surprised.

'Yes. His reputation goes before him. I've never dealt with him but I've heard he's aggressive and difficult. You're not working for him, are you?'

'No. Fortunately, I have a great boss,' she responded enthusiastically, her whole face lighting up. 'He's called Alex Waterford, he's a Junior Partner in the Company Commercial department and he's gorgeous.' She looked quite flushed.

'No wonder you like your job so much!' I teased.

'He's what *you* would call *benfatto.*'

'Handsome. How handsome?' I asked, leaning forward. I was curious and wanted to hear more.

'Very. Well, at least *I* think he is. There's a picture of him in the firm's brochure. Look!' She took a small grey brochure off the table behind her and handed it to me. The page with his picture on it was well-thumbed.

'I suppose he is,' I said, scrutinizing the photograph in the brochure. 'But he's blond. Generally, I don't go for blond men.' I passed the brochure back to Kim and leant back on the sofa. There was a knock on my front door. It was Tammy, back from her interview.

'I thought you must be up here,' she called out to Kim as she strolled through to the reception room from the hall. 'I'm starving and it's freezing cold outside tonight,' she said, pulling off her gloves and rubbing her hands together. She dropped her portfolio on the floor, unzipped her leather jacket, placed it on the arm of the sofa, and took off her scarf and boots. She then sank back into the sofa cushions and put her feet up on the coffee table in front of her. 'I'm bushed,' she said, yawning and rubbing her eyes.

'How did it go today?' asked Kim in a concerned, maternal tone.

'OK. I went to see Tim and then on to that interview in Piccadilly…'

'Tim?' I did not know who he was.

'Tim Lewis from TL Models. He's my agent.'

'Where's he based?'

'Covent Garden. On Long Acre.'

'Has he found you much work?'

'Not much. I took my latest prints to show him today so that I can update my portfolio. I asked him about assignments but he said that it's a very competitive market here in London and there were no guarantees. If I wanted to get on I should expect to go that little bit further.' I presumed Tim meant via "the casting couch".

'How did the interview go this evening?' She handed me a copy of *The Stage* from the previous week and referred me to the advert she had ringed in the Situations Vacant section. The advert read *'West End Club requires hostesses for exclusive clientele...'* and to call after seven in the evening to arrange an interview.

'Did you *actually* go for an interview there?' I was incredulous.

'Yeah. Why?' she replied casually.

'My understanding of these hostess clubs is that they are seedy and not the sort of places where girls like you work.'

'Dick, that's the guy who runs the Club, ran through everything with me. He assured me there's no sleaze attached to his Club. He said his Club is respectable.'

'Did he offer you the job?' asked Kim.

'Yeah. He was very friendly. He said I can fit work around my modelling schedule and I won't have to work the night before I have an assignment,' she said nonchalantly, running those well-manicured fingers through her hair.

'When do you start?'

'Tomorrow.'

'What's the place called?' asked Kim.

'Jensen's.'

'As long as you know what you're getting into.' I was wrong. Tammy *was* that naïve. 'You said you were hungry. Can I make you something to eat?'

'Tea and a slice of your home-made fruit cake would be great.' She followed me into the kitchen.

'What was Dick like?' I asked, cutting her a piece.

'Umm... He was tall but slightly stooped, balding on top and the rest of his hair was greying. He had quite a ruddy complexion too.'

'It doesn't sound as if he has much to recommend him on the looks front, but I meant what impression did you have of him as a person?'

'He seemed really nice.'

'Plausible you mean?' She looked at me vacantly. 'Are you really sure you should be taking this job?' I handed her the cup of tea.

'I can handle myself.' She sounded a bit irritated. 'You're as bad as Kim. You both worry too much. What could possibly happen to me?'

I battled my way out of Bond Street tube station. The escalators were not working, and it was mayhem with people pushing and shoving. No evidence of any Christmas spirit yet, I thought, as a rather hefty man elbowed me out the way. As I walked along Oxford Street I was met by a biting northerly wind. I pulled up the collar of my overcoat and adjusted my scarf, wrapping it around me more tightly to keep out the cold. Oxford Street was heaving with shoppers even though it was still five weeks until Christmas. I glanced at the shops festooned with baubles, Christmas lights and Christmas trees as I hurried down the street. I crossed the road, walked past Selfridges and turned down Duke Street.

The offices of Simons, Snade & Brown were located off Manchester Square near the Wallace Collection. I sometimes went to the Wallace Collection during my lunch hour to wander through the galleries. There was so much to look at from Old Master paintings to Sèvres porcelain, Renaissance bronzes and a fantastic array of armoury. When my mother came to London, we had lunch in Café Bagatelle, the glass-covered courtyard within Hertford House in which the Wallace Collection is housed. My mother liked it there as it had the look and ambience associated with a continental café with its pretty tables and wicker chairs. It was delightful and appealed to her sense of style.

On the odd occasion, a couple of the other assistant solicitors and I would have a drink in the George Bar at Durrants Hotel, a traditional privately-owned English hotel off Manchester Square. It had a certain homeliness about it which I liked. The bar was welcoming and cosy with its leather armchairs, open fireplaces, paintings and friendly ambience. It was the sort of place a woman could go into alone without worrying about being bothered by undesirables.

Unhappily, the position at Simons, Snade & Brown had not turned out as expected. At the interview I was informed that, although I would be predominantly working for Peter Simons, the Private Client and Senior Partner, the firm was actively building up the matrimonial department and this would be a great opportunity for me. However, I discovered on my first day that the Matrimonial Partner, Jenna Philpotts, was leaving due to a falling out with the partnership – taking her two assistant solicitors and caseload with her – which was very disappointing.

During my two years at the firm I had worked almost exclusively for Peter on the Private Client side of things. He dealt with tax planning, investments and offshore trusts, so I had gained phenomenal experience. Unfortunately, he was approaching retirement and I disliked his successor, David Wagstaff. I was not alone – none of the junior solicitors or secretaries seemed to have much regard for him. He was one of those people who made a great deal of noise about everything he did – which was actually very little.

I was amazed at how he had managed to become a Partner in the first place. However, he was very good at licking the right boots and in giving the appearance, to say the least, that he was the best lawyer for the job. In reality, he relied on his Assistants and Counsel. Astonishingly, he also fancied himself as a matrimonial lawyer, but it was obvious he had no talent for that area of the law whatsoever bearing in mind his approach was like a bull in a china shop. Careful client handling was definitely not his *métier*. I could not tolerate working for him after Peter's retirement, so it was time for me to jump ship.

Our offices were situated near an authentic Italian café, where each morning I picked up a caffè latte and croissant on my way into work, and had a brief chat in Italian with the friendly staff. However, this morning as I opened the door, I saw David Wagstaff standing in the queue at the counter at the far end of the café. He had his back to me, but unfortunately he turned around and saw me before I had a chance to make a quick exit. He smiled one of those tight-lipped smiles which are more like a grimace.

He was of medium height and stocky build, but he always referred to himself as 'muscular'. His dark black wavy hair was gelled down into place. Although his complexion was naturally dark, it was obvious he frequently lay on a sun bed because he had a permanent tan. His eyes were quite deep set and, to be honest, I am not sure what colour they were because I had never cared to look at him for very long. Besides, he wore black metal square-rimmed glasses, which in my opinion did nothing to enhance his looks; he had the irritating habit of pushing them up his nose whenever he tried to make a point. And, to cap it all, he constantly wore a supercilious look on his face as if he was in some way superior to the rest of us.

'Alicia. Good morning. What a surprise to see you in here,' he said, looking at me. He pushed his glasses up his nose and strained a smile at me.

'Not really. I always come here for coffee,' I answered blandly as we moved forward in the queue.

'I left some files on your desk last night which I'd like you to look at. There's some interesting research for you to carry out. It really isn't cost effective for *me* to carry out the work, and I think it would be good experience *for you*,' he said, with a slight curl of the lips whilst pushing his glasses up again. Why he did not buy a pair that actually fitted his nose was beyond me. 'It's an interesting divorce case where there are some offshore trusts and I know that you have *some* experience in this area.'

His manner was condescending, and I knew he wanted me to do all the work and that he would take all the credit with the client. I never minded doing research, as it was one of the aspects of my job I enjoyed, but I resented being given instructions by, and having to work for, someone I regarded as a mediocrity, who was determined to keep me down and to use my skills to promote himself.

'Oh right,' I said without any enthusiasm as we reached the counter.

'Can I 'elp you, sir?' asked Gianni, winking at me. *'Buon giorno, signorina.'*

'Buon giorno, Gianni. Come stai oggi? Stai bene?'

'Caffè latte grande,' interposed David. I sensed he was annoyed we were speaking Italian. I took the opportunity to engage in some friendly banter with Gianni knowing that David could not understand.

'Il mio capo non capisce niente. È sempre maleducato. Sei d'accordo con me?'

'Sì. È un tipo incontentabile!' I could not help but laugh at his frankness.

'I want some service here,' interrupted David, pointing his finger at Gianni. 'You're useless. This isn't the time to have a private conversation,' he added and glared at me.

'Sir, 'ere is your caffè.' Gianni placed it down on the counter, trying to keep a straight face and winking at me again. I picked up my coffee and croissant and walked to the door. David followed close on my heels.

'You didn't have to be so rude to him,' I said.

'I don't need lessons in manners from you, Alicia,' he snapped. 'Just because *you* like to engage in conversation with a common shop assistant doesn't mean *I* do.'

'You know, David,' I said, dropping my voice, 'when you point the finger at somebody, there are always three fingers pointing back at yourself.'

'I'll see you later today about those files,' he replied, ignoring my response. He strode on ahead, and as we reached the office, he stormed through the front door which swung back and almost hit me in the face.

Since our offices were in such an old building, the layout was rather higgledy-piggledy. Fortunately, David's office was not on the same floor as mine and, unless he specifically asked me to go upstairs and see him, I never attempted to do so. My office was small but at the back of the building at the end of a corridor which meant nobody walked past and it was extremely quiet. The window was large, so I had a view and fresh air when I wanted it.

Few of the office staff had arrived but, on seeing a light on in Peter's room, I popped my head around the door.

'Alicia. Good morning. How are you?' he asked, looking up at me over his half-rimmed glasses.

'I'm fine thanks,' I replied. 'You?'

'Yes. Very well indeed. Pat and I are going to Adam's Christening on Sunday.' Pat was his wife. Adam was his daughter's son and his first grandchild. He was proud of his family, and there were photographs of them all over his office.

'That's lovely. I have the notes from the meeting with Mr Gilson to discuss with you when you have a moment. Oh…and…David has given me a divorce matter to look at,' I added. He did not comment.

'I have meetings most of the day. I'll speak to you about Gilson later.'

I opened my office door and put my coffee and croissant down on my desk. The files David had mentioned were piled up on it with a yellow Post-it stuck strategically on the top file on which he had scrawled, *'Alicia. See me. David.'* I scrunched up the note and flicked it into my wastepaper bin. I took off my scarf and overcoat and turned on my computer to check my e-mails.

I switched my 'phone to DND (do not disturb) and started to work on David's files. The case was actually very interesting. We were acting for the wife, Rebecca Jacobs. On reading the correspondence file, I noted that Wilson, Weil & Co., Kim's new firm, was acting for the husband. It was not that extraordinary, because there were only certain firms which had the expertise to deal with cases as complicated as this. I knew that Vincent Weil's firm was one of them, and he had an outstanding reputation in this field. David would never be any match for Vincent.

The husband had a number of offshore trusts and some offshore bank accounts. All the matrimonial properties were owned through companies which were also held offshore, so there was nothing in his name. Mrs Jacobs asserted that he had assets abroad, but no attempt had been made to locate and injunct them. I read through the inter-solicitor correspondence; it was evident that Vincent Weil was running rings around David and making mincemeat of his pathetically presented case. By now Mr Jacobs had probably had time to move his assets, and a case for negligence against our firm was looming.

'Morning, Alicia,' said Louisa, my secretary, putting her head around the door. The rest of her followed, albeit slowly, as she was heavily pregnant. Louisa had been working for me for the past seven months, and no sooner had she arrived than she found out she was pregnant; her maternity leave began at Christmas. She had suffered a nasty miscarriage two years before and thought that she would never have children as she was now forty-three. I was going to miss her because she was an excellent secretary in all respects unlike Janet her predecessor. Janet was twenty-six, exceptionally lazy and had showed no interest in her work whatsoever. She had spent most of her time on the 'phone arranging her social life or arguing with her latest boyfriend.

'How are you?' I asked Louisa as she sat down.

'Pregnant,' she replied, laughing and touching her bump. 'David was looking for you as he wants you to see a new client for him. He said he cleared it with Peter yesterday.' I knew that was not true.

'That's odd. Peter didn't mention anything to me this morning. Did David say what it's about and what time the client is due?' I asked, looking at my watch because if there was anything to prepare I might need some time. It was nearly ten o'clock.

'Err… Well, he's waiting outside. David said something about a Children Act application and that it would be right up your street.

Oh…and I've arranged your meeting with Brenda Thomas in Winchester at two on Tuesday. Mr Gilson 'phoned about his investment advice and asked if you could call him, as Peter isn't around; and Meera Ruperelli called, something about wedding plans. Is there something you want to tell me?' I shook my head. Meera was a friend from university and had just become engaged.

'Could you call Mr Gilson and explain that I have to go into a meeting now, but that I will speak to him later today. Who's the client I'm seeing?' I asked, gathering the files together into a pile and clearing my desk.

'Robert Dickson. His wife's with him.'

'OK. I'll be out in a few minutes. Thanks, Louisa.'

'How did the meeting go?' asked Louisa when I walked into the kitchen where she was making tea.

'Oh, it was OK. A bit sad really. They've lost a son and daughter-in-law in the space of three months and are left with a two-year-old granddaughter, Samantha, to bring up. They want me to sort out Probate and residence for Samantha.'

Louisa made me a cup of tea and I hurried back to my office where Mary, Peter's secretary, was rummaging through my filing cabinet.

'Alicia, do you have the Gilson file?' she asked as she looked through the Jacobs papers on the floor.

'No. I gave it back to Peter. Why? What do you want if for?'

'David said that the client called him and he can't find the file.'

'Why did the client call him? He's not David's client. I asked Louisa to call Mr Gilson and tell him I had to go into a meeting, and that I would call him later. David has done this a lot recently. Only last week I caught him going through my dictation pile and then scanning my timesheets. You won't find it there. Those are the Jacobs papers.'

'Yes, but you know what David's like,' she said, standing up, taking off her half-glasses and looking at me. She had very blue eyes and lovely silver hair which she wore in a short sleek bob.

'Is that a question or a statement?' I asked. Mary sighed; the truth was she did not like David either. She had worked for Peter for thirty years and had told me she would retire when he did because she was not prepared to work for the firm if David became head of department, which was likely.

'Alicia, what can I say?'

'There's nothing to say. I'm going out to get something to eat and some fresh air. I'll see you in about twenty minutes.'

I left Gianni's where I had bought a tuna sandwich, and was ambling back to the office when my mobile phone rang.

'Hello…is that Alicia Allen?' I did not recognize the woman's voice which was quite husky. I felt as if she was deliberately attempting to conceal it.

'Who is this?' I asked.

'Is that Alicia Allen?' she repeated, but slightly more insistently.

'Yes, but who are *you*?'

'You don't know me.'

'No. Exactly. That's why I'm asking. *Who* are you?' I asked, slightly frustrated by the roundabout nature of this conversation.

'Let's just say that a friend of yours recommended you. This friend said you're a lawyer and you can help me.'

'It depends what your problem is,' I said cautiously. 'What friend?'

'I can't tell you that over the 'phone.' She sounded agitated and afraid.

'You didn't tell me your name or how you *know* this friend of mine.'

'You can call me Eve. I can't tell you how I know your friend, but you have to promise to help me.' There was a pause. 'I'm sure I can count on you.'

'OK…*Eve*,' I hesitated, thinking that this was absolutely crazy. 'What do you want me to do?' I said in a low voice. Goodness knows why I was whispering and agreeing to help a complete stranger, but I was.

'Nothing, for now. I'll call you again, but you must not speak to anyone about this call or we're both in danger.'

'Hang on a minute,' I replied, but she had hung up. I checked my mobile and the number had been withheld. I felt slightly sick and, all of a sudden, the tuna sandwich did not seem quite as appealing as it had done five minutes earlier. I returned to the office and started to dictate up my notes from the morning meeting, but I could not focus on them as this strange call niggled at me. Obviously the caller's real name was not Eve, but why she was calling me was a mystery.

'You all right, Alicia?' Mary asked, walking into my office with some files. I jumped. 'I'm sorry,' she continued. 'I didn't mean to startle you. You look rather pale. It doesn't look as if your walk has done you much good.'

'No... Err... Yes... I'm a bit tired that's all. I went to bed very late last night.'

'Yes, dear. You young people burn the candle at both ends and you don't eat properly either,' she said, espying the tuna sandwich in my bin and giving me a disapproving look.

David left me alone for the rest of the day and Peter did not return to the office, so I did not have the opportunity to discuss the Gilson file with either of them. I left the office at six and strolled along Oxford Street. Everything looked very festive and in the darkness Selfridges' brilliantly decorated windows came alive, all the lights twinkling cheerfully out into the night. It was bitterly cold and drizzling with rain and, as I waited at the bus stop at the top of Park Lane, I shivered. I wondered whether Eve would contact me again. I was intrigued – who was she, why was she calling me and what assistance could she possibly want from me?

Chapter 3

I was awakened from a deep sleep by a thudding sound outside the door to *my* flat. I glanced at my clock radio; it was four-twenty in the morning. Reluctantly, I dragged myself out of bed, slipped on my yellow towelling robe and staggered into the hall. I peered through the spyhole, which was next to useless because the light was not on in the hallway and I could not see who was standing there.

'Who is it?' I asked cautiously, in a half whisper.

'It's me. Tammy. May I come in?' She sounded slightly choked.

'OK.' I unlocked the door.

'I'm so pleased to see you, Alicia.' She stumbled through the doorway.

'What's the matter?' I said, opening the door. She looked frozen, was shaking and her eyes were smarting from the bitterly cold November night. She was not dressed for the weather, but in denim jacket and jeans. She followed me through to the reception room. 'Are you OK?' I asked, noticing the tea cloth wrapped around her left hand. 'Let me look at your hand,' I said, unravelling the tea cloth. There was a small wound to the centre of her palm. I re-wrapped her hand.

'I've got some dry dressings and a bandage in my First Aid box.' I went to fetch it. I dabbed the wound with cotton wool and a mild solution of Dettol, then covered it with a self-adhesive Melolin dressing.

'Would you like some tea?' I asked as I packed up my First Aid box. She nodded. I went into the kitchen to make it.

'How did you injure your hand?' I asked, walking through to the reception room, placing my cup of tea on the coffee table and handing Tammy her cup.

'The zip on my dress stuck when I was changing. I went to cut the threads with my nail scissors and the scissors slipped. I jabbed the palm of my hand with the blades,' she said, looking down at her hand. 'I'm never going back there, Alicia.' She sounded calm but it was clear she was slightly traumatized by the evening's events as she was still shaking, and I just knew that something else must have happened at the Club to disturb her.

'Do you want to talk about it?' I put the throw from the sofa around her shoulders.

'Before I tell you, you must promise not to tell Kim.'

'But won't she be wondering where you are?'

'She's not here. She's in Bath staying with Sam, one of her school friends, who's over visiting her family. She'll only fuss and I know I can talk to you freely without you judging me.' I felt slightly awkward, if not strangely flattered, that Tammy wanted to confide in me.

'OK. I promise.'

'You were right about the Club being sleazy.' She sighed and slumped back into the sofa and drew the throw around her.

'Go on.'

'I only took the job because Dick made it sound OK. He said it was a gentleman's club and champagne bar and all the guys who came in were members, so it was exclusive. He told me all I had to do was sit with one of the guys each evening, and make him buy loads of champagne. In return I'd earn commission on the number of bottles the guy bought, and Dick would make sure I'd get a good tip for keeping him company.'

'But presumably that's not *all* you were expected to do to earn money?' I guessed that a hostess would be called upon to do more than make small talk to earn a sizeable tip. I could not believe that Tammy had not seen beyond Dick's flannel.

'No.' I noticed she had finished her tea. 'Do you want some more tea?' She nodded. 'I don't suppose you've eaten either. Do you want anything to eat?'

'Toast would be good.' I put four slices of bread into the toaster, boiled the kettle again, and returned to the reception room to listen to what she had to say.

'If I tell you about my experiences at the Club you'll understand why I'm never going back there.'

'I'm all ears, Tammy.'

'My first night wasn't too bad. When I arrived, Dick introduced me to Patti. I think she's the senior hostess. She said Dick had asked her to show me the ropes and introduce me to the other girls.'

'Did you ask her why she worked there?'

'It was difficult to talk to her because she couldn't hear me properly.'

'Why? Because the Club was noisy?'

'No. I mean, yes it was, but the reason she couldn't hear was 'cos she's partially deaf. She told me that she was a single mother and the job suited her.'

'What was she like?'

'Pretty. A mulatto. Tall. Thin. Long dark sleek hair. Elegant. She was wearing a fabulous long black sequined dress which was sleeveless, low cut, and with a side split.' I heard the toast pop up and the kettle click off. I quickly made the tea, buttered the toast and came back into the room. 'Patti and the others were OK. Fen was the one I didn't like.'

'Why?' I asked, handing her the plate of toast. I sat down in my armchair.

'Thanks,' she said, taking a bite. 'She wasn't there yesterday, as she had a night off, but when I went into the changing room this evening she was standing there naked. I just stared at her 'cos she's got these enormous nipple rings. I couldn't help looking – I guess it was the combination of the pierced nipples, cropped bleached blonde hair and the heaviest eye make-up I've ever seen. She accused me of staring at her tits. Then later this evening she made a pass at me when I went to the bathroom.'

'I get the picture,' I said, stirring my tea.

'I made an excuse to Jack, the guy I was sitting with, that I needed to go to the bathroom. I'll tell you about Jack in a minute. I wanted to get away from him. Anyway, Fen was in there. She said if I didn't like boys touching me up I should try a little fun with a girl and she fondled my breasts. I pushed her hands away and told her I wasn't interested. She went berserk and grabbed my hair, pushed me against the wall with her body and forced my dress up. I tried to scream, but she put one hand over my mouth and tried to pull my knickers down with the other. I've got scratch marks from her nails all over my thighs.'

'You couldn't push her away?'

'She forced me back against the wall and she's really strong, but I managed to free my arms and struggled to push her off when Patti came in.' She swallowed another mouthful of toast.

'And then?'

'Fen stormed out, but not before saying I would regret what I had just done.'

'So she threatened you then? What did Patti say?'

'That Fen was in a bad mood 'cos she'd just split up with her girl-friend and was completely screwed up anyway as she takes coke. Apparently, she always tries it on with new girls.'

'Hmm... How very reassuring! You mentioned someone called Jack.'

'Yes.' She swallowed the remainder of the toast and put the plate on the table. 'Patti said Dick had arranged for me to sit with a regular and a big spender called Jack. Annalise, that's one of the other hostesses, said that if I played my cards right I could screw a huge tip out of him.' That was exactly what Tammy was expected to do, I thought. 'She told me she loves working in the Club as it's such easy money because the guys are pathetic inadequates. If they want to give her hundreds of pounds for a bit of tit-and-arse or deep throat she won't say "No".'

'Did Annalise have a view on Fen?'

'Oh yeah. Annalise said that Fen was bisexual, that she had been a hostess, a pole dancer, in a peep show and even a hooker in her time.'

'A bit of an all-rounder then,' I said tongue-in-cheek.

'Apparently, Fen's favourite expression is "dick hard, brain soft" which is the best time to ask the guys for money.'

'Which probably isn't difficult as they're in the Club to spend? What was Jack like?'

'As soon as I saw him he gave me the creeps. I'd say he's about five feet ten 'cos I'm taller than him. He has grey curly hair slicked down with hair gel; and a jowl. He's not very attractive, but it was the way he looked at me, undressing me with his eyes, that freaked me. I sat on the stool next to him at the bar. He moved his stool closer and stroked my knee. He said he'd like to spend some time alone with me in a place where there was some privacy so that he could get to know me. His exact words, Ally.' She sipped her tea.

'Why didn't you leave there and then?'

'I thought I could manage it. Last night was OK 'cos I sat with a group of Americans and they were just really drunk and friendly. I thought tonight would be OK and that I could handle Jack and get my money. I made an excuse to go to the bathroom. That was when I had the run-in with Fen I told you about. When I came back Abbey had stripped down to a sparkly G-string and bra.'

'One of the hostesses?'

'Yes. A Kiwi. She's minute, five feet tall with waist length curly brown hair. Although she's tiny, she has a big personality and she's a good mimic. I heard her impersonating Dick. It was quite funny.'

'Did she strip completely?'

'Oh yes. She approached one of the guys sitting at the bar, Simon I think his name was, and sat on his lap and loosened his tie. She pressed her breasts against him, placed his hands on her buttocks, then arched her back and edged away from him gradually pulling off his tie. She then made him take her underwear off with his teeth. Flic did the same, but with another guy.'

'And she is?'

'Another Kiwi, and Abbey's best friend. She's as tall as Abbey's small.'

'Were you sitting with Jack *all* this time?'

'No. I hovered at the other end of the bar until they had finished. It's so dark in there he couldn't see me.' She finished her tea and put down the cup and lay back on the sofa.

'What happened after that?'

'I went back to sit with him at the bar, but he had arranged to move into one of the booths in the corner. They have red velvet curtains that can be pulled across. Dick brought over some Bollinger and pulled the curtains. Jack had his hands all over me and was kissing my neck. I told him to get off, refused to kiss him and he turned nasty.'

'In what way? Physically?'

'Not at first. It was more verbal. He asked me why I worked in the Club if I wasn't prepared to perform the duties of a proper hostess. I told him I had been given a different impression at the interview and I was sick of being treated like a tart because I'm a model and blonde. I needed to earn some money that's all. He said I was naïve if I thought girls made tips by keeping their legs crossed and by engaging in chit-chat. He was surprised I couldn't earn enough money from modelling. I explained that I was owed a lot of money and told him about Nathan and why I had refused to sign the modelling release and he recommended an IP lawyer to me.'

'How weird. Which firm?'

'I don't remember. A young guy he said. Irish name. Wexford I think. Have you heard of him?'

'No. Kim told me her boss does IP. I'm surprised she hasn't mentioned him to you.'

'I'll ask her. Anyway, Jack said that in the meantime if I needed to earn money he could help me.'

'By helping himself you mean?'

'Yes. He told me that he liked to play with the mind and turn women on that way, that he wanted to make it with me and, if I gave him access, I could command my price.'

'Give him access? Is that we he *actually* said?' I leaned forward in my chair.

'Yes. I said I wouldn't do it and he became very aggressive and started to shake me. He forced me back against the wall and held my chin. He told me that he was used to getting what he wanted and would, whether I liked it or not, and then he forced his hand up between my thighs and tried to push it inside me. I tried to pull his hand away but he was heavy and leaned against me. He said that he wouldn't have to push as hard if I let him in. So I spat in his face, he slapped mine and accused me of being a tight-arsed little prick-teaser. He said I would get what was coming to me. Then he stormed off.'

'Did he tell you why he goes to the Club apart from the obvious reason?'

'He did. Yeah. He said he was divorced eighteen years ago and had a string of failed relationships since. He has his own property investment business and has to fly to New York a lot because he has dealings there. He comes to the Club to alleviate stress.'

'I'm sure. The thing is, Tammy, he's used to putting his money down and buying what he wants. After all, that's what the Club is all about. Look at the other girls. They don't care what they do as long as they get the cash. Did he leave the Club after that?'

'I think so. I didn't see him go, but I went straight into the changing room. Patti left a few minutes after I went in. I was so agitated to get out of there, and that's when I stabbed my hand with the scissors. I couldn't find Dick so I took a clean tea cloth from under the bar and wrapped it around my hand. To leave the Club you have to pass Dick's office. There's a counter like there is in a pub which you have to lift up and the door to his office is behind it. I heard shouting coming from the office, but the only voice I recognized was Dick's.

Although the door was ajar it was impossible to see anything. I didn't want to get involved and made a run for it.'

'You couldn't hear what they were arguing about?'

'No. They all seemed to be shouting at once.'

'The main thing is you're out of there now. You don't have to go back do you?'

'I'll have to tell Dick that I can't work there anymore. I also need to collect my money.'

'When?'

'Monday. That's when he pays.'

'His insurance policy, to make sure girls go back after the weekend!' I said sarcastically. 'Do you want me to go with you?'

'No. You're all right. I'll be fine.'

I turned over in bed and looked at the time on my clock radio. It was just after eight and I felt dreadful. I expected Tammy would be feeling relieved. She had fallen asleep on my sofa and I had tiptoed around the flat so as not to wake her. Dick Jensen had clearly lied about the Club, which was certainly sleazy; the only difference between his Club and other clubs was that his was not *overtly* sleazy. The men that went there were looking for a grope and sex if they could get it.

I now dragged myself out of bed, walked through to the bathroom and glanced in the mirror – not one of my better days. I went back to bed, dozed off again and slept until almost ten o'clock. I was awoken by the sound of the front door clicking shut. Tammy had left.

I walked through to the hall and heard someone drop my post on the mat outside. I opened the front door and picked it up. Among the letters was a postcard from Cesare who was in Dubai and, while the kettle was boiling, I read it. I made tea, toast and marmalade and sat on the sofa to open the rest of my post. I noticed a folded piece of paper on the coffee table. It was from Tammy. It read *'Gone shopping. Catch you when I'm back. Thanks for listening. Don't worry. T x.'*

I heard nothing more from Tammy all day.

I had arranged to meet with Meera on Saturday evening, but she 'phoned me to say that she had a stinking cold and was off to bed with a hot water bottle and some Lemsip. Jo and Will had gone to France for the weekend to see Jo's mother, and Antonia called to say that she was going to the cinema with a couple of her friends and asked if I wanted to meet for dinner afterwards.

At just after eight in the evening Tammy knocked on my front door.

'This is for you,' she said, handing me a bottle of Amaretto di Saronno. 'I know you like it.'

'You're very sweet, but there really was no need.'

'Thank you for listening to me. I felt so much better for talking to you.'

'It was nothing. How are you feeling? How's the hand?'

'I feel heaps better. The hand's OK. A bit sore. What are you up to this evening? Do you want to go out?'

'I'm meeting Antonia for dinner at nine. Do you fancy coming? You can meet her then.'

'If you're sure that's OK.'

'Of course it is. Ask Kim if she wants to come. When did she get back?'

'I don't know. I've been out all day.' She loosened her blue scarf.

'I'll collect you on my way out.'

'Cool,' she said, and ran down the stairs.

My mobile had been switched off and when I turned it back on I saw that I had missed several calls. The numbers were withheld and no messages had been left, and I thought they might be from Eve. I was perplexed by the whole thing and wondered when she would call again. It was difficult to know if she was genuine, but I hoped to find out sooner rather than later.

When I went to collect Tammy, Kim opened the door to their flat.

'You've had your hair restyled,' I said, looking up at the sleek bob. 'It suits you.'

'Do you think so?' she asked, wrinkling up her nose and smoothing the back of her hair with her hand as she turned to look in the hall mirror. 'I had it done in Bath.'

'I told her it looks good,' said Tammy as she appeared in the hall. 'Are we off then?' She pulled her coat and scarf off the coat rack. 'Are you coming, Kim?' She threw Kim her coat and struggled to put hers on with one arm.

'Yes. You can tell me how you hurt your hand and all about the Club.' Tammy looked at me, raised her eyebrows and I turned away.

'Ally! Over here.' Antonia stood up and waved to us as we walked into the restaurant. She was sitting in the far corner with her friends Chloë and Marianne. After the ritual hugging and kissing on both cheeks, I introduced Tammy and Kim to Antonia, Chloë and Marianne.

'You're very different,' said Tammy, looking at Antonia and back at me. 'Antonia is taller and her hair is darker, longer and very wavy. Her eyes are hazel whereas yours are green. You both have the same shaped face though.'

'I have our father's height and our mother's colouring,' said Antonia, 'whereas Alicia has our mother's petiteness and our father's colouring.'

'I think you can definitely tell that Toni and Ally are sisters,' said Chloë. 'They have similar mannerisms and the intonation in their voices has a marked resemblance. But I guess I've known them both since I was eleven, so I know them really well!'

I ordered a bottle of Chardonnay and we ordered our food. The waiter returned with the wine and as he poured it Tammy placed her hand over her glass.

'None for me, thanks. I'll stick with water. I had too much Bollinger last night.'

'What have you done to your hand?' asked Marianne with her

mouth half-full. She had just swallowed a spoonful of prawn cocktail. I disliked her manner and only tolerated her because she was Antonia's friend. She was an in-your-face type of person and very pushy.

'I had a silly accident with some nail scissors at work.'

'Are you a manicurist?' Marianne said patronizingly. Tammy caught my eye.

'She's a model, Marianne. She enjoys the high life. That's why she drinks so much champagne. Did you all enjoy the film?' I asked, changing the subject.

'It was ghastly.' Chloë interjected.

'Put it this way, it was a definite cure for insomnia, I can tell you,' Marianne said as she chewed on a piece of bread. 'How's your job Alicia?'

'The same.'

'Law firms,' Kim sighed.

'It's not as bad as she makes out,' said Tammy, squeezing Kim's forearm. 'Kim has a hunk of a boss.'

'Really?' Marianne leaned forward. 'Is he available?'

'You're more predatory than all the men I know!' said Antonia. The waiter brought our main courses.

'Tell us about him?' asked Chloë, swallowing a chunk of swordfish steak.

'Alicia and I have only seen his photograph in the firm's brochure, but he is very good looking,' Tammy said enthusiastically.

'I gathered that. Does he have a girlfriend?' Marianne was insistent.

'You're incorrigible! Leave poor Kim alone,' said Antonia.

'I don't know much about his private life or his girlfriends really, but he receives loads of calls from women. I think he finds it very easy to attract girls. He's just so…'

'Charming, good looking and knows exactly what to say?' I finished off Kim's sentence.

'And exciting,' added Antonia.

'Mmm… He sounds gorgeous,' said Marianne, positively drooling.

'There's more to him than that. He has that certain *je ne sais quoi* or wow factor. If you met him you'd know what I mean.' Kim was struggling to explain herself.

'What about other people in the firm, Kim?' Marianne asked, yawning.

'What she means is, are there any other eligible men at the office?' Antonia chipped in.

'Nobody like him.'

'How disappointing,' Marianne drawled. 'Oh well, we'll all have to fight over him then,' she added.

'I'll pass. As I said before, he's not my type,' I said, but I was intrigued by Alex Waterford all the same.

It was Tuesday evening and the train from Winchester was late. I walked along the platform where there were quite a few people waiting. I glanced at my watch – ten past six. I wanted to go home and soak in a hot bath because I was tired and freezing cold. I stood on the platform shivering, despite the fact that I was wearing a thick coat, gloves and a scarf. I shuffled my feet and rubbed my hands together in an attempt to keep warm. I had meant to catch the earlier train home but had been delayed because Mrs Thomas, the elderly client whose instructions I was taking for her Will, insisted I stay for tea. I cannot say I minded because she was interesting to talk to, very welcoming and her home-made scones were absolutely delicious.

'Do you know what time the next train will be here?' asked a man standing behind me. The accent was Australian and I turned to put a face to the voice. I looked at the tall, young man with dark straight hair who was wearing a puffer jacket and black jeans. He had an amiable expression and smiling blue eyes. I noticed he was carrying a small backpack and presumed he was on his travels.

'Your guess is as good as mine. The trains are running late.

Something to do with frozen points,' I replied.

'Oh, right. I'll go and get myself a cup of tea then as I'm frozen too,' he said. 'Can I get you one?' I shook my head and he wandered off.

The train arrived at twenty-five to seven. I found a corner seat, took off my coat and scarf, pushed my gloves into my coat pockets and stretched up to place everything including my briefcase on the rack above. My eyes were smarting from the cold and I was glad to be in a warm carriage. I decided to review the notes from my meeting and reached up for my briefcase. Unfortunately, someone else in the carriage had placed a coat and bag in front of mine and, in so doing, had pushed my briefcase to the back of the rack. As I turned around I saw that the Australian man who had spoken to me had settled himself in the seat opposite.

'Excuse me,' I said, addressing him. He looked up from his book. 'Do you mind getting my brief case for me? I can't reach it.'

'Oh, right,' he beamed at me. 'Of course I'll get it for you.' He handed it to me. He beamed again and this time I smiled back.

'Thanks so much.'

'No worries,' he replied. He sat down and returned to his book. I worked for most of the journey but when the train reached Clapham Junction I put my papers away. I looked up, caught the Australian's eye and we both smiled again. 'I saw you working. Are you a lawyer or something?'

'Hmm... Something like that. Why? Does the dark suit and the briefcase give the game away?'

'Thought you must be.'

'Oh, right. What makes you ask?'

'Just curious. I studied Law for one term at university but changed to Sports Science. Law just wasn't for me.'

'I'm not sure it's for me either!'

'You don't enjoy the job then?' He seemed surprised.

'I like the work and the clients. I think it's more a case of not liking the lawyers I've worked with much.'

'Lawyers aren't the most popular people in the world.'

'Nor are estate agents,' I said, laughing. 'Are you travelling around?'

'I have family in Winchester. I've been staying with them for a couple of weeks. I'm starting a job as a personal trainer in London in the New Year, and I think I'm going to stick around in London for a while. I'm coming up to London 'cos some of my mates are over and we're going to France for a few days.'

'Oh, that sounds fun.' The train pulled into Waterloo and he reached up effortlessly to get my coat down off the rack. 'Thank you,' I said as he handed it to me. I put my scarf on and then my coat and did up the buttons. We walked down the platform together and on to the main concourse. 'Well, I hope you have a good trip,' I said, turning to him.

'And I hope you find a better job,' he paused. 'I enjoyed chatting with you.' He grinned and walked away. I stood and watched him and his backpack disappear and it occurred to me that I had not even asked him his name. I walked towards the taxi rank and as I passed a news kiosk I bought an *Evening Standard.* The queue for taxis was not very long and I only had to wait a few minutes.

'Onslow Square, please.' I climbed into the taxi and rested my briefcase and handbag on the floor. I flicked through the newspaper and a headline at the top of page five caught my attention. The words stood out from the page:

'MODEL KILLED IN SAVAGE ATTACK.' I read on: *'Police are today investigating the brutal murder of a young woman whose body was discovered in an alleyway in Soho this morning. The victim has been identified as Tamsin Brown aged 20.'*

Chapter 4

'Oh, my God! Oh, my God!' I gasped, putting my hand to my mouth. I reeled from the shock.

'You all right, luv?' the taxi driver asked, pushing back the glass partition.

'No... I mean, I don't know,' I stammered. 'I've just read something terrible in the newspaper about one of my friends. I need to get home as quickly as possible.'

'Quick as I can, luv.'

I sat and stared at the newspaper headline. It was unbelievable; Tammy was dead.

I picked up my handbag and briefcase, scrambled out of the taxi and paid the driver. I did not bother to wait for my change and, still clutching the newspaper, ran up the steps to the flats. I fumbled in my pocket for my house keys and then dropped them on the steps in my agitation. I bent down to pick them up and saw Kim at her reception room window beckoning me to come into her flat. The door was ajar, I walked straight into the hall as she came rushing out to meet me. She looked as though she had been crying her heart out.

'Alicia, oh Alicia, the most terrible thing you can imagine has happened.' Tears were streaming down her face and she was choking to get the words out.

'I know,' I said softly as she led me inside.

'What do you mean? How do you know?' For that second she stopped sobbing and looked at me quizzically. I realized that she had not seen the evening paper and wondered what I knew. I handed her the paper and pointed to the headline at the top of page five. She looked at it, and dropped onto the sofa.

'I had to identify her Alicia. It was so…so…horrible,' she stammered. 'Her face, it was…' A huge tear trickled down her cheek.

'Don't Kim.' I knelt down on the floor, put my arms around her and hugged her. 'I'm so sorry. What can I say?' The impact of all this had not really hit me and I was on automatic pilot.

'How could anyone hurt her? And why? I can't believe it's true. When the police turned up this morning and told me that they had found a body and thought it was her, I…I…I…lost it.' She started to sob again and put her head in her hands.

'Why didn't you ring me?'

'I didn't want to call you on your mobile and tell you, as that would be too awful. I wanted to tell you in person. I'm so sorry you had to find out by seeing it in the paper…it must have been such a shock.' She looked up at me.

'It has been a terrible shock for both of us,' I handed her a crumpled tissue from my coat pocket. 'What did the police say?' My head was spinning as I came to realize the onus would be on me to inform the police about what had happened to Tammy at the Club.

'That she was savagely kicked in the head. They said something about an assault, but they have to wait for the results of the autopsy…and all the forensic stuff. I can't bear to think of her lying in that mortuary, Alicia. It's all too horrible.' She choked the words out between sobs.

'I know. When did you last see her?' I had not seen her since dinner on Saturday evening.

'Yesterday morning. As I was leaving for work she told me she had a doctor's appointment and that she'd be back late because she was going to the Club to collect her money. I went to bed. I didn't know she wasn't in until this morning when I saw her bedroom door was open and her bed hadn't been slept in. I called her mobile but there was no answer. I didn't think any more about it until the police turned up and I…' She broke down again. 'They've asked me so many questions about her, her friends and her work. I gave them as much information as I could.'

'Do they know if she actually arrived at the Club yesterday evening?' I was cautious over what I revealed to Kim, as she was very distressed and it would hurt her to know that Tammy had not confided in her about her experiences at the Club.

'I asked the police that. They didn't comment. They wanted to look through her things.'

'What about her family, Kim? She has a mother and brother in Australia, doesn't she?'

'Yeah. In Brisbane. I gave the police their details. They said they'd inform the Australian police who'd make contact with the family. Tom called just before you came in and said that the police had turned up on his mother's doorstep and given her the news. They're coming over as soon as they can.'

'It must have been such a shock. How did he sound?'

'Remarkably calm. There's so much to do, Alicia, and then there's the funeral,' she sighed, and put her head in her hands again, resting her elbows on her knees.

'Yes, I know.' I tried to sound reassuring. 'But that's down to Tammy's family, Kim. Is there anything I can do for you? Have you had anything to eat?'

'I couldn't eat a thing. Would you stay down here with me tonight? I don't want to be alone.'

'Of course I will.'

I went upstairs to my flat to shower and change. When I stepped out of the shower I heard my mobile phone ringing so I grabbed a towel off the rail and ran to answer it. I had left it on the coffee table and by the time I reached it the ringing had stopped. I checked the missed calls and, again, the number had been withheld and no voice message had been left. I concluded that this must be Eve. There was a message from my mother on my answerphone about her visit at the weekend. I called her back and told her about Tammy's murder. She was stunned. Then I collected together all the things I needed, slipped my mobile phone into the back pocket of my jeans, closed my front door and ran downstairs. I was outside the door to Kim's flat when my mobile started to vibrate in my pocket. I hesitated before I answered it.

'Ally. It's Meera.'

'Oh! Hello. Are you feeling better?' I am not sure whether I was disappointed or relieved that it was not Eve.

'I'm so much better thanks. Are you OK, Ally? You don't sound your usual self. What's wrong?'

'I'm fine, but something terrible has happened.'

'What?'

'My neighbour's flatmate has been murdered.' I paused. I heard Meera take a sudden intake of breath at the other end of the 'phone.

'That's absolutely dreadful, Ally. I don't know what to say.'

'There's nothing to say. I'm struggling to take it in myself. Murder is supposed to be what happens in other people's lives. It's what you read about in thrillers. Do you know what I mean?'

'Yes, I do.'

'I have to go, Meera, but I'll call you soon.'

'Don't worry about that. Call when you can. Take care.'

Kim's front door was ajar and as I pushed it open and walked into the hall, the 'phone rang. I ran to answer it as I did not want Kim to be disturbed because she said she would take a sleeping pill and go to bed.

'Hello...' I was a little breathless.

'Is that Kimberley Davis?' The voice was male and deep and had a slight Scottish burr.

'No. Who's calling?'

'DS Hamilton. Metropolitan Police. West End Central. You are?' He sounded quite stern.

'Alicia Allen. I'm a friend of Kim…Kimberley Davis.'

'Ah, Miss Allen…right… Miss Davis mentioned you today. You're the solicitor who lives upstairs. We'd like to speak with you about Tamsin Brown. Will you be at home for the next hour or so? We also need to speak with Miss Davis again this evening.'

'I understand. Actually, I'm staying with her tonight. She asked me to keep her company as she didn't want to be alone. Do you *really* need to speak to her, only she's asleep? Can't your questions wait until tomorrow?' I was insistent and he picked up on it.

'It's not a problem. We'll talk to her in the morning, but we'd like to ask you some questions now if you don't mind. We'll be there in about ten minutes.' He rang off.

Almost exactly ten minutes later the video Entryphone buzzed and I went to see who it was. Two men were standing at the doorway.

'Hello…'

'Miss Allen.'

'Yes.'

'Good evening. I'm Detective Inspector Peters.' He held his identity badge up to the video entry system. 'You spoke to DS Hamilton on the 'phone just now.' DS Hamilton also held up his identity badge. 'May we come in?'

'Yes, of course. Please do.' I pressed the door release button. I stood and waited by the door to the flat as they came into the hall, and then I led them through to the reception room. DS Hamilton was about five feet ten inches, medium build, fair hair and eyes, and seemed about my age. DI Peters was taller and well-built, with greying hair and a moustache.

'Please sit down.' They did so, but I remained standing in the middle of the room. 'Can I offer you tea or coffee?'

'Thank you, no,' said DI Peters looking at me very hard. I took it that he was speaking for the both of them or, at least, DS Hamilton had no say in the matter. 'Miss Allen, how well did you know Tamsin Brown?'

'Not that well really.' I sat down a little nervously on the edge of one of the armchairs. 'I only met her in August this year when she and Kim started to rent this flat. I live on the first floor, as you probably know. We bumped into each other the day they moved in, and became friendly, but I'm better friends with Kim.'

'Any particular reason for that?' He gave me a searching look.

'No. Only that Kim and I have more in common in terms of interests and age.'

'Is there anyone you can think of who would wish to harm her?'

'I don't know much about the modelling world. What I do know is that she had a run-in with a freelance photographer called Nathan and problems with her modelling agent, but presumably Kim has already told you all of this?' I looked at them quizzically.

'We took some preliminary details from her, yes.' Clearly they did not want to divulge details of the case to me.

'Tammy did go and work at a club in Piccadilly called Jensen's a week or so ago. It didn't work out and she had to leave...' They were both studying me intently and I felt slightly uneasy.

'What do you mean by that comment, Miss Allen? Can you expand on that for us?'

'Put it this way, her role as hostess wasn't exactly what she expected. The owner expressly stated there was no sleaze attached to his Club, but it seems that there was no shortage of it. She also had a run-in with one of the hostesses who made advances to her, and with one of the clientele.'

'Why did she take the job?'

'She needed the cash and a job that would fit around her modelling schedule.'

'How do you know all this?' asked DI Peters.

'Because she told me.' I was not sure what he was implying.

'When?'

'She knocked on my door in the early hours of Saturday morning. She was a little distressed. She had injured her left hand on some nail scissors while she was changing and I dressed it for her.

A client called Jack had threatened her when she did not perform for him and…'

'In what way threatening? That he would harm her?'

'He said she would regret it as he always got what he wanted.'

'I see. Do you have any idea why she came to you and not to Miss Davis? Miss Davis says she knows nothing about what happened at the Club.'

'I'm not completely sure, although Kim was away that night, and Tammy thought if she told Kim she would only worry.' DI Peters raised his eyebrows. 'I don't know whether this is of any significance, but she alluded to an argument going on in Dick's office when she left, although she didn't hang around to find out what it was about.'

'Thank you, Miss Allen. We'll be interviewing everyone at the Club in conjunction with our enquiries. You will need to come down to the station at some point to provide us with a detailed statement.'

'That's fine.' My mobile was vibrating in my back pocket. 'Oh, excuse me,' I said to them both as I retrieved it. 'Hello.' I was hesitant because I noticed that the number was withheld.

'Miss Allen?' It was Eve, and I almost dropped my mobile. I felt very self-conscious and turned to avoid the gaze of the two police officers.

'Speaking,' I replied airily.

'I told you I'd be in touch. I've been trying to call you, but you haven't been answering your 'phone.'

'We keep missing each other.' I said casually. I wanted to appear nonchalant.

'You've seen the *Evening Standard* then? You know she's dead? Tell the police nothing or you'll put us all in danger, including your friend.' I remained silent. 'You still there?' she asked.

'I have to go now as I'm with some people. I'll talk to you later,' I replied, trying to remain composed and sound natural. At the same time my brain was struggling to work out what was going on and why this strange, husky-voiced woman was calling me, and whether

I should tell the two police officers standing in front of me.

'I'll speak to you…later.' She hung up.

'You OK, Miss Allen,' asked DS Hamilton, peering at me. I must have looked flustered.

'Yes. It was my sister. Boyfriend troubles…'

'Hmm… Yes. Boyfriends. That's a point. Do you know whether Tamsin had a boyfriend?' asked DI Peters.

'She didn't mention one to me, but someone like Tammy would have attracted a great deal of male interest.'

'As *any* very attractive young woman would,' said DS Hamilton, looking directly at me and smiling broadly.

'I suppose.' I unwillingly caught his eye.

'We will be looking into that,' said DI Peters giving DS Hamilton a disapproving look.

'Have you spoken to all the residents here?' I asked.

'We intend to.' DI Peters stood up. 'Could you tell Miss Davis we'll see her here tomorrow morning at eleven?'

'Yes. Certainly.' I led them to the door.

'Goodnight, Miss Allen.' They both shook my hand.

'Goodnight.'

I stood in the doorway and watched them disappear out of the front door. I went back inside, looked in on Kim who was fast asleep, and snuggled down on the sofa with a duvet. I kept thinking about what Tammy had told me and I started to make a mental list of potential murderers. Jack had threatened her, but so had Fen, and who were the people she had heard arguing in Dick's office? Nathan, the sleazy freelance photographer had a grudge against her, she had a lecherous modelling agent, and there may have been others she had knocked back and offended along the way. On top of that, there was Eve and I wondered how she was connected with all this. My imagination was running riot and, with all these thoughts spinning around my head, I was unable to sleep.

Chapter 5

I might as well have not been in the office the following morning because I simply could not concentrate on my work. In addition to being extremely tired, I was feeling rather anxious. I repeatedly looked at my watch, my 'phone and my mobile. Neither Eve nor Kim had 'phoned and both had said that they would. I called Jo to tell her about Tammy.

'Oh, my God! How awful. Did the police speak to you?' She was shocked.

'Yes. I told them what I know and I'm going to give a formal statement.'

'But surely there isn't much you could tell them, Ally? I mean about Tammy's lifestyle and work?'

'Well, that's the strange part Jo because last Saturday for some reason Tammy confided in me about the Club and why she wasn't going back.'

'Club? I thought she was a model.' Jo sounded perplexed.

'Yes, she was, but she took a job as a hostess in a nightclub.' There was a slight pause at the other end of the 'phone.

'Oh, Ally. I can't see that suiting her. What happened to her there?'

'It was sordid. She didn't want to perform the duties that were expected of her as a hostess and things turned nasty.'

'That fits. Who are the police officers who came to see you?'

'DS Hamilton and DI Peters.'

'Oh, I know Angus.'

'Angus?'

'DS Hamilton. The Scottish one. He's a real character.'

'How do you know him?'

'Through Will and his contacts. I met him at a party not so long ago, just before I left the force. If you want to know how the investigation is progressing I'm sure Will can get some information for you. Are you free at the weekend or will you be busy with all of this?'

'My mother's coming up to London with Antonia for Sunday lunch, but apart from that, I've nothing planned. Although, I'd like to be around for Kim in case she needs anything as she was in a really bad way last night and I'm desperately worried about her. I'm not sure when Tammy's mother and brother are arriving from Australia and Kim is going to have to cope with that as well.'

'Whereabouts?'

'Brisbane.'

'If I can do anything you only have to ask. I'll give you a call if Will hears something about Tammy's murder.'

Having spoken to Jo I felt better able to concentrate on my work. I started to read through the pile of post in my in-tray. There was a very detailed letter from Mr Gilson relating to his investment portfolio and a memo from David on Rebecca Jacobs' file. He had taken the file back and would not require any further assistance from me at this juncture. I thought that was rather strange because, from my reading of the file, there was a great deal of action that needed to be taken and as a matter of urgency too. At least that meant I would not have much to do with him, which was a bonus in itself. There was a letter from Robert Dickson thanking me for my advice and requesting a meeting with his daughter Deborah regarding the residence application for Samantha. I became so engrossed in my work that I did not hear Mary walk into the room.

'Are you all right, Alicia?' I almost jumped out of my skin. 'I'm sorry. I didn't mean to startle you. Peter told me about your neighbour. It must have been a terrible shock. Can I get you anything?'

'An injection of pure caffeine,' I said yawning. 'I hardly slept last night.'

'Yes, you do look rather tired and a bit paler than usual. I've typed up that first draft of Mrs Thomas's Will for you since Louisa isn't in today,' she said, handing me the file. 'Peter was with clients all morning and I had some spare capacity.' She smiled at me.

'Oh, thank you,' I replied, taking the file. 'I appreciate your help.'

'You're welcome, dear.' She left the room. About ten minutes later she returned with a caffè latte from Gianni's. 'I thought you needed this,' she said, winking at me, putting it down on my desk and then walking out.

My direct line rang and for a moment I hesitated before picking up the 'phone.

'Hello…' I said.

'Ally?' It was Kim, but I hardly recognized her voice because she sounded very weak.

'Kim. I've been thinking about you. How is everything?' I asked cautiously, not wishing to say anything to upset her.

'Dreadful. I can't come to terms with what's happening. When I woke up it all came flooding back.' She sounded slightly tearful.

'I left you a note about the police. Did they come this morning?'

'I found it, and yes, they did. They asked more questions about Tammy's friends and the Club. They said that they had talked to you last night. I had no idea that Tammy had told you all about the Club? Why didn't she talk to me?' I sensed Kim was hurt that Tammy had confided in me rather than her. I had guessed she would be.

'It was when you were away. I think she needed someone to talk to and I was there.'

'They won't tell me anything. I want to know what's going on.'

'I don't suppose there's anything to tell, well not yet anyway. They probably don't want to say too much until they have evidence. Have you heard when her mother and brother are arriving from Brisbane?'

'Friday morning. Very early. I don't know when to expect them.

I mean there's so much for them to do and then there's the police. I haven't touched her things. The police told me not to. And they had their forensic people all over the flat. I had a problem with work this morning as well.'

'Why?'

'I called Alex to tell him about Tammy's murder. He was really sympathetic, told me he'd tell Diane, the officer manager, and fix up a temp. He said I wasn't to worry and to take as much time off as I needed. Later, Jenny, one of Vincent's secretaries, called to say that *he* said I have to take the time off as holiday otherwise I won't get paid.'

'What? He can't do that. I'm sure that the doctor would sign you off in the circumstances. Did you manage to speak to Alex again?'

'He went to an external meeting and they don't know when he's coming back. These company deals take hours.'

'I'm sure it will be OK. Don't upset yourself over Vincent Weil. You have more important things to worry about than him right now.'

After I spoke to Kim, I decided to go out for some fresh air. I was putting on my coat and scarf when my direct line rang again, and this time it was Antonia.

'*Ciao*, Alicia. It's me. *Sei occupata?* Do you have time to talk?'

'*Con te? Sempre.*' I replied, leaning back against the desk as I did up the buttons on my coat.

'Mamma told me about Tammy when I got home last night. I couldn't believe what I was hearing. It's unreal.'

'I wish it were. But unfortunately, it's not. Are you coming up this weekend?'

'If you still want me to.'

'Of course.'

'I thought I'd drive up with Mamma on Sunday as I can't park anywhere in your borough without worrying about being clamped at any other time.'

'Good idea. See you on Sunday. *Ciao, sorellina. Baci.*'

On Friday evening I left the office and was walking towards Selfridges when my mobile rang and, seeing that the number was again withheld, I was quick to answer it, but it was not Eve. It was DS Hamilton asking when I would be going to the police station to make my statement.

'I could come down now, I suppose, as I've finished work. I could be there in about thirty minutes.'

'That would be very helpful. Ask for DC Owen when you arrive. Thank you, Miss Allen.'

No sooner had I finished the call with him than my mobile rang again and this time it was Meera. As I wandered up Oxford Street towards the bus stop I chatted to her.

'How are you doing?'

'I'm OK. I'm very tired today because I've hardly slept these past few nights. I'm on my way to the police station to give them my statement. What are you up to?'

'I was calling to see if there was anything I could do to help.'

'You're such a sweetie and I appreciate it, but I'm fine, honestly I am. Let's try and get together before Christmas.'

'Yes, let's.'

I arrived home after ten because my statement had taken longer than expected. I was absolutely exhausted. I noticed that Kim's flat was in darkness and the curtains were closed, so I went straight upstairs to my own flat. The light on my answerphone was flashing and there were two messages, one from my mother asking how my day had been, and the other from Kim to tell me that she was OK and was going to meet Tom and Maggie at their hotel. Maggie was Tammy's mother.

I made myself some toast and a bowl of soup and, as I was too tired to face anything else, showered and crawled into bed to watch television. I must have dropped off to sleep because the next thing I remember was the 'phone ringing. I stretched out for the cordless 'phone on the bedside table, and nearly knocked my glass of water flying in the process.

'Hello…' I said half asleep as I picked up the 'phone.

'*Pronto. Ciao,* Alicia. You sound very faint. *Va bene?* You OK?'

'Cesare! Good to hear from you,' I sat up. 'I'm fine. I was just sleeping.'

'Oh, *carina,* I didn't mean to wake you…'

'It's OK. I want to talk to you. Something terrible has happened since we last spoke…'

'*Dimmi subito.*'

'It's Tammy. She's dead.' There was a stunned silence at the end of the 'phone.

'*Come? Quando?*'

I told him everything that I knew, which was in fact very little. It was obvious that Cesare was shocked, although he tried to conceal it.

'*Sai tutto adesso,* Cesare. Tell me how you are? What have you been up to since we last spoke?'

'I'm going back to *Roma* soon. I'll be there for Christmas. Why don't you come out for a break, Alicia? You can stay with my sister, Magdallena, *se vuoi.* It would do you good to get away and London is so grey this time of year.'

'I was thinking of visiting Nonna in Paestum just after Christmas, so maybe I could combine the trip.'

'How's Antonia? Is she still in marketing?'

'She's fine. Yes. She's doing the same job. She loves it. It makes me think I chose the wrong career. She's always saying how frantically busy she is and that the job is very demanding, but she really enjoys it and she has a much better social life than I do. I'm seeing her this weekend. She and Mamma are coming up to London.' I sank back into my down pillow.

'I thought she was still working in *Italia.*' Cesare sounded confused.

'She was. She came back at the end of last month. She's staying with Mamma in Surrey for a little while because she rented out her flat in Bayswater for a year. The tenancy isn't up until the end of February.' I heard a knock on my front door and sat up in bed. '*Un momento*, Cesare. There's someone at the door.' I jumped out of bed and walked to the door still holding the 'phone.

'Who is it?' I asked.

'Kim.' I let her in.

'Sorry, Alicia, I didn't know you had gone to bed,' she said, seeing me in my pyjamas. Then she saw the 'phone in my hand, put her hand to her mouth and whispered, 'Oh! I didn't know you were on the 'phone.'

'It's Kim,' I said, putting the 'phone to my ear.

'Who is it?' she mouthed.

'Cesare,' I replied, putting my hand over the mouthpiece.

Kim raised her eyebrows and looked at me quizzically. I knew that look, it was the one she had when his name was mentioned. What Antonia would class as '*lo sguardo*' – the stare. For once I was not going to berate her about it.

'*Che passa?*' asked Cesare.

'It's Kim,' I replied.

'I know. You just said. How is she?'

'Umm… So-so.' Cesare was quick to pick up the vibes.

'*Capisco.* You can't really talk can you, now she's there? I'll speak with you soon, *carina mia. Baci, ciao ed a presto!*'

'*Baci a te, amico mio.* Thanks so much for calling. I do appreciate it.'

'*Ciao, bella. Buona notte.*'

'How did it go this evening?' I asked, turning to Kim. We walked through to the kitchen. 'Cup of tea?' She nodded.

'Tom and Maggie are really calm. I don't know how they're getting through it all. They saw the police today. They want to sort out the funeral. Tom said that although there has been a post-mortem they have to wait for the body to be released. Is that right?'

'Yes. There'll have to be an inquest at some point, but I believe that can happen later. They can still have the funeral but the coroner has to release the body for burial and, until then, everyone waits.' I handed Kim her tea and the biscuit tin.

'Oh, right, I didn't know that,' she said. 'It's just horrible thinking about it all. What happens at the inquest then?' She leaned against the kitchen units and took a gulp of her tea.

'Well, it's a formal inquiry and held in public. At the hearing the coroner examines the circumstances surrounding the death and makes findings on the identification of the deceased, the time and place of death, and the cause of death. He can also make comments on matters connected with the death. Help yourself to biscuits by the way.'

'Thanks. Tom told me that they've requested the findings of the post-mortem. He didn't say too much about what the police discovered, except that Tammy was beaten, kicked around the head and she had a fractured skull.' As Kim choked out the words she almost choked on her Garibaldi. 'I can't bear to think about how she looked when I identified her.'

'It must be very difficult for them with no family over here.' I noticed a tear trickling down Kim's left cheek which she brushed off her face with the back of her hand.

'No, 'cos Tammy's mother is half-English you see. She was born here. Tammy's grandmother was English and her grandfather Australian. They met when he came over to England to study. They married, had two daughters and moved back to Australia when Maggie was about fifteen. Ironically, Maggie's sister Emily married an Englishman and lives in Suffolk. Near Lavenham, I believe. Tammy visited her several times. Maggie married and had Tom, but stayed with her sister for a few months before Tammy was born. I think there were a few problems in her marriage at that time 'cos I know she divorced when Tammy was a baby.'

'I see. Has anyone tried to contact her father?'

'Tammy said she never heard from him. He moved away and didn't stay in touch. I think he and Maggie just called it a day.'

'Yes, but he should know. I mean he is her father,' I said, helping myself to a custard cream from the biscuit tin. It seemed a little odd that nobody had mentioned a father.

'Don't get me wrong, but that's not for us to decide, is it? He probably doesn't care anyway. Tammy says she never heard from him.' Kim was very matter-of-fact about this.

'Well, that's doubly sad then,' I replied, sighing. 'What about Tom? Isn't he curious about his father? It doesn't square up, that's all.'

'Oh, Alicia you're always looking to resolve everyone's problems but sometimes you can't. Actually, I'm surprised your ears weren't burning this evening 'cos we were talking about you,' she said, changing the subject.

'Me? Why?'

'Nothing bad or anything. Only, I said you were a lawyer and knew all about Wills and stuff like that. Maggie said she wondered whether you wouldn't mind sorting out Tammy's personal affairs for her. She's coming to the flat on Sunday to go through her things. Could you help?'

'Hmm… I'm happy to, although I wouldn't have thought there was much for me to do. I'm around apart from Sunday lunchtime because my mother and sister will be here, but I can make time and I'd like to meet Maggie anyway. There is something about all of this that intrigues me.'

'That's the Machiavellian coming out in you.'

Chapter 6

Jo called on Saturday morning and it was arranged that she would come for lunch at two. I decided to take my car up to the Waitrose supermarket on Gloucester Road to stock up. I was trying to de-ice it because there had been a sharp frost, but the nozzle on the de-icer can was blocked, my fingers were quickly frozen and I was becoming irritated. I saw Dorothy walking down the steps carrying her shopping basket and motioned over to her. She was well wrapped up, wearing a thick camel coat, leather gloves, wool hat, scarf and sheepskin-lined ankle boots.

'Hello, Dorothy,' I called out. 'I'm on my way up to Gloucester Road. Can I give you a lift anywhere?'

'Oh hello, dear. Yes, actually. How thoughtful of you. Are you going to the supermarket?' I nodded. 'That would be very helpful as I do need to buy some groceries.' She walked over to the car, the windows of which I had almost completely defrosted. 'You're looking a little wan,' she said, pinching my cheek. 'This terrible business with Tamsin has been such a dreadful shock to us all. I never thought that something like that would happen so close to home, but you never do, do you?' she said with a shrug. I opened the car door for her and Dorothy seated herself inside. I walked around to the driver's side, opened the door and jumped in.

'No. You don't,' I replied as I tried to manoeuvre my car out of the tight parking space. 'Did the police talk to you?' After about six turns of the wheel I finally managed to move out of the space and headed the car in the direction of the Old Brompton Road.

'Yes, dear. They did. I told them what I saw.' Dorothy pulled off her gloves and laid them in her lap.

'What do you mean? What did you see?' I wiped the windscreen, which had steamed up again, with the back of my glove.

'The car.'

'What car?' I briefly glanced sideways at her.

'The car outside the house.' She turned and looked at me.

'When?' I glanced sideways at her again as I turned into Gloucester Road.

'Several times.'

'When *exactly?*' I began my hunt for a parking space.

'A few times last week. It was the incident with Smoky that did it.' Smoky was Dorothy's Persian Blue cat.

'I don't understand.' I was totally perplexed.

'I was sitting in my armchair in the window brushing Smoky's coat like I always do, when I saw a car pull up on the other side of the road. The driver sat there and stared up at the house. I didn't think much of it because I thought he was waiting for someone. But the other night when I went to the window to pull my curtains, he was there again. Then, on the night that Tammy disappeared, I was woken up by a noise outside. I thought perhaps Smoky had managed to get out as I couldn't see him. I pulled back the curtain in the reception room and I noticed the car yet again.'

'Would you recognize the driver?' I had parked the car now and was undoing my seat belt.

'I don't think so because I didn't have a clear view of his face and it was dark. You must also bear in mind, dear, that the railings slightly obscure my view.'

'The car then?' I asked, pressing her.

'It was large. Not like your one. What model is your car?' She looked around my car.

'It's a Golf. Much bigger than mine then?'

'Oh yes, and very dark. It could have been a BMW but it was definitely a saloon car. I mentioned all this to the police when they spoke to me.'

I thought about what Dorothy had told me and how observant she was, but then she was very sharp, never missed anything and was not to be underestimated just because she was elderly. The super-market was frustratingly busy and to make it easier I suggested Dorothy and I share a trolley. The checkout queues were lengthy but we finally got away and drove home. I helped her out of the car and down to her flat with her three bags of shopping.

'Thank you so much, dear. What are your plans for the rest of the weekend?'

'My mother and sister are coming up for lunch tomorrow and I'm seeing a friend today.'

'Oh. How lovely. I hope you'll have tea with me soon.'

'I'd like that.' I meant it. I enjoyed talking to Dorothy because she had a zest for life, was interesting and always enthusiastic about whatever I was doing.

I had double-parked to unload my shopping and propped open the front door while I ran backwards and forwards from the car with my shopping bags. I bent down and placed a couple of bags in the hall and, as I looked up, I saw Paolo, the friend who had moved into Cesare's flat, coming down the stairs. He stopped, winked at me and asked if he could help me take my shopping upstairs.

Paolo lifted all my shopping through to the kitchen and I started to unpack it.

'The police spoke to me by the way,' he said casually.

'Yes. They said they'd be speaking to everyone in the building.'

'I could tell them nothing.' He shrugged his shoulders. 'I never even met Tammy. I have to go,' he said, looking at his watch.

'Thanks for helping with the bags, Paolo. See you later.'

'*Prego, carina*,' he replied, winking at me as I closed the door.

True to form, Jo arrived exactly on time.

'You're looking pale,' she said as she kissed me. She handed me a bottle of Pinot Grigio and took off her coat.

'That's what Dorothy said this morning. I shall get a complex! Do you want some of this wine?'

'I think you should keep it for later. Coffee would be great.'

'OK. What have you been up to?'

'Helping Will on a case. Have the police spoken to you again about Tammy?'

'Not since I gave them my statement. Has Will managed to find out anything?' I asked tentatively.

'Not yet. He made some discreet enquiries and spoke to Angus, but from what I gather, the police have no major leads. So far they've interviewed Dick Jensen and the girls at the Club and Tammy's modelling agent, Tim Lewis.'

'What about the freelance photographers?'

'They can trace the ones that engaged her through the agency. Any others are proving more difficult.'

'So they have no idea who did this?' Jo shook her head.

'It seems to be a crime without motive.' I did not believe that for one moment. There had to be a reason why Tammy was murdered.

I had told nobody about Eve, but I was very tempted to confide in Jo because I knew I could trust her. However, Eve had actually told me nothing and, on the basis that she had warned me not to involve the police, I did not want to endanger Jo by telling her. I was aware of the risks, but I decided that I would wait and see if I received any further calls and what she said. Subject to that, I would make a decision about informing the police. Consequently, Jo left that afternoon none the wiser.

I wanted to go to a Yoga Ashtanga class on Sunday morning but I overslept and did not have time. I needed to prepare the lunch – roast beef and Yorkshire pudding followed by lemon meringue pie.

Fortunately, Antonia and Mamma were late and did not arrive until one-thirty, enabling me to clear up all the mess. I heard my mother and sister babbling away in Italian in the street below and stepped out onto the balcony and looked down on them. I could see that my mother had brought a basket of 'provisions' with her, just as she always did. She saw me, waved and walked to the outside door with Antonia, who pressed the entry buzzer. I opened my front door and waited for them as they rounded the stairs.

'Alicia. *Arrivo,*' my mother exclaimed, cupping my face in her hands and then throwing her arms about me. 'My goodness, *carina mia,* you are *so* thin. You do not eat enough. *Mangia, mangia, mangia!*' she chided, wagging her finger at me as she came in.

She took off her gloves, scarf and coat. She was always immaculately dressed and today was no exception. Although she was diminutive she was very elegant, had excellent bearing and great presence. She was also very knowing and someone that nobody would get the better of – that included her children – even though she was the most loving mother anybody could have.

She walked through to the kitchen and emptied the contents of her huge basket over the work surfaces while I looked on. She had been to Italy a few weeks before and, among other things for me, had brought back some olive oil, Parmesan cheese, panettone and two bottles of Vernaccia di San Gimignano, her favourite velvety straw-coloured wine. My mother came from Grassina and was proud of her Florentine background.

I brought you the panettone, *carina,* since it's nearly Christmas. I made you a tiramisù as well,' she said, holding up a container, 'and some pasta sauces to put in the freezer.' It was amazing how my mother transported all these provisions from place to place.

'Oh, *grazie,* Mamma.' I laughed.

'I have a *regalino* for you too,' she added, opening her capacious handbag and handing me a very small package. It was a pale grey and blue silk chiffon scarf.

'Something smells good,' said Antonia, walking in to the kitchen.

'It's roast beef, but it's not ready yet. I only put it in about half an hour ago,' I replied. I opened the oven door and took the joint out to baste it. Over the next hour my mother and sister chatted incessantly with me in Italian and English. When the roast was cooked,

Antonia carved it and I served up the vegetables and Yorkshire pudding.

'Is that all you're having?' she asked, looking at my plate as we sat down to eat.

'Don't start, Antonia. You're as bad as Cesare,' I replied. My mother gave me one of her looks.

'Cesare?' she said.

'He's the one who really likes Alicia, Mamma. The one with the ghastly friend, Ivano, who's always after her. *Antipatico*. It's not fair. She has all these men chasing after her and she doesn't want any of them.'

'*Basta*, Antonia. You can't be jealous. You're the one who's never short of a boyfriend.' My mother gave Antonia a withering look.

'Alicia,' she said, putting down her knife and fork, turning to me and sounding very serious, 'I was so shocked when you told me the dreadful news about Tammy. I feel for her poor mother. Have you met her?' Her eyes were full of compassion.

'No. Not yet. Kim said she was coming over today. She may want my help sorting out Tammy's legal affairs in this country. I haven't heard anything.' I swallowed a mouthful of beef.

'*Ben inteso*. Can you help?'

'It depends what's involved. I will if I can.'

We finished eating and as I was clearing the table the telephone rang. It was Kim.

'Ally, I know your mother and sister are with you, but Maggie and Tom have arrived and I don't suppose you could have a word?'

'OK. I'll come down. Give me a couple of minutes.'

'I'm going to disappear for a while so you can talk to them in private.'

'OK.'

When I walked into the reception room, Maggie, who was standing looking out the window, turned to face me. There was no mistaking whose mother she was as she bore a striking resemblance to Tammy.

Her hair was shorter, but she was her equal in height and the bearing was the same. She was wearing well-cut black wool trousers and a cashmere camel turtleneck sweater.

'How do you do?' She took my hand with both of hers and squeezed it.

'I'm so sorry about your daughter, Mrs Brown.'

'Thank you, Alicia. Please call me Maggie.' She indicated for me to sit down.

Although she had lived in Australia for most of her adult life, her Australian accent was imperceptible. I was amazed and impressed by her composure in the circumstances. On observing her closely I noticed how strained and tired she seemed, but I did not suppose she had slept very much these past few nights and she was almost certainly jet-lagged.

'Kim recommends you most highly, Alicia. She says that she has known you since the girls moved in.'

'Yes, that's right.' I glanced at the young man with dark brown hair and brown eyes who walked into the room. He was wearing a black polo shirt and black jeans. I presumed he must be Tammy's brother.

'Tom,' said Maggie, addressing him. 'This is Alicia.'

I stood up and shook my hand, gave me a trace of a smile, but said nothing. He sat down in the armchair opposite and as he did so I wondered whether he looked more like their father because he bore little resemblance to Maggie.

'As I was saying,' Maggie continued, 'I'm looking for someone to help me attend to Tammy's affairs here. The Coroner will release her body soon so we can organize the funeral, but it's everything else that I'm concerned about.' She paused, and I detected emotion in her voice. 'Kim said you're a lawyer and you deal with Wills and Probate.' Her voice quaked.

'Among other things, yes.'

'Could you assist? It would be a great weight off my mind, because I have to return to Australia. As far as I know, there isn't much to be done, but I would feel more comfortable if you sorted out whatever is necessary. Tom is staying on so he can assist you with any queries.'

'I don't see why not, but I do need to know a few things first. I presume Tammy did not have a Will?'

'No.' Maggie shook her head.

'She had a bank account here though?'

'Yes, she did. She also had a few store card accounts and she would have received the money she inherited from my mother.' Maggie glanced at Tom.

'How much and what do you mean by "would have received"? It's just that we'd need to go through Probate if it's over £5,000. At least, that's generally the way it works.' I looked at Maggie and then Tom.

'Our grandmother left us both £10,000 but Probate hasn't gone through on her estate yet, so we haven't received the money,' said Tom, leaning back in the armchair.

'Did your grandmother live here then?'

'My mother moved back to England after my father died.' Maggie answered for him.

'Oh, I see. That makes sense,' I said nodding.

'I'm sorry, I'm not with you.' Tom looked confused. 'What does?'

'Why we need Probate in this country. Since Tammy died intestate we have to apply for what is known as Letters of Administration. As she didn't have a husband or children, under the intestacy rule her parents are the ones next entitled to anything in her estate. So that means you, Maggie, and Tammy's father. Kim told me that you don't know where he is. Only we'd need to contact him.' I paused. 'Even if he wanted to renounce his Letters of Administration, we have to ask him.'

'Would we really need to contact him?' Maggie seemed suddenly flustered. 'Is it really necessary for such a small estate?' I sensed that this was going to be a problem, so what Kim had said about a family estrangement was true. Maggie was visibly upset and I decided not to press the point.

'You have enough on your plate,' I said gently. 'Here's my card.' I pulled a slightly crumpled business card out of my jeans pocket. 'If you decide to take the matter forward, please contact me. You might think about giving Tom Power of Attorney to act on your behalf after you return to Australia,' I said, observing Maggie's expression closely.

'Thank you for your time, Alicia. I expect you will want to get back to your mother and sister now,' she said, dismissing me, and swiftly ushering me out the door.

'Yes… OK… Goodbye.' I was slightly perplexed by the sudden change in Maggie's attitude. As I walked upstairs I thought about what we had discussed. She had absolutely clammed up when I mentioned Tammy's father and I felt sure that there was more to this than meets the eye.

Chapter 7

It was a cold December afternoon and it was spitting with rain. As I walked along the Fulham Road I brushed the fine specks of rain off my nose. My right heel was hurting because my new high-heeled boots were rubbing. Unfortunately, I had not had time to change into a more comfortable pair because I had come straight from the office and, as usual, I was late. At least my trouser suit was comfortable. That was the good thing about being a lawyer – no shortage of black clothes to wear.

I left the bustle of the Fulham Road and ambled through the gates of the Brompton Cemetery and along the pathway to the domed chapel in the centre. I was struck by how still and silent it was. It was so quiet that the only sound was of my footsteps. I looked up at the trees. Autumn had come late this year and there were still leaves on some of the branches; the golden leaves on the beech trees were vibrant and on a dull day such as this the colours seemed more pronounced. The wind picked up and some leaves fluttered to the ground. I glanced at the hundreds of gravestones around me and thought about the people who had walked this path before me. I shuddered.

There were a number of people standing outside the chapel. While I waited for Kim, I observed them. I did not recognize anyone, but there was no reason why I should. I had no means of knowing even if Eve were there. I scanned the faces of all the women, and was so deep in thought that I was not aware that Kim was now standing next to me.

'Ally,' she said, putting her hand on my shoulder. 'You were miles away.'

'I was wondering who all these people are?'

'Oh, right. Yeah. I guess you wouldn't know any of them. I think that's her Great Aunt Jane.' Kim pointed to an elderly lady in a wide-brimmed hat. 'And that's Emily, her aunt. She's quite like Maggie, don't you think? I think the man with her is her husband, Richard,' she said, pointing to the grey-haired man deep in conversation with Jane. 'They must be Tammy's cousins.' She indicated in the direction of two gangly teenagers. 'I think the girl's called Miranda. She's about sixteen, and the boy is David or Daniel or something like that. I'm not sure how old he is, but he must be younger than Tammy or around the same age.'

'Who do you think those men are over there?' I asked, noticing two men standing back and slightly away from the group of mourners who had gathered. One of them was of middling height, medium build and had reddish brown hair, cut very short. I estimated that he was in his late thirties. The other was slightly shorter and quite lean. He had dark straight hair which flopped forward and, as he spoke, he pushed it back off his face.

'I think the red-headed guy is Tim Lewis, the modelling agent. He certainly fits the description Tammy gave of him; the other is probably a photographer.'

The hearse arrived, followed by the chief mourners' car in which Maggie and Tom were sitting. When Kim saw the coffin and the flowers her eyes welled with tears. Everybody walked up the steps into the chapel; the atmosphere was emotionally charged.

'Let's go in,' I said.

Kim and I sat in the second row on the right-hand side. The light was trickling through the skylight in the centre of the dome and reflected dappled light on the flowers. The white lilies on the altar were beautiful, but their sweet scent made me feel sick. Tom and Maggie took their places, the doors to the chapel were closed and the organist started to play.

'What's he playing?' whispered Kim.

'It's Bach,' I whispered back, *'Jesu, joy of man's desiring.'*

The chapel doors opened and we all stood. The priest entered followed by the pallbearers carrying Tammy's coffin. The Order of Service said that he was called Reverend Denning.

'I am the resurrection and the life saith the Lord; he that believeth in me, though he were dead, yet shall he live: and whosoever liveth and believeth in me shall never die...' he read.

Maggie had decided to bury Tammy in a plot at the cemetery and, after the service, the mourners followed the hearse carrying her coffin along the path to the burial plot, which was right at the other end of the cemetery near the Earl's Court entrance. It was raining heavily now and very cold and, on arriving at the spot, everyone huddled together around the grave waiting for the priest to begin the Committal.

'Man that is born of a woman hath but a short time to live, and is full of misery. He cometh up and is cut down like a flower: he fleeth as it were a shadow, and never continueth in one stay. In the midst of life we are in death of whom may we...'

I heard the surreal announcements from Earl's Court tube station in the distance. I caught Kim's eye. Had it not been for the solemnity of the occasion we would have laughed. Reverend Denning continued to read as the pallbearers slowly lowered the coffin into the grave. I shivered, Kim sobbed and Maggie clasped Tom's hand tightly.

'...and for as much as it hath pleased Almighty God of his great mercy to take unto himself the soul of our dear sister Tamsin here departed we therefore commit her body to the earth, ashes to ashes, dust to dust; in sure and certain hope of the Resurrection to eternal life through our Lord Jesus Christ.'

Tammy's family threw handfuls of earth on top of the coffin and Kim a white rose. I glanced at the sombre faces all around me, and as I did so I observed a woman hovering a little way along the path, but I could not see her clearly because the light was fading. I moved towards the path to see her more closely but was unable to see her face because of the hat she was wearing. I tried to slip away, but Kim took my arm.

'I want to introduce you to Tammy's aunt,' she said, dragging me back. My view of the woman was further obscured by the mourners moving away from the graveside.

'What were you looking at?' Kim asked.

'Oh, I thought I recognized someone, that's all,' I replied, straining to see over the heads of everyone in the hope she was still there.

'Oh. Right. Emily, let me introduce you to Alicia.' She was right about the resemblance between Maggie and her sister.

'How do you do?' I extended my hand. She grasped it.

'Kim speaks very highly of you and I wanted to meet you. I understand you'll be helping Maggie sort out Tammy's affairs.'

'Well, I…'

'Emily we have to go now,' Maggie called. I felt she did not want me to talk to Emily.

'Are you coming back with us, Alicia?' asked Kim.

'No. I can't. I have to return to the office.' I kissed her goodbye and hobbled down to the path as my heel was hurting. Much to my disappointment the woman on the path had disappeared.

I left the office earlier than usual because the events of the day had rendered me flat and I had been rather unproductive. I now had a nasty blister on my right heel and felt like the walking wounded. I had arranged to meet Jo in Covent Garden, but since I was in the West End I thought I would fit in some Christmas shopping. Oxford Street was heaving with shoppers and I had to battle along the pavement to Boots to buy some blister plasters, and then through the crowds to Selfridges. I made the powder room my first port of call and sorted out my heel and then went down to the ground floor to buy some perfume for my mother and Antonia: Chanel for my mother and Nina Ricci for Antonia. I took the

Central line from Bond Street to Holborn and changed to the Piccadilly line for Covent Garden. Jo met me on Long Acre.

'Come back to the flat for dinner, Ally. We can talk properly there. It's too crowded here.' Jo looked at her watch. 'Will's back early this evening. He's got some information about Tammy's case for you by sweet-talking his contacts. I'll call him and let him know we're on our way home.'

'Did Jo tell you Angus Hamilton is a good friend of mine?' Will said, filling my glass. 'I had the impression when I was talking to him that he is rather taken with you.'

'What? I've hardly spoken to the man for more than about two minutes,' I paused. 'And that was all in relation to Tammy.' I sipped my wine.

'Two minutes is all it takes, Alicia!'

'Don't tease,' Jo said, leaning over and prodding Will.

'What have you found out about Tammy?' I asked, changing the subject.

'It wasn't some frenzied attack. It was well organized. Tammy's body was found in an industrial refuse sack and her hands and feet were tied. She was dumped in the alleyway, but she wasn't murdered there. Forensics have confirmed that. There's something else too…'

'Which is?' I had the feeling I was not going to like what I heard.

'Tammy was raped.' I gasped in horror. 'The forensic evidence shows that she was repeatedly kicked around her head which is why she had a fractured skull. She had bruises on her arms from where she must have put her hands up to her face to protect herself. Two assailants sexually assaulted her and evidently she was held down during the assault. The marks on her body were consistent with this. It was the head injuries she sustained which killed her…' Will stopped short, as he saw tears rolling down my cheeks.

'I didn't mean to upset you,' he said softly. 'It's hard to stomach for all of us.' He leant over and put his arm around me.

'No. You haven't.' I rummaged in my bag for a tissue and wiped my face. 'I'm fine. It must be unbearable for Maggie and Tom. Kim told me that they asked to be given the findings of the post-mortem examination. It's all so gruesome.'

'From what I've heard about Tammy, I can't get my head around why somebody wanted her dead,' Will said.

'I bet it has something to do with the Club. Don't you think so, Ally?' Jo sounded convinced.

'Whatever it is, find the motive and you're on the way to finding her killer,' I replied.

The next evening I stayed home to decorate my Christmas tree and wrap up my presents. Having done this, I drew up a list of law firms to apply to in the new year. I had almost worked my way through the *Solicitor and Barrister Directory* when Kim knocked at the door.

'What are you up to, Alicia?'

'Not much. Come in,' I replied, walking back into the reception room. Kim closed my front door and followed me through. 'How has your day been?'

'Not bad. Maggie flew back to Australia today. She left this letter for you.' Kim handed me a blue envelope which I opened. I skim read the contents.

'She's given me her contact details and thanked me for coming to the funeral. She doesn't mention me doing any work for her in relation to Tammy though,' I said as I scanned the letter. 'Oh, well. So how are *you*?' I folded the letter, put it back in its envelope and placed it on the coffee table.

'I'm OK. But what you said about Maggie has been niggling at me.' I stood up and walked into the kitchen.

'What do you mean?' I called out. 'Do you want a drink by the way…coffee…tea, or something stronger? I have a lovely bottle of red wine.'

'Wine would be great,' Kim replied as she came into the kitchen. She leant against the kitchen units.

'You can do the honours,' I said, handing her the bottle and a corkscrew. I raided my store cupboard for something to eat. 'I've some nibbles in here,' I said, bringing out a tube of Salt and Vinegar Pringles. 'You were saying about Maggie?' I asked, opening the Pringles.

'When she gave me that note she apologised for being a little abrupt with you.'

'I haven't thought any more about it. I presumed she was under terrible emotional stress. What's niggling you?'

'Well, the other day I asked her if she had informed Tammy's father about her death and she became defensive, like she did with you.'

'I must admit I did think she over-reacted when I mentioned him. I thought it strange but I suppose all this has opened up old wounds,' I said, taking a handful of Pringles and passing the tube to Kim.

'I know what you mean.' She hesitated for a moment. 'Actually, Ally, there's something else I need to talk to you about.' She sounded serious.

'What's that?'

'I'm moving out. I can't afford the rent here on my own and also...' She did not have time to finish her sentence as I cut her short.

'When? You should have said. You could stay with me you if you want and then you wouldn't have to leave.' I felt upset that Kim had not said anything to me about this.

'I'm sorry I didn't tell you before. The six-month break clause came up just after Tammy was murdered and, because of everything that has happened, I missed it. Anyway, I spoke to the estate agent who liaised with the owner. He said that in the circumstances, if I paid up to the date I moved out, that would be OK... I knew you'd say I could stay with you, Ally. You're a good friend,' she said, giving me a hug, 'but Tom and his friend Rob are renting a flat in Earl's Court and I'm going to move in with them. In any case I really have to move away from here... You do understand, don't you?' I knew exactly what she meant.

'Yes. I shall miss you though. I hope the next tenants are as amenable as you two have been...were. When are you planning to move?'

'The new year, but I'll pack up my gear over the Christmas break. What's this?' she said, noticing the list of law firms I had written out.

'My new year's resolution – to find a new job,' I replied, taking the list out of her hand.

'I'm sure something will turn up. Oh, I nearly forgot, do you want to come to a party?'

'When is it?'

'This Friday. Bev Turner is retiring. She's one of Vincent's secretaries and she has worked for him for ten years.'

'Where is it?'

'At a wine bar in Covent Garden. Some of the Partners will be there. Perhaps you could network and you'd be doing me an enormous favour because I don't want to go. I hate work things and you being there would be so nice,' she said in a wheedling little voice.

'OK. So long as they don't mind me coming.'

'Of course they won't. I'll introduce you to Alex.'

'Oh, yes, the famous Alex,' I said looking at her and winking. 'I'll finally get to meet him.'

Chapter 8

Friday evening arrived and I was running late, but my day had been particularly hectic because Peter was out of the office and I had been trying to clear some of the backlog. I made my way down Oxford Street but, as the pavements were packed, I was forced to walk in the gutter to get along the street. I leaped on a number 15 bus, but the traffic was so heavy that the journey took ages. I jumped off when it was halfway up the Strand and walked up Southampton Street and into the Piazza. The wine bar was on the other side of the Piazza in King Street.

I hovered in the doorway, straining to see Kim among the sea of faces.

'Ally. Over here!' She was standing up and waving to me. She made a space for me beside her, and then introduced me to some of the other secretaries. 'This is Carrie Blackstock.' I shook the hand of a mousy-haired middle-aged woman. 'Carrie, this is Alicia Allen, a neighbour of mine. Alicia's also a solicitor.' Carrie smiled broadly so I smiled back. I was conscious of being stared at by a thin-faced young woman who was sitting a couple of tables away next to a rather plump woman with dark shoulder length wavy hair. She wore her straight fine blonde hair long but she had a slightly overgrown fringe which she constantly pushed out the way of her narrow metal-rimmed glasses.

'Who are those two over there?' I asked Kim.

'The blonde one's Teresa James and the other one's Imogen Goede. Teresa is Imogen's Assistant. They're in the Commercial

Property department.'

'If looks could kill. Have you seen the way she's looking at me?'

'You mean Teresa?'

'Yes.'

'She fancies Alex big time and regards any attractive girl as a rival.'

'But that's bizarre. I've never even met him. Where is he anyway?'

'Alex? I don't know, actually. He was here a few minutes ago.' Kim looked around.

'Oh, Anna-Marie,' said Kim, addressing the dark-haired girl edging past, 'this is my friend Alicia.' Anna-Marie nodded at me in acknowledgement.

'Who does she work for?'

'Greg Taylor. He's in the Company Commercial department like Alex. He's a Partner. He's not here tonight. Actually, quite a few of the Partners aren't. I was hoping that either Andy or Graham would be. It's a shame they're not.'

'Andy? Graham?'

'Andy's the Tax Partner. Andy Steinberg. Bit of an oddball, in my view, but brilliant at his job. Graham Ffoulkes is lovely and he's the one I really wanted you to meet. He's the Private Client Partner. Danielle works for him, but she's not here tonight either as her daughter's ill. Mind you, Alex might be able to help you. He's a Junior Partner now. I can't think where he has gone to.' She looked around again.

'Which one is Beverley?' I asked, looking at the group on the table next to us.

'The very drunk cockney one,' she whispered. 'I think she has had too many port and lemons. After working for Vincent for ten years who could blame her?'

'Where is *he*?'

'He came in for about two minutes, mumbled something to Beverley about missing him and then left. Look at poor Jenny. She works for him too. She's run ragged.'

'I must buy a round,' I said and stood up. 'Who wants another drink?'

'One rum and black, one red wine, one port and lemon, one vodka and tonic, two white wines, and two gin and tonics, please,' I asked the barman.

'Looks like you need a hand,' said the man with the cultured voice behind me. I turned, looked up quizzically at the tall, blond young man standing next to me, and recognized him at once.

'I'm sorry. Let me introduce myself. I'm Alexander Waterford,' he said, beaming at me, 'but everybody calls me Alex.' He dropped his well-modulated voice and extended his hand for me to shake, which I did.

'How do you do? I'm Alicia Allen.' I caught his eye and the gaze was warm. 'Actually, I know who you are already.' He looked at me with a puzzled expression. 'I have the advantage on you...I recognize you from your photograph.'

'What do you mean?' He seemed confused.

'Your secretary, Kimberley Davies, is my neighbour. I saw your picture in your firm's brochure. She told me all about you...' I gave him a knowing smile; he nodded and broke into an easy laugh.

'Oh, she would.' He paused. 'I think she's in love with me,' he said, winking at me.

'You're not in love with her then?' I asked whimsically.

'No! She's not my type. I have my eye on mettle more *attractive*.'

'You've been reading too much Shakespeare, Alex. Isn't that what Hamlet said to his mother about Ophelia?'

'Hmm... You're sharp. I like that.' He gave me a sideways glance. 'But I think you know *what* I meant?'

'Don't you mean *who* you meant?' I replied mischievously as I turned to the bar and beckoned the barman over to pay for the drinks.

'No need,' he said. 'It's already taken care of.'

'I don't understand.' I was slightly perplexed.

'Your friend already put his card behind the bar.'

'Friend? Oh…I see.' I turned to Alex. 'Thank you.'

'You're welcome. Actually,' he said, pausing slightly, 'I was about to leave because I was bored, and then I saw you arrive and the evening started to look more interesting.' I caught his eye again and he was looking at me intently. Clearly he liked to flirt and I decided to have a little fun.

'For whom?' I asked, looking up at him.

'We should get these drinks to the others,' he said, picking up the tray.

I sat down next to Alex and noticed that he was wearing a gold torque bangle with some form of inscription on it, but I could not read what the words were.

'What's the bangle?' I could not resist asking. 'I noticed it in your photograph.'

'You're very observant. I always wear it. A friend bought it for me as a present,' he said, toying with it.

'It's very unusual to see one with an inscription.'

'It's supposed to be a sex magnet,' he said, looking up, his eyes twinkling and half-smiling.

'Really?' I replied with a straight face.

'Yes,' he said, and then he changed the subject. 'Carrie says you're a solicitor.' He must have been asking about me. 'What's your area of expertise?' He inclined himself towards me.

'Private Client.'

'Which firm?'

'Simons, Snade & Brown.'

'Just off Oxford Street? I nodded. 'I had a deal on with them a while back. How long have you been there?'

'Too long.'

'That bad?' He took a sip of his wine.

'Yes. I need to move.'

'Hmm… Why don't you write to Graham Ffoulkes. He's the Private Client Partner at WW & Co.'

'I know. Kim told me.'

'I have a better idea. E-mail *me* your CV…I could put in a good word for you.' He dropped his voice again and gave me a penetrating look.

'Why would *you* want to do that? It's not as if you know me.'

'Oh…but I *hope* to.' He handed me his business card.

'Thank you,' I said, taking it. I briefly glanced at the card and then put it in my handbag. 'I'm going to have to make a move actually,' I said, looking at my watch.

'So soon? I was wondering whether you'd like to have a drink somewhere else?' He sat forward and moved closer. I caught a whiff of his aftershave and, although I could not place it, whatever it was really suited him. I hesitated before I responded.

'Yes…OK…I'd like that,' I replied with a nod of agreement. I found him intriguing and wanted to know more.

'Shall we go?' He stood up and put his coat on.

'Give me five minutes. I'll meet you outside,' I said, picking up my handbag and coat.

I stood in front of the mirror in the ladies cloakroom and brushed my hair.

'Off for a date with Alex?' asked Teresa spitefully as she pushed *that* fringe out of her eyes. She was standing behind me and I saw her reflection in the mirror. I decided to ignore the comment and not respond.

'*You'll* never get anywhere with *him* you know,' she said, leaning against the washbasin and giving me a scathing look.

'From what I hear, *you* would know all about that,' I retorted, and walked out.

I walked through the wine bar and beckoned to Kim.

'I'm going for a drink with Alex.'

'Oh.' She seemed surprised by the news. 'Where are you going?'

'I don't know. Are you OK about me leaving you?'

'I'll be right. I'm going soon myself. You'll have to tell me all about it later.' Teresa was standing by the bar and I felt her eyes boring into my back as I disappeared out of view. Alex was waiting for me outside.

'Let's walk down to the Strand. We should be able to catch a cab more easily from there. It's so cold,' he said, turning up the collar on his overcoat. 'Listen, I don't suppose you've eaten and I'm starving. Wouldn't you rather go to dinner? You don't live that far from me actually and we could go somewhere near you if you'd like that.'

'Yes, I would.'

'OK.'

Over dinner I observed Alex closely and had the feeling I was being observed too, albeit subtly.

'Kim told me you're half-Italian. So presumably you're bilingual?'

'Yes.'

'What part of Italy is your family from?'

'Tuscany.'

'Shouldn't the 'c' in your name be pronounced 'chee' like in cheek?'

'You speak Italian?' Alex shook his head. 'Yes, you're right, but it has always been pronounced the English way. My father's choice.'

'I suppose you're an excellent linguist?'

'I can get by in several languages.'

'Davina was a linguist.' His manner was quite matter of fact.

'Davina?' I presumed that this was an ex-girlfriend.

'A long-time girlfriend. Past tense. She studied modern languages for her degree. That's how we met.'

'Oh, I see. What about you?'

'What about me?' He sounded defensive, as if I had touched a nerve.

'Are you a linguist too?'

'Oh, right. No.' I wondered what he had thought I was asking him as he certainly seemed relieved by my response.

'Well, you know how to pronounce your 'c's in Italian.'

'But not much else. Davina used to do all the talking for me...when we were abroad together. So, do you like Italian men then?' he asked, changing the subject. It was evident Alex did not wish to discuss Davina any further.

'In what sense?'

'You know what I mean.' He looked at me hard.

'What? Whether I think Italian men make better lovers? No. That depends upon the individual.'

'I'll tell you one thing I do love.'

'What's that?'

'Italian art and architecture,' he said enthusiastically.

'Really?'

'You needn't sound so surprised, Alicia. A love of Italian art is not exclusive to the Italians you know.'

'I'm sorry, Alex. I didn't mean it like that. Have you been to Italy often?'

'Quite a few times actually. I love Venice. I'm passionate about Canaletto.'

'Do you go to the National Gallery to see them?'

'When I have the chance. Have you been to Woburn?'

'No.'

'You should. Woburn has the largest collection of Canaletto's in England outside the Royal Collection. Maybe...if you fancy it...we could go there one weekend?'

'I'd like that.'

We left the restaurant and walked down the street. It was freezing cold, the wind was biting and I was so frozen that my teeth were chattering. I wrapped my scarf more firmly around my face and, as I glanced sideways, saw that Alex had done the same.

'You look chilled to the bone.' He momentarily put his arm around me. 'We can share a cab as you're on my way home.' Then he stopped right in front of me, put his hands around my shoulders and said, 'I've really enjoyed your company this evening, Alicia. It has been great talking to you.' There was a slight pause. 'I *will* speak to Graham about you…I promise.' We stood there for a moment and I thought he was going to kiss me but the moment passed and we carried on walking. I admit to feeling disappointed. Despite my protestations to Kim that he was not my type I was very much attracted to him.

'That's really kind of you and I would appreciate it, but please don't feel under any obligation to do that for me.'

'No. Don't be silly,' he replied, taking hold of my gloved hand. 'I have an ulterior motive.' I looked at him quizzically. 'When you're offered the job you'll have to go out with me again.'

'Oh, I think I can manage that, Alex.'

'Good. Anyway, you'll have to take *me* out by way of a thank you. Now let's get you home.' He hailed a cab.

'How did it go with Alex last night?' Kim asked as I helped her pack.

'What do you mean?' Sometimes I was not certain what Kim was driving at.

'The two of you did go off together?' Kim was fishing.

'You make it sound like a date. We had dinner and a chat. He said if I e-mail him my CV he will put in a good word for me with the Private Client Partner.'

'Wow! You must have made an impression. What did you think of him?'

'In what respect?' I did not look at her, but proceeded to put some folded clothes into the suitcase on the bed.

'You know?' She shut the lid of the suitcase to attract my attention. 'Tell me!'

'*Benfatto*…you mean?'

'Yes.'

'OK. He *is benfatto*, even though he's blond.'

'You like him then?'

'I do actually.' I watched the look on Kim's face, and she seemed a bit disgruntled.

'Hmm... You wouldn't want to get involved with him though, 'cos he's unreliable...*and* he's going out with someone at the moment.'

'Really? He didn't mention it. But as I said, I only went to dinner with him.'

'Come on, Ally. He wouldn't tell you that he had a girlfriend would he? Not when he's two-timing her by going out with you.'

'But we're not going out. What's the matter?'

'Nothing. I've been around long enough to know that he wouldn't take you out to dinner unless he had an ulterior motive.'

'Don't worry about me. I can look after myself. Anyway, I thought you were a fan of his.'

'Just watch out.'

'How's Tom?' It was time to change the subject.

'I was talking to him about the police investigation this morning. They haven't made any real progress yet. I mentioned your friends Will and Jo and he wants to meet them.'

'Why? What did you tell him?'

'Only that Will's a private investigator.'

'Oh, I see. Give me Tom's details and I'll pass them on to Jo. I'm sure Will can help.'

'OK. Thanks, Ally. Have you finalized your holiday plans?'

'I'm spending Christmas at home. Then I'm going to Rome for a few days and on to see my grandmother in Paestum. I'm not back until mid-January.'

'Cesare's in Rome, isn't he?' she asked, with a mischievous look in her eye. I nodded. 'He *will* be pleased to see you and you him?' Again Kim was fishing.

'Hmm... Yes, of course,' I replied. 'What's Tom's number? I'll programme it into my mobile if you have it to hand. Come to think of it, let's 'phone him now.' Kim gave me his number and I called him.

'Hello,' he said. I could tell from his voice that he was down.

'Tom. It's Alicia... Alicia Allen. How are you?'

'Oh, Alicia. Thanks for ringing. I'm OK. How are you?'

'Fine, thanks. Listen, I'm here with Kim. I understand you want to get in touch with Will and Jo as you'd like their assistance?'

'Yeah. Do you think they'd help me investigate Tammy's murder? I don't feel happy with the enquiry or think enough is being done to find her killer.'

'I think you should speak to Will because he knows his way around these things, especially with the police. The last thing you need is to hack them off. I'll give him your number. Is that OK?'

'Yes, thanks. I'd appreciate that.'

'No problem. How's your mother bearing up?' I was keen to know if she had said anything to him about Tammy's estate and, more particularly, why she did not want Tammy's father involved. I did not feel that it was appropriate for me to question Tom, not least because I barely knew him, but also because I might be opening a can of worms.

'She's not very well actually. I'm worried about her.'

'What's wrong, if you don't mind me asking?'

'She has been really sickly recently.' He was not specific and I did not press the point.

'Tammy's death was a terrible blow. Your mother sent me a note before she left. Are you sure there isn't anything I can do for you in relation to Tammy?'

'Well, actually, there is. I'm going to see that modelling agent, Tim Lewis, this week. Would you come with me?'

'If I can wangle the time off work, I will.' I was curious to meet this Mr Lewis. 'But what are you hoping to achieve? I mean, the police have taken a statement from him, haven't they? Or is it that you just want to satisfy yourself by meeting with him?'

'Something like that.'

'OK. That's settled then!'

Tuesday afternoon at two o'clock and Tom and I were walking down Long Acre on our way to TL Models. The entrance to the Agency was a doorway between some shops on Long Acre itself. There were three plaques on the wall and the Entryphone for TL Models was at the bottom; Tom pressed it.

'TL Models.'

'G'day. I'm Tom. Tamsin Brown's brother. We spoke on the 'phone.'

'Oh, yes. Mr Lewis is expecting you. Push the door. We're upstairs.'

We climbed up the stripped wooden stairs directly in front of us to the first floor and followed the signs to the reception area where we were told to take a seat. As we sat and waited on the low leather black sofa I scanned the room. The name *TL Models* was emblazoned on the back wall in gold letters and beneath it were photographs of models and covers from magazines. It looked like an impressive set up, but then appearances can be deceptive. There were a couple of girls sitting opposite us and I presumed from the portfolios they were clutching that they were waiting to be interviewed. They did not talk to each other as obviously they were in competition. I noticed some withering looks.

'Tom?' drawled the man coming towards us. I looked at him and recognized the redhead Kim had pointed out to me at Tammy's funeral. I remember thinking that it was strange that, although he had come to her funeral, he had not bothered to make her family's acquaintance. Tom stood up. 'I'm Tim Lewis.' He held out his hand and Tom took it. 'Such a terrible thing to happen to your sister. Tammy was a *fantastic* girl... *lovely* girl,' he said, continuing to shake Tom's hand. There was something slightly unpleasant in his speech and I did not take to him at all. He looked at me quizzically.

'Oh, this is a friend of mine.' Tom introduced me.

'How do you do?' he said, scanning me. 'Forgive me, but haven't I seen you somewhere before?'

'Probably at Tammy's funeral,' I replied blandly. For a split second he continued to study my face.

'Coffee?' he asked, leading us from reception to his office. 'I don't know about you but I always need so much caffeine in the mornings,' he drawled and he poured the coffee. 'You said you wanted to talk to me about Tammy…I'm not sure how much I can *actually* help you. As you can imagine, the police have questioned us extensively and we have fully co-operated with their investigation. They took away her file. There's nothing more I could tell you.' He was sitting back in his black leather swivel chair and I observed him closely as he shifted his gaze from Tom to me, and back again.

'Did Tammy ever complain about anyone she had worked with? Can you think of anyone she might have offended or knocked back?' Tom asked.

'As I said, I've told the police everything I know. Of course a girl like Tammy would be noticed wherever she went. I'm sure she had many admirers. She was a very enchanting young woman. Captivating, *I* would say. I'm sorry I can't help you any further,' he said rather abruptly, standing up and ushering us to the door, 'but I can assure you that if anything else were to come to mind I would be the *first* to go to the police.' Tom offered his hand but Tim did not take it. I was not impressed and neither was Tom.

'What do you think?' he asked as we walked up Long Acre to Covent Garden tube station.

'A shady character definitely, but as for being a murderer my money wouldn't be on him.'

'What makes you say that?'

'Call it female intuition.'

Chapter 9

The flight from Naples was delayed, but I was not bothered because I felt relaxed and refreshed after my Christmas holiday. I had spent four days in Rome with Cesare and his family and had then travelled down south to Paestum. I spent the remaining ten days with my grandmother who actually lived in Castellabate. What I loved about Paestum was that, even in the summer, it could be free of tourists and, in winter, it was just perfect. The runs along the deserted sandy beach in front of my grandmother's villa had done me the world of good.

I put my key in the outside door and as I did so felt a tinge of sadness that Kim was no longer there. I looked wistfully at the door to Kim and Tammy's flat as I climbed the stairs to mine. Predictably there was a pile of post on my mat, the bulk of which was junk mail. I was in the middle of unpacking when the 'phone rang.

'Hello, Ally.' It was Kim. 'You're back. Did you have a good holiday?'

'Yes. Thanks. I had a great time with my grandmother. It seems strange that you're not downstairs any more. How are things with you?'

'Not bad at all. Listen, you've got to come over. Tom wants to talk to you. Can you make it this evening about eight? Oh…and…Alex was asking after you. Do you mind if I give him your mobile number?'

'No.'

'I have to go. I need to finish something for Greg. See you later.'

Kim's attitude towards Alex had changed and she seemed much

more relaxed about him now. I wondered whether that was because she had lost interest in him or maybe she was interested in someone else. On my way out I called in to see Dorothy. I was keen to find out who was moving in downstairs and if anyone knew it would be her.

'Hello, dear. How are you?' she asked, opening her door.

'I'm very well. Thanks.'

'I must say you're looking rested.'

'I feel it. I have something for you from Italy.' I handed Dorothy a box of sugared almonds because I knew she liked those.

'Oh, you are a thoughtful girl,' she said, touching my cheek. 'Thank you so much. Won't you stay a while?'

'I'd love to. Only I'm on my way out to see Kim. I dropped by to give you the present. Is anybody moving in upstairs?' She looked disappointed that I could not stay.

'Not to my knowledge, dear. When can you come down for tea?' she asked enthusiastically.

'At the weekend if you like.'

'Yes, I would like that very much.'

'Ally!' Kim opened the door and flung her arms around me.

'Wow! What a welcome,' I hugged Kim back and handed her a bag of goodies.

'Tom's not back yet.' We walked into the reception room. 'Have you met Rob?'

'G'day.' He extended his hand to me. As we set eyes on each other, we both burst out laughing.

'What's the matter?' asked Kim, looking puzzled.

'We've already met,' I said.

'I don't understand, Ally. What do you mean? How?'

'It's quite simple really. It was at Winchester railway station the day I went there for a meeting. I sat in the same carriage as Rob on the way home.'

'The day we found out that Tammy had been murdered?' said Kim, her voice trailing away. I noticed her eyes fill with tears.

'Yes, it was,' I replied, putting my arm around her momentarily.

'We had a good chat as I recall,' added Rob, giving Kim a reassuring smile. 'Such a small world.'

'Yes, what a coincidence. Have you started your new job?'

'I have.'

'Ally! I need your help,' Kim interrupted, taking me by the arm and leading me out of the room to the kitchen. 'You're full of surprises.'

'I do my best. Are you all right? What's been happening in my absence?'

'I'm OK. It's just that it still upsets me when I think about Tammy's murder. I've settled in really well here though, and the boys are great, especially Tom. I've even joined the gym.'

'You really like him, don't you?' I suspected that she had been holding a torch for Tom for years.

'Yes, I do. There was something else I was going to tell you. Jo called Tom and he met up with her and Will.'

'Oh, good. I haven't spoken to her yet. What *else* has been happening?'

'Not much really. Work has been a nightmare. Alex was away over Christmas and I had to work for Andy and he's weird. Has Alex called you yet?'

'No. Did he have a good Christmas?'

'Goodness knows. But I want to hear about your holiday. How's Cesare?'

'Back in six weeks.'

'Ally, that's not what I asked and you know it! Stop ducking and diving.'

'He's fine. Looking really well.'

'And?'

'And what?'

'You and him of course?'

'Still friends. Do we have to talk about him?' I asked, clamming up.

'No. How is your grandmother?'

'Like you!' I replied evasively.

'What do you mean?'

'She asks too many questions.' I heard somebody come in the front door. 'Isn't that Tom?' I went out into the hall.

'Alicia! Hi.' Tom bent down and kissed me on the cheek. 'It's great to see you. How are you?'

'I was going to ask you the same question. Have you managed to find a job over here yet?'

'I'm working freelance for a few sports clubs.'

'Doing?' I had never asked what Tom did.

'I'm a physio. I deal with sports injuries.'

'That's really good. You must be pleased.'

'Yeah. I am. Rob helped me get started. It's amazing how true it is about *who* you know rather than *what* you know. I met up with Jo and Will.'

'Kim just told me. I hope they were helpful.'

'Yeah. I think they will be. I want to have a chat with you about that some *other* time if you can spare me a few minutes?' I nodded. I took the hint; this was not the appropriate forum to discuss such matters and I changed the subject.

'How's your mother?'

'No better. She's going for tests now.' He sighed. He sounded worried and I hoped for his sake that whatever was wrong with his mother was not serious. I tried to be as positive as possible.

'I imagine that all of this has been terrible for you and I don't know anyone who would have coped better in the circumstances. Please send her my best wishes.'

'Tom, can you give me a hand with dinner, please?' asked Kim, popping her head around the kitchen door. I sensed I was not required and wandered back through to the reception room where Rob was watching TV.

'I can't get over what a small world it is,' I said, sitting down next to him.

'I'm glad it is. Otherwise, we would never have met.'
'That's one way of looking at it, I suppose.' I half-smiled at him.

The next morning I called Jo because I wanted to catch up with her, and I was curious about Will's meeting with Tom. I had meant to 'phone her the day before but I had been sidetracked by Kim's call.
'Jo. It's Alicia. How *are* you?'
'I'm fine. Absolutely fine. I didn't expect to hear from you yet. I thought you were away until after next weekend.'
'I decided to come back a few days earlier.'
'How's Cesare?'
'Good. Why?'
'You know why!'
'You and Kim are obsessed. What is it with you two trying to match-make all the time?'
'I'm only looking out for my best friend's interests.'
'I know and I appreciate it. I went to dinner with Kim last night and saw Tom,' I said, swiftly changing the subject. 'When he'd told me that he'd been in touch with you and would tell me all about it another time, I had the impression that Kim has no idea what's going on.'
'No. She hasn't.'
'Why the secrecy?'
'I'm going undercover. Tom asked Will if he would carry out some investigative work. Will told him that everything would have to be done through proper channels. He spoke with DS Hamilton and, to cut a long story short, it turned out that DI Peters had decided to put someone on the inside anyway. The bottom line is that the police believe that Tammy's death is connected with the Club, but they don't know how. That's what I'll endeavour to uncover. Jensen's is closed at the moment as Dick shuts in January so there's nothing I can do on that front yet.'
'I hope you'll be OK.'
'I'm trained to look after myself. Anyway, Dick might not employ

me at the Club.'

'I doubt that, Jo.'

'The police have suspicions about Tim Lewis. I've applied to be a model on the commercial side. It's a bit of a long shot, but we're going to see if Tim will take me on his books. I know I can trust you not to tell anyone.'

'You can.' I bit my lip, and thought about Eve from whom I had not heard since Tammy's funeral.

The next day I was at home doing my chores before I returned to work. My mobile phone was on the coffee table and, because I was hoovering, I did not hear it ring. Fortunately, I noticed the screen light up out of the corner of my eye and ran to answer it.

'Hello,' I said. The number was withheld so I braced myself for it to be Eve.

'Alicia?' I did not recognize the voice at first, but it was male.

'Yes?'

'It's Alex Waterford. How are *you?*'

'Oh. Hello. I'm fine, thanks. How are you?' I asked in my friendliest voice.

'Very well.' He was still formal. He paused. 'The reason why I'm calling is that I wanted to let you know that I passed on your CV to Graham and we had a brief chat about you. He'll call you.' He sounded very matter-of-fact and not at all like he was the day we met. I found his manner towards me rather disconcerting.

'Thank you, Alex.' I tried to sound enthusiastic.

'I have a client waiting, so I have to go. Good luck with Graham. Bye, Alicia.'

'Bye.'

I felt slightly disappointed at the end of the call. I was pleased that Alex had recommended me to Graham Ffoulkes, but when I heard his voice I hoped that he was calling me on a personal basis as I was curious to meet him again. Although I had only met him once and hardly knew him I found myself fascinated by him. There was something mysterious and exciting about him, which was impossible to describe. Maybe Kim was right; Alex had that certain *je ne sais quoi* or wow factor as she had put it. He was aware of himself, but not in the same way as Ivano. Alex was more subtle – and infinitely more charismatic. I was so deep in thought that when the video Entryphone to the flat buzzed I almost jumped out of my skin. On seeing it was Tom, I let him in.

'Thought you weren't in,' he said as he came bounding into the hall. 'I buzzed several times.'

'Sorry, I didn't hear the buzzer. I'm a bit tired. Coffee?'

'Yeah. Great.' He took off his quilted parka and rubbed his hands together. 'It's really cold out.'

'Do you want some lunch now you're here?' I called out from the kitchen.

'No. You're all right. Coffee would be great. I'm sorry to bother you, Alicia, but could you help me out with some paperwork. It's Tammy's stuff.'

'I will, if I can.' I brought in the coffee.

'Did you speak to Jo?' I nodded. 'And she told you that she is going undercover?'

'Yes.' I handed him his coffee. 'Biscuit?' I offered him the tin.

'Yes. Thanks,' he replied, taking it. 'I really hope Jo can find out something,' he said, crunching on a plain chocolate digestive.

'Well, if anybody can she will. I do appreciate you telling me and I won't breach your confidence. Let me have a look at that paperwork,' I said, opening the envelope he had placed on the coffee table.

Tom stayed for about an hour and we chatted, but mostly about his work. I tried to steer him onto the subject of Tammy and their childhood, but it was evident he found it too painful to talk about her, and therefore I let the matter drop. No sooner had I closed the door to him than my 'phone rang.

'Alicia Allen?' The voice was male and unknown to me.

'Speaking.'

'Alicia. This is Graham Ffoulkes from Wilson, Weil & Co. My colleague Alexander Waterford passed me your details. I've discussed your CV with my Tax Partner, Andy Steinberg, and we'd like to meet you. We thought perhaps around close of business on Thursday or Friday. Are either of those days convenient?' I quickly gathered my thoughts and tried to remember what my office diary was like for the week.

'Hmm… Well, Friday would be better for me. Around six?'

'That would be perfect. Do you know how to find us?' My mobile started to ring and it was interfering with the reception on my main 'phone and I turned it off. 'Are you still there, Alicia?' asked Graham.

'Yes, sorry. My mobile rang. You're near Russell Square, aren't you?'

'Yes. That's right. When you come out of the tube station you need to turn left. Walk along the road for a few minutes and across the first set of traffic lights. You'll find us on the next corner. We'll see you then, Alicia. Goodbye.'

'Goodbye.'

As soon as I put down the 'phone I turned my mobile back on. The call was from Jo and I returned it immediately.

'Hi. Jo. It's Ally. Sorry I missed you, but I was on the landline to Graham Ffoulkes from Wilson, Weil & Co. He rang me about going for an interview.'

'Oh. Great. That sounds positive, Ally. When is it?'

'Friday. After work. I think it's worth going for sure.'

'I agree. Guess where I've been?'

'No idea.'

'To see Tim Lewis for a casting and yes, I agree with you, he *is* a creep. I have to wait until Friday to see if they want to take me on their books.'

'It's all happening then.'

'Yes. Tim's assistant, Jane Duncan, 'phoned me on my "Marie" mobile this morning.' Marie Martin was a pseudonym Jo was using for her undercover work. 'She deals with all the bookings. She said that they'd reviewed my prints and wanted me to attend a casting today.'

'How did you find her? I didn't see her when I went there with Tom.'

'Quite pleasant, actually. She introduced me to Tim. He thanked me for sending in my photos and asked me if I had a portfolio. I wanted him to think that I didn't have a clue so I told him I was very new to all this.'

'What did he say?'

'That it wasn't a problem. He made some comment about creating a portfolio to show off my slim, athletic build. He thinks I'm a dancer.'

'Why?'

'Because I told him that my job requires me to be fit, and when he asked me what I do I said I'm a trained professional.'

'Hmm... I have a strong feeling that you'll receive that call on Friday.'

'You and your instincts, Alicia!'

'Not so much that. Having met him I expect he'll conform to type. I'll speak to you soon, Jo.'

'You must, because I'd like to hear how it goes with Graham Ffoulkes.'

'OK. Take care.' I then called Kim to tell her about the interview.

'Ooh. Cool. Alex turned up trumps then. I'll keep my fingers crossed for you. I have to shoot off early on Friday otherwise I'd wait for you, but give me a call when you get home and let me know if it went well.'

'OK.'

'I'd better go, as I have to finish the warranty documentation Alex needs for his meeting. He's hovering. Bye, Ally.'

Chapter 10

On Friday morning I could not decide what to wear for my interview. I had probably tried on most of the suits in my wardrobe, the whole contents of which were strewn across my bed but, in the end, I decided on yet another safe black suit. It was one of those days when nothing went right: I was having a bad hair day, it was raining, all the buses were full on the way into work, my secretary was ill and one of the temps had not turned up.

Consequently, I was glad to leave the office at five-thirty on the dot, jump into a cab and make my way to Wilson, Weil & Co. It was no longer raining but the traffic was heavy and I was lucky to arrive in time. The door to the office was wide open and, as I entered the building, a tall, thin and rather distinguished-looking man with grey hair walked straight into me. He did not turn to apologize, but carried on walking to the limousine waiting for him outside. I knew I had seen him somewhere before, but could not place him. Slightly dazed, I put my head around the door to reception, only to be greeted by the rather officious receptionist Kim had warned me about.

'I'm Alicia Allen. I have a meeting with Graham Ffoulkes at six o'clock.'

'If you'd like to take a seat, Miss Allen, I'll just call through for you,' she replied in a high-pitched voice with pinched vowels which grated on my ears. She gave me an imperious look, as though I was something that she had trodden on. I sat down in reception, picked up the firm's brochure and thumbed through it. It had been updated since Kim had shown me one several months before and some of the pictures had changed. On the first inside page was a photograph of Vincent Weil, the Senior Partner. It was then that I realized he was the distinguished, looking man who had just pushed past me. I turned the page and studied the one of Alex...

'Alicia?' I looked up.

'Graham Ffoulkes. How do you do?' He extended his hand and smiled broadly at me. He was rotund and jolly, looking with a very amiable expression and I warmed to him immediately.

'How do you do?' I replied, standing up and shaking his hand.

'My colleague, Andy Steinberg, is currently on a call, but will join us shortly. If you'd like to follow me...' He led me to a small conference room along the corridor. 'You come highly recommended,' he continued. I looked at him quizzically. 'Alexander Waterford speaks *so* highly of you.' He invited me to sit down. 'I see you have been at Simons, Snade & Brown for three years and before that at Withins & Co. You have the level of experience we are looking for and you have worked for solid firms. Why do you want to move?' I hated all these stock questions, but I supposed I had better provide the stock answers.

'I'm looking to advance my career. I have reached a plateau at Simons, Snade & Brown and need to diversify and gain more experience.' He seemed to like that response and smiled and nodded as if he was agreeing with my sentiments exactly.

At this point the door opened and Andy Steinberg walked in. I stood up to shake his hand. He was not at all like I had imagined he would be. In fact, he looked emaciated and his suit simply hung off him. In addition to that, his cheeks were sunken and I could not help but notice how goggle-eyed he was. I was not sure whether he was staring at me or whether this was his usual expression. I felt a little uncomfortable and his presence rather disconcerting because he sat with his elbows on the table, the tips of his fingers pressed together listening, and he watched me without saying a word. Graham conducted the whole interview single-handed with no input from him whatsoever and I thought it was bizarre.

'Thank you for coming in to meet us, Alicia. We'll be in touch,' Graham said.

I stood up and Graham opened the door, but Andy remained behind the desk. I extended my hand to him out of politeness.

'Goodbye, Alicia. See you *again*,' he said, emphasizing the word *again* and nodding his head in acknowledgment.

'Goodbye,' I replied, thinking that maybe that was his way of saying that I had survived the first round!

I left Wilson, Weil & Co and made my way back to Russell Square tube station. It had started to rain again and was piercingly cold. The underground was packed and I waited for about ten minutes before I could get on a tube. Even then I only managed to squeeze inside the door. I came out of the tube at South Kensington, walked up the steps and switched on my mobile phone. I had two missed calls, one from Jo telling me about her call from the modelling agency and another from Kim asking me how the interview went. I returned Jo's call first but, as I dialled, a number 14 bus came around the corner. I ran to catch it, so when Jo answered I was clambering upstairs on the bus.

'Alicia?'

'Hell…o…Jo…' I replied breathlessly.

'You OK?'

'Yes…fine,' I said, sitting down. 'I was running for the bus. I'm going to the gym on my way home. Tell me what happened at the agency?'

'They've accepted me. I'm amazed. I hadn't heard from Jane Duncan all day and I thought that maybe Tim had decided not to take me on his books after all, but then at six-thirty my "Marie" mobile rang and it was Jane.'

'What did she say?'

'She apologized for not getting back to me sooner, said that they'd been simply inundated and had to sift through a lot of photographs, but that if I was still interested they'd be pleased to take me on their books.'

'What happens now?'

'I have to go into the agency at two-fifteen on Monday to see Tim and meet one of the photographers. Anyway, Ally, that's phase one complete. Now, on to phase two. How did your interview go?'

'It was OK.' I walked down the stairs and jumped off the bus at the traffic lights opposite the gym. 'The Private Client Partner, Graham Ffoulkes, was really friendly. I liked him very much, but can't say the same for the Tax Partner.'

'Why? What was wrong with him?'

'He was weird. Looks apart, his behaviour was very odd. He sat and stared at me the whole time.'

'Oh, well, if you're not going to be working for him, and the other one is OK, it might be worth going back for a second interview. Are the prospects good there?'

'Probably. What's happening about the Club?' I walked through the double doors to the gym and presented the receptionist with my membership card which she swiped through the machine. She handed it back to me along with two towels. I had rented a locker to save me from lugging my kit bag with me when I felt like dropping in at the gym after work. On evenings such as this it had proved to be very convenient.

'Dick Jensen hasn't placed any adverts since December. When the Club opens I'm sure he'll advertise again. If not, I'll apply in person. What are you doing this weekend?'

'Antonia will be here. As you know she was staying with Mamma but she's coming to stay with me for a few weeks until the tenancy of her flat comes to an end. It's easier for her to be in London as she has things to organize. You?' I was now in the ladies changing room.

'I'll be working with Will on one of his projects. I've got to go. Enjoy your workout. I'll speak to you later.'

When I arrived home two hours later I felt much more relaxed. As

I opened the door to my flat I heard my landline ringing, dropped my bags in the hall and ran to answer it.

'Hello…'

'Ally, it's Kim. Did you get my message?'

'Yes. Sorry. My mobile was switched off for the interview, then I was on the tube, and I dashed to the gym.'

'How did the interview go?'

'So-so. Graham was really lovely, but I'm not sure what to make of Andy.'

'Don't worry about him. He's known for being a bit weird! The main thing is that Graham likes you and believe me he is the best of the lot.'

The fact that Andy was a bit weird, as Kim put it, did not bode well, but the way I looked at it, Wilson, Weil & Co. could not be worse than Simons, Snade & Brown or, at least, I hoped not. Besides, Kim worked there so I had one friendly face to work with if I was offered the job.

'I met Vincent Weil too.'

'Did he speak to you then? Strewth. That *would* be a first.'

'No. He was coming out of the front door and walked straight into me. He nearly knocked me flying actually.'

'Well, that's Vincent for you, Ally. Weil by name. Vile by nature. Sure you still want to join the firm?'

During the next two weeks I did not hear from Jo although I had left messages. I presumed her undercover work had taken off. I was not overly concerned because I knew she would return my calls eventually. I was feeling rather jaded again though, as the effects of my holiday in Italy had rapidly worn off once I had returned to the reality of working for David Wagstaff.

I had begun to question whether I wanted to continue working within the law, but this was partly down to the fact that I no longer enjoyed working at Simons, Snade & Brown. David Wagstaff was a major contributory factor. I had not heard back from Graham

Ffoulkes following my interview and I was having doubts about moving to Wilson, Weil & Co.

Meera and I had still not met due to her commitments and, although Antonia was living with me temporarily, I had hardly seen her. She was catching up with all her old friends and had been out most nights. Kim was settled with Rob and Tom and we did not see each other as often, so I was spending considerably more time at the gym venting out my frustrations. A few weeks later, after yet another evening session at the gym, I was lying on the sofa watching television, eating Sour Cream and Onion Pringles. The 'phone rang and I leaned over to pick it up off the coffee table as I swallowed the remainder of my mouthful of Pringles.

'Ally, it's Jo. I'm sorry I haven't got back to you. Would you believe this is the first opportunity I've had to call you? I've so much to tell you and we haven't seen each other for ages. What are you up to?' The sound of traffic in the background made it difficult to hear her.

'I went to a Yoga Hatha class and now I'm vegging out on the sofa eating Pringles,' I replied, clearing my throat. 'Where are you? It's very noisy there.'

'Piccadilly. I've just been to the Club for my interview.' I immediately sat up.

'You know how to grab a girl's attention, don't you?' I chided. 'Do you want to come over?'

'That's why I'm calling 'cos I'm so near you. I'll see you in about twenty minutes.' She hung up.

'You look good.' Jo was dressed in a black polo neck jumper, suede miniskirt, high-heeled suede boots and a black leather jacket.

'I wanted to make a good impression,' she said, winking at me and slipping off her jacket.

'And did you?'

'Well, he offered me the job. Do you mind if I take my boots off? They're killing me.'

110

'You go ahead. What's been happening?' She unzipped her boots and dropped them in the hall. 'The last time we spoke you'd been to the casting at the modelling agency and they'd called you back to meet the photographer.'

'Oh, that's better,' she said, rubbing her right foot as she followed me into the reception room. I flopped onto the sofa, she sunk back in my armchair and propped her feet up on the stool. 'Yes. Rick Steadman.'

'Can I fix you something to eat?' I leaned forward and took a handful of Pringles out of the tube before passing it to her.

'These will do for now. They're just so tasty.' She popped one in her mouth. 'I already knew about Rick because the police interviewed him. He did Tammy's portfolio. I was curious to see for myself what he would be like.'

'And?' I finished off the Pringles in my hand.

'Laid back and rather good looking I thought in a rugged sort of way but not in the least dodgy, unlike Tim.'

'Did you get anything useful out of him?' I asked, walking through to the kitchen. Jo followed me in and perched on my kitchen stool. 'I'm going to make myself a tuna melt. I'm starving.' I cut up a French stick, grated some cheese and put the baguette slices in the oven to warm them.

'During the shoot at his studio in Clerkenwell, I used every opportunity to tap him for information.'

'What did you ask him?' I rummaged around the fridge for the tuna.

'How long he had been a photographer, and whether he had photographed anyone famous. He said he had photographed a couple of the supermodels: Kate Moss and Naomi Campbell. Then, out of the blue, he started talking about Tammy.'

'What did he say?'

'That Tim had a talent for spotting potential and, after meeting Tammy, raved about her.'

'Pity he didn't get her much work then,' I said sarcastically as I took the baguette slices out of the oven, spread over the tuna and sprinkled them with grated cheese. 'Are you sure you don't want anything to eat, Jo?' She shook her head. I turned on the grill.

'Clearly he wanted something out of her first. Rick hinted as much. He made some joke about Tim not being averse to "the casting couch" and told me to watch out. He showed me Tammy's portfolio. She looked fantastic. I found Rick totally professional and there is no reason to suspect he was in any way involved in Tammy's murder.'

'In other words, you don't think he is murderer material?'

'No. Tim Lewis is a more likely candidate, not that there is any evidence to incriminate him either.'

'Quite. Being a lech doesn't make him a murderer; obnoxious and sad, but not necessarily a cold-blooded killer. This is how Tom and I assessed him.'

'One thing's for sure, Ally. Being a model isn't what it's cracked up to be, at least not for those struggling at the bottom of the ladder and having to consider other means to climb to the top. When I went back to the Agency to choose the photographs for my portfolio, Tim made it very clear to me that how well I did would depend upon how flexible I was prepared to be and my relationship with him.'

'We both know what that means.'

'Exactly.'

'What about the Club? Any progress there?' I placed the baguette slices under the heated grill.

'The police have been scanning the 'Situations Vacant' section in *The Stage* for an advertisement from Dick Jensen for weeks. It only appeared last Thursday. I knew what to expect before I went for the interview. I'd had my brief, I'd read your statement and knew what Tammy told you. My initial telephone conversation and the interview mirrored those of Tammy. He uses a lot of stock phrases.'

'What did you think of him?'

'Oh, he's a shady character. As for being a murderer, we shall see.

I hope I can find something out when I go to work there.'

'I hate the idea of you being at the Club, Jo.'

'I know you do, but I've been through all this with the police. If there's something going on at Jensen's, and Tammy's murder is in some way connected, I've got to try and discover what it is. I can only do that if I'm working on the inside. My theory is that she stumbled on something and they bumped her off.'

'But what? I've racked my brains on that point ever since she was murdered.'

'I bet Dick is involved. I really didn't like him at all. He's basically a pimp in another guise and couldn't care less about the girls in the Club. He knows that they are desperate for cash and exploits it.'

'True, but that still doesn't make him a murderer.'

'Well, somebody did it, Alicia, and if I can dig up anything by working there it's worth the risk. Anyway, since I'll be working nights and am going to be good for nothing for the next few weeks I'm going home to spend some *quality* time with my husband.'

'That sounds like an admirable idea.'

Chapter 11

My meeting out of London finished sooner than anticipated and I arrived home early. I opened the door to my flat and my mobile started to ring but, as usual, it had somehow managed to slip to the bottom of my handbag and I could not retrieve it in time. The number was withheld and there was no message but I thought nothing of it until it rang again.

'Hello.'

'Miss Allen.' I recognized Eve's husky voice at once and felt my back stiffen.

'Please tell me what you want, Eve. How can I help you otherwise?' I implored.

'I'm sorry. It isn't the right time. When it is, you'll know. Trust nobody.' Then she hung up. How would I know when it would be the right time? My 'phone rang again. The caller display showed the number was withheld.

'Hello,' I said tentatively, thinking that it was Eve again.

'Alicia?' I did not recognize the male voice.

'Yes,' I said tersely.

'It's Graham Ffoulkes from Wilson, Weil & Co. You sound different. How are you?' He was extremely friendly.

'Oh, hello…I'm fine thank you,' I said, composing myself.

'I hope I haven't called at an inopportune moment?'

'Hmm… Err. No. Not at all.'

'Good. I've discussed you with my fellow Partners and if you're still interested we'd like you to come back for a second interview.'

He paused and I drew breath.

'Oh. Yes. I am actually.' I had nothing to lose by going back for another chat.

'Excellent. There are a couple of points we'd like to run through with you. Can you make tomorrow at six o'clock?' He sounded enthusiastic.

'Umm... Yes. I think so, but I don't have my diary with me to double-check. I'll have to call you tomorrow morning to confirm.'

'We'll be expecting you unless we hear otherwise. OK?'

'Yes. OK. That's fine.'

'Goodbye, Alicia.'

'Goodbye.'

The next evening just after six o'clock I was sitting in the reception at Wilson, Weil & Co.

'Alicia?' I glanced up and saw the tall figure of Vincent Weil standing at the top of the staircase. He was leaning over the balustrade looking down at me. 'You'll have to come up. I'm far too important to come down and get you,' he said arrogantly but oozing charm. I was taken aback because I had not expected to be interviewed by him, and Graham Ffoulkes was nowhere in sight. I climbed the stairs purposefully and he ushered me through the double doors to his office. He shut the doors, sat down at his desk, lit a Turkish cigarette and scrutinized me. The sweet scent of lilies overpowered me as soon as I entered the room and that, combined with the smell of his cigarette, made me feel sick. 'So,' he drawled, 'I hear you come highly recommended. Tell me why you want to join *my* firm?' He leaned back and drew on his cigarette.

'I've been at my present firm for a few years now. There's no room for progression and I'm looking for career advancement.'

'You're ambitious then?'

'There's no point in being on a career ladder if there are no rungs above you is there?'

'Ambition can be an admirable quality, Alicia.' He paused. 'In the right place, of course,' he said, flicking his ash into a large glass ashtray on the desk. 'If you're looking for a mutually advantageous career move,' and he peered at me over his half-rimmed glasses as he spoke, 'you need look no further than Wilson, Weil & Co. We're a forward-thinking firm and with the right attitude and outlook you *will* go far here. *You* can go as far as you want to go, Alicia. Any questions?'

'My firm has a case on with your firm at the moment. The case of Jacobs.'

'Have you worked on it?'

'I have actually. I was a bit worried about confidentiality.'

'No need. We can just prepare a document which states that at no time will you discuss or disclose matters pertaining to that file with members of staff here and vice versa.'

At this point Graham entered the room.

'Alicia. Good to see you,' he said shaking my hand. 'Thank you for coming back. We had a Partners' meeting last week and would like to offer you the position…if you're still interested.'

'Oh.'

'Is there a problem?'

'I'm not used to being offered a position on the spot.'

'Of course, you'll want to go away and think about the terms of our offer.'

'You'll find, Alicia, that in this firm,' said Vincent, standing and walking around his desk, 'we do things rather differently. I'll leave you to finalize everything because I have a meeting now. Well, see you again.' He extended his hand to me. I shook it, he strode to the door, turned and half-smiling at me said, 'I hope you make the decision to join Wilson, Weil & Co., Alicia, and if you play your cards right you'll have an excellent future here.'

Clearly Vincent had a very charismatic side to his personality, which was different from the side I saw when I came to my first interview. I had been doubtful about working at the firm because of Vincent's reputation, but the terms of the offer were highly favourable, the remuneration package excellent and they were offering me the post of Associate, not Assistant. Furthermore, I liked Graham, and Kim and Alex were at the firm so I had every reason to leave Simons, Snade & Brown.

Two days later I received the offer letter from Graham Ffoulkes. If I decided to accept I would need to wait for a few days before I handed in my notice, because Peter was away again and it was better to deal with this upon his return. That afternoon I received a call from Alex Waterford.

'You owe me a drink I believe,' he said nonchalantly.

'Alex?' I was surprised by his casual manner, bearing in mind that the last time I had spoken to him he was aloof.

'Yes. That's me,' he quipped. 'Well?'

'Hmm…' He had caught me off guard.

'You *were* offered the job, weren't you? So when are you going to take me for that drink?'

'When are you free?'

'Any time you like. Actually, I wondered whether you wanted to come to a house-warming party on Saturday night. An old university friend of mine has moved with his girlfriend into a loft conversion in the Docklands. If you're interested I'll e-mail the details to you.'

'That sounds great, but my sister, Antonia, is staying with me at the moment and I'm not sure what her plans are for the weekend.' There was a slight pause at the other end of the 'phone.

'If she's free why not bring her along too? I'm e-mailing the details to you as we speak. I hope to see you there.'

'OK, Alex. Bye.'

I was pleased that Alex had called. This time he had been friendly but I could not quite make him out. It was this mercurial quality that attracted me to him, and I *was* attracted to him. I had no intention of telling Kim about the party, particularly after what she had said to me about Alex, but it was going to be difficult because she was always so inquisitive.

I needed to call Tom to find out what had happened at Tammy's inquest because I had been unable to attend. As it happened, he rang me and arranged to pop around after work for a quick chat.

'How did it go?' I asked.

'Awful. Death by unlawful killing, you know – by person or persons unknown.'

'Yes. It would be. No surprises there then.'

'I don't understand Alicia how all this works. We had that brief hearing after Tammy was murdered and it was adjourned until now. Is that it then?' He seemed distressed.

'What do you mean?'

'That we give up on finding who killed her?'

'No, Tom. The inquest's completely different. It isn't a criminal trial. It's just to establish the facts surrounding Tammy's death and to place those facts on public record. Her killer or killers haven't been found. If the police had charged someone with her murder already then the inquest would have been adjourned at least until after the trial. Then it would be at the discretion of the coroner whether or not to resume the inquest after the trial.'

'Right. Only I'm so frustrated about the lack of progress in the investigation. I know Jo's doing her best, but everything takes so long. How are things with you?'

'Antonia's staying with me at the moment. She'll be home very soon. You've never met have you?'

'No. But you didn't answer my question, Alicia. How are *you?*'

'I'm fine. I've been offered a new job.'

'Really? Are you going to take it?'

'I haven't decided yet. I'm giving it some serious thought.'

'Ally,' Antonia called out as she burst through the front door and rushed into the reception room. 'You'll never guess who I've just bumped into.' She stopped short on seeing Tom. 'Oh, hello,' she said, taking off her coat and smiling at him.

'Antonia. This is Tom. You know. Tammy's brother.'

'Oh. Of course. I've heard a lot about you.' Antonia extended her hand and continued to smile at him. He shook it and smiled back, holding her gaze.

'Oh. Right. Nothing bad I hope.'

'Hardly. How *are* you? Alicia mentioned something to me about the inquest taking place.'

'Yes. That was yesterday. Pretty tough.'

'You'll have to come round to my flat when I move back in. When I've sorted myself out I'm going to have some friends over.'

'Oh. Yeah. That'd be great.'

'How's Kim?' I asked.

'Good. We're going to a party on Saturday night. One of Rob's friends is over. Do you guys fancy coming along?' He was looking at me, but it was clear he was directing the question at Antonia.

'Actually, I've been invited to another party by one of my future work colleagues, so I can't,' I replied, looking at Antonia.

'Oh. That's a shame. How about you, Antonia?' Now he turned to her.

'Hmm… I was going with Alicia.' She paused and looked at me.

'Listen, mine is really a work thing,' I said. 'Why not go with Tom? You'd probably prefer it.'

'Well, if you're sure, Ally?'

'Yes. Quite sure.' I smiled to myself.

'You didn't tell me who it was you met, Antonia,' I asked after Tom had left.

'No, I didn't.' She started to laugh.

'*Dimmi subito.*'

'Guess who?'

'I don't know. That's why I'm asking!'

'Ivano. I bumped into him on the Old Brompton Road when I was having a coffee. I saw him at once and I thought he hadn't recognized me, but then he twigged who I was and came over. He asked me all about you and what you were doing, but I didn't tell him anything. He said he's been out to Rome to see Cesare and that

Cesare's coming back soon.' Antonia gave me a searching look.

'Yes. Next week. He starts his new job in about two weeks' time I think.'

'I find it odd that those two are friends.'

'I'll never understand it, but they're work colleagues and Cesare stayed with Ivano when he first moved to London, so he probably feels he owes him. He's a soft touch, and allows people take advantage of him sometimes.'

'I expect he's really looking forward to seeing *you* again, Ally.'

'Not especially, I'm sure. He has loads of other friends to catch up with.'

'Yes, but the question is whether he's interested in *them*.'

On Saturday evening Antonia left about half past seven and I was about to run out the door when as usual my 'phone rang. It was Kim, and I did not want to tell her that I was going to Alex's friends' party because I knew I would receive a barrage of questions.

'Ally. Glad I caught you before you left. You're not coming out with us then? Had a better offer?' she quipped.

'No. I just had a prior engagement. What makes you ask?'

'Wow. You seem a bit snappy. What's up?'

'Nothing. What's the big deal?'

'Sorry. You seem a bit uptight that's all.'

'No. I'm just running late. Antonia is on her way over to your place now so she'll be there soon.'

'Where are you off to then?' Since I was usually very open about what I was doing she probably guessed that something was up.

'I'll have to catch you later. I must dash.'

I followed the directions that Alex had sent me in his e-mail. The party was at an apartment in a refurbished period warehouse overlooking Canary Wharf. I arrived just after eight-thirty, parked my car and pressed the Entryphone buzzer. Nick opened the door to me, and I soon discovered that he was the friend Alex had mentioned and it was his party. He introduced me to Stella, his girl-friend, and I told them that I was a friend of Alex. They were curious to know how I knew him and it was clear that they did not believe that I was only a friend.

'He's kept *you* quiet,' Nick said, raising his eyebrows and winking at Stella. 'He didn't mention that he had a *new* girlfriend.'

'Oh. No. You've got hold of the wrong end of the stick. Alex is someone I met in a work context. I've been offered a position at his firm. He recommended me.'

'I'm *sure* he did.' Nick laughed as he looked me up and down.

'Go and meet everybody, Alicia,' said Stella. 'Alex is around and about somewhere.'

As I wandered through the apartment I looked for Alex but could not find him. Although it was already crowded with guests it still seemed light and airy because there were so many windows and there were magnificent views out towards Canary Wharf. The open-plan apartment was both decorated and furnished in a minimalist style. I walked into the stainless steel kitchen which was very spacious and beautifully appointed.

'Wine?' said a man beside me handing me a glass of red wine.

'Yes. Thank you,' I replied, taking it.

'I'm Oliver Hampton. How do you do?' He was of middling height, stocky and puggy-looking. I shook his hand limply.

'Alicia Allen. How do you do?' I glanced over my shoulder to see if Alex had appeared.

'Very well. Thank you. So what connection do you have with Nick and Stella?'

'None. I was invited by a friend of theirs.'

'Oh. Who's that?'

'Alex. Alex Waterford. I was looking for him actually,' I said, scanning the apartment.

'What do you do?'

'I'm a lawyer.' I replied disinterestedly.

'What kind of law?'

'Private Client.'

'How tedious having to deal with dead people's affairs.' Perhaps he was trying to be funny, but it was not working.

'Not at all. Death and taxes are the two guaranteed things in life. Are you always this rude?' I asked in a flat voice. He was boring me and I wanted to get away from him. Without giving him a chance to answer I said, 'You will excuse me.' I turned my back on him and returned to the reception area.

I espied Alex on the other side of the room talking to a leggy blonde. From where I was standing it appeared as if he was flirting with her. I hoped he would see me, but his attention was evidently elsewhere and he did not seem to notice me. Somebody then tapped me on the shoulder and I jumped.

'Sorry. I didn't mean to startle you. You must be Alicia. I'm Lydia Lanson. Stella tells me you *know* Alex.' She laughed.

'Yes, but only loosely. On a work basis. How do you *know* him?'

'We were all at university together. I studied Law too, but I went into banking. I'm working in-house now. Alex and I did our traineeship together. So yes, in a manner of speaking, I do know him.'

'We?'

'Yes. Nicky, Oliver, Harry and I were all at York together.'

'Oh. I see. I met Oliver just now. I haven't met Harry. What's he like?'

'He's OK. I'm married to him.' She laughed again.

'What's the joke?' asked the tall skinny man putting his arm around Lydia. I assumed this must be Harry. As he spoke he pushed his glasses up his nose, a characteristic that reminded me of the appalling David Wagstaff. I hoped that was the only similarity.

'Harry, meet Alicia. One of Alex's friends.' Lydia raised her eyebrows.

'How do you know Alex then?' He shook my hand warmly.

'What makes you ask?'

'I'm curious. He has kept *you* very well hidden.'

'You've got it all wrong. Alex and I aren't going out together. He recommended me for a job. That's all there is to it.'

'When you've known Alex for as long as we have then you'd know that that's *never* all there is to it,' said Harry, winking at me.

One of the guests came over to speak to them so I wandered outside on to the balcony. It was still very chilly, but the night was clear and I had an excellent view of Canary Wharf. I leaned forward on the railing and looked up at the night sky.

'So *you're* Alex's latest?' The voice was female; the tone sarcastic. I turned and looked at the young woman in front of me. She was very attractive, about five feet seven with dark shoulder length hair and brown eyes. There was something about the way she held her head that made her seem aggressive. 'His standards must be slipping to want to go out with a stick insect like you,' she said, scanning me. 'I think the phrase "there's more meat on a skewer in a butcher's shop" comes to mind,' she said venomously.

'Sorry. Who are *you?*' I asked, ignoring her spiteful and disparaging remarks.

'Alex hasn't told you about me then? That fits.' She looked at me scornfully. 'You won't get anywhere with him if that's what you think.' Again I ignored the remark. She sounded just like Teresa.

'You didn't say who *you* were.'

'Davina, of course,' she replied, clearly expecting me to know who she was. She had a strong sense of her own self-importance, even if nobody else did. I wondered if she was a lawyer too....

'Oh. It's *you*,' I replied, giving her a withering look. 'I heard about *you*.' I watched her expression.

'Really? What did you hear?'

'That Alex dumped you.' I passed her. 'And from what I've seen and heard of you, I'm not surprised,' I said, turning back and then walking away.

I felt extremely upset by Davina's hurtful remarks and since Alex had ignored me all evening I decided to leave. There was no point in staying to make small talk with strangers, when the real reason I had gone to the party was to get to know Alex better. I retrieved my coat from the bedroom and slipped out.

I called the lift but it seemed to take forever to arrive so I slowly traipsed down the stairs instead. As I reached the bottom of the staircase I saw Alex standing by the main front door. He must have already come down in the lift for some reason. I went to pass him but he stopped me on the steps, stood on the step below me and took hold of my shoulders.

'Alicia. What's wrong? What's the matter? Why are you leaving?' he asked, sounding surprised and looking down at me. Even though I was standing on the step above him he was still taller than me.

'Don't you know?' I replied, charging him.

'No,' he replied earnestly. 'That's why I'm asking you.'

'Oh, come on, Alex. Don't play dumb with me. You asked me to this party and you've ignored me all evening. You've spent all your time with everybody else. You're not interested in being with *me*.' I was incensed. A feeling of anger had replaced the hurt and I wanted to lash out at him.

'Oh, but I *am*, Alicia. Very much so,' he said, continuing to clasp my shoulders.

'You have a funny way of showing it.' I pulled away from him, but he drew me back, cupped my face in his hands and kissed me fervently on the lips. I did not resist, nor did I want to, and I put my arms around the back of his neck and responded, kissing him equally passionately.

'Don't go,' he whispered. 'Please stay with me tonight?' he asked, running his hands up my back. I looked into his eyes and, for a split second, I wanted to say yes, but then, irritatingly, Kim's comments about him and the flirting I had seen during the course of the evening popped into my head and I felt an immediate need to protect myself from him.

'No. I'm sorry, Alex. I can't.' I pushed him away, turned and ran down the steps.

'Why not? What's wrong?' he called out, running after me and grabbing my hand. 'What's the matter with you?' I avoided his gaze.

'Why don't you look at me? Tell me what you want.'

'I can't do this.' I yanked my hand away and ran towards my car leaving him standing by the steps looking bewildered.

Chapter 12

'You look tired,' said Antonia. I was, because I had hardly slept a wink. Antonia, on the other hand, looked as bright as a button and evidently her evening had been a huge success. 'How was the party?'

'Oh. You know. One of those boring work things. I left early and came home. I didn't sleep very well, that's all.' I yawned. 'How about you?'

'I'm fine. We had a great time. I really enjoyed myself. You should have come with us instead. Tom is such fun. I like him a lot.' She sounded very enthusiastic.

'Yes. I thought you did. I noticed that when he was here.'

'I can't hide much from you, Ally. You're too knowing. You notice everything.'

'You'd better be careful of Kim though. I have the impression that she is really keen on Tom. Don't forget she has known him for years and they have Tammy in common.'

'Hmm… I know, but Tom and I have only just met and nothing has happened between us.'

'Yet.'

'Actually, Kim seemed to be more interested in what *you* were doing. She was asking a lot of questions last night about where you had gone. I told her that you were going to an office do. She was very curious. She thinks you've got a mystery man and you're not telling us and is gagging to know!'

'Yes. She would be. There is no mystery man. No man at all in fact. OK!' I felt defensive.

'You're a bit edgy. There's always Cesare,' she teased. Sometimes my sister could be very irritating.

'That's different and you know it. No mystery there. So, did you buy anything at the shops yesterday?' I asked, changing the subject.

I did not expect to hear from Alex but I was unhappy with the way things were left, especially since I had decided to take the position at Wilson, Weil & Co. As we would soon be working in the same firm, I did not want any unpleasant atmospheres. I thought about calling him to clear the air but, on reflection, I decided to do nothing. Deep down I hoped he would contact me. I tried not to think about him as I had other things in my life to concentrate upon.

I confirmed to Graham that I was accepting the position, but explained that I would not be able to hand in my notice until Peter returned from holiday. Although I indicated to Graham that I would tell Peter as soon as he was back in the office, I decided to wait until the end of the week. Unfortunately, Peter did not take the news well.

'I'm sorry to see you go,' he said, scanning my letter of resignation and after I had told him that I would be moving to Wilson, Weil & Co. as an Associate. 'But I think it's a case of jumping from the frying pan into the fire. I wish you well, of course, but I hope you don't regret it. Vincent Weil is known for being an exceptionally difficult person to work for. You would have had an excellent career here, had you chosen to stay.'

On the basis that he was retiring and David Wagstaff would be filling his shoes, that was a distinctly remote possibility. David had no intention of ever promoting me, only to keep me as his little workhorse. I saw little point in contradicting Peter.

'My decision is made. This is something I have to do for me.'

David's reaction was as I had expected.

'Well, Alicia,' he said as he pushed his dark metal-rimmed glasses up his nose, 'I'm very disappointed in you.' Not as much as I was in him. 'You'll never become a Partner unless you stick at it and show true commitment to a firm.'

'Like yourself you mean?' I replied sarcastically. David would not know commitment if it jumped right out at him and bit him on the nose.

'I think you should take a holiday before you join your new firm. Don't you?' he asked. I wondered at the relevance of his question.

'Why? What makes you suggest that?'

'I think a trip around the world would do you good, and when you have found the meaning of life come back and let me know.' Why he always had to be so vicious was beyond me.

'Your comments are of no consequence to me, David. If you'll excuse me I have some work to finish for Peter.'

Peter's secretary, Mary, was very supportive.

'You know, Alicia, I'll be sorry to see you go, but these things happen. Take no notice of what David says. It's sour grapes because he's reliant on you doing all the work. Peter should have realized long ago that if he didn't promote you, at some stage you would leave.'

'I don't know what he thinks. Anyway, I'm going now so that's by the bye.'

'What notice period do you have to work?'

'Two months, not three like most firms, so I'll be leaving in May.'

'I hope your new firm suits you better.'

'It could be worse, but at least I won't have to see David anymore.'

'That will be a bonus in itself! Life does have its compensations after all.'

I had not heard from Jo since the evening after her interview at the Club and I was a little concerned, but then totally unexpectedly she 'phoned.

'How are you? Is everything OK?' I asked.

'I broke my ankle. I fell off my bicycle.'

'Oh. No. When? Why didn't you call? What about the Club and Tim Lewis?' I had so many questions to ask.

'A few days ago. There was a pothole in the road. Apart from the ankle I've a few bruises. The crutches are driving me mad already.'

'Oh! Poor you.'

'No. I'm fine really. We've ruled out Tim now. However, we're still trying to track down Nathan, the freelance photographer. It's a pity Tammy's mobile was never found as we could have checked to see whether she programmed his number in.'

'Something has to turn up soon. What about the Club? Obviously you're unable to work there at the moment because of your ankle?'

'No. I'm not. Come over and I'll tell you all about it. What happened with that interview?'

'They offered me the job and I've decided to take it. I handed in my notice today but it didn't go down very well.'

'No. I bet it didn't. The main thing is that you're happy about it. Alex did you a favour after all. You'll have to take him out for a drink to thank him.' I did not respond. Jo continued. 'Isn't Cesare back soon?' She said it casually, but I knew what she meant.

'Yes.'

'That's good. Can you come over some time this weekend? You have to sign my plaster cast for a start.'

'How about tomorrow evening? I promised Dorothy I'd go down to tea in the afternoon, but I can come over straight after, if that's OK with you.'

'Perfect. See you then.'

On Friday evening Antonia was out with Tom – which she had been most nights that week. She was planning to move back into her flat that weekend and Tom had offered to help. Her tenants had gone and the decorators had been in. She had arranged for her furniture to come out of storage and to be delivered on Saturday. Kim was feeling slightly sidelined because Tom and Antonia had 'gelled' and she was jealous. This again caused tension between us and, when I spoke to her, I sensed that she was holding back. This, and the fact that I did not want to talk about Alex, put an increased strain on our friendship. I endeavoured to steer clear of any discussion about Alex with Kim. Consequently, I was now trying to avoid talking to her at all.

I was about to eat my dinner when there was a knock at my front door. I was not expecting anyone and so I looked through my spyhole. To my surprise it was Cesare and I opened the door.

'*Ciao, bella.*' He beamed at me.

'Cesare!' I exclaimed and gave him a huge hug. 'I thought you weren't back until tomorrow. What a great surprise. Come in.'

'I should go away more often,' he said, smiling down at me. '*Ho un regalino per te, carina mia.*' He handed me a small box.

'Oh. Cesare. Thank you.' I glanced up at him as I opened the box. He had bought me some lapis lazuli and gold drop earrings. 'You shouldn't have bought me anything. You are naughty.'

'*Piacere.* Try them on.' I walked to the mirror and put them on. '*Perfetto.* They suit you.'

'It's good to see you. *We* missed having you around.' I chose my words carefully.

'*Veramente*, Alicia? I hoped you enjoyed your stay in *Roma*. I missed *you* when you left.'

'Have you eaten yet?' He shook his head. 'I've cooked dinner and there's too much as usual. Antonia's out.'

'*Bene.* I mean, how is she?'

'Fine. She moves back into her own flat this weekend. Tomorrow, actually. So, do you want to stay to dinner?'

'Yes.'

'Good. You can tell me *all* about what you've been doing while we eat.'

'*Anche te,* Alicia,' he replied, winking at me. 'I want to hear about *everything* you have been doing.'

'Me?' I said, turning away so that Cesare could not see the expression on my face. Although I was fond of him I could not help wishing that a certain other person was there with me.

Cesare left a few minutes before Antonia returned home.

'What's this?' she said, looking at the two glasses and plates I was loading into the dishwasher. 'You didn't say you were expecting company for dinner?'

'That's because I wasn't. Actually, Cesare's back,' I replied. I continued to load the dishes. 'He popped round and I asked him if he wanted to stay for dinner.'

'I see...an intimate dinner for two. How romantic,' she teased. 'I suppose those earrings you're wearing are from him too?'

'Stop it! *Basta.* You're a right pain sometimes. How was your evening with Tom? You seem to have hit it off with him really well. I think Kim is disgruntled. She isn't talking to me.'

'Sure it's not something *you* said?'

'You know that it's because you're seeing Tom.'

'What's the problem?'

'Oh. Come on, Antonia. You must have noticed how Kim hangs on Tom's every word. Can't you tell she has feelings for him?'

'Like Cesare has for *you.*' She could not resist making the remark, but I refused to react. 'What's the big deal? I thought they were old friends. If she's interested in Tom she's wasting her time because he's not interested in her. Anyway, I thought she was after her boss. What's his name? Alec or something? The one we talked about at dinner with her and Tammy, that night when Marianne was there. Do you remember?'

'Yes. Alex, you mean,' I said, dropping my voice.

'Yes. That's the one. What's he like? You met him, didn't you?' Antonia sat on the kitchen stool.

'Oh. Nothing special,' I replied, biting my lip.

Tom arrived on Saturday morning to help Antonia move her belongings.

'Alicia. Hi. Good to see you,' he said, pecking me on both cheeks. 'How are tricks? Toni says you're on a bit of a downer.'

'No. I'm OK. How's Kim? I haven't spoken to her for a while. When I've left a message she hasn't returned my call. I think she's upset about you and Antonia seeing each other. You know she's keen on you, don't you?'

'No, I didn't realize. Don't get me wrong. She's a great girl, we're mates and we've known each other for years, but I could never think of her in any other way. I'm sorry that my relationship with Toni is putting a strain on your friendship with Kim. The way I feel about Toni is completely different. I can't explain...'

'You don't have to, Tom. Sometimes you can't put into words how you feel. You know if you want to be with someone or not. Kim *is* hurting right now, but she'll be happy for you.'

'Toni makes me really happy.'

'I'm glad. After what you've been through you deserve some happiness. How's everything else?'

'The investigation you mean?' I nodded. 'The police say they are following up leads, but nothing ever seems to happen.'

'We have to keep positive, Tom.'

After Antonia and Tom left, I decided to go the gym. On my way out I bumped into Dorothy.

'Hello, dear. Are you coming down to tea later?'

'Yes, I am. What time? About four?'

'Perfect. I'll expect you then.'

I met Rob at the gym. He was just coming to the end of his shift and stayed to chat to me while I worked out. As I pedalled on the bicycle, I noticed that the name on his identity badge said Richard.

'Have you changed your name by deed poll or something?'

'No, but I can understand the confusion,' he replied, looking down at his name badge.

'What do you mean?'

'Richard's my name, but Rob's my nickname and I prefer it.'

'I gathered that, but why?' I asked a little breathlessly as I continued to pedal.

'Well, you see, my full name's Richard Oliver Bartholomew so my initials are ROB, and it sort of stuck.'

'You're right. Rob suits you.'

'At school I was called Rob Roy,' he said with a laugh. 'Do *you* have any nicknames?

'Many rude ones I don't know about, I'm sure. But at Law school they dubbed me Portia, after Portia in *The Merchant of Venice*. I guess being half-Italian had something to do with it.'

I was about to leave the gym when somebody tapped me on the shoulder startling me. To my chagrin it was Ivano, and he had caught me off-guard because I had not expected to see him there.

'*Ciao, bella,*' he said, following me out of the double doors and eyeing me up and down in his predatory fashion.

'Oh. It's *you*.' I barely acknowledged him. 'Antonia said you were around.'

'You could sound more pleased to see me, Alicia.' He walked beside me.

'But I'm not,' I said, stopping and turning to him. 'Don't you *ever* give up?' He was exasperating.

'No. I always get what I want. *Capisci.* I saw you with that trainer guy. You were flirting with him. *Civetta!* You just like to tease men Alicia. I think you're scared of letting go in case you enjoy it too much. Mamma's little convent girl might have to go to Confession,' he said mockingly. 'Why not enjoy what God has given you and share it with someone who would *really* appreciate it?'

'That's why I'm not going to share it with *you!*' I retorted, quickening my pace and walking ahead of him. I turned the corner of my road but Ivano caught up with me, pulled me round and kissed me forcibly, pushing his tongue inside my mouth. I struggled to break free of him.

'*Lasciami in pace!*' I shouted. I was really angry and used all my strength to push him. away. I bent down to pick up my gym bag which I had dropped when he pounced on me, but he grabbed my arm again. 'Get away from me!' I screamed.

'*Non sono riuscito a resistere alla tentazione...*' He was still holding my arm. 'I don't think you know what you really want…or need. I do…' He bent down and leant forward so that he was within inches of my face.

'*Sei malato al cervello! Ti odio,*' I shouted, wrenching my arm away from him and stepping back. 'Just leave me alone!'

I knocked on Dorothy's door at exactly four o'clock.

'Hello, dear. That was perfect timing. The kettle's boiling. Please go through and I'll bring in the tea,' she said, disappearing back into the kitchen.

As I walked into her reception room I glanced at the table which was covered with a pretty lace tablecloth and napkins to match and laid for tea with sandwiches, scones, fruit cake and a chocolate cake. Smoky was curled up in his basket next to Dorothy's large Victorian armchair. I sat on the sofa and looked around the room. There was an antique skeleton clock and two Worcester vases on the mantelpiece, and I noticed some little silver knick-knacks on a side table. Over in the corner of the room was a Chippendale-period piecrust table and sitting in pride of place on it was a silver-framed wedding photograph of Dorothy and her husband. The sound of the clock ticking on the mantelpiece was very therapeutic. Dorothy walked through with the teapot.

'Do you need any help?' I asked.

'No, dear,' she said, pouring the tea. 'You don't take sugar, do you?' I shook my head. Dorothy beckoned me over to the table.

'Please help yourself to sandwiches.' She handed me a plate and a napkin as I sat down. 'You're looking rather strained. Are you all right?'

'I'm a bit frazzled.' I glanced at myself in the mirror. My run-in with Ivano had disturbed me. ,

'Problems at work?'

'No more than usual, but I'm actually leaving my current firm. I'm on my notice period now.' I put a smoked salmon sandwich on my plate.

'Where are you moving to?'

'Kim's firm.'

'How is she? She must miss Tamsin enormously.'

'I don't speak to Kim very much these days. My sister's going out with Tammy's brother, and it's awkward because Kim is quite attached to him.' I ate my sandwich.

'Oh! I see. Well, that must be rather difficult for you. What a shame. And how about you?'

'What do you mean?' I sipped my tea.

'It's about time you met a nice young man who took you out of yourself. Is there anyone on the horizon?'

'No. Nobody at all. What have you been up to?'

'I have my routine. Have a scone, dear,' she said, noticing that my plate was empty. 'How is the murder investigation progressing?'

'The last I heard, the police were still following up early leads. Tammy did some work for freelance photographers and the police have had difficulty in tracing them. Because her mobile and diary were missing it has made the process much harder for them.'

'What about that one with the Range Rover, dear? Have they found him?'

'Which one? Who are you talking about?'

'I remember the car very clearly because it was a Saturday and I was on my way in. I couldn't see him because the car windows were blacked-out but, whoever it was in the car, was waiting for Tamsin because she came rushing out down the steps almost knocking me over before jumping in the car.'

'It's a shame you didn't see him because you won't be able to provide the police with a description.'

'Oh, I can do better than that, dear. I have his number-plate.'

'How come?' I was incredulous. Dorothy really was a little Miss Marple.

'Well, dear, I remember thinking what a silly number-plate it was.' She chuckled.

'Why? What was it?'

'NAT1!'

'Did you tell the police this when they interviewed you?'

'They never asked. It didn't occur to me to mention it as it seemed irrelevant at the time.'

'We must contact DS Hamilton straightaway so you can give a statement about this now.' I was insistent. 'This is great news. It's possible that the driver of that car is the photographer Tammy fell out with. It could be a major breakthrough for the police. If he isn't involved then at least he could be eliminated from the case officially.'

'All right, dear. If you think it would help?'

'Oh, yes, I do. Let's call him now.'

'Finish your tea first. I'm sure it can wait a few minutes longer. What would you like? A slice of fruit cake or chocolate cake?' she asked with her knife poised.

'Chocolate, please. It looks fantastic, but then we really must 'phone the police.'

'If you insist,' she said, cutting me a rather large piece of chocolate cake. Evidently she thought I needed feeding up too, but it tasted absolutely scrumptious.

DS Hamilton's response was immediate when I rang him. He said he would be around to the flat within fifteen minutes to speak to Dorothy, and he was. Dorothy plied him with tea and cake.

'What do you make of all this?' she asked, after describing the car to him. 'Would you like any more tea?' she added.

'No. Thank you.' He swallowed a mouthful of fruit cake. 'It's very helpful. Lovely cake. We will need to take a full statement though. Would you be able to come down to the station to do that?' He glanced at me.

'I'll take you Dorothy, if you want me to,' I said. 'Then you could go at your own convenience.'

'That would be very kind. I appreciate your offer.'

'Mrs Hammond, while I'm here, are you sure there isn't anything else you remember or that you want to tell me?' asked DS Hamilton.

'I'm not senile you know,' she said in a ticking-off sort of voice. I wanted to laugh at the way she admonished him. 'Just because my name is Dorothy doesn't mean I'm dotty. No. I have told *you* all there is to know, but are you sure there isn't anything else you would like to ask *me?*' He shook his head.

'Be sure to tell us if you do think of anything else when you come down to the station.'

I accompanied him to the door.

'What I said applies to you too.'

'Excuse me?' I replied, looking at him quizzically.

'If you know something that you think *we* should.' Visions of Eve came to mind.

'Hmm... Well, I gave you my statement.'

DS Hamilton left and I walked back into Dorothy's reception room.

'Now, there's a lovely young man. I think he likes you, dear. I noticed the way he was looking at you.' Dorothy smiled at me, but DS Hamilton was the last person on my mind.

Chapter 13

'Ally!' Jo opened the door, leaning heavily on her crutches. I gave her a bear hug.

'How's your ankle?' I looked down at her plaster cast, which had almost been completely covered in signatures. I would squeeze mine in there somewhere.

'The plaster's really itchy. Actually, I think I'm driving Will mad at the moment. I'm so frustrated by not being able to get out and about. I'm too impatient.'

'I know that feeling,' I said, walking into the reception room ahead of Jo, who hobbled in behind me. 'Is Will back later? I want to talk to him about tracing Tammy's father.'

'I'm not sure what time he'll be home tonight.'

'I picked up a couple of DVDs on my way.' I dropped them onto the glass coffee table. 'I want to hear all your news before we watch them. Shall I cook for you? What do you fancy?'

'I thought you wouldn't be that hungry as you had tea with Dorothy and I didn't want you to go to any trouble. I've ordered a Chinese, which means you can eat what I don't, so not much! How was Dorothy?'

'As sharp as a needle. You'll never guess what she came up with today.'

'What?' Jo looked bemused.

'It turns out that she noted the number-plate of the Range Rover of the person who came to collect Tammy from the house last August. There's a good possibility that that's the car belonging to the freelance photographer with whom she had a run-in. Dorothy doesn't miss anything. She says it's because she sits in the window watching the world go by.'

'She's certainly something else. The police can follow up that lead.' Jo's doorbell rang. 'It must be the takeaway. I told them I had a broken ankle, so they said they'd run it round.'

'I'll go,' I said, getting up and running to the door.

'The money's on the hall table, Ally,' Jo called out. I walked through with the food. 'Let's eat now,' she said. 'I'm starving and while I eat, you can talk. I know you, Ally, there's *something* on your mind,' she added, taking the lids off the aluminium dishes. 'You seem distracted.'

'OK, and then you can tell me about the Club,' I replied, winking at her.

'Done,' she said, chewing on a prawn cracker.

'Did I tell you that Antonia's going out with Tom?' I said as Jo toyed with her food.

'Sort of. I mean, I knew that they had hit it off. He mentioned that they'd met her when we spoke. Why? You're not interested in him, are you?' She swallowed a mouthful of rice and sat back with a look of incredulity on her face.

'No, it's nothing to do with Tom or Antonia.'

'What is it then? I don't follow.' She furrowed her brow.

'Kim isn't happy because she's very fond of Tom and that has caused a lot of tension between us.'

'But I thought she was keen on her boss. Alex, isn't it? I'm confused.'

'Well, she was, but there's another problem…'

'Which is?' Jo put her fork down and leaned forward.

'I am.'

'You're what?' Jo stopped short. 'You mean you and him? When? You never said. I know *he's* the one who recommended you for the job, but I thought he didn't appeal to you. Not your type as I recall. Hmm… What's going on?'

'That's it, Jo. Nothing.' I started to wish that I had not told her. 'But something must have happened, otherwise you wouldn't be down about it. I know you. Things go deep with you. Tell me what the matter is.' I relayed to Jo the sequence of events between first meeting Alex before Christmas and running out on him at his friend's housewarming. 'So you didn't sleep with him?'

'No, but I can't say I wasn't tempted.' I helped myself to some rice.

'If it's any consolation, I think you made the right decision. It sounds like he represents short-term pleasure but long-term pain. He's not worth it.'

'I don't know what I think anymore.'

'You find him attractive, stimulating and exciting. I can understand that. But if he's just shallow and preys on women then he's no better than Ivano. Perhaps you should steer clear of him. You're far too sensible to let your emotions get the better of you. Have you heard from him since?'

'No, and I haven't contacted him either.'

'Well, there's your answer. Have you told Kim any of this?' Jo gave me a penetrating look.

'No. She doesn't know what happened at the party. She thinks I have a mystery man. I'm starting work at my new firm soon and I don't want any hassle.'

'Fair enough. Please don't take this the wrong way, but why don't you go out with Cesare as a friend and have some fun. You deserve it. Put Alex on the back burner. If he's interested in you then I'm sure he'll let you know. There's as good fish in the sea as ever came out of it. Don't beat yourself up about some arrogant man who doesn't know how lucky he is that you showed an interest in him. If he doesn't reciprocate your feelings, then that's *his* loss. You don't want to be with someone who will mess you about and hurt you. Excitement is one thing, but sincerity, loyalty and genuine kindness means a whole lot more. I don't mean to lecture you. I'm just concerned for you.'

'I know and I appreciate it, truly I do.' I did; but what I wanted to know was why excitement could not form part of the package. I no longer wished to discuss Alex and changed the subject. 'Are you going to tell me about the Club now?'

'Yes. I managed to pump Patti and Abbey for a few titbits of information. Fen made a pass at me too. Clearly she goes for every new girl who joins, not that she got anywhere with me, but I'll tell you about that in a minute. I met Simon, the one Tammy mentioned and who you refer to in your statement. I had a major run-in with Dick, and I also met Jack. That's a story in itself.'

'You have been busy.'

'Not really, Ally. It sounds as if my time in the Club was productive, but in the scheme of things I actually found out very little, bearing in mind I had to endure it for just over two weeks. I really had to press the girls for information without being too obvious about it. Patti was quite cagey when we chatted, and more so after I told her I was with TL Models. She was reluctant to discuss Tammy at first. Tammy was right about her being deaf though. I had to shout at her all the time.'

'Did Patti tell you anything?'

'Tammy was a taboo subject. Dick said it was bad for business.'

'Well, he would.'

'I asked her whether she thought one of the punters had done Tammy in.'

'What did she say?'

'That Tammy had only been there a few nights and sat with a regular called Jack who was used to getting girls to do what he wanted. Tammy crossed him because she rejected him and he wouldn't have liked that. Other than that she had nothing else to add.'

'What about the other girls? You said that Abbey gave you some information?'

'She thought it was freaky that I worked for TL Models as well. She was a bit of a sensationalist, but that was fine and the main thing is she wanted to talk.'

'What did she tell you?'

'Tammy wasn't the sort of girl she would have expected in the Club. She said that Jack had taken a shine to her, but she wasn't as malleable as he first thought and he turned nasty and threatened her.'

'Which corroborates what Tammy told me. Did you ask her if she thought Jack had something to do with her murder?'

'I did. She didn't know, but threatening her was one thing and murdering her something else. As she rightly said, Fen threatened Tammy too because she rejected her, but that doesn't make Fen a murderer either. According to Abbey, Fen is quite harmless.'

'What do you think? After all she did make a pass at you.'

'Yes she did; it was in the toilets. She's a bully but I'm inclined to agree with Abbey's view of her.'

'She certainly seems to make a habit of stalking models in toilets. What happened?'

'I had just gone in there and one of the cubicle doors was ajar and I heard moaning sounds. I saw Flic giving one of her punters a blow-job. He was so engrossed he didn't see me and I thought I'd make a quick exit, but when I turned around I bumped straight into Fen. She tried to do to me what she did to Tammy, but I was able to twist her around and pin her arms back against the wall. I hurt her badly and she didn't bother me again after that.'

'What about Simon?

'He came in one evening and wanted to sit with me, but Dick had already booked me in with somebody else. He was very persistent though so I stayed with him until the other guy arrived. He told me he was a banker, had loads of money to spend and wanted to spend it on me. He offered me £5,000 to stay the night with him. I just can't buy into the "Club" mentality, Ally. Why does a decent looking guy with prospects need to come into a place like that? It's so bizarre.'

'I agree. Was he helpful?' I finished off the beef chow mein.

'No. He had nothing to tell, except that he goes to the Club often. I asked him about regulars and tried to steer him on to the subject of Jack. He said that Jack always gets first pick of the girls. Simon is only a punter.'

'What was your argument with Dick about?'

'I arrived one evening much later than usual and Abbey said Dick was looking for me and that he was in his office. I lifted up the counter at the bar in front of his office and saw the door was ajar. I heard voices and called out to Dick. He came rushing out towards me slamming the door behind him. He asked me what the hell I was doing there, grabbed hold of me by the elbow and propelled me into the Club. He said that I should know better than to disturb him when he's in his office and that, if I still wanted my job, I should start earning because that was what he employed me for.'

'You didn't see who was in the office with him? He must have been hiding something to react like that.'

'No, unfortunately, and yes, I'm sure he has a great deal to hide.'

'What about Jack?'

'While all this was going on the cabaret was in full swing. Fen had taken to the stage and was doing her pole-dancing routine. She leapt up, wrapped her legs around the golden pole, bent back and laughed as she slowly slipped down again. She was wearing one of her black see through tops, a mini skirt and fishnet tights. Fen beckoned one of the 'gentlemen' at the bar to come up onto the stage with her. He put his arm around her, kissed her neck, fondled her breasts and played with her nipple rings. Guess who it was?'

'Jack.'

'Yes. I sat at the bar and watched the floor show. After the cabaret was over he came up to me. Our conversation revolved around him telling me how he liked to play with the mind and turn women on that way, and how much money he was prepared to pay me if I'd have sex with him.'

'Pitiful. Did you get him to talk?'

'These guys want to talk, so it really isn't that difficult. It's more a question of what they want to talk about. He said he sat with another model a little while back. I asked him what she was like and he said that he had wanted to help her tap in to her own sexuality.'

'He obviously regards himself as a kind of therapist!' I laughed.

'He told me that she wasn't 'compliant' and warned her she would get what was coming to her because it did not pay to reject him. I asked him what happened, but he clammed up and said he wanted to focus on me. He said he'd give me a huge tip but that he expected me to give him something in return, that he was totally at my mercy and I could command my price. I promised I would, but not in the Club.'

'Talk about playing with fire, Jo.'

'I made out I could meet him because I would not be working at the Club for much longer. He gave me a number at a hotel where I could leave a message. He said he was away a lot because he had to travel to the States on business, that I should remember that he always gets what he wants and I had better be playing straight with him as I would rue the day if I didn't. He would be expecting my call and I had better not let him down.'

'What are you going to do?'

'Nothing, until my ankle's recovered.'

'Meeting him outside is dangerous. I know it's your job and you can look after yourself, but do you think that it's worth pursuing? Can he lead you to Tammy's killer? You don't know what you're getting into.'

'I *can* look after myself. There's always a risk, Alicia.'

'What makes you think he's involved anyway?'

'I told you. I saw his reaction when I mentioned Tammy.'

'Hmm… It's a bit of a long shot, isn't it? What about evidence linking him with her murder?'

'Female intuition. I'm following my instincts like you. Now which DVD do you want to watch?' she asked, toying with the two DVDs I had brought with me. She was not going to discuss this anymore.

'How about the thriller.'
'Inspiration you mean?'
'Something like that!' I replied, winking at her.

Chapter 14

I had a very disturbed night as I lay awake thinking about my conversation with Jo, and not only in relation to Tammy, but her pep talk to me. Deep down I knew that Jo was right, but it did not make it any easier to deal with. After making my much-needed early morning cup of coffee, I staggered through to the reception room with it, turned on the TV and watched the breakfast news. My landline rang.

'Hello…' I said, swallowing a mouthful of coffee.

'Ally. It's Jo. You OK? Did I wake you?'

'No. I was up. I slept really badly, that's all. How are you?' I stifled a yawn. 'How's your itchy plaster cast this morning?'

'I'm fine and it's still itchy. I hope I didn't upset you last night. And if I did, I didn't mean to. I'm concerned for you, that's all.' She paused.

'No. You didn't, and I know you are.'

'So long as you're sure. Do you want to come round for lunch? Will's here today and you said you wanted to talk to him.'

'I'd love to but I can't. I'm going to see Antonia.'

'Oh, that's a shame. I'll get Will to call you later then. Have a good lunch and send Antonia my love. Take care, Ally!'

'I will. Speak to you later.'

As I was on my way out, Cesare came bounding down the stairs.

'*Ciao, carina.* Where are you off to?'

'I'm going to see Antonia. She's moved back into her flat in

Bayswater. I told you.'

'*Sì certo.*' He hesitated, and I knew he was working up to say something to me. 'Would you like to come to the opera with me next week...if you're free that is?' He gabbled the words.

'Which opera?'

'*Rigoletto*. It should be an excellent production...and I think you'd enjoy it.'

'OK. Yes. Thank you,' I replied, nodding my head.

'*Veramente?*' He sounded and looked completely astonished.

'Yes. *Rigoletto* is one of my favourites.' I started to run down the stairs. And then turning back I added, 'I look forward to it. Give me all the details later!'

I arrived at Antonia's flat a little late.

'You did what?' she exclaimed. I was standing in the kitchen of her flat. The flat overlooked a garden square not far from Whiteley's. It was in a period building and was well-appointed, although it was quite small. Antonia had refurbished it in minimalist style and the Italian influence was evident throughout the flat. '*Mamma mia*. I can't believe it. *Mi meraviglio di te! Sono stupefatta.* You're *actually* going out with Cesare?' She put her hand up to her mouth in sheer disbelief.

'Yes. We're friends and going to the opera together. What's the big deal?'

'Nothing, only you didn't want to go out with him before that's all. Something must have changed?' She rummaged through the kitchen drawer for a chopping knife, which she handed to me to slice some onions.

'No. Nothing has changed. Not in the way *you* might think anyway. How's it going with Tom?'

'Actually, that was one of the things I wanted to tell you and why I wanted you to come over. Tom's moving in with me...' Now that *was* some news.

'Oh, I see...' I paused to wipe my tears. 'When?' The onions were making my eyes water.

'What's the matter? You don't approve?'

'Don't be silly, Antonia. It's your life and so long as you're happy, I'm happy too. My only reservation would be that you haven't known each other long and Tom's going through a really difficult time at the moment. That's all. I don't want you to get hurt but if it's right then only you know that, and you must do what makes you happy.'

'I know. It feels right and that's what counts.'

'So when's Tom moving in?' I noticed some packing boxes piled up in the corner of the reception room which did not belong to Antonia.

'Oh, he's started to move some of his stuff in already. He's coming round for lunch as he wanted to see you. He should be here soon.'

'Has he told Kim? I haven't spoken to her for a few weeks. I'm sure she'll be OK about it, but I'm concerned for her because the last time we spoke she was feeling low. Tom is her link with Tammy and she really misses her too.' Antonia did not answer me. 'Does Tom want me to help him with any more paperwork?' I washed my hands and dried them on a teacloth.

'Did I hear someone taking my name in vain?' Tom had let himself in and was walking through to the kitchen. 'Hi, Alicia,' he said, pecking me on the cheek. 'Hi, Toni.' He gave her a meaningful kiss on the lips. 'I guess Toni's told you then?'

'Aha,' I said, nodding as I stirred the vegetables in the pan and winked at him. 'I'm very pleased for you both.'

'Well, there's a double celebration. I had a call from DS Hamilton. The police managed to track down that freelance photographer Dorothy spotted and they've taken him in for questioning.'

'Why don't you two go into the other room and chat? I'll finish up in here,' said Antonia.

'OK.' I walked through into the reception room with Tom. 'What did the police say?' I sat down on Antonia's cream sofa, and beckoned to Tom to sit down beside me by patting the cushion next to me.

'They've found Nathan.'

'Really?' I exclaimed. 'Some positive news then?' He nodded. 'Dorothy must have been spot on with her observations then?'

'Oh yeah. She's sharp.'

'Yes, she is. I think she has given more information than anybody else. Have the police told you anything?'

'His name's Nathan Troughton. He's known as Nat hence the number-plate NAT1 on his car. I had the impression from DS Hamilton that he's quite public school. The photographic library work is just a sideline for him because he has other business interests. Apparently they have taken all his files or records to check through.'

'Oh, I see. They must have something on him then.'

'DS Hamilton said that he was helping the police with their enquiries.'

'That's the standard thing, isn't it? I'm sure they'll let you know as soon as there's any news. Slightly changing the subject for a moment, but do you want me to do anything else on the legal side? Only, when I originally spoke to your mother, she asked for my assistance and then she changed her mind.' I was still curious why Maggie had taken against me and I knew it had to have something to do with their father. I was hoping to draw him.

'Yeah, I know. We should sort things out at some point...'

'I hope you don't mind me asking you this, but what happened to your father?'

'He left around the time Tammy was born.'

'I gathered that, but didn't he ever stay in touch with you?'

'He did for a while, but then stopped.'

'Oh, that's really sad. Didn't you ever try to find him?'

'I did once, but Mum was so upset and I promised her that I wouldn't. We sort of came to an agreement that if anything happened to Mum then, at that point, if I wanted to, I would. But I don't.'

'I understand, but didn't you ever want to know what he was like?'

'He wasn't around. I guess it's like some adopted kids. They feel that it isn't necessary to seek out their natural parents as they didn't bring them up. I've never thought about it.'

'What about Tammy? Wasn't she curious about her father? I would be.'

'Tammy always felt that he had abandoned Mum when she was born, and she wasn't curious, no. I suppose she followed my lead. I miss her so much.' Tom slightly choked with emotion. 'I know she has gone, but what I wouldn't give to see her walk through that door. I try not to think about what happened to her.' He put his head in his hands.

'Remember her as she was and why you loved her. That's what I do about my father and brother. Memories are precious and no-one can take them away from you.' I squeezed his arm.

'You're so right.' He looked at me very hard. 'It's very helpful talking to you. You understand.'

'I think that's how most people cope.'

'Anyway, what have *you* been up to?'

'Nothing special. I haven't been up to anything. Worse luck!' I laughed.

Later, on my way home, I mulled over what Tom had said about his father. Kim had impressed upon me before not to probe, but I felt that there was something more to this, not necessarily that it had anything to do with Tammy's murder.

As I drove past the house in search of a parking space, I noticed that Dorothy's curtains were open which was most unusual. She was meticulous in her habits and they were always drawn as soon as it was dark. I thought perhaps that she had left them open since she had caught the crime-busting bug and did not want to miss anything. Maybe she had even gone out, although that was most unlikely on a Sunday night.

I had to park around the corner but as I walked back to the house I observed a BMW car on the other side of the road. It did not register with me at that point that there was anything wrong and I thought that perhaps the driver was looking for a parking space. As I approached, however, whoever it was in the car switched the head-lights on full beam dazzling me and drove off down the road at break-neck speed. I had the sinking feeling that something was seriously wrong and that it concerned Dorothy.

Purposefully, I walked down the stairs to her flat. I heard Smoky miaowing and, as I reached the bottom step, he ran out into the corridor causing me to start. The door to the flat was ajar and there were no lights on inside the flat. I advanced towards the front door with trepidation and a dread of what I might find behind it.

'Dorothy,' I called out. 'It's Alicia.' There was no response, so I edged the door open slightly and peered into the hallway. I fumbled for the light switch, turned on the light, pushed the door wide open and stepped into the flat. I felt something wet and squelchy beneath my feet and then I saw Dorothy lying in a pool of blood halfway down the hall. It looked as if she had been struck on the back of her head, but there was so much blood that I could not make out where it was coming from. For a split second I froze to the spot, and then I started to shake uncontrollably because I thought she was dead. I bent down and carefully felt for a pulse in her neck. My hands were trembling and at first I could not feel one and then I did; it was weak but she was still alive.

'Dorothy, can you hear me?' I asked, trying to stay calm. Her eyes flickered open briefly. I kneeled down on the floor next to her and dialled for the emergency service on my mobile phone. 'You're going to be OK. Hang in there. I'm calling for an ambulance.' I was dubious about moving her because I neither knew the extent of her injuries nor wanted to disturb any evidence but I quickly fetched her sitting room blanket and covered her with it. I then 'phoned DS Hamilton and relayed the events since my return home.

The paramedics arrived within minutes, although to me it

seemed like a lifetime. I was ushered out of the flat while they furiously worked on her, but the door was open so I could see what they were doing. They told me they had managed to stabilize her, and asked me to contact her next of kin. I explained that she had mentioned a niece who lived in Suffolk but I did not know the address.

They were lifting her into the ambulance when DS Hamilton and DI Peters arrived. DS Hamilton said they needed to speak to me, suggested we go up to my flat and a WPC accompanied us. I changed out of my clothes as my shoes, trousers and jacket were covered in blood. I thought they might want to take them away to examine them. By now the area outside the house had been cordoned off and the forensic team was in Dorothy's flat looking for evidence.

'I don't think I can tell you much really,' I said to DS Hamilton. I sat down on the edge of my sofa and pushed my hair off my face.

'What made you go down and see Mrs Hammond?'

'As I indicated on the 'phone, I wasn't immediately suspicious when I saw the BMW outside the house. But when whoever it was in the car drove off like that, instinct told me that Dorothy was in trouble. Unfortunately, I didn't get the vehicle registration number.'

'I see. Well, it's fortunate that you followed your instincts, because you probably saved Mrs Hammond's life.'

'Did they say how she is? I'd really like to know and go to see her at the hospital.'

'She has head injuries. They will have to carry out some tests to ascertain the full extent of her injuries but, although her condition is critical, I understand she is stable. We're not dealing with a murder enquiry… *yet.*' That sounded ominous and clearly they were expecting the worst. 'Can you think of any reason why anybody would want to hurt Mrs Hammond?'

'No. When I found her, I initially thought that she might have been the victim of some bungled burglary, but there was no forced entry, not that there would have been if she knew the assailant. I didn't see anything missing in the flat, although I wasn't really looking and the burglar may have been disturbed.' He did not say anything, but was listening intently. I continued. 'What I now think is that the brutal attack on Dorothy is linked to what happened to Tamsin Brown.'

'What makes you think that?' I was not convinced for one moment that DS Hamilton did not suspect that there was a connection between the two crimes.

'Dorothy, as you know, sees and hears everything. Perhaps she saw something that someone else doesn't want us to find out. Let's face it, she has been a very helpful witness so far and the murderer might not be too enthusiastic about that.' He said nothing.

At that point there was a knock on my door and the WPC opened it. It was Cesare.

'I'm Cesare Castelli. I live upstairs. I've just returned home. I saw all the commotion outside and the police cars. One of your policeman said that Mrs Hammond has been attacked. I want to know how Alicia is and if she needs anything.' He looked over at me with his kindly expression.

'I think we've finished here anyway,' said DS Hamilton. 'I suggest you wait until the morning before contacting the hospital, Miss Allen. You've had a nasty shock and you should probably get some rest. We'll leave you to it then.' He glanced at Cesare as he and the WPC moved toward the front door.

'There is one thing,' I called out. 'Who will be looking after Smoky, Dorothy's cat? I'd like to do it. I don't want her to worry about him while she's in hospital. Also, if you do track down her niece, I'm more than happy to talk to her if that would help.'

'I see no problem. We can deal with that now.' He indicated to the WPC for her to sort it out. Then they left.

'Can I get you anything?' Cesare asked, with the most concerned look on his face as he sat down next to me on the sofa. 'You look very pale.'

'Maybe if I get some sleep I'll feel better. I'm very tired.'

'That's no surprise. You've had a terrible shock. I think you're amazing. Are you sure you don't want anything?'

'No, honestly, Cesare, I'm fine. Thank you though. You're very thoughtful.'

'*Prego, carina.* I'm worried about you. I have some news for you as well. The flat downstairs has been rented out to a friend of mine who you already know.'

'To whom?' I asked, hoping that it was not Ivano because that would ruin everything.

'Paolo.'

'Oh, good,' I said, relieved.

The WPC returned with Smoky and his basket and I settled him down. Cesare left, and I went to bed and called Jo.

'Sorry to 'phone so late but I wondered whether Will was around.'

'No, he isn't. You OK? You sound a bit flat.' I told her about Dorothy.

'How dreadful. I don't envy you walking in on that scene, but thank goodness you did. How is she?'

'Critical.'

'Did you glean *anything* about her injuries?'

'The head injury is severe and they're doing tests. I'm not sure whether she'll make it through. It doesn't look good and she isn't young.'

'I know, but from what you tell me she sounds a fighter and she's in the best hands. What do *you* think about the attack?'

'That it's related to Tammy's. I said as much to DS Hamilton.'

'What did he say?'

'He didn't comment.'

'He can't really I suppose.'

'We should meet up. How about I take you to lunch at Café Bagatelle this week? It's about time I got out and about, and it would probably do you good too. I can move around on my crutches quite well now.'

'I should be free on Tuesday, but I'll call you if I can't make it or when something else happens.'

'You sound as if you expect it to, Ally.' And the truth is I did.

Chapter 15

The next morning I called the hospital for an update on Dorothy's condition, but was able to find out very little because I was not a relative. I decided to go there as soon as I finished work in the hope of seeing her.

About three o'clock Mary told me she had taken a call from someone called Anne Mullen while I was on the 'phone. Apparently she was Dorothy's niece and wanted to talk to me. She had left her mobile number but had said that it would be switched off if she was in the hospital.

'Did she say anything about how Dorothy *really* is?' I asked.

'No, but she seemed quite calm, so hopefully Dorothy isn't any worse.'

'Thanks, Mary. I'll give her a ring.' Her mobile went straight to voice mail so I left a message and numbers for both my direct line and mobile. About half an hour later I had a call from her on my direct line.

'Hello.'

'Is that Alicia Allen?'

'Yes. Speaking.'

'It's Anne Mullen, Dorothy Hammond's niece. I really must thank you for everything you did for her last night.'

'No need. I'm just glad I was there in time to call the ambulance. How is she?' I asked tentatively.

'She has been in intensive care since they brought her in. They've done all the scans and everything. The Consultant said that the blow to her head fractured her skull. There's compression of the brain, and blood between the brain and the skull.'

'Does she have a blood clot on the brain?'

'Yes. That's exactly what she has. When she arrived at the hospital she briefly regained consciousness but she has been unconscious ever since. She had difficulty breathing and paralysis down one side of the body, which is symptomatic of her condition apparently. She's on a ventilator. She's stable and they're going to operate as soon as possible.'

'Do you know when that's likely to be?' I was distressed to learn how critical Dorothy's condition was, because I genuinely cared about her.

'Later tonight, but they told me that due to Dorothy's age…' she paused. I could pick up the anxiety in her voice. She did not have to spell it out as I knew what she was telling me.

'Oh, I see. Are you OK? I mean is there someone with you? Only, if you need anything I could get it for you.'

'That's very thoughtful, but my daughter is on her way here to be with me.'

'Oh. Right. I don't want to intrude but, if it isn't too much trouble, could you tell me when there's some news and if I can help at all please let me know. I'm looking after Smoky, Dorothy's cat, just in case you were wondering who was…'

'Thank you. That's kind. I know Dorothy would appreciate it. I'll let you know how she's progressing.'

As arranged, I met Jo at Café Bagatelle the next day for lunch. I had not heard from Anne Mullen and was concerned to know how Dorothy was and whether she had come through the operation. Jo detected that I was preoccupied.

'I'm sure she'll call you when she has some news.' I toyed with the chicken on my plate.

'You mean no news is good news?'

'Talking of which I have some news for *you*, Ally.' Jo was trying to change the subject to take my mind off Dorothy.

'In relation to what?'

'Nathan. The freelance photographer. Are you going to eat that food by the way?' she said, peering at my plate in her usual fashion.

'What have *you* discovered?' I replied, ignoring the comment.

'You mean what did *the police* discover?'

'OK then, what did they discover?'

'He was brought in for questioning, admitted he had taken photographs of Tammy and produced the contact sheets from the shoots. They discovered that he had sold on some of the pictures and since Tammy hadn't signed any modelling release he is in difficulties on that front. You would probably know more than me about the intellectual property implications of all that. Anyway, so far as the murder enquiry is concerned, he's in the clear because he was in Australia at the time of her murder as confirmed by the Australian authorities.'

'He's eliminated then. Oh well, just a bit shady but not murder material. So we're still no closer to finding out who did it. On the subject of Australia, I want to do some research on Tammy's father. I'd go out there myself, but I don't have the time and I'm not quite sure where to start looking. We know that he was in Brisbane, but I had the impression from what Tom said that he had moved away. I want to trace him and that's where I need Will's help, because he has contacts who can make enquiries for me.'

'You've got a real thing about Tammy's father, haven't you?' Jo seemed baffled by my train of thought.

'I don't know why, but I feel that he's the key to this mystery.'

'Why? You can't think he has anything to do with her murder? There's no causal link and I can't believe the police haven't checked him out.'

'I didn't say that he is connected.'

The waiter brought our coffee and as he put it down I received the long-awaited and expected call from Anne Mullen. She told me that Dorothy had made it through the operation, the blood clot and fragments of bone had been successfully removed, but her condition remained unchanged. She was heavily sedated, on a ventilator, and it was now a question of playing the waiting game to see if she would regain consciousness and whether there was any significant brain damage. I did not say very much, but just listened to what she said. I asked her if it would be possible for me to visit Dorothy that evening. She explained that she was going back to the friend's flat where she was staying for a shower and change of clothes and might not be at the hospital, but would alert the nursing staff in the intensive care unit that I was coming to visit.

'Everything OK?' asked Jo, who had been watching my expression intently while I was on the 'phone.

'Dorothy made it through the operation but she's still on the critical list. I hope she can recover enough to tell the police who did this to her.'

'Hmm... We have to keep positive. At least we know she's in the best hands. What's happening with Cesare? I want to know...'

'What do you mean?' I asked as I sipped my espresso.

'I have a confession to make. I was worried about you and I spoke to Antonia. She told me that you have a date with him.'

'Not a date. I'm going to the opera with him, that's all.' It was typical of Antonia to do that. She was incorrigible.

'Same thing, Ally,' she teased. Jo was no better. 'When is it?'

'Friday. I'm looking forward to it actually.'

'Good,' she said enthusiastically.

'Yes. I like opera and I haven't been for ages.'

I helped Jo into a taxi, crutches and all, and returned to the office. I turned down the corridor and saw David sauntering towards me and, as he did so, he pushed his glasses up his nose. He gave me a deleterious look, and made a point of looking at his watch.

'Taking advantage of being on your notice period?' he smirked. 'It's a bit of a presumption don't you think to go out for a long lunch without Partner clearance?'

'It was in my diary. Anyway, I saw you this morning and told you that I had come in especially early today to make sure there was nothing outstanding as I needed an extended lunch hour,' I responded calmly. He was trying to rile me but I was not going to rise to the bait. He would have liked me to lose my rag and then he could haul me over the coals for insubordination.

'You are a constant disappointment to me, Alicia.' Bearing in mind I only had a few more weeks to work at the firm, it was not worth becoming uptight over his comments and, besides, I had other more important things to worry about. I wanted to tell him how he never failed to live down to my expectations, but I bit my tongue. The fact that I said nothing clearly infuriated him. 'What do you have to say for yourself?' he said aggressively. I had no intention of having a spat with him and ignored his question.

'I have a meeting at three o'clock.' I looked at my watch. At that moment Mary appeared in the corridor. She must have overheard our conversation because we were standing outside the room where she worked.

'Alicia, your three o'clock has just arrived.' She winked at me but David did not notice.

'Thank you, Mary. I'll be about five minutes,' I replied.

'We need to have a word later,' he said brusquely and disappeared down the corridor, seething.

I managed to leave the office on time and picked up a number 14 bus from Hyde Park Corner, which took me straight to the Chelsea and Westminster Hospital. I jumped off the bus, walked the short distance down the Fulham Road to the hospital entrance and through the revolving doors into the main foyer. It was a sunny evening and the light simply poured through the glass roof.

I scanned the information board on the wall on the right hand side of the main entrance. The intensive care unit was on the fifth floor, zone B, so I took the lift and as I came out of the lift I observed that ICU was straight ahead. One of the doors to ICU was open and I put my head around it so I could speak to the male nurse standing just inside.

'Good evening. My name's Alicia Allen. I'm a neighbour of Mrs Dorothy Hammond. She's a patient here. I spoke with her niece who said that if I came by I might see her for a few minutes. I wonder if that's possible.' I noticed from his badge that his name was Paul. He had a genial expression and soft eyes. He was dark, of middling height, quite stocky and muscular – as if he worked out regularly.

'If you wait here, I'll check for you,' he said in what sounded like a French accent. I waited inside the doors until Paul returned to lead me through to the ward. I could see Dorothy in the far corner and she looked very small and frail in the bed surrounded by various machines and all sorts of tubes. I could see she was being ventilated. And, of course, her head was heavily bandaged. I stood for a couple of minutes at the end of her bed and then I sat down next to her and stroked her hand. I was not sure whether she could hear me, but I talked to her about all and sundry. I must have been there for about twenty minutes when somebody tapped me on the shoulder making me jump.

'Sorry. I didn't mean to startle you. You must be Alicia. I'm Anne Mullen,' she said softly and as she smiled I saw the family resemblance. She was a younger edition of Dorothy and, despite the fact she looked rather strained, hollow-eyed and in need of a good few hours sleep, she had that same kind expression. I stood up, turned to face her and she took my hand. 'How do you do? Dorothy mentions you often when I speak with her.'

'How do you do? How is she *really*?'

'The Consultant said the operation was successful, but she's elderly and she has been through major trauma, so we have to wait and see. We won't know what the prognosis is until she recovers consciousness, *if* she ever does.' She hesitated, and although she was trying to put a brave face on it, clearly she was utterly distraught. I reassured her that I would continue to look after Smoky and she was more than welcome to come to my flat anytime. She told me that she would like that very much and appreciated the invitation.

I stayed with Anne and Dorothy for about an hour and then I left. It was a pleasant evening and I walked home as I needed to be out in the air. I had switched off my mobile while I was in the hospital so I checked to see if I had missed any calls. To my amazement there was a message from Kim saying that she had heard about Dorothy and hoped I was OK. I was pleased to receive her call and resolved to ring her as soon as I was home. I slipped my mobile back into my coat pocket. I stopped off at the newsagents to buy myself an *Evening Standard* and had turned the corner into my road when my mobile started to vibrate. I pulled it out of my pocket and observed that the number was withheld.

'Hello,' I said. It was Eve.

'I know who your friend is. I'm 'phoning to warn you.' I sensed the fear in her voice and that she was genuinely frightened. Now she was scaring the living daylights out of me. I felt as if someone had just poured ice-cold water down my spine.

'What are you talking about? Which friend?' I tried to remain calm.

'The one with the broken ankle. As I said, I'm calling to warn you.' Her voice quaked.

'Warn me about what? Why don't you tell me who you are? What do you want of me? What is going on?' I shouted down the 'phone. My head was spinning, my heart was pounding and I was frantically looking all around me and scanning the faces of every woman passing by. Could any of these people be her? Whoever this person was, she seemed to know my every move and that spooked me.

'I can't. If you and your friend don't want to receive the same fate as your model friend, you will have to be very careful.'

'You're not making any sense. Of whom? Of what? Why do you keep calling? What do you *really* want? Are you deliberately trying to frighten me?' I yelled down the 'phone at her. 'You say you are 'phoning to warn me, so why don't you tell me what you know?'

'No! I can't.' She was emphatic. 'Not yet. I don't want any harm come to you, but if you go to the police I can't protect you.'

Somehow I failed to feel reassured by these apparent words of comfort. Then she hung up. I careered along the road and up the steps to the main front door. I was so agitated that I dropped my keys and, as I fumbled for them, somebody came up behind me. Whoever it was lay hold of my shoulder, everything went black and the last thing I remembered was screaming.

Chapter 16

My head felt fuzzy, everything was slightly blurred and I was disorientated. I opened my eyes fully and they were still a bit bleary.
Cesare was leaning over me.

'It's OK, Alicia. You blacked out!' I looked around me. I was in
his flat. 'It must have been the thought of coming to the opera with
me tomorrow,' he quipped and smiled at me. 'I carried you up here,
laid you down and put some ice on the back of your neck. You
feeling OK now, *carina*? You seem troubled these days. I worry
about you. Dorothy's attack has hit you hard. Can I do anything to
help?'

'I'll be all right,' I said, trying to shrug it off. 'You *have* helped.
Thank you for looking after me. I don't know what came over me.
It isn't like me to faint like that.'

'You sure you're OK, *carina*. Only you seemed afraid. I really
didn't mean to startle you. *Mi dispiace*. I insist on cooking you
dinner tonight and I'm not taking 'No' for an answer. *Capisci?*'

'I need to check on Smoky and give him his feed.' I went to stand
up but was still a bit wobbly on my feet.

'I'll do it. You should rest.'

'No. I'd like to and, anyway, I need to call Kim.'

'Everything's OK between you now?' Cesare knew that Antonia
and Tom's relationship had put a strain on our friendship.

'She called to say she was sorry about Dorothy and I'm keen to
catch up with her.'

'*Bene*. That would be good.'

Smoky was really nervy, did not seem very settled at all and plainly missed Dorothy. I fed him, sat down to call Kim and Smoky jumped up on to my lap.

'Ally. How are you? I'm so sorry about Dorothy? Tell me what's going on?'

'I'm fine. Dorothy's hanging in there but they don't know whether she's going to make it through and, even if she gets over the surgery, there's the question of whether she will make a full recovery.' I stroked Smoky.

'Oh, Ally, that's terrible. I know you're really fond of her. And she was so kind to me after Tammy was killed.' She paused. 'I've been meaning to ring you for ages and I'm sorry I didn't return your calls. I've been behaving like an idiot and I don't want us to fall out.'

'I've missed chatting to you. I'd hate to lose our friendship.'

'So would I. You sound deflated. I guess finding Dorothy like that was an awful shock. You sure you're OK?' I was flat; I felt as if a steamroller had driven over me.

'Yes. We should meet.'

'Definitely. We've so much catching up to do. I can give you the full lowdown on the firm as well. Incidentally, did you hear that Maggie's really ill?'

'What?'

'Oh, Ally, I thought you knew…I only found out today from a mutual friend in Brisbane. Tom's really cut up about it and I think he may go back home to stay with her.'

'What's wrong with her?'

'She has terminal cancer, an inoperable tumour on the brain.'

'Oh, my God! How terrible! Poor Tom! I mean, as if losing Tammy wasn't bad enough. This is just awful. Listen, I'm sorry but I have to go as Cesare is cooking me dinner but I'll call you tomorrow. We can chat then and fix something up.'

'Ah… Dinner, eh? What's going on there?'

'Not what you think; I blacked out on my way in this evening and he looked after me. He's determined to cook for me tonight.

We're going to a performance of *Rigoletto* tomorrow evening and, just in case you were wondering, it isn't a date. He asked me and I really want to see that opera and…' Kim cut in true to form.

'Did I say anything? You sure you're OK? It's not like you to stress out like this.'

'I'm really tired. I'll speak to you tomorrow.'

I was very shocked and saddened to hear about Maggie's condition. I tried to 'phone Antonia but she was not picking up her calls. Cesare could not fail to notice my gloomy countenance and knew that something was wrong. He thought that my conversation with Kim had not gone well, and then I told him about Maggie. But I enjoyed the meal with him, I was glad of his company, and for a few hours it took my mind off my other concerns. I arranged to meet him outside the Royal Opera House at seven o'clock the next evening.

On going back downstairs, I checked my answerphone to see if Antonia had rung back but she had not. I presumed she must still be out and went to bed but, although I was completely exhausted, I was unable to sleep as my brain was racing. Thoughts of Tammy and Maggie, Tammy and her father, Tammy and the murder, Dorothy and her attacker, and Eve revolved around my head at such a speed that it was making me dizzy.

What most perplexed me was the latest call from Eve, and I kept turning over her words in my mind. When she said she knew about Jo, did she simply mean she knew who she was, or was she referring to her undercover work? It had to be the latter as that was the only logical explanation and she must have seen us together. Following on from that, was she warning us off or purely trying to protect us? What did she know to make her so afraid, which endangered us and was so bad that she did not want the police involved? I certainly had not noticed anyone watching us, but then I had not been looking out for anybody nor was I ever conscious that we were being observed.

I was supposed to get up at half past six, but I forgot to set my alarm clock, overslept and awoke at eight. Being late for work that morning was not an option as I was due to meet with David at half past nine to discuss my files with him. It was not that I cared what David thought of me, only that I did not want to give him the satisfaction of, or excuse for, having a go at me. Normally I left home before the post arrived but, on this particular morning, because I was late, I found it waiting for me on the front door mat downstairs. Amongst my post was a large brown envelope with the address written by hand. The handwriting looked familiar, but I did not have time to read it there and then, so I crammed it and all my other post into my briefcase and dashed off to the office. Ironically, David had called in to say he would be late because his usual train had been cancelled. I had a meeting with Mr and Mrs Dickson and their daughter Deborah in relation to Deborah's residence application for Samantha at ten, so the meeting with David would have to be postponed until later.

I was completely tied up all morning with my meeting and then client calls, so I did not have a chance to check my e-mails or my mobile until early afternoon or to call Antonia. I scanned my e-mails, which were mostly work related, but there was an e-mail from Kim wishing me better and hoping to speak with me later. There was also one from Will, asking me if I had received the information he had sent me about Tammy's father. I then remembered the post I had shoved into my briefcase, which I had intended to open on arriving at the office but which had completely slipped my mind as my working day had taken hold. I had barely pulled the papers out of the envelope when David burst in to the room with a file.

'Ah, there you are,' he said sarcastically as he pushed his metal-rimmed glasses up his nose. I am not sure where else he expected me to be as this was after all *my* office. 'We'll have to hold our meeting tomorrow. In the meantime, I'd like you to give some thought to this file.' He handed it to me. 'You'll see that our client James McCabe is a very wealthy individual. He's having matrimonial difficulties and wants to know whether anything can be done to protect his wealth in the event of a divorce proceeding. That should keep you busy. I wouldn't like you to think that you could slacken off because you are almost at the end of your notice period,' he added caustically. I ignored his remark.

'What you want me to assess for you is whether he can ring fence his assets to stop his wife getting her hands on them and if this can be done by some form of trust?' He did not answer me. 'I'll read the file and prepare a memo.' I turned towards my computer and thus my back on him, and he left the room. A few seconds later, Mary came running into my office.

'Alicia your 'phone is still on DND and Antonia called. I'm really sorry but she rang when you were in your meeting with Mr and Mrs Dickson and I completely forgot to tell you.'

'Oh, don't worry Mary. I'll come off DND and 'phone her back straightaway.'

Mary left the room and I took the papers Will had sent out of the brown envelope. There were a couple of sheets with data on them, some newspaper cuttings and an article about Tammy's father. It seemed that he was somewhat of a champion in relation to civil rights with a particular interest in Aboriginal rights. No wonder Will had managed to find this information so quickly. I scanned the newspaper cuttings. Two of them related to comments he had made about various landmark cases concerning the ownership of land in Australia and the concept of *terra nullius:* uninhabited wasteland in which no rights to the land were recognized for the Aboriginal peoples. One of these cases was the Mabo decision in June 1992 overturning the concept of *terra nullius* and the other was the Wik decision in December 1996. There was also a mention of an article he had written about the handing back of the Silver Plains property in Queensland's Cape York in 2000. However, by far the most interesting was the article profiling him in *Time Australia* magazine because this provided me with the personal information I was seeking.

His full name was Jeremy James Brown and he was born on 29 April 1950 in Cairns. He had studied Australian Indigenous Studies and civil rights. He married Margaret Rachel Manning in 1976 and in 1980 moved to Brisbane after completing his doctorate when he took up his appointment in the Government Department at the University of Queensland. The article went on to say that he had two children from his marriage but was now divorced. It referred to his work in the area of civil rights and that he had moved to the University of Melbourne in 2001. The article was dated January 2003 so I needed to check if he was still there.

I logged on to the internet to obtain details of staff at the University but when I looked under the heading *Directories* and then the sub-heading *Staff Directory* it seemed to be for internal use only and I could not access them. There was a web centre e-mail address so I decided to send an e-mail to the University from home as I did not want for any response to be e-mailed to the office after I had left the firm.

I became engrossed in all this that when my 'phone rang suddenly it startled me. It was Antonia; in my excitement to read about Jeremy Brown I had completely forgotten to ring her back.

'Ally?' She sounded a little anxious.

'I'm sorry, Antonia, but I didn't get your earlier call and it's been one of those days,' I said guiltily.

'Oh, that's OK. I thought it must be something like that.'

'I was worried about you. I spoke to Kim the other evening and she told me that Maggie is terminally ill...'

'Yes. She was getting terrible headaches and did nothing about it. She put it down to stress but then her vision started to go. She went to the doctor who immediately sent her for tests and they diagnosed the brain tumour. Tom's going home at the weekend. I'm not sure how long he'll be away, but basically Maggie has been told that she only has weeks...'

'Oh, Antonia, I'm so sorry. I just can't believe it. I mean it's only a few months since I saw her. I remember thinking that she was very thin and drawn, but I put that down to Tammy's death as I'm sure did everyone else who saw her at the time. It's such a shame that Tom didn't stay in touch with his father,' I added, slightly tongue-in-cheek. 'At least he has you though, and many friends to support him.'

'It's strange you should mention that, Ally, 'cos when he told me about Maggie I asked him if this would make him reconsider contacting his father. He was a bit non-committal, but I had the feeling that he's tempted. Anyway, we shall see. I'll let you get on as I know you have things to do.'

I was thinking about what Antonia had said and in the process of e-mailing Will to thank him for the information he had sent me when Kim called. I had not managed to 'phone her back either.

'I don't mean to pester you, Ally, but you said you would call and I was just a bit concerned because you were ill yesterday. I sent you some text messages. Did you get them?'

'Ah, that's sweet of you. I'm fine. My mobile has been switched off. I've been tied up in meetings and on the 'phone and bogged down in paperwork. I even forgot to call back my own sister!'

'I wanted to make sure you were OK. I feel happier now that I know you are. How is Antonia by the way?'

'Upset for Tom, understandably. You know how it is.'

'Why don't we meet at the end of the week, Ally? You should come over. I've loads to tell you about the firm. There's never a dull moment working at Wilson, Weil & Co. Only last week Vincent's chauffeur came in with deep lacerations to his face. He said he'd been in a fight down his local but we think he'd had an argument with his girlfriend.'

'She must have enviable long nails.' I wanted to ask her about Alex, but resisted the temptation.

'I wouldn't know. Anyway, how about Friday evening?'

'Sounds good.'

'Great. How's Dorothy today? I'd really like to go and see her but thought I'd wait until she's a bit better.'

'Fingers crossed that she is, Kim, but there's been no news today. Her niece told me that she would let me know as soon as there's any change, so I'm presuming there hasn't been any. If I don't hear within the next day or so I'll call her and find out what's going on.'

I dashed out to buy myself a sandwich and sat at my desk to eat it. For the rest of the afternoon I ploughed through my in-tray. I reviewed the file David had given me, researched the recent case law and provided him with the said memo. I was meeting Cesare at seven and did not have to leave until six-thirty, but my lack of sleep from the night before was catching up on me and I started to flag. I managed to leave the office earlier and revived myself by walking around Covent Garden until it was time to meet him.

As I walked into the Royal Opera House through the entrance from the Piazza and towards the box office area I saw Cesare standing by the doors into the main foyer. He had his back to me so did not see me until I was almost upon him and then he beamed in his characteristic way.

'I managed to get some seats in the grand tier. *Va bene?*' he asked as he ushered me up the stairs where he stopped and bought me a programme. '*Stai meglio?* You don't look very well. Actually, I thought you might cancel.' Judging by the look on his face he seemed really surprised that I had not.

'I'm really fine. Honestly.' I stifled a yawn and laughed. 'I am a bit tired but we had an arrangement and I wouldn't run out on you.'

'You mean we had a fixed *date*,' he said, smiling at me whimsically. It seemed better not to respond.

The production was excellent and the performances from Patrizia Ciofi as Gilda, Carlos Alvarez as Rigoletto and Kurt Rydl as Sparafucile were wonderful. Cesare seemed to be really enjoying it and was quite relaxed. Fortunately, he did not behave as if we were on a date. When the Duke sang "La donna è mobile" I thought about Ivano and I smiled to myself. As I watched the plot unravel on stage, Tammy came to mind, and I supposed it was because there were parallels as the plot revolves around a father and his daughter and I had been reading about Jeremy Brown that day. During the long interval, Cesare and I shared some sandwiches and a bottle of wine. The evening was mild and we sat outside on the terrace overlooking the Piazza. My mind was on other things and he sensed I was preoccupied.

'You OK? You seem very distant.'

'Sorry. I don't mean to be. I was just thinking about the similarities with this opera and Tammy's murder.'

'In what respect?' he asked, refilling my wine glass.

'Think about it, Cesare. Gilda, Rigoletto's daughter, is murdered and her body placed in a sack, just like Tammy's was, but Gilda wasn't supposed to die because she wasn't supposed to be there. She happened to be in the wrong place at the wrong time. Remember the police said Tammy's murder was a motiveless crime.'

'I didn't know. But it's for the police to dig up evidence, Alicia, and you shouldn't worry yourself over this.'

Later that night, as I lay in bed and mulled over the facts in my mind, the more apparent it was to me that Tammy had been caught up in something of which she was not even aware. She had to be disposed of because, whoever it was that murdered her, thought she had either seen or heard something that would do them no good – and therefore they had to silence her. The logical conclusion was that it had to be something to do with the Club, but what it was I simply did not know. Jack and Dick must be key suspects and I was sure the police would have investigated both and knew more than they were letting on. They would not divulge any information if they were still making enquiries. Whatever Jack's sexual proclivities, they did not make him a murderer; no matter how perverse they might appear to some.

As for Eve, her connection baffled me. Then it struck me that I had been following the wrong path completely. Her association was staring me in the face. The only thing that linked Jo and Tammy was that they both knew *me* and worked at the Club. This led me to conclude that Eve also worked at the Club or used to work there. That would support my theory that whoever it was in the Club office that night was responsible for Tammy's murder, and she knew who it was. I would have to break my promise to myself and confide in Jo. Eve might be the only lead we had to Tammy's killer and Dorothy's attacker, and therefore if there was any chance of finding her, I had no choice but to take the risk and the consequences no matter what those might be.

Chapter 17

I was awakened by the sound of Smoky scratching at my bedroom door. The poor little cat was really pining for Dorothy, seemed totally lost without her and followed me everywhere. I sat down at my desk and logged on to my laptop to send an e-mail to the University of Melbourne in the hope that they would pass on the details to Tammy's father. Smoky jumped up onto my lap. I was not quite sure what I hoped to achieve by writing to Jeremy Brown and, moreover, what I would say to him if he ever contacted me, but I would deal with that if and when it happened.

I pondered over the wording of my e-mail. I wondered if I should explain that I was a UK lawyer interested in Australian Indigenous Studies, and while researching that area I had come across some articles written by him and needed to know whether he was still at the University. If so it would be useful for me to have his contact details as I was working on a research project and would value the opportunity to liaise with him. I wrote an e-mail along these lines and then deleted it as it seemed totally ridiculous.

I decided to be straightforward and wrote a short letter, which I forwarded to the University as an attachment to the e-mail, with a request that they pass it on to him. I explained that I was a solicitor and had been trying to locate him as I needed to make contact with him over his daughter Tammy. I did not elaborate and say anything about Tammy's death, because if he did not know that would be a horrible shock for him. But I wanted to create enough curiosity to make him respond. I did not mention that I had known Tammy on a personal basis or that we had lived in the same building.

I left all my contact details to enable the University to respond. As my finger hovered over the send button I hesitated momentarily. Was I doing the right thing? Could I be opening a bigger can of worms? But if I did not send it, I would never know. At that moment, Smoky leapt off my lap and in doing so jolted me, and I pressed the send button. Now it was too late.

I called Jo as I needed to talk with her urgently.

'Ally! Do you know what time it is?' she asked in a very sleepy and slightly grumpy voice. I admit I did not and glanced at my kitchen clock: five-thirty. It was clear why Jo sounded neither awake nor enthusiastic.

'I'm sorry to wake you, Jo, but I *really* need to talk to you.'

'What is it, Ally? Are you OK? What's going on?' Jo immediately picked up from my tone of voice that there was something wrong and suddenly she sounded more alert.

'Can you meet me by the pond in Kensington Gardens this evening, say around half past six?'

'I can manage to hobble over there, now that my plaster cast is off, but why, and why there?'

'I don't want to speak about it over the 'phone. Actually, meet me by the Albert Memorial as you can get a taxi to Queen's Gate and you won't have to walk very far, but please be there. I must see you,' I said insistently.

'All right, Alicia. I'll be there. I promise.'

David wanted to rearrange our meeting for five o'clock but, since I had arranged to meet Jo, and I knew that David would keep me for some time, I had to find a way of cancelling it. After an early morning meeting with Peter I started my leaving notes. It would probably take me the best part of the remainder of the day to work through the filing cabinet and dictate them. I was about half way down the first filing cabinet when, to my surprise, Louisa appeared with ten week old baby Daniel.

'What are you doing here?' I asked, giving her a hug. I peered into his pram and stroked his cheek. He was a cherubic little baby and was gurgling away quite contentedly.

'Couldn't keep away. You know how it is? Anyway, I wanted to see you before you left and for you to meet Daniel. How's it going with the temps?'

'Don't ask. They won't put up with David, so don't stay, but Mary has helped me out as much as she can. Let's not talk about work. How are you?'

'I'm fine, and so pleased to have him after everything. He gets his grisly days and has had a bit of colic, but you *are* a good baby, aren't you?' she said, turning to him in a cooing maternal voice. It was a delight to see how happy she was. 'Do you want to hold him?' she asked, lifting him out of the pram and handing him to me. He was dressed in a white babygrow which had little ducks on the collar, and he looked quaint with his soft and fair downy hair. He peered at me rather strangely but he did not howl and that was a good start.

'Actually, Alicia, Jerry and I were wondering whether you would like to be a Godmother to Daniel.' I was surprised as this was totally unexpected, but I was thrilled to be asked.

'I'd love to be. Thank you. When's his Christening?'

'The end of June.'

'I'll be there. Just tell me where and when.'

At that point David came through the door.

'What's this? A Mother and Baby Club?' He always had to be so derisive. 'I see you've been left holding the baby, Alicia.'

'What's new, David?' I replied, giving him a withering look.

'At least she can handle it. Unlike some,' said Louisa, dropping her voice. 'Do you want to hold the baby, David?' she asked, winking at me.

'No, I don't,' he said, directing his conversation at me and completely ignoring Louisa. 'Alicia, we will have to postpone our meeting until half past five.'

'I'm sorry David but I must leave the office on time today as I

have an appointment.'
'You'll have to cancel it.'
'No, David. I'm afraid that's not possible.' I only had one week of my notice period left so I was not going to be bullied by him.
'I will speak to you later.' He stormed off.
'Oh. Alicia. Well done you. He's such a prig. I have to go. Daniel and I are going shopping, aren't we?' she said, talking to him in the same gentle maternal way. 'I'll be in touch about the Christening, and good luck with the new job if, by some chance, I don't speak to you before.' She kissed me goodbye.

My meeting with David never took place at all. He sent me an internal e-mail, requesting that I have my leaving notes on his desk by the end of the week, but he did not mention my e-mail about Mr McCabe. I presumed he had nothing to add on the subject because he would have made something of it. I knew he would send it off to Counsel anyway.

I picked up the number 10 bus, which took me down Park Lane to Hyde Park Corner and on towards Kensington. I jumped off the bus in front of the Royal Albert Hall and crossed the road to the Albert Memorial. I saw Jo standing to the left of the Memorial, complete with stick, and she waved to me as I walked towards her.
'What's going on, Ally? Why all this cloak-and-dagger stuff?'
'Let's find somewhere to sit and I'll tell you.'
'Sounds ominous. I have the feeling I'm going to hear something I might not like.'
Fortunately it was a bright, dry and mild evening, and we found a seat under a tree not too far from the main path. I relayed to Jo everything about Eve's calls and my theory that she was in some way connected with the Club and knew who Tammy's murderer was.
'Oh, Ally. I can't believe you. You should have told me before. I mean, I understand why you didn't but, if you're right, we're all in danger including this Eve, whatever her name is. It makes sense that

she wouldn't want to reveal her identity. What did she sound like when you spoke to her?'

'Her voice was husky, but she may have been putting it on. I'd recognize it if I heard it again.'

'I'm sure I would too, if you're correct and she was at the Club. In terms of tracing her there are a number of possibilities. As you know, all the girls from Jensen's were interviewed after Tammy was murdered and so the police have their details. But did you know that apart from Abbey and Flic they all use false names?' I shook my head.

'You mean, so they can separate their work life from their real life?' Jo nodded. 'Well, they'd have to, but let's stick with their Club names otherwise I'm going to get really confused!'

'OK. A couple of the hostesses have left. It's unlikely Eve is still working and she's probably moved if she's afraid. But she may be our only lead to Tammy's murderer, so we have to find her.'

'Or murderers, Jo. We don't know that there wasn't more than one. She might still be working at the Club so that she can keep an eye on what's going on. I'm not sure what to think. Watching *Rigoletto* the other night made me think about Tammy's murder.'

'What do you mean? How? I've never seen it.'

'Rigoletto's daughter Gilda is killed by mistake. Basically she's killed because she's in the wrong place at the wrong time. She wasn't supposed to be there.'

'Just like Tammy?'

'Exactly. Ironically, Gilda also ends up in a sack. Tammy said she heard raised voices in Dick's office but she didn't know who was in there, what they were arguing about and never stayed around to find out. It's possible that whoever killed her thought she did, that's all.'

'Yes. True. And Eve knows who that is. Oh, my God! I don't know whether to feel excited or scared to death. Has she ever commented on why she is 'phoning *you* to tell you this?'

'No, she hasn't. But the first time she called she said a friend had recommended me and told her I was a lawyer. Tammy didn't say she had given my details to anyone. Also, I don't practise criminal law, so she can't have selected me on that basis.'

'She doesn't know that, Ally. She probably thinks that if you're a lawyer you can do anything and her prime reason for contacting you would be because of Tammy. When did she first call you?'

'So far as I recall, around the time Tammy started working at the Club. Actually, the day after Tammy went to work there but nothing had happened to Tammy then.'

'That's even more interesting, 'cos it's almost like a cry for help. She must know something about dealings at the Club. Tammy's murder confirmed her fears. No wonder she's afraid. And the timing's perfect.'

'We really need to find her, Jo.'

'Have you told anyone else about this?'

'No. Not a soul. I tried to convince myself at first that she was bogus, but in my heart of hearts I know she isn't. I don't want to put anyone at risk.'

'I don't mean to alarm you, but do you think the house is being watched, particularly after Dorothy and everything?'

'The thought had crossed my mind.'

'Let's hope that she recovers and remembers who attacked her because she's a vital witness.'

'That's why she was bludgeoned in the first place, Jo, for being too good a witness. I don't know about the house, but the night Dorothy was attacked someone in a BMW was lurking outside the house. That ties in with what Dorothy said about the car parked opposite the house the week of Tammy's murder. I can't say that I ever saw the car before that night if, indeed, it was the same car, but I suppose I wasn't looking for it.'

'The question is what are we going to do now?'

'Go to the police. Although Eve said no police involvement, I don't think there's any alternative. I do have reservations about putting others at risk though. I hope the police don't throw the book at me for withholding evidence.'

'You're doing the right thing and I don't think you have anything to worry about so far as the police are concerned. Besides, your information may give them the break they've been looking for. The police can make their own enquiries and reach their own conclusions. Remember, you're the one who has been spooked by the calls.'

'Thanks for trying to make me feel better. I'll ring DS Hamilton when I'm home.'

Jo and I walked down to Kensington Road, albeit very slowly because Jo's ankle was still weak. Jo said that she had arranged to meet Will at the bar of the Mandarin Oriental Hotel in Knightsbridge, so she would take a taxi the short distance there. I made sure she was safely in her cab and strolled off down Queen's Gate towards South Kensington. It occurred to me that Jo might have been seen or was being watched. I felt I was becoming paranoid, but logic told me that it was simply not possible for Eve to follow our every move…but then again, who was to say that we were not being watched by the murderer.

DS Hamilton was, in fact, very supportive and concerned for my welfare. I told him my theories and he certainly did not dismiss them. He asked if I had mentioned any of this to anyone else. I explained to him that, for my own protection, I had confided in nobody except Jo as she had worked at the Club and I trusted her implicitly. He explained that his officers would liaise directly with Jo because of her involvement with the Club and knowledge of the girls who had worked there. They could put a trace on my calls, but if Eve was ringing from different locations and public telephone boxes then it would take longer to track her down. However, he was confident that they would.

I did not sleep well that night either. I was surviving on less and less sleep every night, but it was taking its toll and I felt irritable, agitated and jumpy. My stomach churned over and over and I was on tenterhooks. Smoky was evidently the same as I was, and he was off his food even though I had all sorts of titbits with which to tempt him. He had developed a habit of cowering in the corner every time the 'phone rang or if anybody knocked at my door, and he would scuttle away and start shaking. He was clearly a severely traumatized cat and very withdrawn. Whereas before he had been an adventurous cat, now he would not venture out at all, which was completely out of character. I had bought him a cat litter and a toy mouse to keep him amused as I had not been able to retrieve anything from Dorothy's flat for him, but he was not settling.

The rest of my working week was predictable. I had several meetings with Peter to run through my files, to ensure the handover to my successor would be as smooth as possible. I found Mrs Jacobs' file in my filing cabinet, and presumed one of the temps must have misfiled it, thinking I was still working on it. I knew David was out, so I took the file up to Gloria, his long-suffering secretary. In her mid-fifties, and with her no-nonsense attitude, she was a match for him any day of the week. On the surface she seemed quite brittle, but underneath she was as soft as butter and she had always been very pleasant to me.

'Alicia. What brings *you* up here? You don't come up here very often,' she said in the broadest of broadest Lancashire accents. She winked at me, took off her headset and stopped typing. She knew *exactly* why I always tried to avoid coming up to this floor.

'I found this in my filing cabinet. One of the temps must have put it there by mistake,' I said, putting the file down on her desk.

'What is it?'

'Mrs Jacobs' file.'

'He's been ranting and raving about that file for the past few days. Had a right strop on him he had, throwing himself around the office and blaming us for losing it.'

'What *is* the matter with him? Why does he behave this way?'

'He was born like it, Alicia.'

'Beyond help, then?'

'Definitely. At least he'll stop blathering about it now. Is everything all right, pet? You look very tired. The last few months haven't been good for you have they? You've had a few nasty shocks.' I liked Gloria because she was down-to-earth and genuinely kind.

'It has been a rather strange time, yes. I feel like a character in a novel.'

'And there was me thinking that fact is stranger than fiction! It's probably a good time for you to move on. We all need a fresh start sometimes. Isn't it next week you're leaving?' I nodded. 'Are you having a party?'

'I wasn't going to. I thought I'd try and slip away quietly.'

'Oh, no, you can't do that. You have to say goodbye properly. Anyway, I need a good excuse for a jar or two,' she said, and laughed her throaty laugh.

I intended to go straight home that night as I was completely exhausted. All I wanted to do was check my home e-mail to see if I had had any response from the University of Melbourne, have a long hot soak in the bath and then sleep. My plans went out the window when Antonia called.

'Do you think you could come over tonight? Tom's off tomorrow and I could really do with seeing you.' She sounded down and I could not refuse her request.

'Yes. I'm finishing about six. I'll come then. See you about six-thirty.'

'Good. We can have a proper chat.'

I took the tube to Queensway and ambled down Bayswater Road towards Antonia's flat. I stopped to buy her some flowers from a stall on the way as I thought she needed cheering up. Tom opened the door looking slightly flustered and a bit strained. I could see his smallish backpack in the hall.

'Hiya, Alicia,' he said, kissing me on the cheek. 'Antonia's not back yet.' He looked at the tulips and narcissi I had brought her. 'Shall I take those and put them in water?'

'I can do it,' I replied, dropping my briefcase in the hall. 'I see you're all packed.' I gestured in the direction of his bag in the hall. 'Is that all you're taking?' I asked as I walked through to the kitchen. Perhaps he thought it was going to be a short trip and, if so, that did not bode well for Maggie. He took a vase out of the cupboard and handed it to me.

'I always travel light. I hate carrying luggage. I only take hand luggage.'

'That will be a challenge with Antonia,' I said, laughing as I cut off the stems of the flowers and started to arrange them. 'She always packs everything except the kitchen sink. How is your mother *really?*'

'Not good. Her illness progressed without her picking up on her symptoms. She put the tiredness and headaches down to stress and didn't seek any medical advice until it was too late...' He sounded slightly choked. 'You're looking pretty tired yourself, Alicia. Is everything OK? I was meaning to ask you how Dorothy is.'

'She hasn't regained consciousness yet. We're waiting to see what happens. We don't know whether she'll remember anything, even if she does. What about *you?* How are you feeling?'

'I'm angry that so little progress has been made on Tammy's murder investigation. So angry.' He banged his fist down on the kitchen units and made me jump. I could sense the emotion in his voice and I saw it in his face and from his whole body language. 'I feel frustrated for Mum's sake. If only there could be a break-through, then at least I'd feel there was some justice in this world. Do you know what I mean?' He ran his fingers through his hair, almost in desperation.

'I do.'

'Have you heard anything, Alicia?' I sucked in my cheeks and tried to sound nonchalant.

'As far as I know the police are still following up enquiries.'

'What about any new leads? I called DS Hamilton today and he was a bit non-committal.'

'I suppose he doesn't want to give you any false hope. I expect he will only commit himself once he has something definite to tell you. I'm sure you'll be the first to know.' I heard the front door open and Antonia's footsteps.

'There you both are.' She popped her head around the kitchen door. 'Sorry I'm late. I was about to dash out of the office and had to take a call. You look shattered,' she said, looking at me. I stepped into the sitting room and glanced at myself in the mirror and saw how hollow-eyed I appeared. 'I'm really pleased to see you though,' she added, giving me a hug. 'Did you bring me these flowers? Oh, you are sweet. Thanks, Ally.'

'I have to go out to get a couple of things. Do you want anything, Toni?' asked Tom, walking to the door.

'No. I'm fine thanks,' said Antonia.

'What do you want for dinner, Ally?' she said as she took off her jacket and opened the kitchen cupboard to survey the contents.

'I'm sorry, Antonia, but I can't stay long. I have some work to do. I popped in to see you to make sure you're OK as you sounded a bit down, and I wanted to see Tom before he leaves tomorrow. He's very worked up, but I'm not surprised. What with Maggie and no real positive news on Tammy's murder, he's almost fit to burst.'

'I know. I'm really worried about him. That's why I wanted to see you. I don't know what to do for the best. He's holding it all in, but something has to give soon. I asked to go with him, but he said no. I think he's shutting me out.'

'It's probably something he feels he has to do alone. Just be there for him. He needs your support.'

'You're right. It's a shame you can't stay. Couldn't you hang around for a bit?'

'If you really want me to, I will, and the work can wait, but I thought maybe you'd like to spend the evening *alone* with Tom. As he's going away tomorrow and you don't know for how long, I think you need to have a chat before he goes. I'll only be in the way.'

'Yes. We do need to talk.'

'I'll leave you to it then.'

Chapter 18

I heard nothing more from the police that week and I received no further calls from Eve. Work was quiet so I eased my way towards Friday and, since I had managed to catch up on sleep, I was in a good frame of mind. I even had time to make a lemon tart on Thursday evening to take over to Kim's on Friday for dessert. I had still not received an e-mail from the University of Melbourne in response to mine, which was a little frustrating. I tried to be patient but the waiting seemed interminable.

Antonia had managed to have a proper talk with Tom before he left, so she felt better, which was a relief. I was anxious to hear about Dorothy's progress, and I 'phoned Anne who told me the Consultant's indications were positive. I arranged to go to the hospital to visit her on Saturday. I spoke to Kim on Friday afternoon to confirm our arrangements for the evening.

'Alicia. Haven't seen you at the gym for a while,' said Rob as he opened the door. I had not expected to see him because I thought Kim and I would be alone.

'No. I've been a slacker. I used to be a real gym junkie. I've had a lot of things going on.'

'Hi, Ally,' Kim came rushing through from the kitchen. 'I thought I heard your voice.'

'I'll see you two later then.' Rob took his jacket off the hook in the hall. 'I'll leave you girls alone to talk.' He winked at me, kissed Kim goodbye and disappeared out the door.

'Do I detect romance in the air, Kim?' I asked teasingly as we walked through to the kitchen.

'Hmm...' She went slightly pink. 'We have become very close. Would you like some red wine?' she asked, holding up an open bottle.

'That would be lovely.' She poured me a glass. 'What's this with you and Rob?'

'After Tom moved out, Rob and I spent more and more time alone together. We enjoyed each other's company and it sort of progressed from there really,' she enthused.

'Oh, Kim, I'm so pleased for you. You deserve some happiness. No more tears over Tom and Antonia then?'

'I'll always have a soft spot for Tom, Alicia. I've known him since I was little. He's Tammy's brother, so it's a special bond; but Rob is a gem. You do like moussaka, don't you?' I nodded. 'Good. 'Cos that's what we're having for dinner.'

'I brought dessert,' I said, handing her the tin containing the lemon tart. She opened the tin, lifted it out and took it out of the silver foil in which I had carefully wrapped it.

'It looks gorgeous. Thanks. My favourite. Did you manage to see Tom before he left?' she asked, handing me the plates and cutlery.

'Yes,' I replied, laying the table. 'I went over to Antonia's on Wednesday evening. I had a chat with him. He's under a lot of strain at the moment. There's so much for him to deal with.'

'I think it's partly frustration, about the lack of progress on the murder investigation, and the fact that Maggie is so ill. The pressure on him must be enormous. Have you heard anything lately?'

'No. But the police wouldn't be coming to me would they, not in the first instance, anyway? I spoke to Dorothy's niece today. She said that Dorothy was starting to respond, so let's be hopeful. How's the dinner coming on?' I asked, trying to steer away from the subject.

'It'll be a little longer yet. You can amuse yourself with these while we're waiting,' she said, taking a tube of Hot and Spicy Pringles out of the store cupboard. 'I know how you like your

Pringles. The one thing you're guaranteed to eat!'

'I haven't had these ones for a while,' I said as I delved into the tube, which was already opened and two-thirds empty, I might add. 'I'm not the *only* one who likes them it seems.' Kim was suitably admonished.

After dinner Kim and I chatted about Rob and she briefly mentioned Cesare but did not press me on that subject. Our conversation turned to Wilson, Weil & Co. and, inevitably, the subject of Alex.

'I know what I wanted to ask you. Did you ever go out for that drink with Alex?'

'Well...err...not exactly.'

'I don't follow.'

'After I was offered the job, he 'phoned and asked me if I wanted to go to a friend's housewarming party. I went, but he ignored me throughout the evening and I decided to leave. I haven't spoken to him since.' I did not tell her what happened when I left.

'You never told me that! What odd behaviour. Don't you think so?'

'I'm not sure what I think. I don't know him well enough to make any assessment,' I replied, sidestepping the issue.

'Doesn't matter, I guess, as he isn't your type, is he?' she said laughing. 'So why would you want to get to know him?' The problem was that I did but, because I had been so preoccupied, I had not had time to dwell on him. 'He has no shortage of female admirers. For example, the solicitor acting for the purchaser on this business buyout he's currently working on seems pretty enamoured with him. She finds *any* excuse to arrange meetings with him; and then there's Teresa. Do you remember her?'

'How could I forget? She made her feelings plain when we met at Bev's leaving party.'

'She's obsessed with Alex, but she'll never get anywhere.'

'Is he going out with anyone at the moment, do you know?' I tried to sound nonchalant and my interest not too obvious.

'No. I don't think so, but he only tells me what he wants me to know. He's easy to work for and that's all that matters to me. To be honest, apart from Teresa and Vincent, most of the fee earners at the firm are quite decent.'

'Vincent was really charming when I came for the interview, but I am aware of his reputation, as I said to you before. The fact that I might have to work for him now and then was one of the factors I considered before accepting the position. I'm sure I'll cope, especially as I'll be working primarily for Graham and he seems pretty laid back.'

'He is. You're lucky. The ones I feel sorry for are Peter, the Junior Matrimonial Partner, Angela, Vincent's Assistant and Patrick, Vincent's clerk. They're run ragged by him. You didn't meet them, did you, at Bev's leaving party?' I shook my head. 'I'm lucky too 'cos Greg and Alex are great bosses and we don't work on the same floor as Vincent anyway.'

'Do you know anything about his personal life?'

'I heard that he has been married a couple of times. He's divorced of course. I mean *who* could stay with someone like him?'

'Does he have any children?'

'No. Well, not legitimate ones anyway. Bev used to joke that he probably has children he doesn't know about. He has a penchant for the ladies apparently.'

'I can see the attraction. He's got that charismatic side and he must have been very good looking when he was younger and he's quite distinguished, so he'd be able to draw them in.'

'I know what you mean.'

'It seems that Wilson, Weil & Co. is going to be an interesting career move. I hope I don't regret it.'

'At least it gets you out of Simons, Snade & Brown and you're going to a firm with a better reputation and you've got a much better package. That has to be an incentive. Anyway, nothing is carved in stone and if you don't like it you can just leave.'

Kim did not quite appreciate that, as a legal secretary, she could jump ship with no questions asked, unlike me. For a solicitor, eyebrows would be raised if there were too many moves on a CV. Lawyers, unfortunately, had the reputation of not being the most forward thinking of the professions, although they would like to think that they were. Pigeon-holing and prejudice were the norm for those who did not conform to the stereotypical 'type' that they seemed to look for. Rebels like me were not encouraged.

As I drove home I thought about the firm. I did have reservations, but I would proceed on the basis that no experience is wasted when used constructively. That is how I would regard my time there, but if nothing else I might be able to write a novel about it. I was sure I could weave a plot around my experiences within the law, and I had certainly met enough gruesome characters to enable me to do so.

I turned on the CD player and sang along to 10CC as I drove down the Old Brompton Road and turned into my road. I managed to find myself a parking place near the house, which was a stroke of luck at that time of night, and on Friday night too. I trekked up the stairs to my flat and on reaching the top stair I noticed a small brown paper parcel on my mat. I had picked up my post on my way in from work earlier, so I wondered whom it could be from as there was no writing on it. I shook it and it felt like a little box. I ripped open the package, unlocked my front door and stepped into the hall, almost tripping over Smoky in the process. It was a silver key-ring with a horseshoe attached to it, and there was a note inside from Cesare wishing me luck with my new job.

I had arranged to meet Anne Mullen in the foyer of the Chelsea and Westminster Hospital at ten the next morning. When I arrived she was already waiting for me.

'Alicia.' She clutched hold of my forearms.

'What is it? What's happened?'

'Don't look so worried, dear. Nothing bad at all. In fact, quite the opposite. Dorothy regained consciousness yesterday. I think she's going to be OK.'

'Oh, that's wonderful news. Can I see her then?'

'Of course. She has no memory of what happened to her that night. All she keeps talking about is Smoky.'

'She loves that cat to bits. I suppose it's natural that she would be anxious about him.'

'It's not that. She keeps repeating that Smoky did it and when I ask her what she means she doesn't know.'

'She's probably confused, don't you think? After what she's been through it's amazing she's here at all.'

We took the lift up to the fifth floor. Dorothy was still in intensive care, but they were about to move her to the high dependency ward. Anne said she had arranged to speak to the Consultant and disappeared off down the corridor and I walked towards Dorothy's bed. As I approached her, she inclined her head slightly towards me and peered at me. I was uncertain whether she recognized me at first, and worried that she would not remember me but, as I reached the side of the bed, she looked up at me and smiled.

'Alicia. I *am* pleased to see you, dear.' Not as pleased as I was to see her. She looked minute in her hospital bed and I could see severe bruising underneath the bandage wrapped around her head. Her eye sockets were completely black and her arms also, no doubt from the numerous needles and tubes put into her by the doctors. She spoke coherently, but her voice was weak, which was only to be expected.

'You gave us an awful scare. How are you feeling?' I sat down at the side of the bed and took hold of her hand.

'Disorientated, dear. I can't remember what happened to me, but I am so pleased to see you,' she repeated and squeezed my hand. 'How's Smoky?'

'Don't worry. I'm looking after him. I'll do that until you come home if you want me to?' I asked hesitantly.

'Oh, that would be such a weight off my mind knowing that he is being looked after. He frets when I'm not around. Is he all right?' I did not want to worry her by saying that he was unsettled, so I just smiled.

'Can you remember anything at all Dorothy about that night?' I asked, leaning towards her.

'No, dear. I can't. It's totally unclear. Every time I think about it, all I see is Smoky.'

'What do you mean?'

'I don't know. That's the trouble. All I know is that Smoky was there.'

'Doing what?'

'I can't remember. It's so frustrating.'

'Maybe you shouldn't try to force it, Dorothy. You need to concentrate on getting better. That's the most important thing. Have the police spoken to you yet?' I knew how eager they would be to question her.

'I understand that they want to, but I won't be able to tell them anything more than I've told you.'

'I'm sure they're very keen to talk to you, Dorothy, but they can wait until you feel up to it. Don't worry about them for now. You need to get some rest, so I should leave you be.' I noticed she was straining to keep her eyes open.

'I am very tired,' she said, squeezing my hand again. 'You will come to see me soon won't you, dear?'

'Of course I will. I'll come as often as I can. Oh, I almost forgot,' I said pulling a box of jellied fruits out of my bag. 'I know you like these and can't have anything in ICU, but I'm sure the nurse will allow you to take them with you to the ward,' I whispered in her ear. I left them on the side.

'You're a kind girl, Alicia.'

'My pleasure.'

I stood up and turned to go, but Anne was right in front of me.

'Oh. Alicia. You're not leaving are you?'

'Dorothy's really tired and besides, I don't want to intrude. I thought you'd like to spend some time with her. I've told her that I'll continue to look after Smoky and she seems pleased with that.'

'That's very sweet of you. Did she say anything to you about the attack?'

'No more than she said to you. What did the Consultant say?'

'That the operation was successful and she should recover physically. Although she's suffering from memory loss at the moment, they hope that this will be temporary because she can remember everything else.'

'Did he say how long she'll be in here?'

'A good few weeks. She's going to need a lot of therapy to get her up and running.'

'I suppose she'll need physiotherapy.'

'Yes, she will.'

'What about long-term care? I know she's fiercely independent, but will she be able to manage at home? Would she feel safe living there after what has happened?'

'Oddly enough, those were my thoughts. Somehow I think she'll need to come and stay with me for a while to recuperate. But in the long term she'll want to go home. As you say, she *is* fiercely independent. It'll be interesting to see what the police think about her continuing to live there while the investigation is pending.'

'The main thing is she recovers soon.'

When I arrived home there was a removal van outside the house. I remembered that Paolo was moving into Kim and Tammy's old flat and, as I walked up the stairs, caught sight of Paolo in the hall through the open door. I continued up to Cesare's flat. I could hear the sound of opera – *Turandot*, to be precise – so he must be home. I knocked at the door.

'Alicia,' he said, beaming at me and holding the door wide open.

'I wanted to thank you for the key-ring. It was a lovely surprise and I really appreciate it.'

'*Prego, carina. Buona fortuna!* I hope it helps to bring you luck.'

'That was very thoughtful of you.'

'Would you like to go to the opera again sometime soon?'

'With whom?' I teased. He looked confused. 'Joke, Cesare.'

'Oh, OK.' He smiled.

'I wouldn't mind seeing this opera.'
'That's settled then.'

Antonia was missing Tom and decided to spend the weekend with Mamma. She asked me if I wanted to drive down with her on Friday night, but I had already made arrangements to visit Dorothy. Also, I needed to dash into the office to pick up my precedents and Saturday evening seemed a good time to collect them. Mamma 'phoned to see how I was, but I did not tell her that I had blacked out after finding Dorothy as I knew she would only worry. I had not mentioned the incident to Antonia because she could never keep a secret.

I went to the supermarket on Saturday morning and spent the rest of the day window-shopping on the Kings Road. I did not buy anything, but I stopped off at The Stockpot for an iced coffee. I liked the friendly atmosphere in there and sat in the window and watched the world go by. After an early evening workout at the gym – Rob having pricked my conscience about my infrequent attendance – I drove to the office as it was easy to park at that time of night.

By the time I returned home it was very late and I was too tired to eat properly. I rummaged through my kitchen cupboard and found an unopened tube of Salt and Vinegar Pringles. I logged on to the internet to check my e-mails and munched some crisps while I scanned through them. My eyes lit up on seeing a response from the University of Melbourne. Due to a system error the University had only received my e-mail the day before; they apologized for the delay in responding.

Unfortunately, Dr Jeremy Brown was no longer with the University and they were not at liberty to give out his contact details without his authorization, in accordance with University policy, but would forward my contact details to him. My initial euphoria was replaced by disappointment that he was no longer there. Whether he would contact me was another matter, but I remained optimistic because there was always the possibility that he might.

The final week of my notice period at Simons, Snade & Brown simply flew by and my last day was soon upon me. I was in the process of clearing my desk when Mary came running through the door.

'Alicia. I'm sorry to do this to you, but David insists on you sitting in on a meeting with him.'

'But that's ridiculous, Mary. It's my last day and what's the point of me meeting a client only to say 'hi' and 'bye'.' I was annoyed.

'I know, but he wants you to take notes or something.' She shrugged her shoulders.

'Where is he?'

'In the small conference room.' This was the conference room on my floor.

'OK, Mary,' I said, reluctantly. 'I'll be there in a few minutes.' I picked up my notebook, slowly made my way down the corridor and braced myself as I turned the door-knob to the conference room.

'Surprise!' they all shouted, and I almost jumped out of my skin. I was not expecting a leaving party. Mary and Gloria must have arranged it behind my back.

'I'm sorry I did that to you, Alicia!' said Mary, laughing and putting her arm around me, 'but I didn't want you to know that we'd organized a party for you and, don't worry, David's not coming.'

'Have a drink, darling,' piped up Gloria. 'You deserve it.' She handed me a glass of champagne.'

'And now for your present,' said Louisa, handing me a large envelope, a bottle of champagne and a box.

'Oh, Louisa, how sweet of you to come. And to think you were only in last week.' I gave her a hug and proceeded to open the box.

'Waterford champagne flutes. Oh, thank you. Hence the bottle of champagne.' I took the card out of the envelope and read all the signatures. David's was conspicuous by its absence, but it would have been hypocritical of him to have signed it.

'Thank you so much everybody for the card and lovely present. I'll always think of you when I use them!'

'Our pleasure, Alicia,' piped up Jen from accounts. 'These are also for you,' and she produced a large bouquet of spring flowers.

'David's that tight he wouldn't give to your collection, but no loss,' said Gloria. 'Now, let's get some champagne inside you.'

A few glasses of champagne and a few hours later, I had almost forgotten about David, and it was finally time to leave, but I had to return to my office to pick up my personal possessions. I was unaware that David was still in the building but, as I opened my office door, I saw him standing in the corridor outside. I went to walk past him, but he stood in front of me, blocking my way.

'Excuse me,' I said politely, but he did not move.

'I hope you're not thinking of taking any of the firm's clients with you,' he scoffed, looking at my flowers, and the bottle of champagne and the box.

'What *is* your problem, David? I feel really sorry for you, truly I do. If you can't say anything pleasant to me, why say anything at all?'

'Moving to Wilson, Weil & Co. is the biggest mistake you'll ever make in your career, Alicia. I hope you don't regret it.' He moved aside to let me pass.

'Yes, you do. That's why you're saying it,' I said, turning back and stopping in front of him. '*Goodbye.*' He stood motionless, and for the last time I walked away.

Chapter 19

My first day at Wilson, Weil & Co was indeed an experience; although not an entirely unexpected one given what I knew. On arriving at the office, the receptionist with the high-pitched voice and pinched vowels, who was called Tilly, told me to wait in reception for Diane, the office manager. Although Diane had asked me to come at quarter past nine there was no sign of her, and so I sat flicking through copies of *Country Life* while I waited.

At about ten minutes to ten I heard some commotion upstairs, raised voices and the slamming of doors and then about five minutes later what sounded like two sets of footsteps walking down the main staircase. I could not distinguish between them, but I knew that one set of footsteps belonged to Vincent because I recognized his booming voice. It seemed about fifty decibels higher than the other one and, it was evident from this, he was extremely angry with the person he was bawling at.

I was sitting under the stairs and could neither see him nor the person with him. I leant forward and saw him stride towards the front door followed two paces behind by a man whom I presumed to be his clerk, Patrick Kelly. If it was Patrick I was unable to see his face as he had his back to me, but I sensed from his whole demeanour that he was very tense and under pressure. It was as if he was cowering in Vincent's presence. A few minutes later I heard another set of footsteps and then I saw a burly looking individual carrying some black brief bags. I thought he must be Vincent's chauffeur but he looked more like a bouncer with his shaven head and black attire. I was unable to see his face, but judging from the back of him, I would not have wanted to be on the wrong side of him.

Diane finally appeared just after ten o'clock looking suitably harassed and flushed.

'Alicia,' she said, running her fingers through her grey and unkempt hair. 'I'm sorry you've had to wait so long, but we've had a crisis here this morning.' I could only describe her as a bit fey.

'Oh, right. Nothing serious I hope?'

'No. And all resolved now. Anyway, I had a quick word with Graham. He suggested that after I've taken you around and introduced you to everybody, Danielle should go through all the office procedures with you. Have you met Danielle?' I shook my head. I knew she was Graham's secretary because Kim had told me at Beverley's leaving party. 'That should take up the rest of the morning and Graham will touch base with you this afternoon.'

'Fine,' I replied, picking up my briefcase.

The office was situated over several floors. On the ground floor were the reception area, several meeting rooms and Diane's office. There was a narrow staircase leading down from the ground floor to the basement where the general office was located, the accounts department, the kitchen and the cloakrooms. Diane introduced me to the junior clerk, Tom Spencer, who was busy photocopying documents. He looked equally as harassed as Patrick. He shot me a fleeting glance and a weak smile, and carried on with the task in hand.

Michael Shaw, the accountant, was on the 'phone when we walked in to his office. He put his hand up to acknowledge us and we stood hovering in the doorway until he finished his call. His office was large and there were filing cabinets situated in the alcove and a safe was located at the near end.

'Alicia!' He stood up and shook my hand, 'If you can let me have your P45 in the next day or so I'll put you on the payroll.' I did not like the way he averted his eyes and avoided my gaze. It was disconcerting, and it did not help that he had beady brown eyes and a faux smile. I disliked him, for there was something about him I found shifty and made me feel uncomfortable.

'You can have it now,' I replied, opening my handbag, taking it out and handing it to him.

'Thanks,' he said, taking it from me and catching my eye for a split second, 'Good to have you on board,' he drawled.

We walked up to the first floor. This was where I would be working because the Matrimonial and Private Client departments were situated on this floor. Vincent's office was at the front of the building and twice as large as and grander than anyone else's. I had already seen his office at my second interview and, as we walked past it, I picked up the scent of lilies and the strong aroma of Turkish cigarettes the combination of which was always guaranteed to make me feel bilious.

Peter Crawford's office was along the corridor and Angela Pritchard's office was next door to his. Diane introduced me to Peter first. There was a framed photograph of a woman on his desk and another one of him with two small boys. I presumed she was his wife and they were his children. Peter seemed to be of a similar ilk to Graham and consequently I warmed to him immediately. It was not that he looked like Graham. Physically, he was completely different, for he was tall and thin with dark curly hair. He had a very open face, kind expression and the same quiet approach as Graham and that was what made them alike. Although it was evident from the state of his office and the amount of paperwork on his desk that he was extremely busy, he took the time to have a brief chat with me, and I appreciated that.

Angela was not around so Diane took me down to Graham's office. My office was next to his at the back of the building, which was better because it was quieter.

'Alicia,' he said, smiling at me, jovial as ever. 'Danielle will go through all the office procedures and the systems with you. After

198

that we can talk about the files you can start working on straightaway. Is everything OK?'

'Fine. Thanks.'

'Good. I'll see you later then.'

Diane acquainted me with the four secretaries for the Matrimonial
and Private Client fee earners.

'Alicia. This is Carrie Blackstock.' She gestured towards the
secretary sitting in the far right hand corner. 'She's going to be
working for you and also takes the overflow from the Matrimonial
department.'

'We've met,' she said. 'I remember you. You were at Bev's leaving
party.'

'Yes, that's right.' Kim had introduced us.

'I hope you settle in well,' she said with a smile at me.

'This is Danielle Griffiths,' Diane continued. Danielle sat
opposite Carrie. She had a photograph on her desk of her daughter
who was the spitting image of her mother. She had the same rosy
colouring and dark auburn hair.

'Give me a shout, Alicia, when you're ready and I'll show you
everything you need to know. It's all quite straightforward really.'

'Thank you.'

'Let me introduce you to Jenny Milton and Amanda Jones,
Vincent's secretaries.' Diane turned to the two other secretaries
sitting opposite who had not stopped typing the whole time I had
been in the room. 'We're a bit short staffed on the Matrimonial
front at the moment, so it's all hands on deck really.' Jenny looked
even more harassed than when I saw her five months before and her
brown hair was turning grey. Amanda looked very strained and it
was evident that she was under great pressure and had no time to
talk. They both briefly took off their headsets to say "Hello" but
then carried on typing. It seemed odd they stayed if the job was that
bad, but then they must have had their reasons.

The Company Commercial ('coco') and Commercial Property departments were located on the second floor and this was where Kim and Alex worked. Andy Steinberg's office was also on this floor because, although he worked in conjunction with Graham, he was actually attached to the Company Commercial department. As we entered he was sitting at his computer typing and he swivelled around to face me, goggle eyes to the fore.

'We must have a chat once you're settled in,' he said, with a self-satisfied grin, which pulled his face so tight that his skin seemed completely stretched over it. 'Have you met everybody up here yet?'

'Not quite,' interjected Diane.

'I know Alex Waterford and his secretary, Kimberley Davis. I've met Teresa James before,' I replied.

'Yes. He recommended you to us,' he said, turning back to his computer.

Teresa was sitting at her desk marking up documents. Her fringe was still hanging over her eyes and it amazed me how she managed to see beyond it.

'I understand that you and Alicia have already met,' said Diane innocently.

'Oh, yes,' she replied, tight-lipped, as she pushed her metal-rimmed glasses up her nose which reminded me of David Wagstaff. 'I *wondered* if you'd get the job,' she said, scrutinizing me. 'I *knew* you would though.'

'I think it would be a good idea if you and Angela could take Alicia out for lunch today as it's her first day. Angela's out at the moment, but I think she's due back soon.'

'I'd love to,' she said, between gritted teeth. 'I can tell Alicia *what* to expect here.' She spoke sweetly, but insincerely. 'I'll come down for you about one.'

Imogen Goede, Teresa's boss, was the complete antithesis to Teresa. She rushed out from behind her desk to greet me and was friendly and welcoming. As she was well-upholstered, when she bounded towards me she almost set me off balance.

'So good to have you on board, Alicia,' she said, shaking my hand with her rather fleshy one. 'We'll have to organize some welcome drinks for you.'

'Thank you.'

'I suggested to Teresa that she take Alicia out to lunch today,' piped up Diane.

'Good idea.'

Kim shared an office with Gemma Hughes, Teresa and Imogen's secretary, and the paralegal Ella MacDonald. The atmosphere in this room was much lighter than on the first floor and Kim winked at me as we walked into the room.

'Hi, Alicia,' she said.

'Oh, yes, of course, you know each other, don't you?' said Diane, looking at Kim. 'Kim. Would you mind finishing off for me? I'm interviewing secretaries in about fifteen minutes time and I need to make some calls.'

'No worries.' Diane disappeared. 'So how's it going?' asked Kim.

'Fine. Diane's been showing me around and introducing me to everyone.'

'Aren't you going to introduce Alicia to us?' asked the gamine girl with short blonde hair.

'Oh, I'm sorry,' said Kim, turning to her. 'This is the long suffering Gemma who works for Teresa and Imogen.' I shook her hand. 'And this is Ella, our efficient paralegal, who takes flak from nobody, not even from Vincent, so you had better stay the right side of her.' Kim laughed.

'I'm not that bad, but I won't have any nonsense. Hope you settle in OK. You have to give it to Vincent straight. I told him I'm not having it!' I liked her attitude, and her rebellious streak really appealed to me.

'Where are you from?'

'My grandparents came from St Lucia. Have you ever been to the West Indies?

'No.'

'Think about booking a holiday there. If you work here, you'll need one before long.'

'Thanks. I'll bear that in mind.'

'I'll take you to meet the rest of the gang,' said Kim, walking to the door. 'Alex isn't here today. He's on a course.' As we passed the door to his office, I was not sure whether I felt disappointed or relieved. 'I'll introduce you to Greg. You'll like him. How are you finding it?'

'OK. I haven't done any work yet. What was all that shouting upstairs this morning?'

'Vincent went ballistic. He couldn't find a file he needed for court and said that all work in the office had to stop until it was found. He started accusing everybody and abusing Patrick. Diane was helping him look for it. This is a usual occurrence, Ally, but it doesn't really affect us upstairs.' She knocked on the door to Greg's office.

'Come in,' he said in an authoritative voice.

'Greg, this is Alicia Allen, our new Associate. She's starting today.'

'Oh, Alicia, how do you do?' He stood up to shake my hand. He was quite rugged looking with dark hair greying at the temples but his face was lined in a way which added character.

'How do you do?'

'I expect our paths will cross as this department needs tax advice all the time. Have you met Andy Steinberg our tax whizz?'

'Yes. He and Graham interviewed me.'

'Good. I'll leave you in Kim's capable hands and no doubt see you later. Oh, and Kim, I need that disclosure document this afternoon.'

'No worries.'

I left Kim and returned to my new office. No sooner had I put down my briefcase and taken off my jacket, than there was a knock at my door and a larger than life character bounced in. The first thing I noticed about her was her curly red hair; there was so much of it.

'Hi. You must be Alicia. I'm Angela.' She extended her hand which I promptly shook. She smiled at me with the widest of smiles revealing deep dimples. 'I'm sorry I missed you. I've only just come back from court. Peter was saying you have experience in matrimonial law as well, so two strings to your bow,' she said with enthusiasm.

'Some experience. When I was at Withins & Co., the Partner I worked with did both and, inevitably, so did I. How do you find working here?'

'The quality of work's excellent and I enjoy it.'

'What about Vincent?'

'To say he is difficult to work for would be an understatement, but Peter keeps the balance and, if I have a problem, I always go to him. We're all cool, calm and collected at the moment because Vincent's out. You'll see the difference when he's back. It gets really tense up here especially if he's having a bad day. But I'm getting excellent experience here and he pays very well, so it's not all doom and gloom. It'll be good having you here though and someone of my own age to chat with.'

'What about Teresa? Do you see her much?'

'Umm… We don't socialize.' That did not surprise me in the slightest as I would not want to socialize with Teresa either.

'What about Alex?'

'He has a busy social life of his own. Diane said you're going out to lunch with Teresa. I'd love to come, but I've a mountain of work to get through before Vincent returns from court. It's going to be a sandwich at my desk for me today. Maybe we can have a drink sometime this week?' I suspected that even if she had no work, she would want to avoid lunch with Teresa. I cannot say I blamed her, as I was not exactly revelling in the thought of our little repast myself.

'I'd like that.' Danielle popped her head around the door.

'I'm ready when you are, Alicia.'

It took an hour or so for Danielle to run through all the office practices with me. She covered the accounts procedures, billing, computerized time recording, precedents and office packages. While we worked we talked and I discovered very quickly that Danielle liked to chat. Within the space of that hour she had given me *all* the office gossip. She told me that Imogen was divorced and Vincent had acted for her. Apparently her husband had run off with his secretary, but Imogen was still in love with him. Vincent did not have much respect for her because he thought she was weak over the divorce settlement. Imogen was lonely; her life revolved around her daughter and that was why she continued to work there.

Danielle disliked Teresa, and so did all the other secretaries. Although Teresa was not a matrimonial lawyer, she took her cue from Vincent in how to treat people. She was very ambitious, cut-throat and egotistical and for some unknown reason he was nurturing her. She felt confident about being unpleasant to everyone since she was secure in his favour. Danielle warned me to give her a wide berth – but I already knew what an unpleasant character she was from our first meeting.

Danielle told me that Greg was an incredibly likeable man, but kept out of Vincent's way because he found Vincent impossible to deal with. Peter had managed to negotiate a fairly decent package with Vincent and so was prepared to put up with the grief that he gave him on a regular basis. As for Andy and Alex, Danielle did not know much about either of them. Andy had worked for the firm for just under a year and Alex slightly less. Andy generally kept very much to himself and held his cards close to his chest, as did Alex.

Jenny hated working for Vincent, but she was now fifty-six, widowed and needed the money. Amanda was twenty-eight and saving up to get married. She had started off as a temp but because it was difficult to find a secretary who would tolerate Vincent's behaviour, and Amanda seemed able to manage him, Diane asked her if she would stay on. To make it worth her while they had offered her a good package.

'You ready to go to lunch?' asked Teresa, pushing open my door. I glanced at my watch – one o'clock on the dot. She was punctual; I would say that for her, if nothing else.

'Yes,' I replied, putting on my jacket. I had been reviewing the precedents on the system while I waited. 'I met Angela earlier. Unfortunately, she couldn't make lunch today as she's too busy.'

'Hmm… Yes she always *says* she's frantically busy. She's just disorganized, that's all.' She was cutting and dismissive. 'I thought we'd go to the wine bar around the corner.' As we walked along the street I tried to make small talk. I asked her how long she had worked at the firm and she told me that she had been there for nearly four years. Apparently she had acted for a friend of Vincent's who had praised her so highly that Vincent had head-hunted her. Halfway through the meal she started probing me about Alex.

'How's Alex?'

'Well, you'd know that better than me. You're the one who has been working with him.' I swallowed a mouthful of salad.

'I see. So you haven't seen him since the party?'

'No, I haven't.' Strictly speaking this was true, although what she meant was Bev's leaving party and it was actually at the house-warming party that I had last seen him. In any case it was none of her business.

'Oh, right. He recommended you for the job, didn't he? That's the trouble with men, isn't it? You never really can tell if it's on merit,' she said as she leant back, sipped her water and glowered at me through her metal-rimmed glasses. 'I wouldn't want to take a job *if* I didn't feel that I had been offered it because of my *ability* to do it.'

'Neither would I.' I knew exactly what she was implying with her snide remarks.

'Men are so easily influenced by *other* factors. At my last job this used to happen *all* the time. In fact, I understand it happens everywhere.'

'Really. I've not come across it,' I answered coolly, with no intention of rising to her bait.

'It happens here you know. How do you think *you* got the job?'

'Think what you like Teresa. It really doesn't matter to me!'

Chapter 20

Almost one month had passed since I joined Wilson, Weil & Co. and during that time there had been a number of developments both in and out of the office. I was so engrossed in my new employment that I had actually not given much thought to Tammy's murder investigation. I suppose the fact I had not received any further calls from Eve had something to do with that. It was strange that, after a series of calls, she had suddenly stopped 'phoning, and at the time I contacted the police too, which I found unnerving. If that was the case, then she knew my every move, which was disquieting.

Jo told me that the police had been making discreet enquiries about the girls at the Club. They were evidently proceeding with caution because they did not want to frighten Eve off or put anyone else in danger. She was likely to go undercover again as her ankle was fully recovered. Three of the girls had now left the Club: Abbey, Fen and Patti. Fen had moved, but she had been tracked down drinking with her girlfriend at the Candy Bar in Soho. Apparently she was working as a pole dancer at a club in Mayfair. Abbey's landlady told the police she had gone to Amsterdam and that was being checked out; and Patti had disappeared from her flat in Tottenham without leaving a forwarding address.

'When did Abbey go to Amsterdam and when did Patti disappear?' I asked Jo.

'I don't know, Ally. What's the relevance?'

'Think about it. When did the calls from Eve stop?'

'After you contacted the police…'

'Yes. But more crucially, Jo: the date. It has to be significant. From what you've told me, my money is on either Abbey or Patti being Eve. It has to, by a process of elimination. How did they both sound? Come on, Jo. Think. It's important.'

'Abbey's a Kiwi and Patti's a mulatto. They both have deep voices. Abbey was a good mimic though. She used to imitate all the other girls so she could have put on a voice to conceal her identity.'

'Tammy told me she was a mimic. We need to find them, Jo. I'm worried that they've disappeared. What if they're dead?' I left Jo with that cheerful thought and agreed to meet her again later in the week. She said she would 'phone me to arrange a date and time.

Dorothy had made excellent progress: I had visited her several times at the hospital and each time she seemed brighter and stronger. She was now well enough to be discharged but, because she required a great deal of aftercare, she was going to convalesce with her niece in the country. She still could not remember what happened to her the night she was attacked; all she could recall was Smoky screeching. I packed him into his little basket and his niece came to collect him in order that he could be with Dorothy. After he left I missed him because I had become accustomed to him being around.

Antonia had taken a few weeks holiday and flown out to Australia to be with Tom as the news on Maggie was not good. She wanted to be there to support him, which in the circumstances could only be the right thing to do. I had not heard from Jeremy Brown and was slightly disappointed because I felt that this was the piece of the jigsaw missing from Tammy's life. Cesare's grandmother had died and he had returned to Rome for the funeral. He was staying on for a few weeks with his family. It was unlikely he would be back in London until the beginning of June and, in a curious way, I missed him too.

My first few weeks at Wilson, Weil & Co. had gone well, in that working for Graham was a breeze compared with my working life at

Simons, Snade & Brown. Although Vincent had had a number of tirades since I started, as yet none of them had been directed at me, even though I had had a few exchanges with him. Due to the high profile nature of his work it inevitably involved tax, trusts and offshore assets. I observed from his dealings with others that he was a chameleon character and exceptionally charming one minute and a complete beast the next. He could be very charismatic with his clients, particularly the female ones, but for a man of fifty-one he was extremely good-looking in a rakish sort of way. He had a certain air about him, which money, confidence, reputation and power bring.

I told Graham I wanted to gain more 'tax' experience and he delegated some of his files to me, which required detailed research and tax planning advice. I welcomed the experience, but the drawback was that I had to have far more contact with Andy Steinberg and I did not feel at all at ease in his presence. Unfortunately, most of the relevant research material was in his room and it was necessary to make regular trips to the second floor. Towards the end of my third week I needed to review a volume of *Simon's Taxes*, the tax reference volumes. Kim e-mailed me to tell me that he was in a meeting, so I hotfooted into his office and proceeded to locate the volume I required. I was about to take it down off the shelf when the door clicked shut. I turned and there was Andy standing with his back to the door. He had returned early and I had not heard him come in.

'What are you researching today?' he asked, moving towards me and looking at the spine of the volume I was holding.

'I'm looking at something in relation to non-residence.'

'Oh, I see. Let's not talk about work,' he said, taking the book out of my hand and placing it on the desk. 'Let's talk about *you*.' He walked around the side of his desk, with his goggle eyes staring at me, and sat down.

'Sorry? Did I miss something?'

'What *really* interests you, Alicia?' he asked, leaning forward.

'What are you *passionate* about?' Where this conversation was leading I did not know.

'What do you mean?'

'A half-Italian girl like you must have many passions.'

'OK. How about truth?'

'You say that because you're a lawyer.'

'No. Lawyers deal with the evidence, the facts before them. Truth is different.'

'How very philosophical of you,' he said sarcastically. He stood up and walked towards me. I picked up the volume of *Simon's Taxes* and edged towards the door. At this point someone opened his office door. It was Alex and, as he strode in, he bumped right into me and I dropped the book.

'Alicia!' He sounded embarrassed. 'I'm terribly sorry. Are you OK?' He bent down and picked up the book and handed it to me. As he did so he caught my eye and, unless I was mistaken, he winked at me.

'I'm fine. No damage done.' I was pleased Alex had appeared when he did as it gave me the opportunity I needed to excuse myself. 'I had better get on with my research. I'll return the book when I've finished,' I said, addressing Andy. 'I haven't seen you since I arrived, Alex,' I said, turning back towards him as I walked out the door.

'No. I've been frantically busy,' he replied sheepishly. We both knew that he had been avoiding me.

'We'll have to catch up.'

'Yes, we will.'

I relayed my conversation with Andy to Carrie and Danielle.

'He's unhinged that man. A bit unstable,' said Carrie.

'Like most of the Partners here then!' Danielle laughed.

'Graham and Peter are OK, aren't they?' I chipped in.

'Yes. True. They are,' conceded Carrie. 'But it was Graham who told me that Andy was unhinged. He never says anything nasty about anyone so there must be some truth in it.'

'Funny old place this, as Alicia is no doubt discovering,' said Danielle.

'You can say that again,' I replied, raising my eyebrows. I was about to discover how much.

Andy was on holiday the following week and he had allocated some files to me. He left some notes explaining he wanted me to review a number of investment portfolios, consider the tax position and then revert to him with my comments upon his return. Graham told me Andy had had a word with him before he left and the work was not urgent, but it would be very helpful if I made a start on it. I was about to do just that when Alex burst through the door to my office.

'Alicia,' he said, looking flustered.

'Alex,' I replied, looking up from my desk. 'Is there a fire?' I asked calmly and quietly, but with a hint of sarcasm.

'What?' He looked perplexed.

'You seem in a bit of a rush, that's all.' I looked at him, eyes wide. 'I thought perhaps the building was on fire. What can I do for you?'

'You can do me an enormous favour.'

'I take it this is professional, then?' I asked, tongue-in-cheek.

'Yes. Look, I have this deal on,' he said, running his fingers back through his hair. His blond hair was cut slightly shorter and it suited him. 'Let me explain what it is.'

'Please do. I'm waiting.' I sat with my arms folded on my desk. He hesitated. 'It's not like you to lose your tongue, Alex. You use it very effectively…' I paused, 'so far as I recall.' He broke into his easy laugh and sat down in the chair on the other side of my desk. He took a sharp intake of breath.

'I'm acting on the acquisition of a business. My client's Italian and, although he does speak English quite well, it's very technical. I don't want anything to go wrong and…'

'You would like me to be your interpreter?'

'Yes. Please.' He gave me a winsome smile. 'I'd be *really* grateful to you if you could.'

'I'll have to clear it with Graham, but subject to that I don't see why not.'

'You'll let me know?'

'Yes. How urgent is this.'

'It's all go right from now really. Oh and umm…there might be some long nights.'

'Whatever.'

'Thanks, Alicia. You're a gem.'

'Just doing my job, Alex.'

Graham gave me the go ahead to help Alex out. He was all for teamwork and thought this would be a good opportunity for me to 'diversify and grow as a lawyer'. Kim was pleased because it meant that, in the likely event she would have to work late, she would have me there for company. Alex said it would be helpful if I read the background documentation, so I went up to his office to collect the paperwork. In the corridor I passed Teresa who gave me a scathing look. Alex was on the 'phone but smiled, pointed at the papers on his desk and made a thumbs up sign at me. I picked them up and as I clicked the door shut behind me Teresa stopped short in front of me.

'Working with Alex now? How cosy.' She was vicious.

'Not at all. Unless you categorize hard work and late nights at the office as cosy.'

'You did well to engineer that.' She really was pathetic, as clearly having a go at me would not make a blind bit of difference so far as her amorous intentions towards Alex were concerned.

'Umm… I think that being an Italian speaker had something to do with it actually, since our client is Italian. I mean, please feel free to volunteer yourself, Teresa. I'm sure Alex would be *most* grateful. Oh. Silly me,' I lightly touched her shoulder. 'I forgot. You *can't* speak Italian, can you?'

'She must have hated that,' said Kim, when I told her. 'But she deserved it. She's such a bitch. I'm sorry, Alicia, but she really is.'

'Don't apologize. I should know. All part of life's rich tapestry. Anyway, sticks and stones. I've worked with worse people than her and no doubt will again. I expect that somewhere down the line she'll be involved in this matter as, if we're dealing with the acquisition of a business, there will be commercial premises to transfer.'

'So enter Teresa. The walking commercial property textbook,' said Ella sarcastically. 'I'm telling you, if she spoke to me the way she spoke to you she'd get the rough edge of my tongue. Make no mistake. I wouldn't stand for that.'

'She did!'

'I'd watch your back if I were you,' piped up Anna-Marie. 'Teresa's a stirrer, Alicia. She doesn't like you and she doesn't like the fact that Alex does.' The latter point was debatable. I did not pick her up on it, but I did wonder why she thought that he did. 'And believe you me, at the first opportunity she'll drop you in it. Remember, she's in favour with Vincent, so doubly dangerous.'

'Can we have less drama please? I'm not quaking in my boots. I'll just play it by ear and see what happens.'

'We mean it well with you,' said Kim. I was chastened.

'I know, but I can deal with Teresa.'

There was more than a grain of truth behind what Teresa was implying, although I had no expectations or illusions after what had happened at the house-warming party. Anyway, I was in no mood to complicate things now we were working together on this deal. Our relationship needed to be conducted on a professional footing, and if anybody was going to make the first move then it would have to be Alex.

Our client, Mr Baldini, was buying a chain of restaurants, and everything looked straightforward. On reading the documentation I noted that Imogen was dealing with the commercial property side. Teresa was annoyed because she had lost the chance of working closely with Alex, not that it would have done her much good. Between us, Graham and I would be able to advise on any tax aspects. Later that afternoon, Alex sent me an e-mail to say that he was finalizing some documents for a meeting with the client that evening and that it would be helpful if I could meet with Mr Baldini to talk through the documents.

Mr Baldini was of Sicilian origin and his English was far better than Alex had indicated. In fact, his comprehension of the negotiations was impressive and he hardly needed me to translate for him at all, which begged the question why Alex had really asked me to come on board. On the other hand, perhaps I was being harsh and Alex was just covering his "legal" back. I had been given my brief and would interpret if necessary, and it was an experience in spite of the late nights, which, as I recall, was one of the reasons I never wanted to be a company commercial lawyer in the first place.

Alex had been working on the deal for a few weeks, but now things were moving full steam ahead and this had been a heavy week for him with several late night meetings. My translation services were not required all the time, so most evenings I busied myself on my own work while I waited. It was Friday evening and the end of Andy's first week away. I had rather neglected the files he had allocated to me and I could not locate the notes he had left. I looked on the computer system and although we were networked, on scanning all his folders, I could not find them anywhere. I decided to search in his room because, being extremely meticulous, he kept hard copies of everything. He had left his office very tidy and, in his in-tray, there was a pile of papers. Among them there was a plastic folder with holiday notes in it, so I flicked through it and came across what I presumed to be the sheet I wanted; at least it looked like it. There were some scribbles on it, but on the top right hand corner were the words '*As amended*' so I thought it must be the right one.

I returned to my office and logged on to the system to see what details were on there. I knew Andy was punctilious and he would have created computer records with all the relevant data on them. I input the client access code for the first client file from his list and, as luck would have it, the details of the portfolio came up on screen and so I printed it off. I continued doing this for the other files apart from two files where I was unable to access the system at all. Every time I entered the client code the words 'ACCESS DENIED. UNAUTHORIZED USER' appeared. The file numbers were 1769/1DAW and 1769/2DAW. I checked and double-checked the client codes and Andy's list. There had to be a mistake somewhere but as I was tired perhaps it was me who had made the error. I was musing over this when Alex 'phoned asking if I could join the meeting. I had to leave my work until Monday morning and, if I still had the same problem then, I would speak to Graham about it.

This was the final meeting and the deal clincher. Alex had already thrashed out the main points and it was now a case of dotting the 'i's and crossing the 't's. He wanted me to go through all the final amendments and any outstanding legal points with Mr Baldini, before he signed the paperwork. As is customary at the end of any deal, Alex cracked open the champagne, which he had asked Kim to put on ice. She had not stayed late that evening because she had a terrible headache. After Mr Baldini had finished thanking me profusely, and the legal team acting for the vendor had finally left, it was only Alex and I who remained. He had returned to his office to organize the final documentation, while I cleared away the champagne glasses and the debris from the conference room. I made my way down to the kitchen with the glasses and had finished washing them up when Alex appeared.

'I found this going spare in the conference room fridge. Fancy sharing it with me?' I turned. He was holding up a bottle of champagne. 'Oh, good,' he continued, seeing the glasses on the draining board. 'Clean glasses.'

'I think I should go home,' I replied, glancing at my watch. It was after one in the morning. 'I'm really tired. I'm sorry, Alex.' I went to walk past him.

'Oh, come on,' he said, putting his left hand on my right shoulder to stop me. 'Just a quick drink and then we'll order you a cab home. I'd like to have a chat to catch up with you, as we haven't really spoken for *so* long,' he said in a wheedling voice. That was because he had completely ignored me since the house-warming party, of course. I supposed I could have a drink with him. After all it was *only* a drink.

'It's really late, Alex, and I must go home.'

'I wanted to celebrate the end of the deal with you and to thank you for your help.'

'You just did,' I responded, being deliberately difficult.

'OK, let me put it this way. I'm suffering from a bad attack of insomnia and you could help me out.'

'Oh, you mean I could bore you to sleep?'

'Something like that. So?'

'Oh, all right then. You've persuaded me.' Not that he had, as I would not have stayed unless I wanted to.

We went upstairs to Alex's office and he poured the champagne. I put my jacket on the back of the chair and sank back into it. I was genuinely very tired and, after only one glass, bearing in mind I had drunk several after the deal had completed, the champagne went completely to my head. I was feeling slightly the worse for wear and started to giggle.

'Well, you're certainly better looking than the Assistant I had to work for when I was a Trainee.'

'Is that your idea of a compliment, Alicia?'

'No. I was making a statement, actually. But you are.'

'Why? What was he like?' Alex leaned forward, elbows on the table.

'He was short, dumpy and plain,' I said, probably slightly slurring my words, 'and he always latched on to Trainees and tried to make them go out with him.'

'I take it you didn't fancy him then?' Alex sat back in his chair and looked at me intently as he sipped his champagne.

'No.' He topped up my glass.

'What do you fancy, Alicia?'

'Don't you mean *who?*' I smiled at him, head on one side. The alcohol had really kicked in and I felt very light-headed. 'I need to go to bed.' Alex raised his eyebrows.

'So do I. You know I rather like you when you're like this.' He came around to my side of the desk.

'You mean you don't like me when I'm not like this?' I slightly slurred the words.

'Did I say that? Stop analyzing everything I say. Take off your lawyer's hat for once. It's a different side to you. It's very appealing.'

'How do you look so good this time of the morning?' I asked, peering at him.

'That's supposed to be my line, isn't it?'

'No, Alex. That's only if we spent the night together.'

'I'm game if you are, Alicia.' He rubbed my knee.

'You're not trying to take advantage of me, are you?' I removed his hand. Actually I was rather hoping he might.

'Of course I am. But rest assured I will always behave like the perfect gentleman, unless invited not to be so.' He stood up and put on his jacket. I did the same, except I was a little unsteady on my feet. 'Let's get you home. I'll order a cab.' He reached for the 'phone. I went to the cloakroom and splashed my face with cold water. When I came out Alex was standing waiting for me in reception. He said the cab would be there in five minutes and when it arrived to my surprise he got in with me.

'I thought you lived in the opposite direction?'

'I want to make sure you're home safely,' he said, stretching his arm out along the back of the seat behind me.

'Oh. OK.'

'Did I tell you I moved?' Since he had not spoken to me for months clearly I did not, but he made it sound as if I ought to know.

'No. Where to?'

'I've bought an apartment near Tower Bridge. I moved in last month. Would you like to come over?'

'What for? Are you having a house-warming party?' I asked slightly sarcastically, remembering what had happened the last time he invited me to a party.

'No. For dinner. Tomorrow night, at eight. Here's my address and mobile phone number.' He pushed a piece of paper into my hand. 'Call me if you need directions. Well, this is you,' he said, as the taxi driver pulled up outside the house, and he kissed me on the cheek.

'You're not coming in then?'

'Maybe some other time.'

'Oh, OK.' I fumbled for my house key as I scrambled out of the taxi. As usual it had fallen to the bottom of my handbag.

'Tomorrow night then,' said Alex, pulling the door of the taxi shut. I did not respond because I was stunned by this sudden invitation to dinner. The taxi driver waited until I was inside the front door before he drove away. I meandered up the stairs to my flat and heard the squeak of the taxi's brakes as the driver paused at the end of the road before turning. Kim told me it was never *just* a drink with Alex and it looked as if I was about to find out what that meant.

Chapter 21

I could not find the piece of paper with Alex's address on it and I had searched for it everywhere. I repeatedly checked the pockets of my suit jacket and emptied out the contents of my handbag, but it was nowhere to be found. I must have dropped it as I stepped out of the taxi because I remembered Alex pressing it into my hand before we reached my flat. Unfortunately, I did not recall what I had done with it after that.

I was feeling restless and slightly claustrophobic, so I decided to take a walk. I needed the air and to clear my head as I actually felt quite groggy, even though I had slept in. I ambled along Queen's Gate towards the park and wandered through Kensington Gardens. It was a lovely early summer's day, and warm with just a slight breeze, and it seemed a waste not to make the best of what was left of the day. While I walked, I thought about the murder enquiry. Obviously there was no further news on Eve, since Jo would have informed me of any developments.

I found a shaded spot under some trees and sat down, but I felt quite tired and lay down to rest my head back for a few minutes to relax. The next thing I knew, it was nearly six and I had been asleep for almost two hours. I was not particularly bothered though, as I had no definite plans for the evening and I felt refreshed after my sleep.

I let myself into the flat and put my keys in the bowl on the hall table. I was about to walk through to the bedroom to change my shoes, when I noticed a folded piece of paper on the floor and picked it up. It was the piece of paper with Alex's address on it, which must have fallen off the table where I had placed it absent-mindedly the night before. How could I have missed it? I looked at my watch; nearly seven and if I wanted to go to dinner I needed to be quick about it. There were of course no 'ifs' about it as I very much wanted to go, out of curiosity if nothing else, and keen to see Alex in situ. It is amazing how little time a woman needs to get ready when she has the right incentive and puts her mind to it. By seven thirty-five I had showered, dressed, finished my make-up and hair and was ready to leave.

Kim called me as I was tottering along the street to my car.

'I tried you at home. Are you out?' She could not fail to hear the sound of my heels clicking along the street.

'Yes. Why?'

'I wondered what you were up to this evening, that's all. I thought you might like to join Rob and me for dinner, and maybe catch a movie after or something.'

'That's very sweet of you but I'm actually going out to dinner. I'm on my way there now as it happens.'

'Anyone I know?'

'It is actually.'

'Who?'

'Alex,' I said blandly.

'You're joking. Oh, Ally. How did that come about? You're a dark horse.'

'Not at all. We finished the deal last night and afterwards we sat chatting and finishing up the champagne. He asked me if I wanted to come to dinner tonight at his new apartment. I think he's just being friendly.'

'Maybe. As long as you know what you're getting yourself into, Ally.'

'Oh, come on, Kim. It's *only* dinner.'

'Yes, but yesterday it was only a drink. Be careful. I don't want you to get hurt.'

'Don't worry. Nothing is going to happen to me. I can look after myself.'

'That's what Tammy said, Ally, and look what happened to her.'

'Don't be so dramatic! You make it sound like Alex is a murderer or something.' A sobering thought at the best of times, but I bit my tongue as soon as I said it. It was not something to joke about.

I was running late, the traffic was heavy and the journey seemed interminable, so I decided to call Alex to let him know I would be there a little later than anticipated. There was no reply, I was diverted to voice mail and left a message saying I was on my way and presumed he was still expecting me.

Alex lived at Lloyds Wharf SE1, and the building in which his apartment was located was a warehouse conversion. There was a small courtyard in front of the building where I managed to find a parking space. Although I was not sure whether I was allowed to park there I did so anyway, as I could always move my car if Alex said I needed to. I pressed the video Entryphone buzzer for Alex's flat, the door clicked open and I walked in. The building had porterage, although there was no evidence of any porter this evening. The interior of the building was very plush, with mirrored walls and pot plants. There was a lift directly ahead of me which I took to his floor. As the lift doors opened I found Alex standing opposite me, leaning nonchalantly in the doorway of his flat and wearing a striped butcher's apron.

'Glad you could make it,' he said, smiling as he glanced at me. 'You look fantastic.'

'Thank you,' I replied, smiling back at him. 'Sorry I'm late. Did you get my message?' He nodded.

'I had to nip out for a couple of things.'

'I parked my car in the courtyard. Is that OK?'

'It's fine.'

'These are for you.' I handed him a box of Lindt chocolates.

'My favourites,' he replied and bent down to kiss me on the

cheek. He was wearing *that* aftershave again but I could not place it. 'Please come on in,' he said, standing back to let me through the door. 'Let me take your jacket.' He helped me off with it and hung it in the cupboard in the hallway to the left of the door. He led me into a quite sparsely furnished reception room, which I estimated was about thirty feet long, and had stripped wooden floors and halogen down lighters. The room had two large low cream sofas with down cushions, an oblong smoked glass coffee table and a long glass dining room table with six black dining room chairs. I noticed that the table had been set for two, so clearly I was the only one expected for dinner. There was a wide-screen television in one corner and a stereo system in the other.

'It's a lovely apartment,' I said, turning around. 'It's so spacious.'

'Thanks. I bought it 'cos I was looking for something different. Have a look around while I sort out dinner.' He disappeared into the kitchen. I followed him in. It was vast, stainless steel and with state-of-the-art appliances.

'Are you sure I can't help you?'

'No. Everything's under control. You relax and enjoy,' he said, pouring me a large glass of red wine. 'Is this OK for you?' he asked, handing it to me. 'I have white if you would prefer?'

'No. That's perfect thanks,' I replied, taking it.

'And help yourself to these.' He pointed to some nibbles on the table.

'Something smells good. What are you cooking?' I peered at the oven.

'You'll have to wait and see. Please make yourself at home.'

I wandered around the apartment and the first thing that struck me was how unlike a home this was because, although it was beautifully appointed, there were no individual touches. There were no ornaments or photographs or a trace of anything of a personal nature, but maybe that was just how Alex liked it.

There was another hallway behind the reception area with a number of rooms coming off it. I opened the first door to the right.

This had to be Alex's bedroom, I thought. It looked like the master bedroom from the size of the bed. The bed linen was white and there were some blue cushions on the bed. There was a wrought iron table on either side of the bed and I noticed that there were some art books on one of them, including a book on Canaletto. On the opposite wall were cupboards with mirrored doors floor to ceiling, running the length of the room. There was another door leading off the bedroom into an en-suite bathroom with a mirrored wall opposite the shower. I caught a glimpse of myself in the mirror and toyed with my hair.

'What do you think?' I jumped. Alex had walked in behind me. I pushed my hair behind my ear nervously. 'Sorry. I didn't mean to startle you. You forgot your wine,' he said, handing it to me.

'Oh, thanks,' I turned around to take it from him. He had taken his apron off now and I observed he was wearing black Armani jeans. I noticed his pert bottom and those jeans certainly enhanced it. His shirt was Sea Island cotton and mid-blue and the colour really suited him. I could smell that aftershave again, but still I could not place it.

'Alicia,' he said, moving closer, taking the glass of wine out of my hand and placing it on the bedside table. 'You're lovely,' he whispered softly, inclining his head to kiss me.

'What's that awful smell? Is something burning?' I moved my head.

'Oh no. The Béchamel sauce!' He rushed out of the bedroom in the direction of the kitchen and I followed him. As he opened the kitchen door the smoke billowed out. Evidently the sauce had boiled away and burnt the bottom of the saucepan.

'Can I help?' I asked, laughing.

'No. My mess. I'll sort it! You finish looking around the flat.'

I sank back into the soft down cushions on the sofa and sipped my wine. The meal had actually been delicious, three hours had passed and we had chatted about nothing in particular. We had touched on a number of subjects such as the firms we had worked for, our favourite holiday destinations and embarrassing moments in our lives, but none in any depth and it was as if we were skirting around each other. I felt that although Alex was friendly, he was holding back and not being completely open with me. The conversation suddenly went quiet and Alex looked hard at me. I wondered what he was thinking. He had been laying lengthways on the sofa opposite me, leaning on one elbow with his glass of wine in the other hand. Now he got up, came over and sat next to me.

'Would you ever consider living in Italy?' He moved closer and ran his fingers through my hair. He stroked the back of my neck.

'Quite a few people have asked me that. I don't know. I've lived here all my life and, although I'm half-Italian, my home's here.'

'Don't you ever think about breaking free, spreading your wings and leaving the law? Wouldn't you like to do something else?' He turned, took the glass out of my hand and placed it on the coffee table. 'Let's have some champagne.' He walked through to the kitchen to fetch it and came back with a bottle of Moët and two glasses. 'I was asking you about whether you would like to do something else?'

'Oh yes. I'm sure most lawyers do. Wouldn't you? My sister's in PR and I think she has a better lifestyle. She travels quite extensively. She's in Australia at the moment actually.' Alex popped open the bottle of champagne, poured me a glass and handed it to me.

'On business?' he asked, leaning back and running his hand along the back of the sofa behind me.

'No. Her boyfriend's Australian. His mother has terminal cancer and Antonia has gone out there to be with him.' I held the glass up to the light. 'I have some glasses like these. They're lovely,' I said turning the glass around in my hand. They were Waterford Crystal, like the ones that I had been given for my leaving present.

'Thanks. I'm sorry to hear about your sister's problems. That's awful. Whereabouts in Australia has she gone?' He sounded genuinely concerned.

'Brisbane.'

'So her boyfriend's from Brisbane, like Kim?'

'Yes. Let me explain the connection. Antonia's boyfriend, Tom, is a really good friend of Kim's.'

'Which is how Antonia met Tom?'

'Yes. But there's a bit more to it. You remember that Kim's flatmate Tammy was murdered.'

'Yes. Of course I do. That isn't something I'd be likely to forget,' he said, sitting up. 'She was a model, wasn't she? I nodded. 'I remember Kim asking me one day about some modelling release that Tammy had refused to sign for a photographer. Actually, you just reminded me of a call I received from one of Vincent's contacts asking me a similar question. I remember because he thought my surname was Wexford. Sorry, Alicia. I interrupted what you were saying.'

'That's OK. I was going to say that Tom is Tammy's brother. He came over here after Tammy was murdered and later he and Antonia met. Kim was a bit put out to begin with as she really liked Tom. Mind you,' I said teasingly, 'I heard she used to have a crush on her boss. It must be that magnetic charm which attracts the opposite sex to you, Alex. I understand that they are queuing up for you.'

'I was thinking the same about you. I feel lucky to have you here.' I wanted to believe him, especially now he was kissing my neck and it felt so good.

'How do I know you're sincere? You have quite a reputation.' He kissed me softly on the mouth.

'You should know better than to believe everything you hear, Alicia. Things are sometimes not what they seem. Nor people.' He was very serious suddenly and I felt he was trying to make a point, but about what I was not sure. 'How do you know that I'm who I say I am?' He put his arm around my back.

'I don't.'

'Exactly,' he said emphatically.

'And the point you are trying to make, Alex?' I swivelled around to face him.

'Well, for instance, I'm known as Alex but that's actually my second name. My first name is Duncan. It's a family name and I don't like it; so I chose to be known as Alex. You take my point?'

'I do. You worried me there for one minute. I thought you were going to tell me you were a spy or something,' I replied with a slightly suppressed laugh.

'How would you feel if I was? I'm still the same person,' he said, rubbing my back. He removed his hand, looked down, toyed with his gold torque bangle, looked up and stared hard at me. It struck me as an odd thing to say and then a rather distressing thought came to mind. Alex's initials were not ADW but DAW, the same initials as those files I could not access. I tried hard to dismiss the thought, because it was ridiculous and files were always based on a client's name and he was not a client. On top of that, I liked the feel of his hand stroking my neck and him kissing me, but those thoughts niggled at me and I felt slightly uncomfortable. There was also something else he had said that disturbed me. Jack had mentioned an IP lawyer called 'Wexford' to Tammy. Alarm bells started ringing in my head which made me jump to the conclusion that Alex was somehow involved in all this. He noticed that I was deep in thought.

'Alicia? You still with me?' he asked, stroking my forehead and brushing my hair off my face. 'You looked as if you were miles away.'

'Oh, I'm sorry, Alex. I feel very tired and as if I've hit a wall. I don't know what's wrong with me. I can't think about your question right now.' I laughed but it was a nervous laugh. 'Oh,' I said, looking at my watch. 'Is that the time?' It was nearly midnight. 'I really should be going.' I wriggled to manoeuvre myself off the sofa and stood up. 'Thank you so much for the wonderful dinner and the great company afterwards. I've really enjoyed myself this evening. It's been great to relax and chat.'

'Good. But you *don't* have to go home,' he responded, catching my hand and sitting me down again.

'I think I should,' I replied, looking directly at him and feeling slightly more agitated.

'But you don't want to and I don't want you to go either.' I glanced away. 'Oh, come on, Alicia. I think we've spent enough time together to know that we're attracted to one another.' With one of his hands he had begun undoing the buttons of my blouse and the other hand was gently insinuating itself around my breast. My self-control was dwindling. 'You know, Alicia, the true test is the breakfast test,' he said, looking at me intently.

'The breakfast test?' I quizzed, gathering my thoughts and stopping his hand.

'Yes. You know. Whether we would have anything to talk about in the morning, and I think *we* would have plenty to talk about. Don't you?'

'Like whether you prefer marmalade or jam on your toast, Alex?' I wanted to sound flippant.

'That's why I like you, Alicia. You have this way with you. You look vulnerable but you're actually very tough. It's very seductive,' he said, stroking the back of my hair. 'I want to be with you and I'd really like you to stay.'

'I'm sorry, Alex. I can't. I have to leave.' I stood up and tried to do up the buttons of my blouse.

'Don't go, Alicia. Not like this.' But I did. I rushed out to the hall, grabbed my coat from the hall cupboard and opened the front door. I ran down the stairs but this time Alex did not come after me.

I felt sick to my stomach and, as I drove home, I attempted to justify my actions to myself. Although Alex's initials were DAW it was purely coincidental that these were the initials on the files I could not access, and perhaps I had overreacted. It might not be at all remarkable that Jack would have called Alex to ask him about an IP matter, bearing in mind he had IP expertise and was listed as up-and-coming in *Chambers* Law Directory. There had been no necessity for me to leave and I wished now I had not acted so hastily. I presumed that I had blown it with him. I turned on my car radio and the strains of Kylie Minogue singing *Can't Get You Out of My Head* came blaring out at me. That was the last song I needed to hear as it was like rubbing salt into a wound that I had opened. I flipped channels only to hear Al Green's *Tired of Being Alone* playing, so I switched off the radio and drove the rest of the way home in silence.

Chapter 22

Monday morning came around all too quickly and I was not ready for my alarm clock to go off at six-thirty. I was unsure how Alex would react to me after Saturday night and how I was going to face him was another matter. Kim had also 'phoned me several times on Sunday and I had not returned her calls, so she would be wondering what had happened.

I needed to work on Andy's files and to find out what or who DAW stood for. Once again I inputted the details of the two investment portfolios, but the same words came up for two of them: ACCESS DENIED; UNAUTHORISED USER. I looked through Andy's filing cabinet but could not find the files although all the others were there. I decided to speak with Graham.

'I'm sorry Graham, but in all the commotion last week over Alex's deal I mislaid the original print-out Andy gave me. This was all I could find when I looked in his office.' I handed him the sheet I had taken from Andy's in-tray. 'The thing is I can't access these files,' I said, pointing to 1769/1DAW and 1769/2DAW on the sheet. 'Every time I input the codes the words "ACCESS DENIED; UNAUTHORISED USER" appear.' Graham did not seem the slightest bit concerned.

'You'd best have a word with Michael, Alicia. If there's a problem, he's the one to sort it out for you. Clearly the two files relate to the same client so perhaps there's just a glitch with the system.'

I went down to Michael's office in the basement. I knew that Vincent had been there that morning because I could smell his

Turkish cigarettes. Michael was particularly grumpy and almost snapped my head off as I entered. I wondered whether it was because he had climbed out the wrong side of the bed or had had a run in with Vincent.

'Yes. What is it?' he said abruptly, without looking at me properly and continuing to input data into his computer.

'I'm sorry to trouble you, but Andy left some files for me to work on in his absence and there are two files I can't seem to access on this list. Graham said I should speak to you.'

'What files might those be?' He stopped what he was doing and looked at me hard with his beady brown eyes beneath his furrowed brow.

'These two.' I handed him a copy of the sheet and pointed to the numbers of the two files I was unable to access.

'Where did you get this?' he asked aggressively, vigorously waving the piece of paper at me.

'I told you. From Andy.' His manner changed towards me.

'I think there has been a mistake. There's nothing here for you to worry about. These files shouldn't have been on the list. They're not live. They've been archived.' He gave me a strained smile.

'Oh, right. Well, I'll leave it then.'

'You do that.' He turned away from me and returned to his computer. It was not what he said, but something in his voice made me feel something was amiss. From the moment I had met him I had mistrusted him, and this feeling now increased.

I continued to work on my other files for the rest of the day. However, about five that afternoon the door to my office was flung open and Vincent stormed in looking like a thundercloud. To say that he was furious would be an understatement.

'What the hell do you think you're playing at?' he bellowed, breathing cigarette smoke into my face and banging his left fist on my desk with such force that it made me jump. His fingers were so tightly clenched that his knuckles were white, but his face was as red as a beetroot.

230

'Who gave you the authority to look at those files?' he bawled. 'What do you think you're playing at, trying to access archived files?'

'Well...' I wanted to say they were Andy's, but he would not let me get a word in edgeways and shouted over me, drowning out my words.

'You had no business requesting those files. You hear me. No business at all,' he repeated, drawing heavily on his cigarette and leaning forward so that he was within inches of my face. His manner was menacing and, bearing in mind I was sitting at my desk and he towered over me at the best of times, I felt truly intimidated.

'But I...' Again he would not let me explain. Talk about manic behaviour.

'If you value your job you'll keep your nose out of matters which don't concern you. Is that clear?' he said, pointing his finger at me. I looked at him but did not respond. As much as I wanted to say something I could not get the words out. 'I said, "Is that clear?"' he screamed once again, coming within inches of my face. I recoiled. I nodded meekly and he charged out, slamming the door behind him and leaving me feeling as if I had done ten rounds with Mike Tyson.

A few moments later Carrie opened the door.

'You OK, Alicia? I heard all the shouting. What's going on?'

'Your guess is as good as mine,' I replied, trying to regain my composure. 'You said that Vincent would lose it with me sooner rather than later. He just did. I feel sick.' I fanned myself with the papers on my desk.

'Don't worry, Alicia. Storm in a teacup, I suspect. Vincent has been ranting all day. Both Jenny and Amanda were in tears earlier and poor Patrick has had an ear-bashing as well. We're all keeping our heads down. Go home, have a long hot soak and forget all about it. That's what I would do. It'll blow over. It always does.'

I did not feel that it was a storm in a teacup. Vincent's reaction had been extreme in the extreme even for him, and I knew there had to be more to it. Clearly he did not want me to know about those two files and it was reasonable to suppose from his behaviour that he had something to hide. My gut feeling had been correct and I felt slightly less guilty about walking out on Alex. Whether or not Alex was actually involved was another matter, but there was cause for concern.

I called Jo to tell her what had happened because she was the only one I could trust.

'Ally, I'm so sorry.'

'Don't you think Vincent's behaviour was bizarre?'

'Not if he has something to conceal, although you'd think that he'd be a bit more subtle about it. By shouting at you he has merely heightened your suspicions.'

'I think he deliberately wanted to frighten me. He's pretty intimidating.'

'I'd love to see this man. I'll have to come to the office. Why don't I pick you up after work tomorrow?'

'OK. If you want to.'

'You can introduce me to Alex. What's happening with him?'

'I've blown it. I helped him out on a deal last week as he needed an Italian interpreter. I went to dinner at his place on Saturday evening, things were going well and then he mentioned the fact his first name was actually Duncan and not Alex, and I freaked because his initials are DAW like on those files. I put two and two together and made five, panicked, and had to get out of there. I suppose I over-reacted, but after Vincent's reaction today I know that there's something going on at the firm even though I don't know what.'

'For what it's worth, I think I'd have done the same as you. Alex could be involved. The trouble is you like him, you don't want to believe that he is and you feel torn,' she said knowingly.

'True. I have a lot of other things on my mind as well. I haven't heard from Antonia yet and I'm concerned. She said she'd call if there were any developments. What's the news on Patti and Abbey?'

'There isn't any. Don't worry. Something will turn up. You'll see. I'll be at your office at five-thirty. Get some sleep!'

I was lying back on my sofa in my jumpsuit contemplating my lot, munching Ready Salted Pringles, when my video Entryphone buzzed. It was just after eight and I was not expecting anyone, so it gave me a start. I suspected it was probably somebody pressing the buzzer to the wrong flat, but I dragged myself off the sofa to check. I was astonished to see that it was Alex; he was the last person I thought would be ringing my doorbell. I was not sure whether to be nervous or excited or both.

'Alex,' I said, opening the door cautiously.

'Forgive the attire,' he remarked as he wiped his feet on my front door mat and ran his fingers back through his hair, 'but I came over on my scooter. It's so much easier for nipping through the traffic, and parking. Do you mind if I put these down somewhere?' he asked, referring to his backpack and the crash helmet he was holding in his hand.

'No. Anywhere you like.' He took off his jacket and shoes and left them in the hall. As he walked into the reception room he glanced up at my Venetian mirror and readjusted his hair which had been slightly flattened by the crash helmet.

'I thought you could do with this,' he said, pulling out a bottle of wine from inside the backpack, 'and, I don't suppose you've eaten yet? Well, not *properly* anyway,' he added, noticing the opened packet of Pringles on my coffee table. From inside his backpack he pulled out a couple of plastic containers.

'What on earth do you have there?'

'Dinner. Show me the way to your kitchen and I'll cook it for you.'

'Do you do this often?' I asked in bewilderment as I watched him take out pieces of veal, a lemon, breadcrumbs and some potatoes.

'I wanted to make up for the rotten dinner I cooked the other night.'

'I told you it was lovely. The meal turned out fine in the end. There's nothing to make up for.'

'I disagree. I wasn't happy about the way you left.' He paused and caught my eye, but I did not respond. 'As for this evening, I thought you needed cheering up.'

'Oh, you mean Vincent? Par for the course, isn't it?' He raised his eyebrows but said nothing. 'Anyway, it was a long way to come without checking I was in. It's really appreciated though,' I said, hovering in the doorway watching him while he prepared the meal.

'Calculated guess. Somehow I didn't think you'd be out this evening.' I said nothing. 'What's the matter? You seem withdrawn? You are OK with this, aren't you? You're not offended or anything?' I was uncertain how to react because he had completely swept aside the events of Saturday evening.

'No. It's one of the sweetest things anyone has ever done for me. But I am surprised because I didn't expect to see you after Saturday night.'

'I told you, Alicia, people aren't always what they seem. As I said, you shouldn't believe everything you've heard about me.' He turned to me and smiled.

'Do you need a hand with anything?' I asked, still feeling slightly awkward.

'No. I have two.' He laughed. 'You just relax. Now where do you keep your pots and pans?'

'You're a great cook,' I said as I savoured another mouthful of veal.

'Thanks, but I'm sure you didn't really think that the other night and you were being polite. Anyway, someone has to save you from all those Pringles!'

'What scooter do you have, Alex?' I changed the subject.

'A Scarabeo Aprilia. Black. Do you approve?'

'Yes.'

'You'll have to come for a ride sometime.'

'I'd like that.'

It was now his turn to change the subject. 'Spill the beans. Why was Vincent shouting at you today?' I was not sure how to respond. Was he concerned or was he fishing?

'He thinks that I was trying to access files on the system for which I have no authorization and he went berserk,' I replied, scrutinizing the reaction on his face.

'You were trying to access files…' I could not tell whether Alex was making a statement or asking me a question.

'Andy gave me a list of files to work on while he's away, mainly the ones with investment portfolios. They were on the list.'

'What list?' I wondered whether I should tell him but decided to take the risk.

'Andy gave me a print-out but I mislaid it. I couldn't find it anywhere on the system, so I looked in his office and I found another one in his in-tray which looked the same – but maybe it was a slightly different list. I don't know. I only did what I was told to do.'

'Well, it's hardly your fault then, is it?'

'Try telling Vincent that. Has he ever shouted at you?'

'He shouts at everyone. I feel slightly guilty because I recommended you for the job and you're probably regretting accepting it now.'

'Oh, Alex. Please don't. Anyway, I chose to accept it. That's the way life goes. I am curious though. Why do *you* stay there?'

'Because it suits me. There are some things I need to do before I move on.'

'Such as?'

'Nothing that you need worry about. Watch your back, Alicia.' I did not have the opportunity to ask him exactly what he meant by that last remark because there was a tap at my front door. I looked through the spyhole, saw Cesare and opened it.

'*Ciao, carina,*' he said, giving me a hug.

'*Ciao,* Cesare. I didn't expect you back yet. This is a lovely surprise. *Stai bene?* Is everything OK?'

'*Sì.*'

'Come in.' I lead him into the reception room. 'Cesare, let me introduce you to Alex Waterford. Alex is a colleague of mine.' I turned to Alex. 'Alex this is my neighbour Cesare Castelli.' They shook hands, but not warmly. 'Won't you stay for a drink, Cesare?'

'No. I didn't realize you had company,' he replied uneasily. 'I only wanted to give you these tickets for *Turandot*,' he said, handing them to me.

'Oh, thank you. That's really sweet of you. Please stay for a drink?'

'No, really. I'll speak to you later. *Buona sera, carina.*'

I walked to the door with Cesare and when I returned I noticed that Alex had a rather sour expression on his face.

'What's the deal with your neighbour?' He sounded put out.

'Nothing.'

'You two seem pretty friendly, that's all. I saw the way he was looking at you.' Surely Alex wasn't jealous?

'We are. He's a very good friend. What's the matter Alex? Is there a problem?'

'My mistake,' he said curtly, rising from the sofa, walking into the hall and picking up his crash helmet and backpack.

'Don't go. Not like this,' I said, grabbing him by the arm. 'This is ridiculous!'

'So I'm ridiculous now am I, Alicia?'

'That's not what I meant, Alex. Why are you behaving this way? Especially after the lovely dinner you made for me, which I really appreciated.' I felt disappointed because I thought Alex and I had made it up after I had blown him out on Saturday evening.

'I'm tired. I need to go home. It isn't you. It's me. I've got a lot on. I'll see you at work tomorrow,' he replied, and walked briskly to the front door. He turned, paused for a second, and from the way he looked at me I sensed he wanted to say something to me, but he just sighed heavily and left. I was confused and I did not know what to think about him or what to expect next.

236

Chapter 23

'Josephine Brook has arrived for you,' Tilly rasped down the phone. Her voice was more grated than usual and she sounded very weary. She had taken her fair share of abuse from Vincent that day, although that was nothing new. I looked at my watch and it was five-thirty on the dot. Jo was always punctual.

'Thanks, Tilly. I'll be down in a minute.'

Vincent's office door was shut as I walked past and I presumed that he was with a client. He generally did not leave the office until late, so Jo and I needed to hover around long enough so she could get a glimpse of him. I had not seen Alex all day and when I called his direct line it went straight to voice mail. I had left a message asking him to ring me but he had not returned my call, and until Jo had arrived I had been too busy to try again.

Jo was dressed in chocolate brown and cream, which really suited her *café au lait* complexion. 'Hi, Ally,' she said as I walked into reception, and stooped to kiss me on both cheeks. 'How was your day?' she asked as she followed me up the stairs to the first floor.

'No repercussions from yesterday, if that's what you mean. I haven't seen *him* all day. You're looking great, Jo.' We walked past Vincent's office and the door was still firmly shut. 'You've had your haircut. It suits you.' It was about eight inches shorter and now shoulder-length.

'Thanks, Ally.' She touched the back of her hair. 'Easier to manage I thought. You're looking thin. It amazes me how someone who eats so many Pringles manages not to put on weight. You clearly have a metabolism faster than anyone in the universe!'

'You're as bad as Alex.' We walked down the corridor.

'Perhaps he and I should exchange notes on the subject,' she teased. We had nearly reached the door to my office when I saw Teresa, who must have come down the stairs, walking straight towards us. As she did so, she stared so hard at Jo that she almost bored a hole through her. It would have been rude of me not to introduce Jo in the circumstances.

'Teresa, this is my friend Jo.' Jo extended her hand first and smiled at her.

'Pleased to meet you.' Teresa limply shook her hand, but her face was like stone.

'I'd love to stay and chat,' she replied as she pushed *those* metal-rimmed glasses up her nose, 'but Vincent is waiting for me. *Some* of us have work to do,' she said, looking pointedly at me.

'Please don't let us detain you,' interjected Jo.

'Yes,' continued Teresa, ignoring Jo and directing the conversation at me. 'You remember that property client I mentioned to you on your first day?' I nodded. 'He's in with Vincent at the moment. My expertise is required.' She pushed her fringe out of her eyes and walked off.

'Expertise in how to be a complete bitch?' asked Jo as we walked into my office. 'Do I get to meet Alex?' At that very moment the door to my office opened and none other than Alex walked in.

'Alicia, we need to talk,' he said, and then he saw Jo. 'Oh, I'm terribly sorry,' he continued, looking slightly embarrassed. 'I didn't realize you were with a client. Please excuse me.' Jo laughed.

'It's all right, Alex. This is a friend of mine. Jo, this is Alex Waterford. Alex this is Josephine Brook, my closest friend.'

'Oh, I see. How do you do?' He shook her hand.

'How *do* you do, Alex? I've heard *so* much about you.'

'Really? How come?' With a seriously worried expression he looked at me.

'How you recommended Alicia for the job and have made her

feel *so* welcome.'

'Oh. That.' He was momentarily speechless. 'I'll leave you two to chat. I'll speak to you later, Alicia,' he said, and disappeared.

'Cute. Very cute. Great bum. Nice eyes. The list goes on,' she teased. 'I can see the attraction.'

'Don't start,' I said reprovingly. 'He turned up at my flat last night on his scooter, completely out of the blue and insisted on cooking dinner. Towards the end of the evening Cesare appeared with tickets for *Turandot* and Alex just upped and left. I can't make him out. It's as if he's two people.'

'I'm sure he thinks the same about you, but he definitely likes you. Just leaving the subject of Alex for one moment, did you get anywhere with those files?'

'No.' I paused, as I thought I heard Vincent's door open. I moved to the door and opened it quietly. The office was deadly quiet now and, even though I was at the far end of the building, I was able to hear what was going on at the end of the corridor. 'If you want to see Vincent, Jo, now is your chance. I heard his door open. He'll be coming out any minute.'

Jo reached for her bag and jacket, and we tiptoed along the corridor and peeked around the corner. Teresa, Vincent and the client, whoever he was, were standing outside Vincent's office, but it was not possible to see Vincent's or the client's faces.

'I want to take a closer look at that middle one,' said Jo, straining to look at him.

'That one isn't Vincent.'

'No. I know he's not.'

'What are you talking about, Jo? You've never seen Vincent before, so how do you know it's not him?'

'Because I know who the middle one is.'

'You're not making any sense.'

Teresa shook the client's hand and he and Vincent started to walk down the stairs, but Teresa turned back in our direction.

'Start walking,' said Jo, 'or she'll be suspicious. Ask her who that client is?'

'Why? What's the relevance?'

'Just do it.' She was insistent.

'You still here?' said Teresa as she approached.

'Looks like it,' I replied sarcastically. 'Good meeting?'

'Excellent.' She sounded pleased with herself.

'So who's the client?'

'Mr Warrener. I must get on. Things to do,' she snarled, and swaggered off.

'Come on,' said Jo. 'If we hurry we might get another glimpse of him before he leaves.'

Jo and I reached the end of the corridor, stood in the stairwell and peeked over the banister. We could see down into the main foyer by the front door where Vincent was standing talking to Mr Warrener. Jo became visibly pale and spun around so that she had her back to the banister.

'What's the matter Jo? What's going on?'

'Ally. It's him?'

'Who?'

'Jack. He mustn't see me,' she gasped.

'Jack?' I asked in utter astonishment. 'You mean from the Club?'

'Yes. Where else? We'll have to go back to your office until he leaves. Actually, we had better wait until they both leave in case Vincent asks you who I am.' We scurried back to the office and shut the door.

'Are you sure that was Jack?'

'As sure as I've ever been about anything. That was Jack all right. Those features are a dead giveaway. Mr Warrener *is* Jack. He told me he was in the property investment business and he's probably doing some shady deal or something.'

'Tammy told me he was a property speculator. Maybe he and Vincent are in on some scam and those files I can't access have something to do with it.'

'Hang on, Ally. You're jumping the gun.'

'Coincidence is all very well, but there are just too many coincidences here, don't you think?'

'OK. I take your point.'

'It might even be more than that.'

'What are you saying, Ally?'

'What if it was Vincent and Jack whom Tammy heard arguing that night at the Club, and they thought she overheard them and they murdered her to silence her? Maybe that's what Eve knows.'

'It can't be. Surely not?'

'Think about it, Jo. It makes sense.'

'OK. But where's your proof?'

'I know this is all rather circumstantial. I realize we need concrete evidence but I'd like to look at those unauthorized files because then we may have some idea of what Vincent is up to and whether Jack is involved. We need to hack into the computer system; but I wouldn't have a clue how to do it.'

'Ah, but Will would. Let's get out of here. This place is starting to give me the creeps. You go home and I'll see you later. If Kim speaks to you, don't breathe a word to her.'

'You mean, what she doesn't know can't hurt me? I had no intention of telling her anyway.'

'Something like that; and that applies to Alex too. I'd stay clear of him too. In fact, we can't afford to trust anyone.'

I walked along the street to the tube station and mulled over my latest theory. I thought through what Jo had said and I shuddered. Maybe I was completely wrong, but my instincts told me otherwise. It was imperative I get back into the office, hack into the computer system and access those files. It would be a risk, but if Will could help me and it gave us some clues, then it would be one worth taking. I was concerned about Jo because, if anyone recognized her, she would be in danger as well. I was so deep in thought that I was totally unaware of the people around me. I was standing on the kerb at the traffic lights waiting to cross when all of a sudden somebody came up behind me and shook one of my shoulders. I almost jumped out of my skin, took a sharp intake of breath, and gasped.

'Alicia. You OK?' It was Alex.

'You shouldn't do that.' The lights changed and I started to cross the road with him in tow.

'What?'

'Come up behind people like that. You frightened me to death,' I snapped.

'I'm sorry. I really didn't mean to startle you. Where's your friend?'

'Why?' I was on my guard bearing in mind what Jo had just said.

'Just wondered. What are you up to later?'

'Why?'

'What's the matter with you? You seem so bad tempered.'

'I'm not. Anyway, this isn't the way home for you so why are you here?' I gave him a sideways glance.

'I wanted to talk to you. Remember? I really want to clear the air. I went to have a coffee around the corner and waited for you as I know you pass this way.'

'So you're following me now?' It was my turn to be acerbic. We crossed to the other side of the road and I doubled my pace to get ahead of him, but his strides were long and he managed to move in front of me, turn around, and block my way.

'Come on, Alicia. Talk to me. Tell me what's wrong,' he said, gently shaking my shoulders. I looked at the expression in his eyes and all I could see was genuine concern and for one second I wanted to tell him everything. I needed to believe that he was sincere, but I could not endanger so many people even if that meant jeopardising a relationship with him.

'I told you. Nothing's wrong. I have things to do and I need to get home. I'm sorry, Alex,' I said abruptly, trying to shrug him off. He looked deeply hurt and I had to school myself to maintain an air of detachment.

'Fine.' He took his hands off me and raised them in the air, palms outstretched, in a dramatic gesture. 'I'll leave you alone then.' He stormed off. I stood for a few moments watching him walk along the street. He hailed a taxi, I saw him slam the door with a vengeance, and I continued looking as the taxi disappeared down the street.

I sifted through my post hoping that there might be a letter from Jeremy Brown, but I was again disappointed. There was an invitation from Louise to baby Daniel's Christening, which cheered me up; I placed it on the mantelpiece. I felt unsettled and disturbed about the events of the day and, in particular, my exchange with Alex but, as much as I tried, I could not take my mind off him. In an attempt to do so, I decided to call Dorothy's niece to find out how Dorothy was progressing.

'Alicia. Lovely to hear from you,' said Anne. 'Dorothy's making excellent progress. I know she'll want to talk to you.'

'Oh, please don't disturb her on my account.'

'She'll be cross if she doesn't speak to you. It isn't any bother. She can use the cordless handset.' I waited a few minutes while Anne walked through with the 'phone. I heard her telling Dorothy who it was and then she picked up the 'phone.

'Hello, dear. How are you?'

'I'm fine,' I said lying and pretending to sound cheerful. 'But, more to the point, how are you?'

'Better. The doctors are pleased with my progress, though I miss being in my own home.'

'Yes. I can imagine. Maybe soon. How's your memory coming on?'

'It's strange you should ask, dear, but something happened the other day which triggered it.'

'What do you mean exactly?'

'It was the gardener you see?'

'No, I don't. Explain it to me, Dorothy.'

'Smoky must have climbed up on to the table by the French

doors that lead out to the garden, naughty little thing, as he's not supposed to do that. The gardener obviously startled him when he knocked on one of the doors to attract my niece's attention. He opened it suddenly and Smoky flew at him and scratched his face. I was sitting in my armchair opposite the windows so I saw everything. You know how I like to sit by the window?'

'Yes, I do. I don't follow. How did this trigger your memory?'

'At the very moment Smoky leapt up at him, I had a picture in my head and I was back in the flat that night and I saw his face quite clearly.'

'You mean whoever it was that attacked you?'

'Yes, dear. I knew that my recollection of Smoky had to be relevant.'

'But you were struck from behind. How did you see his face?'

'I can only think that he entered the flat from the garden as the door was ajar. It always is, as you may know, because Smoky likes to go in and out that way. I remember seeing the man in the hall. He was coming towards me and I turned away from him and tried to make for the front door but I don't recall any more. I suppose that was when he attacked me.'

'Your recollection of the events that evening sounds amazing to me. Would you recognize this man if you saw him again?'

'Yes, dear. I think so.'

'Have you spoken to the police?'

'They're coming tomorrow. I'm sorry I won't see you on your birthday. Isn't it next week? Are you going to have a party?' My thirtieth birthday was the last thing I was thinking about; there were more important things on my mind.

'There isn't much wrong with your memory,' I said with a laugh. 'I'll try to get up to see you soon if you'd like that?'

'That would be lovely. Now tell me about your new job. Are you enjoying it?'

'There's lots of variety. Something unexpected happens every day.'

I did not have much time to muse over what Dorothy had told me because five minutes later Jo and Will arrived on my doorstep.

'We tried to call you to let you know we were on our way, but your landline was engaged and you weren't answering your mobile. I was a bit worried,' said Jo, bending down to kiss me. Will did the same.

'Oh, I'm sorry. I was in a meeting earlier today out of the office and I switched it off. With all the commotion I forgot to switch it back on.' I reached for my handbag, pulled out my mobile and turned it on. It went to *diverted call* straight away. 'That must be your message.' There were no other calls. 'I was on the 'phone to Dorothy. That's why my landline was engaged.'

'Oh. How is she?' asked Jo, sitting down on the sofa. Will sat next to her.

'Better. And her memory of what happened to her that night is coming back. She recalls Smoky scratching her attacker's face and she thinks she could identify him if she saw him.'

'That's excellent,' said Will. Some positive news for a change. I heard what happened at the office today. So you think there's a connection between Jack, Vincent, Tammy and the Club?'

'I think it's a strong possibility. I don't know for sure. I want to find out what Vincent and Jack are up to and see where that leads us, but to do that I need your help.' I sat down in my armchair opposite him.

'What is it you want me to do?'

'Can you hack into computers?'

'That's what I do all the time. What about access to the building?'

'Easy. The security is very lapse. There's an alarm, but the cleaner has set it off so many times that nobody bothers to do it anymore. Vincent keeps threatening to sack her but he never does. All we fee earners have keys to the building, so that would pose no difficulty.'

'How about Friday night? Does anyone work late?'

'Alex does if he has a deal on, but he's quiet at the moment. Teresa invariably works late during the week, but she goes away at the weekends and doesn't like to hang around on Friday evenings. The rest of us get out of there as soon as possible, so that shouldn't be a problem.'

'I'll pick you up about ten 'cos at the moment it isn't dark until then and we don't want to risk being noticed. In the meantime, see what else you can find out about this Mr Warrener and let me know if anything turns up.'

After Jo and Will left, I went to bed and fell asleep straightaway. It was only the sound of my landline ringing that woke me and, as I turned over and looked at the clock radio, I saw it was five o'clock in the morning. I wondered who was calling me so early. I reached for the 'phone and knocked it off its base. As I picked it up I could hear Antonia's voice saying 'Hello'.

'*Pronto.* Antonia.'

'*Va bene,* Alicia?' she asked, and from the sound of her voice I knew that all was not well.

'I'm fine,' I replied, lying through my teeth; there was no point in worrying Antonia when she was on the other side of the world. 'How's everything? How's Maggie?'

'Oh, Alicia. She's dead. She died this afternoon.' I nearly dropped the 'phone again. I knew that Maggie was terminally ill but I had not expected her demise to be so swift.

'Oh, Antonia. I'm so sorry. Poor Tom. How is he?'

'He's doing remarkably well in the circumstances. I think that it hasn't sunk in yet.'

'No. I'm sure. What are you going to do? I mean about the funeral and everything?'

'I think we'll stay out here for a few weeks as there's a lot to sort through, so I won't be back for your birthday at the weekend. Do you mind?'

'My birthday's the last thing I'm worried about. Stay with Tom and do what you have to do.'

'Don't say anything to Kim yet because Tom wants to tell her.

246

He's been 'phoning all the family. It's very tough. I'm glad every-thing is all right with you though.' If only she really knew, I thought. 'And the job – it's going well?' It was definitely neither the time nor the place to go down that road.

'It's all go, go, go, at the moment,' I replied, trying to sound enthusiastic. 'I'll speak to you soon. You take care, OK. I'll tell Mamma so that she doesn't worry about you. I love you. Send my love to Tom.'

'Will do. Love you too. *Baci. Ciao.*'

There was no point in trying to go back to sleep, after hearing that news. I watched breakfast television for a short while and then decided I might as well go in to work. I had barely locked my front door when I heard Cesare's footsteps behind me. I had forgotten that he always left for work at the crack of dawn, and I was certainly not feeling very chatty, or wanting to answer any questions.

'Alicia,' he said, catching up with me on the stairs. 'You're very early this morning.'

'Yes. I'm in a bit of a rush actually. We'll have to catch up later. One piece of good news for you, though,' I said, turning as I reached the outside door. 'I spoke to Dorothy last night and she's making an excellent recovery.'

'*Bene. Va bene?*' He must have sensed my agitation.

'Yes. I'm just a bit preoccupied. Have a good day.'

'You too. Don't forget the performance of *Turandot* on Friday; that is if you still want to go.'

I sensed that he was really asking whether I wanted to go with *him*. Because he had seen Alex with me, I knew that he must be curious about the nature of my relationship with him. But it was not entirely the case of forgetting that the performance was on Friday, just that, because of my set-to with Alex, I had not looked at the date on the tickets when I had arranged with Will to go sleuthing at Wilson, Weil & Co that evening. Consequently, I would have to forego his invitation and make some reasonable excuse about being unable to accompany him. I could deal with that later as it was only Wednesday, for now I needed to concentrate on catching Tammy's killer.

Chapter 24

I picked up the milk from the office doorstep on my way in and took it downstairs to the kitchen. It was only half past seven and nobody had arrived, not even Teresa. I walked past Michael's office and tried the door handle in the hope of having a quick look around, but unfortunately the door was locked. I walked back upstairs to the ground floor.

Since Tilly made all Vincent's calls for him and for several of the other fee earners, she kept a record of the telephone numbers of all the firm's clients and any other relevant numbers in an enormous address book. It was kept in reception, which was a room just off the main foyer and to which all the fee earners had keys. Tilly regularly updated it so that she would have the details at her fingertips if required to make a call. Without this information to hand, her life would not have been worth living. I unlocked the door and found it on top of her desk. I turned to the "W" section and thumbed through the pages in Tilly's neat handwriting until I found the details I was looking for. The first line of the entry read: *Mr Daniel Warrener, Jackdaw Investments Ltd.*

The details leapt out of the page at me. This must be Jack's company. I wondered whether Jack was in fact a nickname and that his initials were DAW. That would make sense because the two parts together made up the word JACKDAW. I recalled my conversation with Rob at the gym when he explained how he became known by that name because of his initials. I felt a mixture of anxiety and relief: anxiety about the true implications of this and what I might discover, and relief that, if I was right, this had nothing to do with Alex.

On the second line there was a mobile phone number but no other contact details, which slightly surprised me. I took a yellow Post-it note off the pad and a biro out of Tilly's pot of pens and scribbled the details down. I placed the address book back where I had found it, locked the door to reception and walked upstairs to my office.

I logged on to my computer to carry out a company search on Jackdaw Investments Ltd, as the firm had an account with Companies House and that meant we could access their database and do online searches. Unfortunately, I could find no trace of a UK Company by that name, and I searched to see if Jack held any directorships but none were listed. I suspected that any business dealings he had were offshore.

I then logged into the accounts system to check for files under the client code for investment advice with the client reference "WAR". It was the practice within the firm for files to be opened using the first three letters of the client's surname and then a matter number would be allocated to it depending upon the type of work to which it related. Up came the client names WARNOCK, WARTON, WARWICK but no WARRENER, but then I was not really expecting it to, as that would be too obvious and too easy. I carried out a general search of the firm's clients to see if anything turned up, and opened the appropriate screen but found nothing. I needed to call Will and tell him what I *had* found out, but it was too risky to do so from the office in case someone walked in on me. I was popping out for a croissant and a coffee anyway, and now was as good a time to go as any.

It was already half past eight and several other members of staff had arrived as I could hear movement in the building. I made sure I had logged out of the accounts system, put on my jacket and picked up my handbag. I was about to open the door to my office when I heard a commotion and shouting in the corridor. Evidently

Vincent had arrived early this morning, in even more of a foul mood than usual, and was shouting and swearing at Patrick who was shouting and swearing back. I heard the door to his office slam shut and then there was silence. I opened the door to my office and walked along and around the corridor and down the stairs. Patrick was standing at the bottom of the stairs by the open front door looking extremely red-faced and drawing heavily on a cigarette.

'What's the matter this morning?' I asked.

'Is it any wonder I'm losing my hair?' he replied, in the broadest of broad Southern Irish accents. 'I'm tearing my hair out every day working for him.' He looked at me with his Celtic blue eyes. He did look rough and indeed appeared to be losing his hair. I was sure he had more hair than that when I arrived and that was only a matter of weeks before.

'Why the foul mood today?'

'He's going on holiday to Barbados at the end of the week and he's panicking about getting all the work done. He's always like this before he goes away.'

'Really? I thought he was like this every day. Is that why Mr Wilson left? I always wondered where he went.'

'Derek retired ten years ago. He'd had enough of the law. Well, you would. I mean working here, that's for sure.' He sighed.

'Yes, but I guess part of the problem with Vincent is he takes on too much work, isn't it? And also non-matrimonial work?' Patrick looked puzzled. 'You know like Daniel Warrener, the client who was in with him yesterday evening, the property speculator.' Patrick was just about to respond when Vincent, who was looming at the top of the stairs, bellowed down at him in a voice which made both of us jump out of our skin.

'Patrick! Where the hell have you been? I need you this instant.' Patrick stubbed out the cigarette on the doorstep outside and shifted slowly up the stairs. Vincent then addressed me. 'Ah. If it isn't the lovely Miss Allen,' he said in a sycophantic sort of way. 'Are you gracing us with your presence today *or not?*' He dropped his voice and sounded sarcastic.

'Of course,' I replied. 'But I…' I did not have a chance to finish what I wanted to say, because he shouted over me.

'Get back upstairs and do some work then!' he bawled. He returned to his office and slammed the door. I walked out of the building and straight into Teresa.

'Leaving already,' she remarked. 'Part-timers. Really can't get the staff.'

'Yes. That's what I was thinking about you,' I replied, looking at my watch. 'Eight forty-five. Oh dear. You're late. You're slipping.' I brushed past her.

On my way to the coffee shop I 'phoned Will.

'Hi, Will. Sorry to call you so early.'

'Not at all. What is it, Alicia?'

'I've discovered that Mr Warrener's name is Daniel and his company is Jackdaw Investments Ltd. I did a search at Companies House but it isn't UK registered. I think it must be offshore. Anyway, could you do some digging and see what you can find out? Oh, and I heard Vincent is going away to Barbados at the end of the week.'

'No problem at all. You OK? You sound a bit agitated?'

'I am a bit. I'm concerned about Antonia. We spoke this morning. Maggie's dead.'

'Oh, my God! That's awful. What terrible news. Poor Tom.'

'Yes, particularly since we don't seem to be any further forward on Tammy's murder investigation. I'm sure that DI Peters is going to go ballistic when he finds out what I've been doing.' I was also agitated about Alex but did not want to tell Will.

'I know why you want to do it this way, Alicia.'

'You do?'

'I had the impression that you think DI Peters doesn't take you seriously, so I understand that you want to find evidence to ram down his throat!' I laughed, but he was not far off the mark. 'I'll see what I can rake up about Warrener and get back to you. Something will turn up I'm sure.'

On Thursday morning I had another early morning wake-up call from Antonia to tell me that Maggie's funeral had been arranged for the following Monday and she and Tom would return about a week or so after that. Kim was very distressed about it all so I arranged to go for a quick bite to eat with her after work in Covent Garden but, as was invariably the case with Kim, the evening turned out to be a much longer one than I had anticipated. I did not mind, though, because I had only intended to go to the gym, Kim was always good company and I had missed our little chats.

Inevitably, I knew the subject would turn to Alex, because Kim would be curious about the evening he invited me to dinner; but I did not want to have that conversation. In any event, I was not in a position to explain to Kim what was going on.

'Alex has been like a bear with a sore head these past few days. What did you do to him, Ally? Is your meal OK? My vegetables are a bit hard.' We were having fillet steak with a selection of vegetables.

'Nothing,' I replied. 'Dinner went well and he popped over on Monday night. Everything was all right until Cesare dropped in. My vegetables are fine.' I swallowed a mouthful of carrot.

'Why?'

'Alex reacted adversely and went off in a strop. I haven't been able to sort it out with him,' I said, skirting around the facts.

'Why did Alex pop around? It's a bit out of his way, isn't it? What happened at dinner? You didn't say.' She beckoned the waiter over.

'No, I didn't.'

'Oh, come on, Ally. This is Kim you're talking to.' The waiter came over to our table. 'Could you cook my vegetables a little more please?' He nodded and took them away.

'There's nothing to tell. It's as simple as that.'

'But why did he come over on Monday?'

'Because I left my fountain pen at his flat,' I said ad-libbing.

'Were you taking notes on him or something?' She laughed. 'Why didn't he give it to you at the office?'

'I don't know. Why don't you ask him?' I replied, trying to conceal my irritation and stabbing my steak with my fork.

'As if. He'd bite my head off! What did Cesare want?'

'Oh, my goodness. The tickets!'

'What tickets? What are you talking about Ally?'

'I completely forgot. Cesare gave me tickets for *Turandot* tomorrow evening, except I can't go.'

'Why not? What are you doing?'

'Oh, I have to see an old friend of the family who's over from Italy for a few days and tomorrow is the only day he can meet me,' I said, lying. 'Why don't you take the tickets?'

'Won't Cesare be disappointed?'

'It would be a pity to waste them and I'm sure he won't mind.'

'It's not exactly my thing, Ally, and Cesare and I probably don't have anything in common.'

'I'm sure you'll get on perfectly. You're both so easy going. Please. You'll be doing me an enormous favour.'

'OK,' she said reluctantly, 'but if I'm bored stiff all evening you'll owe me.'

'It's the opera, Kim, not tooth extraction!'

'Tooth extraction is probably less painful.'

'Where's Rob tonight?' I asked, changing the subject.

'Working late at the gym as usual. What did Antonia say when she called?' The waiter returned with her vegetables. Kim stuck her fork into a piece of cauliflower. 'That's better,' she said, chewing it.

'Not much. She told me about the funeral arrangements and said she would call at the weekend.'

'For your birthday, no doubt. What plans have you made?'

'None. I don't feel like celebrating in the circumstances.'

'Oh, Ally, you have to. You're only thirty once and, despite everything that's happened, we've got to celebrate. All this has made me feel that I shouldn't waste a moment. Don't feel guilty about it.

Antonia and Tom wouldn't want you to be unhappy on their account. Tammy loved a party. You should celebrate for her sake.'

'OK. Maybe we can do something after all then.'

I returned home very late and, on checking my answering machine, I had two messages. One was from Dorothy about her interview with the police and asking me to ring her when I had a moment. The other was from Will urging me to call him no matter how late I returned home as he had some information for me. I 'phoned him back immediately. He answered the 'phone.

'Ally. Thanks for calling back.'

'Oh, no problem. Sorry it's so late but I went for a meal with Kim and the evening went on and on. You know how it is?'

'You mean when women start talking?' he said, laughing.

'No comment. What's happening?'

'Jackdaw Investments Ltd is an Isle of Man company. You were right; it's offshore and because of that I haven't been able to ascertain the extent of its assets. However, I carried out a land registry search on the firm's premises and guess what?' He paused for a second. 'Jackdaw Investments owns the premises leased to your employer. And there's something else as well, Alicia.'

'Which is?'

'Mr Warrener's company owns the premises leased to the Club.'

'You're joking? I know you're not, but the police must have checked out the Club when they made their initial enquiries?'

'I can't answer that, but so far as I understand it, they had neither reason to suspect that Dick was carrying on anything untoward at the Club, nor to investigate the company with ownership of the head lease.'

'I don't believe that. My guess is that the police are investigating, but not telling us, which probably means they do know something. If you can't find out, then it must be big.'

'Maybe. But it was only because Jo recognized Jack at your office, and you discovered that he had a connection with the firm, and his company was Jackdaw Investments, that we started to link Jack, Vincent and the Club. That was when our suspicions were aroused, wasn't it?'

'True. I hope we can access the computer system because I'm sure there's money laundering going on, and maybe different types. The fact that Jackdaw Investments owns the premises leased to the firm makes me suspicious, but we'll need to follow the audit trail to get the evidence.'

'We'll have to try to hack into the system and see if we can obtain some.'

'Now that you have told me Jackdaw Investments owns the premises leased to the firm, I'll dig around in the office tomorrow and see if I can turn anything else up.'

'OK, Ally, but be careful.'

'Always.'

Friday morning had finally arrived and, because it was Vincent's last day in the office before his two-week holiday, he was being particularly manic even by his standards, which was saying something. He was abusing all the staff. Peter, Angela, Patrick, Jenny and Amanda all looked terribly harassed and the atmosphere in the building was extremely tense. Even Graham, who was usually so cool and calm, seemed slightly flustered. It did not help that it was an extremely humid summer's day and tempers were frayed more than usual.

I needed to call Cesare to tell him that I was unable to accompany him to the opera after all and did so as soon as I arrived at the office. Admittedly, I had a legitimate excuse, but I could not explain what it was and I felt slightly awkward lying to him.

'*Meno male, carina.* It can't be helped. But are you sure Kim wants to go?' he asked, sounding slightly dejected.

'I know she hasn't been to the opera before, so it will be an experience for her,' I replied, avoiding the question. 'I'll give her your number. Hope you have a good time and I'll catch up with you over the weekend.'

'Yes,' he said, sounding more cheery. 'You will. *A presto.*'

Unfortunately, Kim was still unenthusiastic.

'I'll go, Ally,' she said, taking down Cesare's work number. 'But I'm not really into all that opera stuff. You owe me for this. Don't forget.'

'How could I. You keep reminding me.'

I was completely occupied on a large probate matter all morning and had neither the opportunity nor the time to try and speak with Alex to see if I could at least salvage our professional relationship. Around midday I had broken the back of my work and I popped up to his office, but he was not there. Clearly Lady Luck was not on my side because, as I turned, I walked straight in to Teresa. She was carrying a pile of files and in doing so I sent those files flying.

'Oh. I'm terribly sorry,' I said, bending down to help her pick them up from the floor.

'Don't you ever look where you're going?' she barked, glaring at me and pushing those horrible glasses up her nose. 'But I suppose you only have eyes for Alex?' she sneered. I ignored the remark.

'It was an accident. I just didn't see you. It was hardly deliberate,' I retorted, trying to be both apologetic and polite, though it was difficult to remain civil with her.

'Then maybe you should have your eyes tested, Alicia,' she replied spitefully and stared right into them.

'I don't need to have my eyes tested to *see* what kind of person *you* are,' I snapped back. I had had enough of her snide remarks and I was not going to tolerate them any longer. 'I saw right through *you* the first time we met and I've *seen* enough of you to know that I really don't like *what* I see. Now, if you have a problem with me fine. But actually you're the one with the problem, not me. I heard about you before I arrived, but *seeing* really is believing.'

'We'll *see* about that,' she hissed back spitefully as she wrenched the file I was holding out of my hand, stepped into her office and slammed the door shut.

'What on earth was all that noise,' asked Imogen as she opened the door to her office and peered out into the corridor. 'Alicia. What's the matter?'

'I had a misunderstanding with Teresa. I'm sorry if it disturbed you.'

'Make sure it doesn't happen again,' she said as if she was ticking me off, reminding me of my physics teacher at my school – obviously the reason why I loathed the subject.

'It won't,' and I paused, 'provided Teresa keeps her remarks to herself. Then we can all get along.'

'I don't want to discuss this further, Alicia,' she said, like an old school ma'am. With that she returned to her office and closed the door firmly.

I wanted to speak to Gemma, Teresa's secretary, and ask a few discreet questions about Jack and Jackdaw Investments. Since I was up on that floor I decided to take the opportunity to ask her but, unfortunately, she was not in her office. Neither was Kim and the only one in there was Ella, who appeared to be typing at the speed of light.

'I couldn't help overhearing your conversation with Teresa just now. Good one,' she said, pausing, looking up and winking at me.

'Mrs Goede didn't think so.'

'Who gives a stuff about what she thinks. She's weak. Teresa gets away with her behaviour because she's Vincent's little protégée and Imogen is too scared to do anything. Teresa's a bully, but if you stand up to her she backs off. When I first arrived she talked to me like dirt and I wasn't having that. One day she came in accusing me of not doing some research properly, said I was thick, that my job was hanging by a thread and she could snip it at any time. So I gave it to her straight. I told her that if she tried to pull a trick like that, I'd pull my black card right out of the hat and have her for racial discrimination. You have to play dirty with people like her, Alicia. Playing by the rules gets you nowhere even if it does go against the grain. Remember she has no conscience. Like Vincent, she's ruthless, and thinks nothing of crushing anyone who stands in her way.'

'So I gathered. You're all alone? Where have Kim and Gemma gone?'

'For an early lunch. Why? Do you want to speak to Kim?'

'No. Actually I wanted a word with Gemma.'

'Anything I can help you with?' I could not risk saying anything to Ella and it was not because I did not trust her. Out of all the people who worked in that office, apart from Kim, whom I obviously knew on a personal basis, she was the only one I trusted. Telling her was not an option.

'No. Don't worry. Could you just ask her to call me when she's back?'

'No problem at all.'

I needed to finish off my notes for Andy, who was returning on Monday and since I had an external meeting at half past four I only had time to slip out to the nearest coffee shop for a sandwich. I missed Gianni's. I had forgotten my sunglasses and was squinting because the light was so bright but, as I rounded the corner to the office, I saw Gemma. She was sauntering along the road only a few steps in front of me, so I quickened my pace to catch up with her.

'Hi, Gemma. How are you?'

'Hot,' she replied, fanning herself with the magazine she had bought. 'How are you?'

'Frazzled. In more ways than one! Where's Kim?'

'She said she had to go and buy something. Why? Did you need her for anything in particular?'

'No. You actually. Do you have a minute?'

'I'm in no hurry to go back into the office, that's for sure. Not with the atmosphere in there today. Have you heard Vincent shouting? I don't know where he gets the energy from, especially in this heat. What do you want to chat about?' she asked, sweeping her sunglasses up into her blonde hair and wiping the perspiration from the side of her nose.

'Andy asked me to look at some investment portfolios while he was away and there were a couple of property investment files among them. I was unable to locate details of those files but I couldn't find the client folders on the system and I wondered whether Teresa organizes her files differently.'

'No,' she shook her head. 'Who was the client anyway?'

'Daniel Warrener. I think his company is Jackdaw Investments.'

'I'm sure he's not a client, Alicia. I think he's a sort of freelance consultant. I've certainly never typed up anything for Teresa relating to him.'

'Oh. How strange. Andy must have made an error.'

'I can ask Teresa if you like.'

'No. Don't worry about it. I'll ask Andy when he returns.' I was not going to wait that long though, as Will and I would be back that night.

Chapter 25

I continued with the work that I wanted to finalize before I left for my meeting. The fan in my room was on full blast and the large sash window wide open, but there was no breeze and the heat was simply stifling. I felt lethargic and drained, not only by the torrid weather, and furthermore my shoes had become extremely uncomfortable because they pinched my toes. I fetched myself a glass of water from the water bottle in the corridor and when I returned to my office there were papers all over the floor. The air circulated from the fan must have blown them off my desk and I bent down to pick them up. I was in the process of doing this when Vincent stormed into my office.

'Alicia,' he bellowed. I clambered up off the floor clutching the pieces of paper I had gathered together.

'Yes,' I replied, remaining calm, standing back and away from him.

'I told you not to meddle in matters which are none of your business,' he shouted, leaning forward, snatching the papers out of my hand and throwing them down on to the table.

'I don't follow,' I replied, trying to maintain my cool. Gemma must have mentioned something to Teresa about our conversation earlier on and she had told Vincent, which was why he was standing in my office bawling at me.

'Did I not make it perfectly clear to you before that there are certain matters in this firm which are no concern of yours?' He pointed his finger at me as he walked towards me, causing me to walk backwards so that I was now standing against the wall. He put his arms on the wall either side of me, so effectively I was pinned against it with him standing over me.

'Yes,' I responded, looking up at him.

'Then what the fuck are you doing asking Teresa's secretary questions which are of no relevance to your work here?' he screamed. He was so close to me that I could smell his tobacco breath and I turned my head to the side to avoid it.

'There must be some misunderstanding,' I replied. 'I'm only carrying out the work Andy left me.'

'You couldn't leave it alone, could you, Alicia?' He was menacing. 'You know what they say about people who mess with fire?' he added, taking his arms away from the wall. He reached into his right suit pocket, took out a lighter and repeatedly flicked it open and shut within millimetres of my face. 'They get burned.' I closed my eyes for a second, then opened them and swallowed hard. My heart was pounding, I felt hot and sick and I could not speak. He paused. 'And we couldn't have that happening to you, could we?' he said, cupping my chin in his fingers and pushing my face up and back against the wall. He was hurting me. 'Such a pretty face too!' he added sadistically, and then he let go of me and strode to the door. As he reached it he turned back and said as if to taunt me, 'You're an excellent worker, Alicia,' he continued, looking me up and down lecherously, 'and a lovely girl. It would be such a waste if anything *happened* to you.' He left the room.

I sank to the floor for a minute as my legs had become like jelly. I felt faint and desperately needed some air, so I dragged myself to the window, pushed up the sash as far as it would go and sat on the window ledge trying to catch my breath. I managed to make it down to the cloakroom and ran my wrists under cold water because I felt so hot and flustered. Then I burst into tears. It was as if I had had so much pent-up emotion inside me for weeks and I had released it in one go. I wiped my eyes, splashed my face with cold water, and went and sat in a cubicle for about ten minutes until I had regained my composure. Amazingly, nobody came in during this time. I returned to my office to pick up my jacket and the papers for my meeting. I was about to leave when Tilly rang me wanting to put a call through.

'Alicia. I have a new client enquiry for you,' she wheezed. She suffered from asthma and the hot weather did not agree with her.

'I'm sorry, Tilly. I'm running late. Could you take the details and I'll ring whoever it is back on Monday.'

'She sounded very insistent and anxious. She says she needs to speak with you urgently. It's about her child.'

'Can't she speak to Angela or Peter, as it's a family matter? I would take the call but I'm really pushed for time.'

'They're all busy with Vincent, but in any event she specifically asked for you. She said a friend recommended you, she knows you will want to help her as her case will be of interest to you.' Tilly pressed me, 'She did sound desperate, Alicia…'

'Are you sure that's what she said?'

'Yes. Definitely.' I do not know what it was that made me decide to speak to her, but I felt compelled to.

'OK. Please put her through, Tilly, but if it's an injunction she needs we're stuffed as I was supposed to leave the office ten minutes ago and it just isn't going to happen today. Oh, and did she say what her name was?'

'Yes. Miss Kingston.'

'Hello. Alicia Allen speaking,' I said, with my 'phone on loudspeaker because I was packing my briefcase and not sitting at my desk.

'Good afternoon, Miss Allen,' she said. As soon as she uttered those four words I knew who it was. I would not mistake that husky voice; the voice of Eve. I rushed to pick up the 'phone but in my agitation I dropped it, which was something I seemed to be making a habit of lately.

'Hello. Are you still there?' I asked as I picked up the receiver. I was slightly breathless because I was flustered, very anxious and on tenterhooks, especially after the day I had experienced.

'Yes. What's going on? Is everything OK?' she asked, sounding suspicious.

'Yes. My 'phone was on loudspeaker and I didn't want to have a conference call with you that anyone else might hear. I went to pick up the receiver, but dropped it in the process. You disappeared? What happened to you?'

'I had to make sure my daughter was safe. It was too dangerous to 'phone. I know you told the police as they've been sniffing around looking for me. It doesn't matter now though. I'll explain everything when we meet.'

'Meet? You want to meet now?'

'Yes. Sunday night. Nine o'clock at the Trocadero, Piccadilly Circus. Be there. I'll find you.'

'OK,' I said reluctantly.

'And, oh, Alicia…no police.' She hung up.

I did not have time to think about 'Miss Kingston' at that point because I was so late for my meeting and I was still reeling from my run-in with Vincent. I asked Carrie if she would call the firm of solicitors I was dealing with and explain that I was on my way, but that I would be about half an hour late. I ran down the stairs, popped my head around the door to reception and told Tilly that I would not be back for the rest of the day. I asked if she could please put all my calls through to Carrie and wished her a good weekend.

The main front door was open and as I walked out on to the street I espied Alex getting on to his scooter in the parking bays just along the road. I desperately wanted to talk to him but, unfortunately, he was a fair distance down the road from me. I could not run after him as I was wearing those ridiculous shoes and although I shouted out to him he did not hear me because he was already wearing his crash helmet. I stood and watched as he rode off into the distance. I waited ages for a taxi, no doubt because it was so hot and nobody wanted to walk. Finally, I managed to hail one and arrived just twenty-five minutes late for my meeting.

I had a splitting headache and took some painkillers as soon as I returned home. It was such a relief to kick off my shoes, which were now consigned to the back of the wardrobe. My feet were killing me and my little toes were red from where the shoes had rubbed against the skin. After a long cool shower, I felt much more refreshed and lay on my bed to rest, but I was so tired I fell asleep. But when I awoke at half past nine my headache had gone.

As Will was not coming to collect me until ten o'clock, I had plenty of time, and as I was starving – because I had not felt like eating the Coronation chicken sandwich I had bought at lunchtime and had thrown it away – I now made myself some toast and an espresso. I had just swallowed the last mouthful when I heard the roar of Will's motorbike as he turned into my road and pulled up outside. I peeked behind the curtain; he saw me and waved. I grabbed my handbag and the silk scarf my mother had bought me and ran down the stairs. I was passing Paolo's flat when he opened the door.

'*Ciao, carina.* Are you going clubbing?' It may have had something to do with the fact I was dressed completely in black.

'No, why?' I asked, slightly defensively.

'I thought you were going to the opera with Cesare tonight.' Cesare must have mentioned something to him. That was the trouble with Cesare having a work colleague who also happened to live in the same building.

'No. I couldn't make it. Kim has gone with him. I'm going for a late night supper with a family friend who's over from Italy. Actually, I have to dash as he's waiting for me.' I sped off out the front door to avoid any further conversation with him.

'*Buon godimento,*' he called after me. 'You're looking very good by the way!'

'*Ciao,* Paolo.'

Will was leaning back against his motor bike waiting for me.

'I'm very pleased to see you,' I said, and gave him a hug.

'You OK, Alicia? What's happened?'

'Today has been a complete nightmare from start to finish. I had a set-to with Teresa this morning. At lunchtime I asked her secretary Gemma about Mr Warrener and Jackdaw Investments, but she must have mentioned something to Teresa who told Vincent because he exploded like Vesuvius this afternoon and threatened me.'

'He did what? What did he say?'

'That something nasty might happen to me, if I didn't keep my nose out of affairs that did not concern me. And he wasn't joking. He half scared me to death.'

'He's definitely a man with something to hide. Are you sure you're feeling up to going in there tonight?'

'Yes. Let's do it,' I replied, putting on his spare crash helmet.

It was just after ten-thirty when we arrived at the office, which was in complete darkness. Will parked his motorbike and we walked up to the office together.

'Put these on,' said Will, handing me a pair of gloves.

'But they'd expect my finger prints to be on everything and besides Vincent's hardly going to call the police is he and drop himself in it?'

'Don't argue with me, Ally!' Will scolded and handed me a torch.

I took the office key from my pocket, opened the front door, switched on the torch and led Will down to the basement to Michael's office. The door was locked, but Will picked the lock easily and opened it. He did a quick reconnoitre around the office and switched on Michael's computer. I was not exactly sure what he was doing, but whatever it was seemed to be taking ages. I was fidgety and started to walk backwards and forwards.

'Alicia. Can you stop pacing about please? You're making me nervous.'

'Sorry. I'm just melting in this heat.' There was no ventilation in the basement at the best of times, but with both doors to the area steps and the back entrance closed it was worse than ever. 'Don't you find it unbearably hot down here?' I asked, taking my scarf off, dropping it on the table and wiping my forehead with a tissue.

'OK, I'm in,' said Will, ignoring me. After a moment he said, 'Hey, look at what we have here?' and beckoned me over to the screen. There was a list of files including my two DAW files. 'Let's see if we can access these,' he enthused, and it was then that we heard a noise. 'What the hell was that?' Will looked up. 'I thought you said the office would be empty?'

'It should be, but it sounds as if there are some people upstairs,' I whispered. 'I can hear voices and I think they're coming down the stairs.' My heart was beating so hard that I thought it was going to leap out of my chest. Palpitations were not the word for it. Perhaps I should not have had that espresso before I came out.

'Quick,' said Will, turning off the computer. 'Let's hide in the big gap behind those filing cabinets,' he said, shining the torch into the alcove. 'We can squeeze in there. Hurry!' I grabbed my handbag, and wriggled in behind the filing cabinets. Will crammed in beside me, squashing me into the corner so that I could barely breathe let alone move. It was then that I remembered I had left my chiffon scarf on the desk and started to panic.

'Will,' I whispered.

'What?' he whispered back.

'I left my scarf on the desk.'

'Oh, Ally, no! We had better hope and pray they don't see it 'cos there's no way we can go back and get it now. Shush. I can hear footsteps. They're almost downstairs. Don't breathe a word.'

It was not possible for either of us to see anything from where we were hiding but we could hear most of what was said. There were three of them and I could pick out the voices of Vincent and Michael, but not the third. They were talking about some deal they had done on the stock market and how nobody would ever be able to trace the source of the funds. Vincent was laughing at his own brilliance and how he had orchestrated the whole thing almost single-handed, although he did concede that without the assistance of his two companions he would not have been able to pull it off.

Since we had been disturbed before completing our investigation Michael's office was unlocked and open. Vincent went berserk over this, and accused Michael of being incompetent, and they had an altercation which seemed to go on for ages. Michael insisted that he had locked the door, but Vincent continued to berate him about failing to do so. The first of them to walk into the office, and I thought it must be Michael, turned on the light. I was praying that he would not discover my scarf.

'Let's get on with it,' I heard Vincent say. 'I haven't much time and a number of matters to attend to before I leave for my holiday.' I presumed it was Michael who walked towards the safe, which fortunately was on the wall behind the first set of filing cabinets and not anywhere near where we were hiding in the alcove. I heard him turning the combination lock, twisting it from side to side as he entered the code, and then the door spring open. He was rummaging around in the safe, took something out of it and threw whatever it was on to his desk. It sounded like bundles of bank notes. He walked to and fro repeating this exercise several times. As he was placing the cash on the desk, I expected that at any minute he would catch sight of my scarf and suspected that we would be exposed. I was petrified and started to shake. I waited for that moment to come, but nothing happened and I supposed for some bizarre reason he could not have seen it. Then I heard Vincent's voice again.

'Just look at that, Jack,' he said. Now we knew for sure that Jack was involved which fitted in with everything we had discovered so far. 'Who would ever have thought it would be this easy?' continued Vincent. 'Let's go to the Club and relax. We can select a couple of girls from Dick's bevy of beauties to entertain us. There's something I need to discuss with him which has to be dealt with urgently before I go away.'

'Sounds good to me,' responded Jack. I heard Michael lock the safe, put the money into a bag and then they all walked to the door. It was sweltering behind that cabinet, I was feeling claustrophobic and could not bear being squashed in for much longer. But evidently Vincent lingered for a few more moments at the door.

'Have you taken to wearing perfume?' he asked scornfully, I presumed to Michael. 'Can't you smell it in the air?' He must have smelt the perfume on my scarf and picked up the fragrance. 'So which of the girls have you *had* down here today?' he mocked.

'Sounds intriguing,' I heard Jack say. 'Why? Are there actually any attractive ones here?'

'You mean, as opposed to Teresa?' Vincent scoffed. Jack laughed too, a very lewd laugh. Vincent continued. 'She makes up in brains what she lacks in looks. She's ambitious and eager for promotion so she does what I need her to do.'

'I'd agree with you there,' said Michael. 'She was a bit short-changed on the looks front.' Although Teresa had been vile to me I actually felt sorry for her when I heard how they were referring to her. She had been naïve to think Vincent wanted to use her for anything other than furthering his own interests. 'Tell you who I wouldn't mind doing though,' added Michael with enthusiasm. My ears pricked up.

'Who's that?' asked Vincent.

'Alicia. She's feisty that one. I bet she's good; all that Italian passion lying beneath that English cool and between those slim thighs. A right little goer, I'd imagine.' If he wanted passion he might get it – but not the kind that he was seeking. I could hardly contain myself, but Will put his hand over my mouth to prevent me from yelling out. 'I was having a chat with the clerks about the girls in the office the other day and we all agreed that she'd be at the top of our list of those we'd like to screw. When I first met her I thought that Vincent would have trouble concentrating on his work with her around.'

'Yes. The thought has crossed my mind on a number of occasions.' He drawled the words as if he was dwelling on the thought. 'But she's trouble that one. Big trouble. She needs taking in hand.'

'Well, from the sound of her,' said Jack, 'I'd be happy to take her in hand *any time*. I'd love to meet her. Maybe we could arrange a foursome some time,' he said licentiously, sounding very excited at the prospect. I supposed he wanted to 'play with my mind'. He certainly was not going to get the chance to do that, but he was definitely going to get his just deserts, if I had my way. They all were.

'Let's go to the Club, now. I feel in the mood for some fun. Dave will take us,' said Vincent. One of them turned off the light, the door was locked and at last they had left. After a few minutes Will started to shift his legs. I felt numb from the waist down.

'They've gone,' he said. 'You all right, Alicia?' I probably looked green.

'I just need some air,' I replied. Will nodded. He eased back the filing cabinet and inched his way out and then I did the same. I tried to stand up but I had severe cramp in my right thigh. I sat down on the floor and Will rubbed my thigh vigorously for a good few minutes.

'Hopefully that will be better now. I'll see if I can find you some water. Stay there.' Because we had been locked in Will had to pick the lock again before he could leave the room. A few minutes later he returned with a glass of water and knelt on the floor next to me while I drank it. 'The coast is clear you'll be pleased to hear. How are you feeling?'

'Better now, thanks. Have you seen my scarf?' I asked, standing up.

'I can't see it, Ally. Are you sure you left it on the table?' he said, directing the torch across the room.

'Positive. Hey, Will, look. There it is on the floor. It must have slipped off the table when they came into the office. Oh, thank goodness.' I breathed a sigh of relief. He picked it up and handed it to me.

'That was a narrow escape, Ally. You weren't the only one with your heart in your mouth. OK. Let's try to finish what we came here to do,' he said, turning the computer back on. 'I didn't have time to log out properly and just pulled the switch, so I expect the computer crashed. We were lucky that Michael didn't try and log on, as then he would have known someone had been in here.'

Will managed to hack back in to the system and re-access those files. On scanning the transactions on the files it was evident that the client accounts for them were being used as a bank account.

'I knew it, Will. Vincent is definitely money laundering. Look at that,' I said, pointing to the screen. 'You can see that invoices are being rendered on files, paid in cash into client accounts and then transferred out.'

'Yes, of course. Allowing his business to be used to launder the proceeds of a crime makes him a money launderer.'

'Michael is too. This must be his secret record of what's going on.'

'Yes, Alicia. Clearly Michael's in on it as he's the one creating the bogus invoices. Let's print everything out,' he said as he began to do just that, 'and take it to the police.'

'There's more to it. You know when we were stuck behind that filing cabinet and Vincent mentioned a great deal on the stock market?'

'Yes.'

'I've been racking my brains trying to link everything together and then it came to me. Tammy told me that Jack said he had had dealings in New York, and at the time it didn't register with me.'

'Well, it wouldn't.'

'Then we discovered who Jack was and that his company was offshore and it reminded me of a very similar case I read about recently in the FSA *Money Laundering Sourcebook*. Because we advise on investments, Graham has all the Law Society *Money Laundering Updates*.'

'You're losing me. What case?'

'It doesn't matter what case, but the facts were similar and that's what triggered something in my mind. I've been trying to piece the jigsaw puzzle together ever since, but didn't work it out until now. I think what they're doing is running a very clever racket. On the face of it, it looks as if Vincent is advising on investment opportunities. But what probably happened is that Jack set up a number of offshore bank accounts in the name of Jackdaw Investments, a bank account in London and a corresponding bank account in New York, which is why he referred to dealings there. My guess is they've made credits from the offshore bank accounts to the deposit account in New York, then invested in blue chip stocks and transferred some of the monies to London. They may have used those monies to fund property purchases because we know from Teresa that she has acted for Jack on a number of them.'

'So what you're saying is that the money from the bank accounts in *London* is used to finance the property purchases in the UK?'

'Yes. Exactly. So it looks legitimate.'

'OK. But it's amazing they could get away with it without detection.'

'Maybe, but they've created quite a complex web of financial transactions to disguise the audit trail as well as the source and ownership of the funds. Moving money by electronic transfers out of an offshore company to an ordinary bank account isn't exactly easy to trace. There are literally hundreds and thousands of these going on every day across the world, most of which are legitimate anyway and who's to say how clean or dirty the money is on any transfer? Then, of course, with all the complex dealings on the stock exchange it becomes even more difficult to trace and by the time the money comes into the UK Bank who's any the wiser.'

'What do you think the original source of the money is?'

'That I don't know. It could be cash from the Club, or drugs. But Michael is always betting on the horses and he may use cash from illicit dealings at the Club to gamble. When he legitimately wins he could put the money in the offshore account, then transfer it, buy stocks, sell them, transfer the money back to the UK and buy property. He seemed to be shifting around a lot of cash in that safe tonight.'

'Let's get out of here.'

By the time Will dropped me off at home it was one o'clock in the morning and I was exhausted.

'Do you have those papers you printed off in a safe place?' I asked him.

'Of course I do. You worry too much!' he said, laughing. 'I'm fully aware we have to report this straight away, otherwise we could be charged with having knowledge of money laundering and doing nothing and get a prison sentence. I have no intention of doing time for Vincent Weil and company! I'm familiar with the economic crime unit of the National Crime Intelligence Services. I'm as eager as you for them all to get fourteen years imprisonment for breaching the Criminal Justice Act.'

'You know your stuff, Will.'

'I also do research, Ally! After you mentioned your suspicions of money laundering to me, I boned up on it. It helps to know what you're looking for.'

'It would be great if we could get Vincent. Now we've discovered that he has connections with the Club and dirty dealings he wants to keep covered up, I think he must be involved with Tammy's murder. I'm convinced of it. We just need to prove it. Do you think Jo would be willing to meet with Jack and set him up?' I said, yawning.

'Does your brain ever stop? You should sleep.'

'Do you think she'll do it?'

'Yes,' he sighed. He sounded exasperated. 'If the police agree, she will. Let's talk tomorrow. You look dead on your feet. Oh, that reminds me,' he said, pulling an envelope out of the inside pocket of his jacket. 'Jo and I wanted to be the first to wish you a Happy Thirtieth Birthday.' He handed it to me. 'Happy Birthday,' he said bending down to kiss me. 'Goodnight, Alicia.'

Chapter 26

'Happy Birthday to You! Happy Birthday to You!' Antonia sang down the 'phone.

'Thanks, Antonia. It's so sweet of you to call.'

'Did I wake you?' she asked. It was eight o'clock.

'No. I've been up for ages; I couldn't sleep.' I had been awake since six thinking about the revelations of the past week and my head was buzzing.

'I thought you might be having a lie-in today.'

'Oh, you mean now I'm thirty I need all the beauty sleep I can get to stop those premature wrinkles from developing!'

'No, Ally. Not at all. You know I didn't mean that.'

'I hope not. How are things with you?'

'Tom and I have been sorting out Maggie's belongings. It's been difficult, but we're getting there. I should go. It was only a quick call to wish you a Happy Birthday and to say I love you.'

'Thanks, darling. You take care. Bye now. *Ciao, sorellina.*'

Among the usual junk post was a birthday card from my mother, a note from my grandmother in Paestum and a long letter from my aunt – my mother's sister – asking when I was coming out to visit her in Florence to visit her. There were also cards from my father's side of the family, and I felt slightly guilty because I had not seen them for ages and I knew I ought to make the effort to do so. I would talk to my mother about arranging some form of family get together when I was next home for the weekend. Dorothy had sent me a card as well which was really thoughtful of her in the circumstances and that reminded me that I had not returned her call.

I was standing in the bathroom brushing my hair and contemplating whether I should have a haircut when my mother 'phoned to wish me a Happy Birthday and to chat. I told her that everything was fine, but I had the feeling she sensed that all was not well, as mothers do with their sixth sense. I prattled on about nothing in particular and promised that I would come home the following weekend. No sooner had I put the 'phone down than my video Entryphone buzzed.

'Miss Allen. Flowers for you,' said the man at the door. I saw he was holding a huge bunch of something through the video entrance screen.

'I'm on the first floor,' I replied, letting him in the outside door. I opened my front door and watched him come up the last few steps to the landing.

'Is it your birthday?'

'Yes. It is,' I said, taking the bouquet of flowers from him. It was composed of freesias, roses, carnations, irises and gypsum and a few other flowers I did not recognize.

'Happy Birthday. I won't ask you how old you are. I know it's impolite to ask a lady her age.' I laughed.

'Thank you,' I replied, and shut the door. There was no card saying who had sent them, just the florist's card and number, so I called to see if I could find out but, apparently, they had been sent anonymously. For one second I hoped they might be from Alex, but then again I did not suppose he knew when my birthday was and, after the way I last spoke to him, I could hardly expect him to send me flowers. That was wishful thinking, but whoever the flowers were from they were beautiful, the fragrance magnificent and I took pride in arranging them in an oasis in my hearth.

I 'phoned the hairdressers to ask for an appointment but was told they were fully booked. I explained that it was my thirtieth birthday and I desperately needed a re-style and, as a favour, they said they could squeeze me in at four. I was on the point of ringing Kim to ask her how the opera had gone with Cesare when she called me.

'Happy Birthday, Ally,' she chirped. She sounded happy, so the opera could not have been that bad.

'Thank you. I was about to call you to see how it went last night.'

'I've been trying to get through to you for ages, Ally, but your 'phone has been permanently engaged. I suppose everyone has been calling to wish you a Happy Birthday.'

'No. Not really. Only Antonia and my mother. I was making a few calls out. Was the opera OK?'

'Well, yeah, actually. It was sort of different and I quite enjoyed it.'

'Oh, good. Not that bad then? What about Cesare? Was he OK?' I was concerned that he was a bit disgruntled over the whole thing.

'Yeah. He was right as rain, although he wanted to talk about you all the time and asked a few questions about Alex. I knew my life wouldn't be worth living if I talked about you so I blanked him,' she said in her usual no-nonsense manner.

'What did he want to know?'

'Whether you two are an item. Ally, the guy is smitten. It's killing him. Anyway, far be it for me to tell you what to do. I'm not even going there. Just remember you owe me for last night.'

'Yes. I wondered when you were going to remind me of that.'

'I was thinking that since it's your birthday we should go out for dinner. I know you don't want a fuss but you can't let your thirtieth birthday pass by without doing anything.'

'Where were you thinking of going? And what about Rob?'

'Working again. Why don't you come around here about half past seven and we can play it by ear.'

'All right. I was thinking that I might see Jo.'

'What tonight?'

'For lunch, but if she wants to come tonight that's fine by me.'

'Great. That's settled then. Why don't you give her a call now and find out what she's up to.'

'I will.'

276

'What are you doing *now?*'

'Now? I thought that, if Jo isn't free for lunch, I'd go and do some retail therapy. I'm going to the hairdressers at four so I've a few hours to shop around.'

'Oh, OK. I know what I was going to ask you, Ally?'

'What's that?' I replied, sounding slightly defensive.

'How did your late night supper go with your Italian friend?'

'Fine. I'm sorry, Kim, but I've got to go.' I cut her short. 'There's someone at the door. I'll speak to you later.' There was nobody at the door but I did not want to lie about where I had been the night before.

'We've been trying to call you,' said Jo when I rang her.

'Sorry. I've been on the 'phone all morning.'

'Well, it's good to be popular, Miss Birthday Girl. How's my best friend today? How does it feel to reach the grand old age of thirty?'

'You were there first so you would know all about that!'

'Very funny, Miss Allen. What are you up to?'

'I was going to ask you that. I really wanted to catch up with you after last night. Has Will told you what we found?'

'Yes, Ally. He has. We should meet.'

'There's something else I need to tell you. It's important.'

'OK. Don't worry. I want to see you today anyway as it's your birthday. What are you up to?'

'Not much really. Retail therapy and a haircut. Kim wants me to go out to dinner and you and Will are more than welcome to come along. I'm not really in the mood for celebrating.'

'You must. It's your birthday.'

'I'd have to even if I didn't want to. I owe her for going to the opera with Cesare last night. Are you free for lunch? I'd rather see you than go shopping.'

'Yes. I'll make my way over to you, 'cos if you come out to us you won't get back in time for your hair appointment. I'll leave straight-away. See you soon.'

'Who are the flowers from?' asked Jo, espying them in the hearth as she walked into the reception room.

'I don't know. There was no label and I called the florist and she said she couldn't give me the details.

'Hmm... Cesare maybe, or Alex, or another secret admirer? Perhaps they're even from Michael in your office!'

'Will told you what he said, then?' Jo nodded. 'Don't even go there. That's not a pleasant thought.'

'Well, whoever they're from they're beautiful. Are you ready?'

We wandered down the Old Brompton Road to find a place to eat. It was another boiling hot day and everybody was seated outside, so we had no problem finding a quiet seat inside. We both ordered Salade Niçoise. Jo ordered a glass of champagne for each of us and a bottle of mineral water.

'Your very good health,' she said, picking up her champagne glass. 'Cheers.' We clinked our glasses together. 'Will contacted NCIS. He also spoke to DS Hamilton this morning and then I spoke to him about going undercover again. He's with him now. The police will want to talk to you later. I'm quite prepared to contact Jack to see if we can flush him out. I can call him to arrange a 'date'. The police are keen on this. Oh, and Vincent did get on his flight this morning. That gives us two weeks to gather all the evidence together and nail him for money laundering.'

'Did Will mention to the police what I said about Tammy's murder and Dorothy's attack all being related?'

'I had the impression from what Will said, and I'm sure he'll tell you himself, that the police were already making enquiries about Vincent's dealings. Either somebody had tipped them off, or they had someone working for them, but I don't know any more about that. As for the murder investigation, it's a question of proof. We still need to track down Patti and Abbey.' Our salads arrived and we both paused for a moment while the waiter served us.

'That's what I want to tell you,' I said as I picked up the pepper mill. I had to have cracked black pepper on my salad. 'Black pepper?' I asked as I handed it to her.

'Thanks. What do you mean?'

'Eve contacted me again.'

'When?'

'Yesterday afternoon; after my run-in with Vincent. I was about to leave the office when I received a call from someone who said her name was Miss Kingston. She told Tilly that it was about her child and that she only wanted to speak to me. She said a friend had recommended me and that I would want to speak with her because her case would be of interest to me. She wants to meet me tomorrow night at the Trocadero,' I said, and then swallowed a mouthful of salad.

'Did she say she had a daughter?'

'Yes. Why?'

'It must be Patti. She was a single mother. Do you remember?'

'Now you mention it. The mulatto?' Jo nodded.

'Patti was the one in the changing room the evening Tammy hurt her hand, wasn't she?'

'Maybe Tammy wasn't alone in the Club that night. What if Patti was there, Jo?'

'Patti may have heard what Tammy's killer *thought* Tammy had heard, in which case it is no wonder that she has been hiding because she doesn't want to suffer the same fate as Tammy.'

'Doesn't she have a hearing problem though?'

'Trust you to bring that up, Ally!'

'Well, it is a relevant point.'

'It all makes sense though. You have to tell the police.'

'She said no police and the thing is, Jo, I don't want her to run again.'

'It could be done discreetly. Think about it. You have no choice but to tell them.'

It was just after six when I returned home and I had plenty of time before dinner. I had not seen Cesare all day nor had he wished me Happy Birthday and I thought he might be annoyed with me because of Alex, not that he had anything to be irritated about as nothing had happened. I showered, changed, tinkered with my newly cut hair and called Dorothy.

'Happy Birthday, dear.'

'Thank you, Dorothy. I'm sorry I missed you the other night but I was out and it was really too late to call when I returned home. How are you?'

'Much better, dear, and eager to talk to you.'

'Why? What's happened?'

'After we spoke I kept thinking about his face.'

'The attacker's?'

'Yes.'

'I went to bed and woke up with a start. I saw his face as clear as day. I'm positive that he was the man in the car.'

'Which car? Not Nathan?'

'Not him.'

'The car that was outside the house the week Tammy was murdered?'

'Yes.'

Alarm bells started ringing in my head because I had a strong idea who Dorothy's attacker was. I recalled something Kim had told me about Vincent's chauffeur, Dave, which I dismissed at the time as unimportant. Around the time Dorothy was attacked, Kim commented that Dave had come in to the office with lacerations to his face. It would make perfect sense if it was him.

'How would you describe this man? Would you say he looked a bit like a bruiser, really big, bald, with broad powerful shoulders? Was he wearing a silver earring in the shape of a cross?'

'I only looked at him briefly before he attacked me and I can't say I remember the earring, but apart from that your description sounds very similar to what I remember. Do you think you know who my attacker is?'

'It's just a theory I have. Make sure you tell the police everything you have remembered.'

'Oh, I intend to.'

'Good. I have to go now but I'll speak to you soon. Take care and get well.'

It was a sweltering summer's evening and, as usual, I could not decide what to wear, but after some thought settled on a pale blue Armani shift dress which I had picked up in a sale when I was last in Florence. I made my way over to Kim's apartment and rang the doorbell; Kim came running to the door.

'Happy Birthday!' she said, opening it, kissing me and giving me a hug. 'You look lovely and I like the haircut.'

'Thanks, Kim. It was getting too long and needed shaping.'

'Champagne?' I followed her through to the kitchen.

'You go and make yourself comfortable in the other room. I'll bring these glasses through.'

The sitting room door was closed. As I opened it there was a tremendous noise.

'Surprise!' they all shouted. Kim had secretly arranged a small party for me and invited Jo and Will, and Carrie, Danielle and Ella from the office. Rob was standing at the far end of the room with Cesare and a couple of his friends.

'Happy Birthday, Ally, for the second time today!' Jo said, giving me a hug. 'You didn't really think we would let your big day pass without some form of celebration, did you?'

'Many Happy Returns,' said Will, handing me a glass of champagne and kissing me on both cheeks. Cesare walked forward and did the same.

'*Buon compleanno, bella*,' he said, and I gave him a hug and he hugged me back. 'You look very pretty this evening. *Che bel vestito! Molto elegante.*'

'*Grazie mille, Cesare. Sei molto gentile.* Did you enjoy the opera last night?'

'*Così, così.*' But I would have preferred it if you had come,' he said, nudging me with his elbow.

'I'm sorry, Cesare. I couldn't make it, but I think Kim enjoyed it.'

'Ally. Can you come here a minute,' Kim called across the room. 'This is for you,' she said, handing me a huge card, 'and this,' she said passing me a small Links bag, 'is from all of us to wish you a really Happy Thirtieth Birthday.' Then the doorbell rang and Kim disappeared for a moment.

'Oh, thank you,' I replied, delving into the bag and taking out an oval box tied with navy blue ribbon. I undid the bow and gently eased off the lid. I pulled out a wadge of navy blue tissue paper to find a little soft felt drawstring pouch. 'Wow,' I said as I opened it. 'What a fantastic present.' Inside was a gold bracelet on which hung a number of charms.

'It was Cesare's idea to buy the bracelet and we each chose a charm for you,' said Kim returning to the room. I felt guilty that I had thought negatively about Cesare, and berated myself as I should have known better. The charms they had chosen were a mobile phone, sunglasses, teddy bear, a heart, and a gold letter A. 'We hope you like them.'

'They're gorgeous Kim. I'm really touched. Thank you all so much.' I noticed Ivano and Paolo enter the room with another man I did not recognize.

'Put it on,' said Will.

'How does it look?' I asked as I slipped it on my right wrist.

'*Meraviglioso,*' said Cesare.

'*Sempre meraviglioso,*' Ivano said. What was he doing here? Surely Kim had not invited him? I turned around and faced him.

'Oh. It's you. *Che fai?*' I asked coldly.

'I came to wish you a Happy Birthday,' he replied, with his usual oily charm and bent down to kiss me, but I moved my head to the side and away from him. He reeked of aftershave. I think it was *Egoiste*, which was quite appropriate.

'*Ti sta bene,*' he said as he eyed me up and down. 'I had hoped since it was your birthday that you would come in your birthday suit. You have such great assets. You should always show them off. And now you have even more charms,' he said, looking at my bracelet.

'Who invited you?' I replied icily and brushing aside his remark.

'I came with Paolo. Kim invited him.'

'Who's your other friend,' I asked, looking at the tall man with the dark straight hair which flopped down over his forehead and who was loitering behind him.

'Alicia,' said Ivano with a dramatic gesture. 'Let me introduce you to my friend Simon.'

'How do you do? You have my deepest sympathy.' Simon furrowed his brow and looked slightly confused.

'Why?' he asked, looking over to Ivano and then back at me.

'To have the misfortune of knowing Ivano!' I replied. However, Simon was distracted by something and was not listening to me but looking over my shoulder and staring hard across the room. I spun around and observed that he was looking directly at Jo. Then, ignoring my comment, he walked towards her and tapped her on the shoulder.

'Marie?' I heard him ask. Jo did not say a word but I could tell from her expression that something was wrong. 'Marie. It *is* you,' he said. 'I wasn't quite sure at first. I mean I didn't recognize you. You've changed your hair. That's what it is.' He stood back and gazed at her.

'I'm sorry,' I heard Jo respond, 'but I think you must be confusing me with someone else. We've never met,' she paused, '*ever.*' She swivelled around and away from him but he grabbed her by the shoulder and pulled her back.

'I'd never forget *you.*' And then he started pointing at her saying, 'Oh, I get it. You don't want them to know what you do in your spare time.'

'I don't know what you're talking about. Please let go of me.'

Will was on the other side of the room talking to Cesare and had not seen Simon talking to Jo. I quickly dragged him away from

Cesare to tell him what was going on.

'See that man over there with Jo,' I whispered in his ear. He nodded. 'His name's Simon and he's a banking friend of Ivano, but I think he's *the* Simon that was in the Club. He has recognized Jo as *Marie* so can you get rid of him?'

'OK. I've got the picture.'

I stood back while Will strolled over to where Jo and Simon were standing. Jo had obviously not wanted to make a scene and continued to deny that she was Marie and insisted that Simon had made a mistake.

'So it's you who's been keeping my wife from me?' said Will nonchalantly.

'Your *wife?*' quizzed Simon, looking perplexed. 'You mean you two…?' he said, pointing from one to the other.

'Yes. I'm Will Brook. How do you do?' He extended his hand to Simon. 'And this is my wife Josephine.'

'Simon Evans,' he replied, shaking Will's hand. 'I was just saying to your *wife*,' he stressed, 'that I'm sure we've met some place before,' and he gave Jo a piercing look.

'He's mistaken,' said Jo, turning to Will. 'I've never seen him before. I must have one of those faces.'

'If my wife says she *hasn't* seen you before, she hasn't seen you before. You understand.'

'My mistake,' said Simon, wandering off towards Ivano. Will put a reassuring arm around Jo's shoulder and then I saw her disappear in the direction of the kitchen. I went to follow her to find out if she was OK, but Kim intercepted me.

'Ally,' she said, handing me my birthday card. 'You forgot to open this.'

'Oh, so I did.' I tore open the envelope and started to read the messages, but out of the corner of my eye I was watching Simon. He was talking to Ivano and then pointed over in the direction of Will and I surmised they must be discussing Jo.

'You haven't got a drink,' said Kim, touching me lightly on the arm. 'I'll get you some more champagne.' She also disappeared off towards the kitchen. I put my card down on the table and wandered out on to the patio. I had seen Rob go out there a few minutes before to set up the barbecue. It was smoking but I did not know where he was. The flat Kim and Rob were renting was the garden flat so they had some extra outside space and it was perfect for summer parties. I thought I was alone and then I was suddenly conscious of Ivano standing next to me and he startled me.

'Leave me alone,' I said. '*Va'!*' I moved back and away from him.

'I didn't touch you,' he replied, holding his hands up as he walked towards me and making a stupid face at me. '*Ho tenuto le mani a posto!*' he said mockingly.

'You didn't keep your hands off before. Anyway, I meant generally.'

'I hear your friend is a bit of a goer. Is that the correct English term?' he scoffed. 'Maybe I chose the wrong one to pursue.' His manner was taunting as he circled me.

'What? I don't know what you're talking about,' I replied, following his eyes as he walked.

'Oh, Alicia, I think you do. I know you girls discuss everything together and as for best friends…'

'If you've got something to say, spit it out, Ivano. I'm not in the mood for this,' I snapped. 'You're spoiling my party.'

'No. You're never in the mood, Alicia.'

'Not when it comes to you. No!'

'I heard she's a hostess. Who'd have thought? *Mamma mia.*'

'You mean an air hostess?' I responded as quickly as anything.

'*Sei pazza!* Very funny, Alicia. No. A girl who works in a nightclub. A tart. *Una sgualdrina.* That's what I heard.'

'Well, you heard wrong!' I retorted.

'Simon told me.'

'Well, he's mistaken. Why would Jo be working as a hostess?'

'Maybe her husband isn't enough for her.'

'Don't be ridiculous. Jo and Will are very happy together. Anyone can see that. You're perverse.'

'But sometimes people need a little bit extra. They need more excitement, Alicia.'

'People like Simon who have to go to Clubs because they can't get it anywhere else?' I countered.

'Everybody needs excitement, Alicia. I know you need it too. I see the passion in you.'

'Oh, *diamine!* Don't start that again. Go away! You're ruining my birthday.'

'What's going on out here?' said Kim, walking out and hearing raised voices. 'Oh, Ally, there you are. Have you seen Rob? He's in charge of the barbie tonight.'

'He can't have gone far. You really shouldn't have gone to so much trouble Kim on my account.'

'No trouble. Perfect night for a barbie,' she replied and winked at me. 'And, oh,' she said, turning to Ivano, 'I think your friends are looking for you. They're leaving.'

Ivano left with Simon and Paolo and I felt relieved. According to Cesare, Paolo had arranged to meet his girlfriend at some other party but Ivano and Simon were going on to a nightclub. As soon as they disappeared I went in search of Jo. I found her in the kitchen with Kim and Danielle, helping out.

'Do you mind if I steal her away from you for a few seconds?'

'No worries. You carry on,' said Kim.

'You OK, Jo? They've gone.'

'Yes, I'm fine. It was just a bit of a shock to see him.'

'What can you expect when Ivano comes along? His friends are probably all as suspect as he is.'

'Cesare isn't, is he, Ally? Theirs is such an unlikely friendship.'

'Yes. True. But going back to Simon,' I said, returning to the point, 'there's no way you can work undercover in the Club again because there's a risk that Simon might be there. If he tells Dick he saw you, and Dick asks where, and he mentions me, then I'm sure this is going to arouse their suspicions. It won't take long before they put two and two together. They'll know we're friends and I work at Wilson, Weil & Co and you worked at the Club under a different name, so they'll be on to us which means we're in danger.'

'It's all coincidental, though, Alicia. I mean, when you started working for Vincent, we had no idea that he had any connection with the Club.'

'Yes, it is and no, we didn't, but they're not going to be bothered about that, are they? Only if we know anything, and what to do about us. Vincent has already threatened me.'

'It's unlikely, though, don't you think, that Simon would say anything to Dick?'

'I don't know. Simon was quite a regular at the Club, wasn't he, and he was really put out by you this evening. He was pretty insistent that you were Marie. I watched him talking to you and then I know he spoke to Ivano, because when I was outside just now Ivano remarked that Simon had told him that you were a nightclub hostess. Cesare said that Simon and Ivano are going on to a nightclub. How do you know they're not going to *the* Club? After all, Simon's a member.

'I don't.'

'Quite. I'm going to call DS Hamilton tomorrow morning. I'm in way over my head and I'm really frightened.'

I was determined to enjoy the rest of my birthday party and forget about Vincent Weil and the Club for a few hours. Everyone kept pointing out to me that life was for living and for all I knew I could be dead tomorrow. For tonight I was going to live for the moment, not that I would have slept with Ivano even if he had returned to beg me. Living for the moment was one thing, but there are limits even to that.

After we had finished eating, Kim disappeared and a few minutes later returned with a birthday cake for me on which she had placed thirty candles.

'You shouldn't have gone to so much trouble,' I said, fingering the charms on my bracelet.

'Don't be silly. I didn't make it. I bought it from Marks & Spencer, but I've had this cake before and it's delicious.' She started to sing 'Happy Birthday' and then everyone joined in.

'Make a wish before you blow out the candles, Ally,' said Carrie.

'Come on, Ally,' said Will. 'You must have made your wish by now. One, two, three…blow,' he said, and I did, managing to blow out all the candles on the cake with one deep breath.

'There you go. You just extinguished the flames of desire Ivano has for you,' Rob teased and started to laugh.

'Don't you start!'

'I saw him with you earlier that's all and observed his manner.'

'Predatory you mean?'

'Something like that.'

'A toast,' said Will. 'To Alicia. Happy Thirtieth Birthday!'

'To Alicia!' they said, raising their champagne glasses.

Chapter 27

I was blissfully in the arms of Morpheus when I was awakened with a bang by a colossal thunderclap overhead. Even the copious amounts of champagne I had imbibed at my birthday party were insufficient to enable me to sleep through that tumultuous crash. The curtains were not completely closed and, as I lay in bed, a flash of lightning outside streamed through the gap, across my bed and my face, illuminating my bedroom. I jumped out of bed, drew back the curtains more fully, peered outside and watched the rain pelting against the window. The last time we had a summer thunderstorm like this was the first time I had met Tammy.

That was ten months ago at a time where events were contriving to change my life completely. In retrospect, none of what happened felt real, even though it was all real. I had become innocently embroiled in something so dangerous that Tammy had been murdered for it, Dorothy had been bludgeoned for it, and Patti was terrified of being killed for it. I felt very frustrated that Tammy's murderer or murderers had not yet been brought to justice.

I fetched myself a large glass of water because I felt suddenly dehydrated, climbed back into bed, and lay there thinking about Tammy's murder. I was convinced that Vincent had a hand in it, but I had no proof; I was quite sure that it was his brute of a chauffeur who had attacked Dorothy, no doubt on his instruction. Jack and Dick were Vincent's associates and very dubious characters to say the least. I knew that Jack was involved in money laundering and I suspected that he was also a party to the murder, and that Dick was mixed up in all of it as well. Motive and proof were what we needed and I pinned my hopes on Patti providing both.

True to my word, I called the police and DS Hamilton and DI Peters arrived at ten. I told them everything I knew but it was clear they were not prepared to do likewise. I presumed, however, that was for my own protection.

'So, Miss Allen,' said DI Peters, tweaking his moustache, 'you believe that Vincent Weil is a murderer as well as a money launderer?'

'Well, we know he's a money launderer because we have the evidence for that. It's the murder and Dorothy's attack for which we don't. Did Dorothy tell you that she thinks she could identify her assailant?'

'Mrs Hammond is very definite about what or should I say who she saw, but bearing in mind her age and the memory loss how do you think any identification will stand up in court? The Defence will attack her evidence on both fronts and it would be better if we had something independent.'

'OK. Point taken,' I continued. 'Then Patti's evidence is crucial as she may lead us to the truth. My main concern, though, is that she said no police involvement and the last thing we want is for her to run scared.'

'We can wire you so that we have a record of what she tells you,' said DS Hamilton. 'But it's in her interests to come to us. If she's at risk it would be better for her to be under our protection.'

'I have no problem with being wired. Are you going to arrest Vincent and the others for money laundering? I understood from Will that you have had suspicions of their money laundering activities for a while and that you've had someone on the inside helping you.' I probed because I wanted to know who it was, but I did not really expect that they would divulge their sources to me. Clearly DI Peters was not impressed with the way I was questioning his investigation. I watched his back stiffen and I heard the irritation in his voice.

'We could arrest them for that, but we don't want to alert them to the fact that we have suspicions in relation to Tamsin Brown's murder. We plan to arrange a set-up to flush them out. That's where Jo comes in and *you*, if you're willing to take that risk. It's up to you,' he replied, tweaking his moustache again. I saw the expression on his face and detected the air of expectancy in his voice, and I knew he was hoping I would accord with his view and assist them in whatever it was they were planning.

'What risk? What *exactly* do you want me to do? So far as I'm aware there is a strong possibility that I'm at risk anyway but, if it helps you catch them, I'll do it.'

'OK. As long as you're sure?' interjected DS Hamilton. 'We want you to call Jack, say that you're a friend of Marie from the Club, that you know about his business dealings and ask him for money to keep quiet.'

'Blackmail him you mean?'

'Yes. Inform him that Marie will meet with him at the Club and that she will call Dick to make the arrangements.'

'Won't he want to know who I am?'

'We're sure he will. Tell him you're Jo's insurance policy and if anything happens to her you'll go straight to the police.'

'Yes, but they're not stupid. They're going to put two and two together. These people have been engaging in pretty serious money laundering, have already killed one person and attempted to kill another. They're not going to stop at doing away with me if it means saving their own hides.'

'Yes. You are in grave danger. We need to emphasize that. That's why we're saying you don't have to do this.' DS Hamilton squeezed my arm. DI Peters shot him a disapproving glance.

'Essentially what you're saying is that, if they dispose of me first and I'm Jo's insurance policy then they can get rid of her and nobody will be any the wiser? But hasn't she blown her cover over that incident with Simon the other day? I don't really understand how this can work.'

'Leave the finer points to us. Are you willing to do it?'

'Yes. But what about Jo? It can't be safe for her to do this now?'

'Don't concern yourself with Jo. She has her brief and knows the risks. It goes with the territory.'

'I realize that, but she's still my best friend and I can't help worrying. I'll do it but on condition I 'phone Jack from here.'

'OK. We'll be back in about an hour with the equipment and the operators. We'll run through it all with you again and, when you're comfortable, you can make the call.'

After they left I was unable to settle and paced up and down while waiting for them to return. I considered the implications of the task I was about to undertake. I had always told myself that I would take any step necessary if it meant catching Tammy's killer and now I had to act on my words. To say I was nervous about making this call would be an understatement. My heart was pounding, my stomach felt tight and I wanted it all to be over.

Everything was ready and I had gone over my instructions with DS Hamilton several times. We discussed a number of possible scenarios, although I did not suppose we could prepare for everything. After all, I had no idea how Jack was going to react and what he might say in response to me.

'When you're ready,' said DI Peters.

'I'm as ready as I'll ever be.'

'Try to relax into it. Imagine that we're not here,' said DS Hamilton. I have a vivid imagination, but that was something even I did not think I could manage in the circumstances. I cleared my throat, dialled the number the police gave me, and they put on their headsets and switched on the recording equipment. His 'phone rang several times before he answered.

'Hello,' he said aggressively. Certainly he had a very abrupt telephone manner. I took a deep breath.

'Mr Warrener?'

'Who wants to know?' he replied aggressively.

'I'm a friend of Marie,' I continued, trying to remain calm but I was very nervous and the agitation was apparent in my voice.

'Marie?'

'Oh, perhaps you don't remember her. She worked at Jensen's. Tall, thin, long dark hair, long legs, *café au lait* skin.' Although there was a time lag of probably no more than a few seconds before he responded, to me it seemed like forever.

'Oh! Marie. Oh yes. I remember *her*,' he drawled. From the way he said the words I could tell that he was recalling every single detail about her in his mind. 'Who are *you*? Do I know you?' He sounded suspicious.

'No. We've never met. I'm ringing on Marie's behalf.'

'Why doesn't she ring me herself?'

'She's away at the moment.' I hoped that was the right thing to say.

'What do you want?'

'To talk.'

'What about?'

'Jackdaw Investments.' There was another short silence before he responded.

'I don't know what you're talking about.' Now he was defensive.

'Oh, I think you do, Mr Warrener. All that money being shifted about from account to account,' I paused for a second, 'with a little help from your friends, and without the authorities knowing. It would be a tragedy wouldn't it if it happened to be leaked to them?'

'You don't know anything,' he replied. 'You're bluffing.'

'Ah, but can you take that risk?' I swallowed hard. My mouth was dry and my cheeks were burning. Again there was a pause. For a second I thought I had blown it and he had hung up.

'What do you want?' He *was* still there. I took another deep breath.

'I told you. To talk.'

'No,' he replied. 'You don't make a call like this just wanting to talk. What do you *really* want?'

'Money.'

'You mean you want me to *buy* your silence?'

'You could call it that.'

'How about blackmail?' he shouted down the 'phone.

'Call it what you like. It amounts to the same.'

'How much do you want?'

'£50,000 – in cash.' He didn't comment on the amount or when we should collect it.

'How do you want me to get the money to you?'

'Marie will call Dick on her return and arrange to come to the Club at a convenient time.'

'How do you know I'll give it to her and that nothing will happen to her?'

'Because I'm her insurance policy and you know I'll go straight to the police.' Again there was a pause.

'I'll tell Dick to expect her call then.'

'You do that.' DI Peters indicated to me to hang up and I did.

'I can't breathe,' I said, standing up from the table. 'I put my hands up to my throat. DS Hamilton pushed open the French windows to the balcony and I stepped outside for a few moments to catch the air, but it was raining so hard that I came back in. I started to hyperventilate.

'Try and stay calm,' said the WPC as she sat down next to me on the sofa. She was very reassuring. 'Breathe slowly and steadily. You're having a panic attack. You did so well.' She put her arm around me.

'Yes, she did. You kept it together, Alicia. You did a fantastic job.' Unless I was mistaken, and he had a twitch, DS Hamilton had winked at me. At least he sounded appreciative, which was more than I could say for DI Peters who always looked stern.

'What happens now?' I asked, looking at him.

'We wait and see if Jack does anything. I'd rather you weren't alone. I've arranged for a WPC to stay with you.'

'But I want to be on my own if you don't mind. I can't live my life like this. I have to go out, go to work and carry on as normal. I'll be fine. Don't worry I'm not backing out on you. I'm still meeting with Patti tonight. Send whoever it is you need to wire me up for that.'

'I really don't think it's a good idea for you to be here alone right now,' urged DS Hamilton.

'Look. I appreciate your concern for my welfare, but I'll take my chances. I'll be OK. I need some space. I'll see you later.' I stood up and led them to the front door.

'Any problems and you 'phone,' insisted DS Hamilton pausing momentarily. 'If you are thinking of venturing out today be sure to let us know.'

I needed to compose myself for my meeting with Patti. I turned on the television but there were no decent films showing and nothing else I really wanted to watch. I flicked through my DVDs but none of those appealed to me either and I could not concentrate on reading or listening to music as I was too restless. I decided to go to the gym and vent out some of the frustration and aggression that had been building up inside me. It was only five o'clock and if I went there for only a couple of hours I would be back in plenty of time before the briefing with the police about my meeting with Patti.

I toyed with 'phoning DS Hamilton and telling him I was off to the gym, but it seemed ridiculous to bother him and I elected not to call. Besides, his number was programmed into my mobile 'phone which I took with me in case I needed to contact him. It was raining heavily when I left the flat, but I walked because I was not going far from home. There was hardly a soul about and the gym was quite empty, but that was normal for a Sunday evening, and then I spotted Ivano lifting weights in the far corner.

I pretended not to see him and started running on the treadmill, but I sensed he was watching me out of the corner of his eye. I waited, but he did nothing, and I thought that perhaps he had finally given up trying to seduce me. As I came off the treadmill, he suddenly walked straight in front of me blocking my way.

'Oh, Ivano. *Stai bene?*'

'*Sì. Tu?*' I nodded.

'What did you get up to last night after you left? *Ti sei divertito molto?*' I asked in a friendly manner.

'*Stai bene*, Alicia? It's not like you to be so *amichevole*.'

'I'm fine. Thank you. I just think that it's time we tried to rub along together, after all we're both friends of Cesare and are going to continue to see each other.'

'I've been trying to rub along with you since I met you, Alicia.' I ignored the remark.

'Didn't you go to Simon's club and rub along with any of the girls there?'

'No. We went to a bar and Simon got very drunk. I didn't feel like going on to his club with him. Not my scene. Don't look surprised. I don't need to go to places like that. I've never needed to pay for it and I've no intention of starting now.' I felt that my rapprochement with him was not going to last. How silly of me to think otherwise.

Clearly Simon had gone alone to the Club and the chances were he had told Dick about Jo, and me. Now that I had made that call, it would not take long for Dick and Jack to work out who we were.

I left Ivano in the gym and went for a swim. The pool was empty and I floated on my back without a care in the world imagining that I was in Italy swimming in clear blue waters beneath an azure sky. This moment of total relaxation was all too fleeting as my peace was disturbed by someone jumping into the pool. It was Simon and he swam over to me.

'Oh, it's you.' I started to swim back to the side of the pool, as I did not wish to engage in any conversation with him. There was something about his demeanour that made me uncomfortable and, since there was nobody else around, I was loath to stay alone with him in the pool. But he swam back with me and we reached the side. I pushed my goggles up and looked at him.

'It's good to see you again, Alicia.' He pushed his wet hair back off his face. 'I stayed with Ivano last night and he got me a guest pass for today. It's not a bad health club this one.' He paused for a second. 'Actually, I wasn't quite sure it was you. You look different. I guess I'm not used to seeing you without many clothes on,' he said, peering down my front. The strap of my costume had slipped so I pulled it back onto my shoulder.

'You've only met me once so you've hardly seen me at all. You seem to make a habit of mistaking people. It's amazing you recognized me really,' I replied, trying to be disarming.

'You mean last night and your friend? Sometimes Alicia you meet people once, they make a lasting impression and you don't forget them. Your friend isn't who she says she is.' He scanned my face.

'Hmm... Well, I'd love to stay and chat,' I said, ignoring his remarks, 'but I need to get home as I have things to do.' I clambered out of the pool.

'See you again, Alicia.'

'I don't think so,' I mumbled under my breath.

By the time I left the gym it was nearly seven. It was pelting with rain and, although it was a June evening and should have been exceptionally light, it was grey, murky and decidedly cold and miserable. I was probably about half way home when I heard Ivano calling after me.

'*Aspetta,* Alicia. I want to talk to you.' I stopped walking and waited until he had caught up with me.

'*Cosa vuoi da me?* What do you want?' I asked, and started walking again.

'I need to tell you something. Will you wait a moment? *Aspetta!*' he exclaimed, catching up with me and taking hold of my arm. I paused for a moment.

'Look, I'm running late and I need to get home,' I said, pulling my arm away as I reached the kerb. The road looked clear so I started to cross.

'Alicia!' shouted Ivano.

'Leave it, Ivano,' I called out spinning around. 'I don't have the time right now. I thought we could try and be friends but I don't know how it's ever going to work.' I was halfway across the road.

'*Attenzione! Sei in pericolo!*' he screamed frantically, running out into the road towards me. I recall he went to grab me; I turned and, as if from nowhere, a car appeared and whoever was driving suddenly accelerated and drove directly towards me at top speed with the car headlights on full beam. I was dazzled by them and could not see what car it was or who was in the driving seat, but I knew that there was no time for me to get away and that the driver intended to kill me. I remember the sound of the engine revving and the smell of burning rubber as the car careered in my direction and then I think I was thrown – but after that I remember nothing.

Chapter 28

'Where am I?' I asked, hardly able to get out the words as I struggled for breath and tried to pull whatever it was on my face off. I could not lift my head because any movement was restricted by the collar supporting it.

'It's OK. You've been in an accident. You're in an ambulance on your way to hospital. It's just an oxygen mask.' I managed to open my eyes for a few seconds and looked at the person standing over me. 'I'm Jess. I'm a paramedic. You were knocked down. Are you in any pain?'

'I can't breathe,' I wheezed, trying to lift the oxygen mask off. 'My chest. The car came from nowhere. I didn't see it. Where's Ivano?'

'Try not to talk,' she said, stroking my forehead, and putting the mask back on. 'We've arrived.'

I must have lost consciousness because the next thing I recollect was waking up in a side room at the hospital with a doctor peering at me from the end of my bed.

'I'm Dr. Morgan. Senior Registrar. In the accident you broke several of your ribs and one of them punctured your left lung causing a pneumothorax. We've carried out a procedure to re-inflate your lung. You have extensive bruising and you hit your head when you fell. I'm going to send you for a CT scan just to make sure.'

'Is there anyone you want us to call?' asked the nurse beside him. Her name badge said Nurse Templeton.

'Cesare. His number's in my mobile.'

'Your boyfriend?' she asked, smiling at me.

'No. A friend.'

'I'll call him for you.'

'Where's Ivano? What's happening?'

'Try and rest. I'll 'phone Cesare.'

'What time is it? I have to be somewhere at ten o'clock.'

'You're not going anywhere.'

'But you don't understand. *She's* depending on me.'

I had my scan and was returned to the ward and must have drifted off into drug-induced sleep. When I awoke Cesare was sitting by my bed.

'How long have you been there?' I asked.

'Not long. I'm sorry. Did I wake you?'

'Where's Ivano? Nobody will tell me what has happened to him.' Cesare turned ashen and put his head in his hands.

'He's gone, Alicia.'

'What? What do you mean?' I squeezed his hand.

'They couldn't save him. His injuries were too extensive. He took the full impact of the car.'

'He told me to wait. He said he wanted to tell me something. He saw the car before I did. I think he grabbed me. I can't really remember. It all happened so quickly. It's my fault,' I gasped, as it was painful to breathe with broken ribs. 'The police told me not to go out alone. I should have called them. That stubborn streak of mine always gets the better of me. And now he's dead. It was meant to be me.'

'It's your determination and independence that makes you who you are, Alicia.' He wiped a tear off my cheek.

'Will you call my mother for me please, Cesare?' I said breathlessly.

'Of course. What do you want to do about Antonia?'

'Oh, nothing. She can't know. It's already Monday in Australia and she'll be preparing for the funeral. She has too much on her plate right now.'

'Excuse me,' said the nurse coming into the room. She had a slight Scottish accent. 'A DS Hamilton and DI Peters are waiting outside to speak to you. You don't have to speak to them yet if you don't want to.' I looked at her and then Cesare and at her again. 'You have a think about it and I'll pop back in five minutes.'

'You heard what she said, Alicia. You don't have to speak to them yet.'

'Yes, I do. I have to get this over with. Could you go and tell the nurse that it's OK?'

'*Certo, carina.* I'll be outside. I'm going to call your mother anyway.'

A few minutes later DI Peters and DS Hamilton walked into the room with Nurse Baxter.

'You can have ten minutes with her, and then she needs to rest,' she said, smiling at me with her twinkling blue eyes.

'Thanks,' replied DI Peters, closing the door. He stood at the end of the bed while DS Hamilton pulled up the chair beside it.

'I'm sorry about Patti,' I paused for breath. 'I let you down.'

'You were lucky not to be killed this evening.' For once I actually detected compassion in his voice.

'I went out alone when you told me not to.'

'We'll come to that in a minute. Can you remember what happened?' DI Peters pressed me. He was stern as ever in his approach.

'I stepped off the kerb and a car appeared from nowhere. Ivano was shouting at me to look out and he went to grab me. I can't give you any description because the headlights of the car were shining in my face. I couldn't see the driver or the car. I saw nothing.' I struggled to speak as every time I moved it was agony.

'I think we all know who is behind this.' DI Peters was very matter of fact.

'We warned you making that call was a risk which is why we

cautioned you not to go out on your own, but what's done is done.'

'What about Patti?'

'When you didn't show up to be wired and we couldn't find you and you weren't answering your mobile, we contacted Jo. She was adamant that something must have happened to you and then of course we received word that you'd been involved in a hit-and-run. She agreed to go to the Trocadero and point Patti out. Patti didn't show up until about ten-thirty and our plain-clothes officers intercepted her in the crowd. We told her that she could come in voluntarily or be charged with obstructing us with our enquiries. She's at the station now.' DI Peters sounded very satisfied with himself.

'Will she co-operate?'

'She already has.' I was pleased to hear that news. At least now we had Patti we might be able to progress on the murder investigation.

'What did she tell you?' I really wanted to know but it seemed I would have to wait a while longer.

'Time's up, gentlemen,' said Nurse Baxter, opening the door. 'Alicia needs to rest now.'

'We'll be back tomorrow.' DS Hamilton turned and smiled at me as he walked out the door. I forgot to ask them Patti's real name.

Cesare was waiting outside.

'*Va bene?* Did it go OK?'

'Hit-and-run.' I could not tell him the real reason why I had been run over, not just yet anyway.

'I called your Mamma. She wanted to come up immediately, but I told her to wait until the morning. She's leaving first thing.'

'How did she sound?'

'Calm.'

'Poor Mamma. It must have been a shock. Ever since my brother and father were killed in a car crash she worries over me driving.'

'But you weren't driving.'

'I know, but it was still a road accident and...'

'Don't upset yourself. You can't change what has happened.'

'What about Ivano's parents?'

'I called.'

'Oh, Cesare, you had to do that too!'

'I didn't mind. It was better they heard it from me rather than a stranger. I appreciate you never liked Ivano, but beneath all that machismo he had many good qualities. If he did a lot of bad things in his life he made up for it by what he did for you.'

'It shouldn't have been like this, Cesare. When we were at the gym I told him we should be friends, but it all went wrong. I wish I could turn back the clock and...'

'That's life. You can't change what's already done. We have to move forward now. I should go. You need to get some rest.'

'What about you? You'll be so tired tomorrow.'

'*Niente affatto!*'

He left and Nurse Baxter came in to do my obs and check that I was comfortable.

'He's a good egg that one.'

'What do you mean?'

'Anyone can see by looking at him how much he cares for you. You're a lucky girl to have someone like that.'

'Right now I'm thinking I'm lucky to be alive.' I started to cry. I only said the night before that I was going to live for the moment because I could die the next day, and how close I had come to that.

'What's the matter, sweetheart?' she asked as she finished doing my blood pressure.

'The man who died was his friend. I never liked him. My squabbles with him all seem so petty now. Why does it take for someone to die to realize what is really important in life?'

'Because we're human; and it's part of our human condition to take things for granted until they're taken away from us. Oh, to have a crystal ball! Now press the bell if you need anything.'

'I will,' I replied, and this time I would do as I was told.

When the police returned to see me early the next morning they told me that for my immediate protection I would be moved to a safe house where I would continue to receive medical care. They intended to leak the word that I had died in the hope that the killers would relax, mistakenly thinking that Jo's insurance policy had expired.

'That's very comforting to hear. When did I die?' I asked, wincing because I was in pain.

'This is not the time to be flippant, Alicia!' I did not appreciate being admonished by DI Peters.

'I wasn't trying to be funny,' I replied, getting together as much breath as I could muster to answer him back. 'Somebody tried to kill me yesterday evening, and that's why I'm lying here now and, if you haven't forgotten, somebody did actually die. I'm willing to assist with any plan you have if it catches the perpetrators of these crimes.'

'What's going on in here?' asked one of the nurses as she came into the room. 'Are you OK, Alicia? Do you want them to leave?'

'No. It's fine. We need to sort something out,' I replied, trying to drag myself up in the bed.

'Let me help you,' she said, raising the back of the bed, re-arranging my pillows and moving me. 'I'll be right outside if you need anything.' She cast disparaging looks at both DS Hamilton and DI Peters and went out shutting the door behind her.

'So what you want is for me to play dead for a while in an attempt to entice the killers out of the woodwork? My mother is about to arrive any minute and somehow she's going to catch on that this wasn't just an ordinary hit-and-run. What are you going to do? Tell her I'm dead too, so that her grieving looks genuine? I want to help you, but there is no way I'm agreeing to that. I couldn't put her through that kind of torment. Anyway, she'd want to see me and I don't think I could hold my breath for that long!' I was in pain and upset, and sarcasm seemed my only outlet. I was surprised that my mother was not there because it was nearly midday and I was anxious that there had been no word of her.

'Please don't distress yourself, Alicia.' DS Hamilton was trying to reassure me. 'That's not what we are suggesting at all.'

'Then what are you suggesting and what about the firm? Do they know I'm dead yet?'

'We've already spoken with your mother and she has said she will assist.'

'Really? I don't understand. When?' I had no idea what they had been doing or why.

'We sent some police officers to her home this morning before she left.' I imagined the scene when my mother was told who they were. She must have been frantic. 'She understands the situation and what's at stake. She made the call to the firm. She informed your employers that you died in the night as a result of your injuries after a hit-and-run. We brought her to London.'

'Can I see her?'

'Yes. She's waiting outside now.'

'What about my friends?'

'They can't know. To be convincing they have to believe that you're dead.' I wondered how Cesare and Kim would react at the news, particularly bearing in mind Cesare had sat with me into the early hours. And what about Dorothy?'

'It's just as well my mother was trained in the dramatic arts then, wasn't it? But my sister's in Australia at the moment. Her boyfriend's mother died of cancer last week, and if she thinks I've died too, do you have any idea of what that's going to do to her?'

'When is she back?' asked DS Hamilton.

'Next week, I think.'

'It should all be over by then.'

'But you don't know that. And I don't know how long I'm supposed to be dead. I want to see Jo.'

'Later.'

'OK. When will I be moved?'

'As soon as you've seen your mother, we'll make the arrangements.'

'It doesn't look as if I have any choice, bearing in mind you have presented me with a *fait accompli,* and the firm already thinks I'm dead, but it will be worth it if it delivers the results you need,' I said, smiling at DS Hamilton.

It was now Friday and I was starting to feel much better and recovering well. My main problem was my mobility because my ribs were bound and I was severely bruised. I was feeling frustrated though, because nobody had told me whether any progress had been made with the investigation or whether the set up had been arranged. I appreciated that I was supposed to be dead, but I did not want to be left to rest in peace. I simply hated being cooped up and kept in the dark. Then, when I least expected it, I had a visit from Jo.

'What are you doing here, Jo? Is this allowed?' She nodded.

'It's OK. I persuaded them to let me come because your assistance is required.' She gave me a gentle hug. 'Besides, everyone thinks you're dead. Your mother is very convincing, Ally.'

'I can imagine. When's my funeral?'

'Next week, I think; if it goes that far.'

'What about Cesare and Kim? How did they take it?'

'Devastated. Cesare is heartbroken.'

'Oh, no! How do *you* know?'

'Because your mother mentioned him when we were chatting about you. Don't forget she and I are the only ones who know what's going on, and we have to carry on as normal. I don't have much time because there are things I have to prepare, but I came to update you.'

'Good. The police have told me nothing. What is this assistance you require?'

'I'll come to that. First let me tell you about Grace.'

'Grace?'

'Sorry, Ally. Grace is Patti's real name.'

'Let's stick with Patti. Forgive the pun, but I've been dying to know what she told the police.'

'She worked at Jensen's for three years and although Dick made out the Club was clean there was always drug-dealing going on.

Vincent and Jack were frequent visitors to the Club and sometimes Michael. There were habitual late night meetings in Dick's office. Do you remember I told you that when I worked there Dick bawled me out for going near his office?' I nodded. 'Well, according to Patti, on the night that Tammy was murdered one of these meetings was taking place. Patti said she saw Tammy in the changing room and she was upset about Jack. Patti thought Jack had gone, but he returned. When she walked out into the bar to say goodnight to Dick she saw him sitting at the bar and she had a word with him.'

'Jack, you mean?'

'Yes. As she was leaving, she thought he asked her if Abbey had left; but in retrospect he must have said Tammy.'

'That fits with her hearing problem.'

'Yes. Anyway, she had left her mobile behind and went back into the Club to retrieve it.'

'How? Once she was outside, the door would have shut on her surely? I presume it would have had one of those fire exit release bars on the inside.' This was pure conjecture as Tammy had never mentioned it.

'Good point, Ally. You're right about the door.'

'So how *did* Patti get back in?'

'She didn't leave. She was only halfway up the stairs when she remembered that she had put her mobile and her bag down on the bar while she was talking to Jack.'

'But what about Dick and Jack? How was it they didn't see her?'

'The door to Dick's office was closed by this stage. She was at the bar when she heard raised voices and saw the door to Dick's office open, so she hid behind it. Dick went into the outer office but when he went back into the main office he didn't close the door properly and it was left ajar. Patti said she was too far away to hear what they were talking about, although one of them, whom we believe to be Vincent, was shouting about something that had not been done. It was at this point that Tammy ran out of the changing room. When Patti saw Tammy hurrying to the side of the bar she ducked down, so Tammy didn't see her. She was wearing black, there was little light and Tammy wasn't expecting her to be there. She saw Tammy pick up a bar towel and wrap it around a cut on her hand and walk towards the exit.'

'Why didn't she let Tammy know she was there and tell her not to go? I mean she must have realized there was trouble brewing by the fact she didn't want to be seen herself? Plus she noticed that Tammy had hurt her hand.'

'She said she was frightened, and it didn't occur to her that anything really nasty would happen to Tammy.'

'What happened next?'

'Tammy tripped as she reached the top of the stairs and made a noise opening the door. Dick and Jack came rushing out, but she had gone. Patti ducked behind the bar, but she couldn't resist peeking and saw the distinguished-looking man making a call. She thinks it was to Dave and he told him to follow Tammy in the car.'

'As she has such bad hearing how could she be sure what she heard?'

'He was shouting and it was her best side.'

'Presumably the 'distinguished' one she is referring to is Vincent?'

'Yes.'

'Maybe Dave followed her home? Dorothy said that there was a car loitering outside the house sometimes during that week. Did Patti mention anything else?'

'Such as?'

'What they intended to do about Tammy.'

'No.'

'That's a real shame. How did *she* get out without being seen?'

'She didn't want to run the risk of leaving in case Dave saw her, so she stayed there.'

'What, all night?'

'No. Only about four hours. She was locked in after they left. When the cleaner arrived after seven in the morning, she scarpered.'

'And I suppose it was only when she realized that Tammy had

been murdered that she surmised that they were the ones who had contrived to kill her or to have her killed. Patti first rang me after Tammy started working at the Club, and the next time was the day after the news of the murder. But how did she get my details, and why call me?'

'We asked her that. She chatted with Tammy and told her that she needed a lawyer to help her out with a problem. Tammy said she had a neighbour who was a lawyer and gave her your mobile.'

'What problem?'

'She didn't tell Tammy, but it was in relation to the dealings at the Club.'

'Tammy never mentioned that conversation to me when we spoke about the Club. Maybe she overlooked it. If she had done we'd have known who Patti was right from the start. She must have been trailing me because she seemed to know my every move.'

'Yes, she did watch you, but it wasn't that difficult because your life has a routine.'

'Hmm… You mean boring?'

'Ally! You can hardly say your life has been boring recently.'

'Well, it's the regularity of going to work every day, isn't it? It's just easier to follow the man who always takes the 8.15 a.m. train from Paddington, than the man who works as a freelance; but I take your point. It isn't as if Patti actually witnessed the murder. We need something more to link them to the crime.'

'A confession would be good,' she said, screwing up her forehead.

'How are you're going to get that? What's happening with this set-up? Jack thinks you want to blackmail him for money laundering, so you're going to have to draw him in and convince him that you know more than you do. It's a risky strategy because he thinks that I'm dead and that your insurance policy is now null and void, in which case he may feel safe because he can dispense with you and no-one will be any the wiser. My instinct tells me that Jack will be only too willing to brag to you. It's all a game of cat-and-mouse now. What they don't realize is that we still have Patti and they don't know how much she knows. You could use that.'

'You and your instincts, Ally.'

'Maybe, but I haven't done too badly so far have I?'

'No. Dead on cue.'

'Befitting my current status.' Jo laughed. 'So when are you going in?'

'Tonight. We had to wait because Jack was away. I called Dick and it was evident that Jack had spoken to him. He said that he understood we had some unfinished business and an account to settle; and he told me to come to the Club at three in the morning. This is where you come in.'

'Me?' I wondered how, in my condition, although I was eager to help if possible.

'I want you to be there, Ally.' I furrowed my brow.

'In what capacity?' I did not know what she meant.

'I know it sounds ridiculous but I need your support. I told the police that I would only do it if you could be outside with them. I'm sorry. I should have spoken to you first. I don't expect you're well enough to make it.'

'I'll be there, but I don't think DI Peters likes me too much. He thinks I interfere with his investigations!'

'He had no choice but to agree to my request or I wouldn't do it. He wants the kudos for solving this case, Ally, and so it was in his interests to accommodate me. I'll tell them we've discussed matters and they'll sort out the arrangements to get you to Piccadilly. I have to run.' She bent down and gave me a kiss.

'Keep safe.' Jo was about to walk out the door when she paused, turned and came back over to me.

'There's something else I meant to tell you, which I think is going to surprise *even* you.'

'What's that? I'm lying down now. I think I'm beyond being surprised.'

'You remember the police said they suspected Vincent of money laundering and had someone working on the inside?'

'Yes.'

'You'll never guess who it is?'

'I asked the police, but they wouldn't tell me.'

'It's Alex.'

'What? Alex Waterford?' I could hardly believe it.

'Yes. The very same. I only found out today or I would have told you before, I can assure you. He's been assisting the police for some time. But I really have to go,' she said, glancing at her watch. 'Get some sleep. We have a busy night ahead.'

I felt slightly guilty for suspecting Alex was involved in shady dealings, when all along he had been working as a police mole. I had misjudged him, but then again, I could hardly be blamed for mistrusting his motives. I suppose he had been trying to tell me something when he stressed to me that people were not always what they seem, appearances are deceptive and that I should not believe everything I had heard about him. This latest revelation would certainly explain his behaviour, but it was still a shock to learn of his involvement and I wondered what else could possibly happen to surprise me.

Chapter 29

At quarter to three in the morning everything was set, and I found myself seated in the back of an unmarked police car with WPC Jones. DS Hamilton was sitting in the front passenger seat and another plain-clothes officer called Nick, whom I had not met before, was driving. We drove down Piccadilly, across the Circus and into Shaftesbury Avenue, all of which were buzzing with those nocturnal creatures who thrive on London's night-life and kept people like Dick in business. We turned off Shaftesbury Avenue into the one-way street where the Club was, and parked just across from the entrance. DI Peters was with Will in another car along the street. My understanding was that backup was at hand if required, which provided some reassurance, however minimal.

It was a couple of minutes to three when I glanced at my watch, but there was no sign of Jo and I hoped all was well. Then I heard the sound of her footsteps behind us as she strode up the street. I saw her pass by on the opposite side of the road and approach the door to the Club. It was three o'clock precisely and she was on time. She disappeared into the Club. The police officers and I had been chatting in the car, but as soon as Jo appeared everybody fell silent. All of us were really keyed-up and the atmosphere felt very charged, but I had an ominous feeling that all was not going to go well.

Jo had been wired so we could hear her every move, and we listened to the sound of her shoes as she walked, purposefully, down the stairs in the Club. DI Peters spoke to all units on the police radio.

'OK, everyone. Here we go. Let's see if she can get the information we need to arrest them, but any sign of trouble and move.'

'I hope that Jack and Dick don't find the wire on her.' If they did it would be the end for her.

'At least not until she's got what we need,' responded DS Hamilton.

'That's very callous,' I snapped. 'I'm surprised at you. After everything that has happened. She's the one risking everything, not you.'

'She knows the score.' As did I, but that did not remove the fact she was in mortal danger by going into that den of iniquity.

'Good evening, Marie,' I heard Jack drawl. 'So,' he paused, 'we meet again.'

'Ah. If it isn't the lovely Marie,' I heard Dick say sarcastically.

'Dick, I presume?' asked DS Hamilton.

'Yes,' I replied.

'And what can we do for *you*, Marie?' Jack continued in his lewd manner, just like I had heard in the office basement that night.

'You know why I'm here.' She was calm and I don't know how she retained her composure.

'I was rather hoping you were missing me,' we heard Jack say in his usual slimy way, but with a real sting in the tail. 'We do *indeed* have unfinished business.'

'He's playing with her.' DS Hamilton sounded annoyed.

'Give her a chance,' I said, irritated by him. 'Let her do her job.'

'My friend spoke to you on the 'phone. She told you what we want.' Jo remained controlled.

'We?' he quizzed. 'I heard your friend was dead. Hit-and-run they said. People really don't drive carefully anymore. What a tragedy! – and for it to happen to one so young. A shame about the young man though. Bit of a risk you coming here, don't you think, in the circumstances?'

'I don't know what you mean.'

'Good girl. Play it cool,' I heard DS Hamilton murmur.

'Oh, I think you *do*, Marie. Your insurance policy expired… literally,' he taunted. He must have been standing very close to her face as the reception was in stereo.

'Come on, Jo. Drag it out of him.' I could hear Will's agitated voice on the police radio. I was sitting on the edge of my seat.

'For goodness sake!' I said. 'Wait.' There was a pause before Jo replied.

'But what about Patti?' she asked.

'What about her?' Dick replied dismissively.

'She knows everything about the business dealings with Jackdaw Investments and…' she hesitated, 'Tammy. Her murder, that is.'

'You're bluffing,' shouted Dick.

'And all about my friend. What Dave did to her?'

'What does Patti know?' asked Jack in a sort of frenzy, and it sounded as if he was shaking Jo because we could hear the movement through the wire and the sound became distorted. I detected slight panic in his voice.

'Can't you see she's bluffing you?' Dick said, trying to press the point on Jack.

'How much do you want?' asked Jack.

'We told you. £50,000.'

'What are you doing?' We heard Dick remonstrating with Jack. 'You're not seriously considering paying her are you. You know this is not what we agreed with Vincent…' and he paused.

'Vincent?' asked Jo. 'You mean Vincent Weil, don't you? What did you agree with him?

'You idiot!' Jack shouted.

'She doesn't know anything! What's your problem?' Dick retorted.

While all this was going on, a car drew up outside the Club and Dave, Vincent's chauffeur and Michael, the accountant both got out. I did not recognize the car as this was not the usual car he drove, well, not to the office anyway. This was a BMW and it appeared to be midnight blue; he normally drove a black Mercedes.

Maybe that was the BMW I noticed outside the house on the night of Dorothy's attack and the one that had been used to run me down. We watched Dave swagger into the Club followed closely by Michael who shuffled in behind him. The next thing we heard was Dave's gruff voice.

'What's with the shouting?' he growled.

'She says that Patti knows everything about Vincent and Tammy's murder,' responded Jack.

'It's not going to save *her*.' I recognized Michael's voice. His next comment was directed at Jo. 'What she knows can't help *you*. You hear,' he bawled. 'Do you really think anybody's going to worry about some little tart who worked here as a hostess? It won't take long before we catch up with her and give her some very personal service.'

'You haven't yet, and the police haven't given up on Tammy's murder investigation and *she* worked here. If anything happens to me, they'll investigate that too.'

'You're all two-a-penny,' Dave said menacingly. 'Put a bag over your heads and nobody would know the difference between any of you. Isn't that right, Jack?' I could hear Jack cackle. 'I wouldn't mind doing her myself,' he added.

'Oh, no,' I said. 'Stop this.' I was frantic. 'Get her out.' DS Hamilton was radioing DI Peters.

'He says not yet. Give it a few more minutes,' he said.

'It might be too late by then,' I urged.

'Shush! Jo's saying something.' WPC Jones interrupted me.

'Is that what you did to Tammy? Jo continued. 'Raped her and then silenced her?'

'The stupid little bitch had it coming to her,' said Michael.

'And Mrs Hammond?'

'Her head cracked like a nut. I had my instructions.' Dave's voice again. I knew deep down that he was Dorothy's attacker and now he condemned himself from his own mouth.

'Are you going to kill me too?' Jo sounded afraid now.

'You're going the way of all the others. Vincent doesn't like any loose ends.'

We heard what seemed to be a scuffle and then an eerie silence.

'What's going on? What's happened to the wire? Why don't you do something? ' I screeched at DS Hamilton. 'Give me the radio.' I mustered all my strength and tried to grab it off him.

'Calm down, Alicia,' he said. 'This isn't helping.'

'No, I won't. He could be killing her.' I felt hysterical. 'Do something!' I screamed at him.

Our attention was diverted by about a dozen people emerging from a nightclub further along the road. They were rolling up the street in the direction of Jensen's, shouting and singing. They all looked rather the worse for wear and could barely stand, and then one of the young men vomited into the gutter. As they walked past the doors to the Club we saw Dave and Jack appear carrying something heavy. Unfortunately, our view of them was partly obscured by the drunken clubbers and we could not see what was going on.

'What the hell's that?' asked DS Hamilton. 'What have they put in the boot of the car?' Dave closed the boot.

'Oh, my God! They've got Jo. It has to be. Pray she's still alive.'

'We're going in,' I heard DI Peters say, and something about all units taking up their positions. However, they were not quite quick enough to intercept Dave and had to push past the group of drunken clubbers who impeded their progress. This enabled Dave to get into the car and speed away in the wrong direction down the one-way street.

'Turn the car. Turn the car,' DS Hamilton shouted, but our path was suddenly blocked by a refuse truck which, in that split second, had turned into the street from Shaftesbury Avenue and was slowly driving up the street. I heard DS Hamilton talking frantically on the police radio and describing Dave's car, Dave, the direction in which he was travelling and stressing that Jo was believed to be in the boot.

'What's happening?' I asked WPC Jones.

'He's requested urgent back up. They'll be sending the IRVs in.'

'IRVs?' I questioned.

'Instant Response Vehicles. Pursuit cars.'

'Come on,' said Nick, repeatedly sounding the horn. 'Come on,' he shouted, banging his fist on the dashboard. 'Police. Back up. Back up,' he yelled out the window at the driver through a megaphone. The driver was slow to react and seemed to have been asleep, but at this time of night it was not surprising. Eventually he reversed into Shaftesbury Avenue, we passed the truck, and sped off in hot pursuit of Vincent's chauffeur with the siren wailing and blue lights flashing, and with me in a state of nervous agitation.

DS Hamilton received news on the radio that Dave had been seen driving down Piccadilly and through the underpass. He was being pursued by one of the IRVs and was now heading in the direction of Knightsbridge.

'Put your foot down, Nick,' DS Hamilton said to him. It was as well I was strapped in because we were travelling at such speed that I was being thrown around. My damaged ribs were hurting badly and I could hardly breathe.

It felt unreal to be in the back of an unmarked police car, in the early hours of a Saturday morning, driving at full speed through red lights, and dodging traffic, in London's West End in pursuit of a murderer. Nick was driving so fast that, as we drove down into the underpass and into the dip, it felt as if the speed carried us and momentarily lifted the back wheels of the car off the road, making my heart miss more than a few beats. We sped past the Lanesborough Hotel and towards Knightsbridge.

The radio messages came fast. Dave had passed Knightsbridge tube station and turned left into the Brompton Road, and was driving towards Harrods. In seconds we followed into the Brompton Road, and saw him just ahead of us. Dave accelerated as he passed Harrods and had to swerve, clipping the side of a car parked outside, losing his wing mirror and nearly hitting a taxi just pulling away from outside.

'Between all of us we can head him off,' shouted Nick. 'We have cars coming along the Cromwell Road and Thurloe Place. The faster we drive the faster he'll drive and we can net him.'

'Where do you think he's heading?' I asked.

'Probably for the M4,' replied DS Hamilton, 'as he's making for the Cromwell Road.'

We followed close on his tail. I saw a police car coming up Thurloe Place, and another coming along the Cromwell Road. Dave accelerated along Cromwell Gardens and then, unexpectedly, he moved on to the wrong side of the road. I presumed this was in an attempt to avoid the police car steering towards him.

'Oh, my God!' I said. 'He's going to hit that police car.' I put my hands over my eyes.

'No, look, Alicia, he's turning into Exhibition Road,' cried WPC Jones.

The angle was too acute, he could not hold the turn, and I heard the screeching of his brakes as he tried to take control. It was too late and he crashed straight into, and through, the railings of the Natural History Museum at a speed of probably more than one hundred miles per hour. He plummeted forward and down the ten feet drop into the gardens and hit the ground with such a thud that the front of the car collapsed like a concertina. I knew he must be dead and feared that Jo must have suffered the same fate as she could not have survived the impact.

In an instant we were at the crash scene along with the other pursuit cars. The car with DI Peters and Will arrived a second after us, and Will literally leaped from the car. Black smoke billowed from the engine of Dave's car, the horn was sounding, and I supposed he had slumped forward onto the steering wheel.

'Get down there,' he shouted. 'Get her out,' he called as he stood by what was left of the railings.

An ambulance and a fire engine were there within moments and all I could see were flashing lights, police, paramedics and firemen swarming everywhere. Two of the firemen clambered down to the car. I watched Will standing by the broken railings. WPC Jones helped me out of the police car and, as I hobbled over towards him, I saw the skid marks where Dave's car had swerved. There was an acrid smell of burning rubber. I reached Will, took hold of his hand, stood with him and looked down on the car. The impact had indeed completely crushed the front of it, the windscreen had shattered and there was metal and glass everywhere. I could not see anything of Dave except for his arm, which was hanging limply, palm upwards, out of the car door; it was covered in blood.

I observed as one of the paramedics ran to the front of the car, looked inside, and shook his head, presumably to confirm that Dave was indeed dead. The boot was jammed and the firemen were prising it open, but they were proceeding with caution because they did not want to take any step which might endanger Jo. If, miraculously, she had survived the crash it was clear that, at the very least, she would be severely injured after that impact. Will let go of my hand and climbed down to where the car lay, and even though it was only a few seconds before they managed to open the boot, it seemed like an eternity. I watched as they carefully lifted her out. She was wrapped in what looked like a red velvet curtain. It was presumably one of the curtains to the cubicles in the Club that both Tammy and Jo had described.

'Please, God. Don't let her be dead,' I mumbled under my breath as they gently released her from the folds of cloth. I could hardly bear to look and then I felt light-headed, everything turned black and my legs gave way under me.

'Alicia. Alicia. It's OK,' said WPC Jones, catching me. 'I think you need to sit down.' She slowly led me back to the police car and helped me inside. 'It's the shock.'

'What about Jo? Is she alive? Please find out what has happened to her?' I beseeched.

'OK. Don't worry. I'm sure it'll be all right,' she said, trying to reassure me.

While I was sitting in the car waiting to hear news of Jo, DS

Hamilton walked over to me.

'If she's dead it will be because DI Peters didn't go in sooner.'

'That's what I came to tell you.'

'Tell me what?'

'It seems there was a car blanket in the boot and the curtain Jo was wrapped in cushioned her, which in turn softened the impact. We don't know the extent of her injuries yet, but she *is* alive. It's amazing. We should get you back now.'

'How much longer do I have to go on like this?'

'Jack, Dick and Michael are in custody now. Officers raided the Club and arrested them. The only one we don't have is Vincent. He's going to be away another week but that gives us time to work on them. It won't be much longer, Alicia.'

'I want to go home. I want to see Mamma; and my sister will be returning home from Australia soon.' He did not respond. 'Keep me informed about Jo, please, and let me know what you manage to extract from them.'

'Yes. I'm sorry you had to go through this, Alicia, especially after your accident. I know this hasn't been easy for you.' I tried to move, but I was in pain and I winced. It was now after four; I was exhausted and did not have the energy to answer him back. All I could think about was the sound of that car as it hit the ground, and the fact that Dave was dead but Jo was still alive.

Chapter 30

Four days had passed since the crash and Jo was still critical. She had suffered some horrendous injuries: a torn spleen and cracked pelvis requiring emergency surgery because she was haemorrhaging internally. She had lost so much blood that she had received two blood transfusions. As a result of being thrown about in the car she had also sustained severe bruising. Not surprisingly, when Will visited me, he looked strained and hollow-eyed.

'How's Jo? What do the doctors say? I've been so worried. I can't stand being cooped up here much longer not knowing what's going on.'

'I've come straight from the hospital actually, Ally. She's very weak and she has a long way to go, but they think she'll pull through and make a good recovery.'

'I only hope the police are grateful for what she did for them. Job or not, what she did was very brave. You must have been beside yourself with worry?'

'I was, but I'm fine. Your mother came and stayed with me at the hospital while Jo was in theatre. She has a very calming influence. It helped having her there.'

'She has and it would be. Jo's like a daughter to her. She has known her nearly twenty years.'

'Antonia called apparently.'

'Really? What did Mamma tell her?'

'Only that you were out and she was staying with you for a while.'

'Did she say when Antonia's coming back?'

'Not until next week and after Vincent returns, so that gives us more time. Your mother told me that she felt awful lying to Kim and Cesare. They're both gutted.'

'I hate all this subterfuge. It's so cruel to let them think I'm dead. Don't get me wrong. I understand why the police want to proceed this way, and I want to catch Vincent as much as they do, but this is unbearable.'

'I know, but the police don't want any more slip-ups.'

'Have you heard from them? Has Angus told you what is going on with the beastly threesome?'

'Michael, Jack and Dick, you mean?' I nodded.

'All that material we printed out in Michael's office tied in with the evidence Alex Waterford gathered on Vincent's crooked dealings, and enabled them to complete an audit trail. Alex has been assisting NCIS for a while. Following the audit trail and tracing the accounts back to New York has been difficult. With this latest evidence they have proof of Vincent's complicity. You were right.'

'I was wrong about Alex though. I completely misjudged him. I thought he was involved.'

'Well, he was, even if it wasn't in the way you suspected. Don't beat yourself up about it. You had reason to be suspicious. Sometimes issues get clouded, particularly where emotions are involved,' he said, dropping his voice and looking at me hard. 'I had the impression Alex led you a bit of a dance. He wasn't supposed to get involved with anyone. It wasn't part of the job description,' he paused. 'It will all come out in the wash I'm sure,' he said, smiling.

'Like the laundered money you mean!' I winced.

'You OK?' Will sounded concerned.

'Yes. Did DS Hamilton tell you anything about the murder investigation?'

'They've already spoken to Jo, to ask her what happened after the wire went dead.'

'I don't suppose she can remember much.'

'Only that Dave shook her so violently that the wire came loose and he punched her left side. She thinks he must have knocked her out.'

'I suppose they intended to take her out of the Club and kill her elsewhere.'

'That seems to have been the idea. The punch to her left side is the likely cause of the tear to her spleen. She was probably saved by the fact she was unconscious and limp when she was being thrown about in the back of the car. She was also wrapped in a velvet curtain from the Club and placed on a car blanket.'

'Yes, I saw that when they lifted her out. I'm surprised she didn't suffocate. She was wrapped so tightly.'

'I know. It doesn't bear thinking about. I think the police will be coming in to see you later today. I have to go,' he said, looking at his watch and bending down to kiss me goodbye. 'I've errands to run and I need to buy a few bits and pieces for Jo. Is there anything I can get you?'

'No. Thank you. Please send my love to Jo.'

'Of course.'

After Will left I sat on the sofa in my room reading, but was unable to concentrate on the book. My thoughts were on Vincent instead, and I visualized him lying on a beach sunbathing, blissfully unaware of the turn of events in his absence. I imagined him sipping an exotic cocktail with some young former female client who was no doubt blonde, bronzed, big-breasted and rich. I hoped he was enjoying his freedom *while* it lasted.

'Penny for your thoughts?' DS Hamilton was standing in front of me. I jumped. 'You were miles away. I didn't mean to startle you. Good book?'

'It's only a collection of Italian short stories; but I wasn't reading. I was thinking about Vincent.'

'And?'

'That it's three days until his return. I saw Will Brook. He told me how the information we obtained has helped with completing the money laundering audit trail. That's excellent news.'

'Yes, it is.'

'You don't even have to worry now about putting Dorothy through the trauma of an identification parade. You have Dave's admission of guilt on tape and Vincent's complicity in the crime of attempted murder on Dorothy. Jo can bear witness to what he said anyway. It wasn't clear from Jo's conversation in the Club which of them actually murdered Tammy, was it?' I looked at him expectantly.

'Dick was the easiest one to break. He wanted to save his own hide. We were able to use the money laundering evidence to squeeze him and he cracked under pressure. He said that Vincent had been blackmailing him and he had no choice other than to do what he said. He was more than willing to talk.'

'Why? What was he blackmailing him for?'

'Vincent had photographs of Dick in compromising positions.'

'Well he *is* in that kind of industry.'

'He didn't want his family to know apparently.'

'What a hypocrite!' I exclaimed. 'Talk about double standards.'

'What he told us ties in exactly with the information Patti gave us about that night at the Club.'

'Which is?'

'That Vincent thought he saw a glimpse of someone passing the door. You remember Patti said that after Dick came out it was ajar?' I nodded. 'Well, they heard a noise on the stairs and Vincent called Dave and asked him to see who it was. Dave confirmed that it was Tammy, and Vincent told him to follow her to see where she lived. Vincent was convinced that she had overheard their conversation about buying more property with the money from the stocks and shares they had sold, and about their next transfer. He said that she had to be dealt with. Dave trailed her for the next few days.'

'That corroborates Dorothy's evidence about seeing a car outside the house, doesn't it?'

'Yes. He said that Vincent was insistent that Tammy was sorted out, and Dick agreed that he would call Dave and tell him when she came in to the Club again. Of course, we know she only went back to collect her money the following Monday night and Dick told them this.'

'That's why he was so amenable to her returning to collect her money, I suppose?'

'Yes, but he denies prior knowledge of Vincent's intentions to harm her. He alleges that he thought she was just going to get warned off.'

'Oh yes. I really believe that. I mean you would, wouldn't you?' I said with sarcasm. 'This isn't something he's going to slide out of.'

'He also denies being there when Tammy was killed,' added DS Hamilton.

'Doesn't he mean murdered? Well, he may not have been there, nor may he have been the one to kick her head in, but I'm damn sure he knew all about it. He can't deny his complicity in all this and, besides, I bet Jack and Michael aren't going to let him off the hook that easily.'

'Yes. You're right about that. They confirmed that Dick knew what was going to happen to her but he wasn't at the murder scene. They said they weren't there either and allege that it was Vincent and Dave who killed her.'

'But what about the DNA of the men who assaulted Tammy? I mean somebody raped her.'

'I was coming to that, Alicia.'

'Sorry. So many clues have been going around in my head for weeks and I want to know what happened, that's all. Patience was never my strongest point!'

'As I was saying,' he continued, giving me a slight smile, 'their DNA samples matched the ones taken from Tammy, so we accused them of her murder. Under pressure they confessed to raping her in turn. Neither showed remorse, particularly Jack who seemed to revel in it, telling me *exactly* what he did to her. In fact, once he started talking about her he couldn't stop. They both denied murdering her, though Jack said that after Tammy left the Club that Monday night, he and Dave waited for her in the car. As she was walking down the street in the direction of Piccadilly, Dave drove down slowly behind her; Jack opened the car door and dragged her in. She struggled a bit but they soon put a stop to that and they went to Hampstead Heath where they met Michael and Vincent.'

'Vincent didn't rape her, did he?'

'There is no forensic evidence to show that and, according to both Jack and Michael, Vincent prefers to watch, which he did while Dave held her down.'

'Oh, that's almost worse.' I felt revulsion at his voyeurism. 'That's so sick! Maybe he needs that to turn himself on and to give himself kicks. Did he kill her?'

'They're pinning it on Vincent. He was the one to kick her to death they said and he kicked her and kicked her and kicked her. I saw the pictures, Alicia. They were horrendous.'

'What kind of man is he?'

'An evil one.'

'Yes. To exact pleasure the way he does. Kim had to identify her and it's no wonder she was traumatized. They're all evil. What about Dorothy's attack?'

'They deny having anything to do with that. They say Vincent must have instructed Dave to do it.'

'What about the attack on me?'

'We suspected that if you made that call to Jack it wouldn't take them long to work out who you were. According to Michael and Jack, on the Friday night before Vincent went away, which was the night when you and Will were in the office looking for evidence of money laundering, Vincent told them what he intended to do about you.'

'When? It wasn't in the office.'

'No. It was on the way to the Club.'

'That would fit because Vincent said I was trouble, Jack and Michael were discussing what they would like to do to me, and I heard them saying they were going to the Club.'

'They allege that Vincent instructed Dave to dispose of you and it was coincidental that you made the call to Jack as Dave already had his brief.'

'Yes, and killed Ivano instead of me. He has that to answer for as well. This is all too awful for words. And Jo? Who's idea was it to go after her?'

'After you 'phoned Jack, he and Dick spoke to Michael. They called Vincent and he told them to do it.'

'Do you believe them?'

'I do now.'

'What do you mean? How? I don't understand.' I was confused.

'On reviewing the funds received from the money laundering and, with assistance from Alex, we have established that Vincent has been shafting them all and not giving them their fair cut. True to form they wanted their revenge.'

'Which was what exactly?'

'To set him up.'

'He isn't stupid though. He's a rat and he can smell one from a long distance. It did cross my mind that if Vincent tried to 'phone any of them while he was away he would be suspicious if they weren't around to take his calls. I mean he'll be expecting Dave to pick him up from the airport, won't he?'

'He'll get a nasty shock then won't he, Alicia, when we turn up? I can see your mind has been working overtime as usual. As for Dave, we understand that he generally takes his leave when Vincent is away and would not be expected in the office.'

'But what about the others? How are you managing to keep this quiet? After the crash the press must have been sniffing around?'

'The identities of the parties in the crash have not been released. We cannot afford any leaks because too much depends upon it. As I said to you, Michael, Dick and Jack have helped us to set Vincent up.'

'How?'

'We arranged for them to 'phone him to tell him that both you and Jo had been successfully disposed of, and that everything had gone as clockwork.'

'Which naturally you recorded, like you did when I called Jack?' He nodded. 'What did he say?'

'He was very pleased that all obstacles had been removed, and the path was now clear for them to move forward with their plans. I think his exact words about you were "that little bitch should have known better than to cross me, but now she's gone the way of all the others." He commented that it did not pay for anyone to stand in his way because they would be crushed. There was no stopping him because he was invincible.'

'Clearly the man is more deluded than *even* I thought.' I wondered how many others there had been. Maybe ones we did not know about. That was certainly a sobering thought. 'What happens now?'

'We wait until his return.' I stood up, thinking DS Hamilton was about to leave. 'Actually, I have some other news which may be of interest to you'

'What? Something more? I thought I'd heard all the revelations today has to offer.'

'This is one I think will please you.'

'Really? What is it?'

'I understand you have been waiting to hear from someone for a while.' I did not know who he was talking about and I looked perplexed.

'Who?'

'Jeremy Brown.'

'What? Who? I mean, I know who you mean. I'm surprised to hear his name. I had completely forgotten about him with everything that has been going on.'

'You're not the only one who was trying to track him down, although by all accounts you did very well. Why did you want to contact him, Alicia?' I had always had a sneaking suspicion that the police must have been looking for him too.

'This is going to sound ridiculous in light of what we know about Vincent's involvement in Tammy's murder, but after she died, Maggie asked me to help her with Tammy's affairs. When I said we needed to make contact with Tammy's father she clammed up and showed me the door. It seemed odd. I was curious about him. I had a feeling there was something more to it. I supposed I got it wrong, but my instincts still told me otherwise.'

'I can understand why you thought that. When we spoke with Maggie, we also thought it rather strange that she did not want to divulge any details of the father. She was very defensive about the whole issue and we were slightly suspicious. We had to find him to eliminate him from the enquiry as we didn't know anything about Tammy's background in Australia. We've had people working for us out there, making contact with all and sundry who knew her. Then, of course, the investigation turned towards Vincent Weil so we focused our attentions on him.'

'When did Jeremy Brown turn up? I sent him an e-mail weeks ago, and he never responded to me.'

'He's not been in Australia for eight months. He's been overseas and only returned to Melbourne last week. When he came back into the country he was stopped at the airport. All his details had been left with the Australian authorities as we still wanted to interview him, although by this stage he was clearly off the suspect list. He was informed that Tammy had been murdered, and he asked for Maggie's details. He told the Australian police that he wanted to put them in touch with us because he wanted to find out about the enquiry and come over to London.'

'That's strange. Tom said that after Tammy was born he upped and left. He never had any contact with Tammy at all and he didn't want to see Maggie.'

'He then heard the news that Maggie had died.'

'Poor man. To have two shocks, one after the other like that. But what about Tom? Has he seen his father, especially as he's in

Australia at the moment?'

'Not yet, apparently. When I spoke to Jeremy Brown he told me that he had picked up the e-mail you sent him and was curious. Apparently he's had problems with the e-mail account to which it was forwarded while he's been overseas and rarely uses it. He had forgotten to inform the University of that though. He wanted to know what your real involvement in all of this was. When I explained, he indicated he wanted to meet you.'

'What did you say, bearing in mind I'm supposed to be dead?'

'It all depends upon what happens on Saturday.'

'You mean when Vincent returns?'

'Yes, and because that's the day Jeremy Brown is due to arrive.'

'Oh, I see. He's not here yet.'

'No.'

So, after all this time, I was finally going to come face to face with Tammy's father.

Chapter 31

I was awakened by the sun streaming through the gap in the curtains and across my face. There was a bee buzzing behind the curtain, which must have flown in through the window I had left ajar. I opened my eyes and squinted because the light was so bright, and then I realized it was Saturday morning: the day of Vincent Weil's return from Barbados.

That morning at ten, DI Peters, DS Hamilton and I were waiting at Heathrow airport in the Arrivals hall. There were other policemen milling about in the terminal. I looked at the arrivals board for his flight and read the words "LANDED". Then a short while later "IN BAGGAGE HALL" appeared, and I looked across first at DI Peters who remained as impassive as ever, and then at DS Hamilton who had an air of expectation about him. As for me, I was like a cat on hot bricks – the wait seemed interminable.

The automatic doors opened, and I watched with anticipation as they repeatedly opened and closed and the holiday-makers traipsed through one after the other, but there was no sign of Vincent. Five more minutes passed and then the doors opened again and I espied him pushing a trolley, laden with suitcases, and accompanied by a tall leggy blonde who was well-endowed and probably half his age. He was deeply tanned, and wearing a patterned open neck, casual shirt and light cotton trousers. He looked as arrogant and self-satisfied as ever.

I was standing a little way from DI Peters and DS Hamilton and wearing dark glasses and followed Vincent with my eyes as he passed me. I knew he would not recognize me because he believed that I was dead and had no reason to suspect otherwise. I observed him looking round for Dave, over the heads of those waiting, and saw him glance at his watch and make some remark to his companion. He seemed rather irritated by the fact that Dave was not there to collect him.

I merely wanted to witness the arrest, and I stood and watched the two policemen as they purposefully strode over to where Vincent was standing. He was ranting and raving over the fact that Dave had let him down. This was the least of his worries now, I thought. I looked on as he was arrested on counts of money laundering, murder, aiding and abetting, and blackmail. As he was cautioned, I watched his face for any sign of emotion or remorse, but there was none. In reality, I had expected nothing less from him and I listened while he asserted – in no uncertain terms – that they had no case, he was going to trounce the whole lot of them and bring a case for unlawful arrest. Of course, he did not know that Dave was dead, his partners in crime had turned against him or that Jo and I were still alive. I felt nothing as he was led away to the police car waiting outside. I did not see where his holiday companion had gone. She had disappeared at the first sign of trouble, and I cannot say I blamed her.

'Alicia!' I turned. It was WPC Jones. 'You'll be needed at the station later.'

'I didn't know you were here,' I replied. 'Is it concerning Vincent Weil's arrest?'

'Hmm…' She paused for a moment. 'Not directly. Actually, it's to do with Jeremy Brown. DS Hamilton told you he was arriving from Australia today, didn't he?'

'Yes, though I wasn't sure what time. He's arrived then?'

'At six this morning. He's at the station helping us with our enquiries.'

'What do you mean? I thought he had been eliminated.'

'It isn't quite that simple, Alicia. I'll come to collect you later.'

'I don't understand. Don't you think that when he finds out that his daughter's killer is at the station, there'll be hell to pay?'

WPC Jones did not respond and I was confused. I knew that Vincent would continue to deny everything, safe in the mistaken knowledge that Jo and I were dead and that Jack, Michael and Dick would corroborate his evidence. However, it would not be long before he realized that the game was now up. I supposed this would be when I was miraculously resurrected from the dead. I did not understand what 'enquiries' Jeremy Brown could possibly be helping the police with as I thought we finally had all the pieces to the jigsaw puzzle.

WPC Jones arrived as arranged; I was taken to the station to meet with Jeremy Brown and ushered into an empty office where there was just a desk and two chairs. We did not need to be introduced. Tom was the spitting image of him, albeit a younger version. They both had a bewitching smile.

'You must be Alicia,' he said, as I walked into the office and towards the tall, fit looking man with salt-and-pepper hair and deep tan. He held out his hand and I shook it warmly. His accent was, of course, Australian, but very soft. He spoke gently and I could hear Tom in his voice for the intonation was the same. I could not see Tammy in him at all, but then she had looked like Maggie.

'Yes. How do you do?' He looked at me hard. We sat down.

'You knew Tammy well?' he asked.

'I wouldn't say well. I knew her. We were neighbours. But she did confide in me about her troubles.' I paused. 'I'm really sorry, Mr Brown, about your daughter. It must have been a terrible shock for you to find out that she had been murdered and then to hear that Maggie had died.'

'Please call me Jeremy.' He paused for a moment and cleared his throat. 'The thing is, Alicia, I never knew Tammy. Her mother and I split before she was born. The year before we broke up Maggie came back to England for a while. Our marriage was going through a rocky patch and when she was over here she had an affair.'

'Oh. I didn't know. I'm sorry.'

'Don't be. It happened. She wrote to me from England telling me that she was leaving me for this other man and that she was pregnant with his child. When he discovered her condition he threw her over. I suppose he'd had his fun. Somehow he didn't seem the commitment type. She wanted me to take her back and I would have done, but I couldn't.'

'The pregnancy?'

'Yes. I couldn't bear the fact that she was pregnant with another man's child. I loved her so much and I felt betrayed and angry. She was determined to have the baby and I couldn't accept it.'

'And the baby was Tammy?'

'Yes. So you see I'm not Tammy's father at all. My name may be on the birth certificate, but I'm not her natural father.'

'But what about Tom? He's your child and you left him.' I bit my lip. 'I'm sorry,' I said. 'That's judgmental and it's not for me to comment.'

'I tried to stay in touch, but I was blocked all the way and I didn't want to go to court over it. It all seemed so unpleasant, but I hoped that one day Tom would contact me. I felt, rightly or wrongly, that Maggie poisoned him against me after I left because she thought I should have forgiven her.'

'Oh. That's sad. But there's still time for you and Tom. It's not too late.'

'Maybe.' I was going to tell him that Antonia and Tom were seeing each other but I thought better of it. I left it for the moment.

'This other man. The father. Do you know who he is?'

'Yes. Why don't you read this,' he said, handing me an envelope. 'And then I think you'll have all your answers.'

I took the envelope, pulled out the letter inside, opened it and scanned it. It was the letter Maggie had written to him all those years ago telling him she was leaving him and that she was pregnant with this other man's child. I needed to sit down. I folded the letter, put it back in the envelope and, as I handed it back to him, said, 'You've already shown the police this, haven't you?'

'Yes. Why?'

'I knew there was something strange going on when WPC Jones told me you were helping them with their enquiries. I thought you must know something, but I wasn't sure what.'

'I provided the police with a DNA sample.'

'I see. And that proved conclusively that you weren't Tammy's father, as if you needed confirmation.'

'Yes, but they did. I was going to leave this letter with my Will for Tammy. I suppose I wanted to redeem myself. I didn't want her to think that I had abandoned her. I wanted her to know the truth.'

'It's a pity you and Maggie didn't tell her the truth when she was alive, because now Tammy will never know.'

'I appreciate that. The truth has been hidden for far too long.'

DI Peters poked his head around the door and looked over at Jeremy.

'She knows,' he said. 'I told her.'

'Alicia.' DI Peters turned to address me. 'We need to have a word.'

'Excuse me.' I smiled at Jeremy, stood up and walked to the door.

'What's going on?' I asked DI Peters, who was characteristically tweaking his moustache.

'I'd like you to do something.'

'In relation to Vincent?' He nodded and furrowed his brow. He peered down at me with a very serious expression. 'How is it going with him?'

'Well. He's dug himself into a pit and there's nobody to pull him out of it this time. I want him to confess to Tammy's murder.'

'It isn't like you to be so emotional.' It was clear that DI Peters really wanted to throw the book at Vincent. 'I see you're human after all. He doesn't know I'm alive yet and you want him to see me?' DI Peters nodded again.

'OK. What do you want me to do? If you think it will help, I'm more than willing to try.'

I had my brief and I knew what to expect. DI Peters opened the door to the interview room and I followed him in. The interview had paused when DI Peters had left the room and now it recommenced. Vincent and his solicitor were sitting directly opposite me as I walked in the door. DI Peters moved across to the table. I remained stationary and stared at him with a fixed expression. Vincent seemed visibly shocked by my reappearance and for a moment I thought I detected a slight quivering of his lower lip. His solicitor was shuffling around uneasily in his seat, and awkwardly straightened his tie.

'What?' stammered Vincent, pointing at me with the forefinger of his right hand. 'What?' He repeated. 'How the hell? What is she doing here?' he asked, turning to DI Peters. 'I thought...' and then he paused.

'What did you think, Vincent?' He was sweating and beads of perspiration appeared on his forehead. He glared over at me. The look was of pure hatred, but I stared back; he then glanced at his solicitor and over to DI Peters. I watched him wringing his palms.

'What did you think, Vincent?' DI Peters repeated. 'Did you think she was dead?'

'No! No! No!' he shouted.

'Yes,' continued DI Peters. 'You did. You arranged to have her murdered.'

'No!' Vincent bawled.

'Don't deny it. We have evidence against you for all the crimes you have committed. Your chauffeur is dead, your cohorts have confessed, we have tape recordings, we have the evidence of Miss Allen, Mrs Brook, Mrs Hammond and the audit trail is complete.'

'No!' he screeched. His cries were pathetic.

'And so we come to Tamsin Brown's death. You had no cause to murder her. That's the irony. She saw and heard nothing. You murdered her for nothing! I have three pieces of evidence to show you.' DI Peters laid the first one down on the table in front of Vincent. It was a copy of the letter from Tammy's mother to Jeremy Brown. 'Read it!' he said, pushing it forward. I watched Vincent's face as he scanned the letter, I saw his expression change and all of a sudden his tan no longer seemed so bright.

'No,' he yelled as the letter was passed to his solicitor. 'It's not true. It can't be true.'

'Look at this then,' DI Peters continued, putting down the second piece of evidence in front of him. It was a DNA result, not Jeremy Brown's but Vincent's. Vincent had been so convinced that his DNA would take the police nowhere that he had not protested about agreeing to the test. He did not realize why they had asked for it. 'The test is conclusive.'

Vincent put his hands up to his face. 'It can't be true,' he raged, banging his fist on the table, making me start and move backwards.

'You're a lawyer. Let's look at the evidence of what you did.' DI Peters laid down the third and final piece of evidence. It was a sheet of card and on it were pinned photographs of Tammy's battered head. It was a horrendous sight. 'Look at them, Vincent. Look at what *you* did to a beautiful, vivacious girl. Take a look.' Vincent turned away. 'Do it!' shouted DI Peters, shoving the sheet towards Vincent's face. 'Look at what *you* did to *your* daughter!'

It was hard to believe that Tammy was Vincent's daughter. Maggie's letter named him as the father. He was the man with whom she had had the affair all those years ago. The DNA test showed that Vincent was her biological father as he had all of the paternal DNA fragments. Maggie had given a DNA sample, as had Tom, at the beginning of the murder investigation. Forensics had Tammy's DNA and so they had been able to compare Tammy's DNA profile with her mother's. They knew that the DNA fragments in Tammy's profile, which were not present in Maggie's, must have been inherited from her father, and that was now proven to be Vincent.

The realization that Vincent had murdered his own daughter and the sight of her battered head was too much even for him, and he had hurled the sheet of card across the table at DI Peters. He stood up, punched the air with clenched fists and then broke down and whimpered. I felt only contempt for him and wondered how many of those tears were for Tammy, or for the frustration of knowing that it was because he had murdered his daughter that he had engineered his own downfall.

Six weeks had passed since the day of Vincent Weil's arrest and it was now the beginning of August. I had recently returned to London, after recuperating and staying with my mother. Fortunately, I had been well enough to attend baby Daniel's Christening at the end of June which had pleased me enormously. Antonia and Tom had returned from Australia the week after Vincent was arrested. I had persuaded Tom to meet his father, and although there were bridges to rebuild, they had made a start. Since my sister was dating Tom it had been easier than I had thought.

My reappearance had been as much a shock for Kim and Cesare as it had been for Vincent, but it was reassuring to know that they were pleased that I was back in the land of the living. Kim and Rob became engaged at the end of July and surprised us all. They had decided to move back to Australia and start their married life there. Cesare and I remained close friends. He had visited me several times at my mother's home, and I never divulged to him that I knew of his true feelings for me after he thought I had died. Subsequently, he put his flat on the market as he intended to move to New York. Dorothy had returned home to London with Smoky now that it was safe. She had made an amazing recovery. Jo was progressing well, but it would be a while longer before she was fully recovered.

As for Wilson, Weil & Co., that was a chapter in my life which was now firmly over, although I missed Alex. I wondered what he was doing, where he was, and if I would ever have the opportunity to apologize to him for misjudging him. On returning home I decided to make a trip to the Brompton Cemetery, to visit Tammy's grave and to pay my respects. I had told the police I would be in London that day and, as I was walking down the front steps to the house, I saw DS Hamilton pull up in his car.

'I'm glad I caught you, Alicia. How are you?'

'I'm well. Thank you. Do you need to talk to me?' I felt he wanted to say something.

'I was passing.' He paused. 'Vincent could barely remember Tammy's mother when questioned. We had to dredge the facts up for him. Maggie had apparently met him at the party of a friend. She had told him of her matrimonial difficulties and he had said he could help. He took advantage of a young woman in distress and of course dumped her when she found herself pregnant.'

'That goes to show what kind of man he is, doesn't it? She meant nothing to him. I don't suppose he ever gave her a second thought. No doubt she was a diversion for him. That's the irony; he's probably giving Tammy and Maggie a great deal more thought now.'

'Your instincts were right after all, Alicia.' I looked at him quizzically. 'About Tammy's father being the missing piece of the jigsaw puzzle,' he added.

'But I didn't know about Vincent, did I? I always felt her father was the key but I thought it was to do with Jeremy Brown.' He smiled at me.

'It's good to see you better. Where are you off to?'

'Actually, I'm on my way to Tammy's grave.'

'Can I offer you a lift?'

'No. Thank you. It's a lovely day and I'd really like to walk. Besides, I have to buy some flowers.'

'OK. I'll leave you to it then.'

The weather was very different from the last time I had been at Brompton Cemetery. Then it was winter and cold and wet, but today it was warm and bright and sunny. As I stood in front of Tammy's grave I felt the heat of the sun on my back. I laid the flowers I had bought on the grave and turned to walk back down the path when I heard a voice. It was Alex.

'You're looking remarkably well for someone who is supposed to be dead,' he said with a quirky expression on his face.

'Very funny,' I replied, walking towards him. 'How's life treating you, Alex?'

'I really can't complain. But seeing you has given *me* a new lease of life,' he said, winking.

'Still the same old Alex? Charming as ever.'

'Not so much of the *old* if you don't mind, Miss Allen.' I laughed.

'Not working at Wilson, Weil & Co. anymore then, Alex?'

'No! I've closed the door on that one.'

'Teresa *will* be disappointed.'

'I'm not interested in Teresa, Alicia. I've never been interested in her.' He smiled winsomely at me.

'How did you know I was here?'

'The police told me you were coming back. Your neighbour said you might be here.'

'You mean Dorothy?'

'Yes.'

'She's very knowing. She must have guessed. Actually, I'm glad you found me. There's something I've been meaning to say to you.' He looked at me expectantly. 'I'm sorry I misjudged you. I didn't realize that you were working with the police.'

'I know, and I couldn't tell you. It wasn't allowed. It goes with the territory. Mind you, you were doing a fair share of sleuthing yourself. If I'd known you had a date with a murderer, well…but it goes to show that what I said is right.'

'And what's that Alex?'

'That people aren't always what they seem, Alicia. There's certainly a lot more to you than meets the eye. Those flowers are lovely,' he said, pointing to the freesias I had laid on the grave. 'Did you receive *my* flowers?'

'*Your* flowers?'

'The flowers I sent you for your birthday!' So those flowers were from him after all.

'You really are full of surprises. I didn't know who they were from. The florist said they were sent anonymously so I couldn't thank you. They were beautiful.'

'Don't you think we should put all this behind us and start afresh?' He looked at me earnestly.

'We can't rewrite the past and there's no point in looking back,' I replied. 'What's done is done. But I agree that it *is* time we closed this chapter and looked forward to a new one.'

'To new beginnings then?'

'Something like that, Alex,' I replied as he took my hand.

THE END

Read the second part of the trilogy…

ALICIA ALLEN INVESTIGATES 2

WILFUL MURDER

By Celia Conrad

Soon after starting at a new law firm, Alicia Allen, a young London solicitor, acquires a new client, Isabelle Parker, who has lived in Australia most of her life. Unhappy with Holmwood & Hitchins, the firm dealing with her English grandfather's multi-million pound estate, Isabelle instructs Alicia to draw up a Will in contemplation of her marriage. Isabelle tells Alicia that she believes her brother and grandfather were murdered. On a journey to Brisbane, Alicia meets a Partner from Holmwood & Hitchins who is travelling on to Melbourne, and when she changes planes in Hong Kong learns that Isabelle's fiancé has been killed in an explosion in London. Subsequently she hears that the partner at Holmwood & Hitchins has been discovered with multiple stab wounds. Isabelle implores Alicia to investigate, and as devastating revelations about Isabelle's family history come to light, Alicia realizes she is looking for a psychopathic killer guilty of premeditated and wilful murder…

ISBN 978 09546233 3 3 (0 9546233 3 9)
PUBLISHED BY BARCHAM BOOKS
£10.99
ORDER YOUR COPY NOW

Read the final part of the trilogy…

ALICIA ALLEN INVESTIGATES 3

MURDER IN HAND

By Celia Conrad

Through her Uncle Vico, a New York attorney, Alicia Allen, a young London solicitor, is introduced to Fabio Angelino to deal with the Probate of his mother's English estate. Fabio's father once worked with Vico at the New York firm of Scarpetti, Steiglitz & Co., but sixteen years earlier disappeared in Sicily, the Italian police concluding that he was murdered by the Mafia. After a trip to the Amalfi Coast, Fabio tells Alicia someone has tried to kill him. When Fabio's sister, Giulia, is found callously murdered, Alicia investigates their father's disappearance, and is convinced that Giulia's research on the Angelino family background in Lucca holds the key to the mystery. Finding evidence of massive corruption in both London and Italy, Alicia determines to expose the criminals. But in her bid to entrap them, has Alicia taken on malevolent forces too great, and will this be her last investigation?

ISBN 978 09546233 4 0 (0 9546233 4 7)
PUBLISHED BY BARCHAM BOOKS
£10.99
ORDER YOUR COPY NOW

Celia Conrad was educated at King's College at the
University of London and now lives and writes in London.